# 2004

## A BRAND-NEW YEAR—
## A PROMISING NEW START

Enter Sydney Omarr's star-studded world of accurate
day-by-day predictions for every aspect of your life. With
expert readings and forecasts, you can chart a course to
romance, adventure, good health, or career opportunities
while gaining valuable insight into yourself and others. Offering a daily outlook for 18 full months, this fascinating
guide shows you:

- The important dates in your life
- What to expect from an astrological reading
- How the stars can help you stay healthy and fit
- Your lucky lottery numbers
  And more!

Let this expert's sound advice guide you through a year of
heavenly possibilities—for today and for every day of 2004!

### SYDNEY OMARR'S® DAY-BY-DAY
### ASTROLOGICAL GUIDE FOR

**ARIES**—March 21–April 19
**TAURUS**—April 20–May 20
**GEMINI**—May 21–June 20
**CANCER**—June 21–July 22
**LEO**—July 23–August 22
**VIRGO**—August 23–September 22
**LIBRA**—September 23–October 22
**SCORPIO**—October 23–November 21
**SAGITTARIUS**—November 22–December 21
**CAPRICORN**—December 22–January 19
**AQUARIUS**—January 20–February 18
**PISCES**—February 19–March 20

## IN 2004

# SYDNEY OMARR'S®

## DAY-BY-DAY ASTROLOGICAL GUIDE FOR

# SCORPIO

## OCTOBER 23–NOVEMBER 21

# 2004

### With Carol Tonsing

A SIGNET BOOK

SIGNET
Published by New American Library, a division of
Penguin Group (USA) Inc., 375 Hudson Street,
New York, New York 10014, U.S.A.
Penguin Books Ltd, 80 Strand,
London WC2R 0RL, England
Penguin Books Australia Ltd, 250 Camberwell Road,
Camberwell, Victoria 3124, Australia
Penguin Books Canada Ltd, 10 Alcorn Avenue,
Toronto, Ontario, Canada M4V 3B2
Penguin Books (N.Z.) Ltd, Cnr Rosedale and Airborne Roads,
Albany, Auckland 1310, New Zealand

Penguin Books Ltd, Registered Offices:
80 Strand, London WC2R 0RL, England

First published by Signet, an imprint of New American Library,
a division of Penguin Group (USA) Inc.

First Printing, June 2003
10  9  8  7  6  5  4  3  2  1

# CONTENTS

# INTRODUCTION

# Leap Year and What It Means

It's Leap Year 2004! What better time to ask how February 29 came to be associated with women "popping the question" to their sweethearts?

As one legend goes, it all started in Ireland. Beloved St. Bridget complained to St. Patrick that women had to wait for a man to propose. In response, St. Patrick solved the problem by declaring that women could propose to men on the day of February 29, a day outside the domain of normal customs.

For hundreds of years, February 29 has been a window of opportunity for lovelorn lasses. In the thirteenth-century Scotland passed a law that allowed women to propose on this day, and if a man declined he had to pay a fine. In twentieth-century America cartoonist Al Capp invented Sadie Hawkins Day, a day when women were allowed to trap their man by any means at hand—no doubt inspired by former Leap Year traditions.

It is a romantic custom that a man should ask for a woman's hand in marriage, going down on bended knee. (And writers of books like *The Rules* would agree.) Today, though, it's accepted practice for a woman to ask a man out on dates, lure him into bed, and even pop the question herself—never mind waiting for Leap Year.

How does astrology say a man would react? An Aries would admire her courage. A Leo would be flattered. A Cancer might want her to meet Mother first.

To celebrate Leap Year 2004, we've included some helpful astrological tips for seducing every sign. Just knowing the other person's sun sign can give you many clues to how to make your relationship a happy one. You

1

can troubleshoot problems in advance and, if they crop up, find a way to make them work for you. This autumn, as Jupiter moves into Libra, the marriage sign, is a great time to fall in love and march down the aisle.

There are other challenges ahead in 2004. What about the possibility of changing careers? And how about coping with a midlife crisis? In this book we'll deal in many ways with the question of timing. There are the potentially difficult times, which also present positive challenges, there are the times with potential for delays and misunderstandings, and there are the best times to take risks.

For those who would like to know more about astrology, there is basic information to start you on your astrological journey. Then you can put your whole astrological portrait together by looking up the other planets in your horoscope.

Anyone with access to the Internet has a world of astrological connections available. We'll show you the best astrology Web sites, where you can find wonderful free information. And if you're interested in connecting with other astrologers, we provide an extensive resource list of contacts and organizations as well as computer program recommendations for fun or serious study.

Bring astrology into your life every day with Sydney Omarr's astonishingly accurate day-by-day forecasts for eighteen months ahead. Let this book become your astrological partner and companion, ready to enhance every aspect of your life. Here's wishing you love, happiness, health, and success in Leap Year 2004!

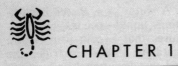

# CHAPTER 1

# What's New in 2004?

## The Dance of Uranus and Neptune

Last year, the slow-moving planet Uranus moved into Pisces. Uranus will remain in Pisces until 2011. Whenever a slow-moving planet changes signs, there is a deep influence on the collective atmosphere. The Uranus transit through Pisces also creates a new dynamic with planet Neptune, which is continuing its slow transit through Aquarius.

Planets Uranus and Neptune are doing a kind of astrological dance, called a "mutual reception." In this mutual reception Uranus is in Pisces, the sign ruled by Neptune, while Neptune is in Aquarius, the sign ruled by Uranus. Mutual reception is generally considered beneficial, as the two planets support each other. When this seven-year dance of Uranus and Neptune is over, it is very likely that the world will be in a very different condition politically and socially.

## Uranus in Pisces

Uranus, known as the "Great Awakener," tends to cause both upheaval and innovation in the sign it transits. During previous episodes of Uranus in Pisces, great religions and spiritual movements have come into being, most recently Mormonism and Christian Fundamentalism.

In its most positive mode, Pisces promotes imagination and creativity, the art of illusion in theater and film, the inspiration of great artists. A water sign, Pisces is naturally associated with all things liquid—oceans, oil, alcohol—and with those creatures that live in water—fish, the fishing industry, fish habitats. Pisces also rules the underdog, the enslaved, and the disenfranchised, whose status has been illuminated in previous Uranus in Pisces periods.

The last time Uranus was in Pisces was early in the twentieth century from 1919 to 1927, during the "roaring 20s." Prohibition of alcohol (Pisces-ruled) began in 1920, causing secret bootleg industries and speakeasy clubs where racy dancing and upbeat music signaled the "Jazz Age." A unique American music evolved, with great musicians like Louis Armstrong and George Gershwin. It was a time of innovation in the Pisces fields of film and theater, which extended to the electronic inventions of radio and television. In literature, the "Lost Generation" of American writers began publishing. Socially, the underdog triumphed. Women finally won the right to vote in 1920. Gandhi began the peaceful noncooperation movement against the British in India. Yet the underworld also thrived, such as the Mafia's secret "Cosa Nostra" and the precursor of the IRA in Ireland.

The nineteenth-century period of Uranus in Pisces, from 1836 to 1843, a time of widespread Pisces and Aquarius issues, might also give us a preview of what to expect. At that time, as the Victorian Era began, there were rumblings of women's rights. Victoria Woodhull, who would later be the first female to run for U.S. President, was born. The issue of slavery was coming to a head. The slave ship *Amistad* mutinied and ran aground on Long Island, New York, in 1839. A legal battle ensued that went to the Supreme Court, where former President John Quincy Adams argued for the rebel slaves' freedom and won. The saga of the *Amistad* has inspired books, an opera, and a major film. The Cherokee "Trail of Tears" march to Oklahoma was another dramatic and sorrowful episode. Baseball was invented. Financier J. P. Morgan and John D. Rockefeller, founder of Standard Oil, were born. Many great artists and composers, such

4

as Cézanne, Monet, Renoir, Winslow Homer, and Tchaikovsky, were born. The Cunard Line celebrated its first Atlantic crossing. There were great inventions in photography, such as the stereoscope and the daguerreotype. The Opium Wars erupted in China. Wars between the Afghans and the British resulted in the British being driven from Afghanistan. In America, Mexicans defeated 182 Texans at the Alamo.

These moments from history could give us clues about what to expect in the current Uranus in Pisces transit. Perhaps the first woman president of the United States will be elected, and the emancipation of women in Arab countries will proceed.

Pisces rules the prenatal phase of life, which is related to regenerative medicine. The controversy over embryonic stem cell research should continue to be debated.

Petroleum issues, both in the oil-producing countries and offshore oil drilling, will come to a head. Uranus in Pisces suggests that development of new hydroelectric sources may provide the power we need to continue our current power-thirsty lifestyle.

Just as we saw in the previous eras, there should continue to be a flourishing of the arts. We are seeing many new artistic forms developing now, such as computer-created actors and special effects. The sky's the limit on this influence.

Those who have problems with Uranus are those who resist change, so the key is to embrace the future. Those born in early Pisces, February 20 to 26, are most likely to have Uranus changes in their lives this year. Go with the flow!

# Neptune in Aquarius

Neptune is a planet of imagination and creativity, but also of deception and illusion. In recent years there have been dramatic scams and scandals, especially in the high-tech area associated with Aquarius.

Neptune is associated with hospitals, which are acquiring cutting-edge technology. The atmosphere of many hospitals is already changing from the intimidating and sterile environment of the past to that of a health-promoting spa. Here alternative therapies such as massage, diet counseling, and aromatherapy are available, which tells of the Neptune and Pisces trend. New procedures in plastic surgery, also a Neptune glamour field, and antiaging therapies should restore the illusion of youth.

Those born February 1 to 5 will feel the foggy influence of Neptune this year.


# Pluto in Sagittarius: Religious Intensity Continues

The slow-moving planet Pluto is our guide to life-changing, long-term trends. In Sagittarius until 2008, Pluto is emphasizing everything associated with this sign to prepare us philosophically and spiritually for things to come. Those born from December 11 to 14 will be feeling the force of Pluto this year.

Perhaps the most pervasive sign of Pluto in Sagittarius over the past few years has been globalization in all its forms. We are re-forming boundaries, creating new forms of travel. A space station may soon be one of the brightest objects in the sky.

In true Sagittarius fashion, Pluto will shift our emphasis away from acquiring wealth to a quest for the meaning of it all, as upward strivers discover that money and power are not enough and religious extremists assert themselves. Sagittarius is the sign of linking everything together. Therefore, the trend will be to find ways to interconnect on a spiritual, philosophical, and intellectual level.

The spiritual emphasis of Pluto in Sagittarius has already filtered down to our home lives. Home altars and private sanctuaries are becoming a part of our personal environment.

Pluto in Sagittarius has expanded the experience of religion into other areas of our lives. For example, vast church complexes are now being built, which combine religious activities with sports centers, health clubs, malls, and theme parks. Look for an expansion in religious education and religious book publishing as well.

Sagittarius are known for their love of animals, especially horses. Horse racing has become popular again, thanks to charismatic horses like War Emblem. America has never been more pet-happy. Look for extremes related to animal welfare, such as vegetarianism, which will become even more popular and widespread as a lifestyle. As habitats are destroyed, the care, feeding, and control of wild animals will become a larger issue, especially where there are deer, bears, and coyotes in the backyard.

The Sagittarius love of the outdoors combined with Pluto's power has already promoted extreme sports, especially those that require strong legs, like rock climbing, trekking, or snowboarding. Rugged, sporty all-terrain vehicles continue to be popular. Expect the trend toward more adventurous travel as well as fitness or sports-oriented vacations to accelerate. Exotic hiking trips to unexplored territories, mountain-climbing expeditions, spa vacations, and sports-associated resorts are part of this trend.

Publishing, which is associated with Sagittarius, has been transformed by the Internet, with an enormous variety of books available. Internet publishing is coming of age and should continue to develop under Pluto in Sagittarius. It is fascinating that the on-line bookstore Amazon.com took the Sagittarius-influenced name of the fierce female tribe of archer-warriors. There should continue to be more inspirational books, aimed at those who are interested in spirituality outside of traditional religions.

# Jupiter: Who's Lucky in 2004?

Good fortune, expansion, and big money opportunities are associated with the movement of Jupiter, the planet that embodies the principle of expansion. Jupiter has a twelve-year cycle, staying in each sign for approximately one year.

When Jupiter enters a sign, the fields associated with that sign usually provide excellent opportunities. Areas of speculation associated with the sign Jupiter is passing through will have the hottest market potential—the ones that currently arouse excitement and enthusiasm.

Those born under Virgo and Libra, the signs through which Jupiter is moving in 2004, should have many opportunities during the year.

However, the key is to keep your feet on the ground. The flip side of Jupiter is that there are no limits. You can expand off the planet under a Jupiter transit, which is why the planet is often called the "Gateway to Heaven." If something is going to burst (such as an artery) or overextend or go over the top in some way, it could happen under a supposedly "lucky" Jupiter transit—so be aware. A current Jupiter-favored celebrity is embroiled in a devastating scandal because of a foolish slipup. Don't let it happen to you!

Those born under Pisces and Aries may find their best opportunities working with partners this year, as Jupiter will be transiting their seventh house of relationships.

# Saturn in Cancer

Saturn gives us the rewards we work for. But first we must put in the time, be focused and disciplined. There are no shortcuts with Saturn.

Saturn is currently transiting the sign of Cancer, which has special significance for Americans. The United States is a Cancer country, born July 4, 1776, and President

George W. Bush was born under Cancer (July 7, 1946). So this country is likely to experience the restrictive influence of Saturn, but also the rewards and maturity that come after being tested.

Other Cancer areas under Saturn's influence will be: domesticity, the home and homeland, the food supply, digestion, motherhood, milk, dairy products, hotels, restaurants, boating, cruise ships, waterways, water-related industries, crabs, seafowl, the tides, the moon.

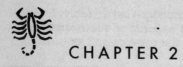

# CHAPTER 2

# Timing Secrets of the Stars: How to Pick the Best Time to Make Your Big Moves

Have you ever wondered if there was a lucky time to plan big events, schedule meetings and medical appointments, even change your hairstyle? Maybe you could benefit by timing an event to happen on an astrologically auspicious day.

For instance, when mischievous Mercury creates havoc with communications, you'll back up your vital computer files, read between the lines of contracts, and put off closing that deal until you have double-checked all the information. When Venus passes through your sign, you're the romantic flavor of the month. That's when your sex appeal is hottest. Get a knockout new outfit or hairstyle, then ask someone you'd like to know better to dinner. Venus timing can also help you charm clients with a stunning sales pitch or make an offer they won't refuse.

Coordinating your schedule with the stars couldn't be easier, thanks to this book! In this chapter you will learn how to find your best times as well as which times to avoid. You will also learn how to read the moods of the moon and make them work for you. Use the information and tables in this chapter and in chapter 4 on the planets, and also use the moon sign listings in your daily forecasts.

Here are the happenings to note on your agenda:

- Dates of your sun sign (high-energy period)
- The month previous to your sun sign (low-energy period)
- Dates of planets in your sign this year
- Full and new moons (Pay special attention when these fall in your sun sign!)
- Eclipses
- Moon in your sun sign every month, as well as moon in the opposite sign (listed in daily forecast)
- Mercury retrogrades
- Other retrograde periods

# Your Birthday Starts Your Solar Cycle

You should feel a new surge of vitality as the powerful sun enters your sign. This is the time when predominant energies are most favorable to you. So go for it! Start new projects, make your big moves (especially when the new moon is in your sign, doubling your charisma). You'll get the recognition you deserve now, when everyone is attuned to your sun sign. Look in the tables in this book to see if other planets will also be passing through your sun sign at this time. Venus (love, beauty), Mars (energy, drive), and Mercury (communication, mental sharpness) reinforce the sun and give an extra boost to your life in the areas they affect. Venus will rev up your social and love life, making you seem especially attractive. Mars amplifies your energy and drive. Mercury fuels your brainpower and helps you communicate. Jupiter signals an especially lucky period of expansion.

There are two "down" times related to the sun. During the month before your birthday period, when you are winding up your annual cycle, you could be feeling especially vulnerable and depleted. So at that time get extra rest, watch your diet, and take it easy. Don't overstress yourself. Use this time to gear up for a big "push" when the sun enters your sign.

11

Another "down" time is when the sun is in a sign opposite your sun sign (six months from your birthday). That's when the prevailing energies are very different from yours. You may feel at odds with the world. You'll have to work harder for recognition because people are not on your wavelength. However, this could be a good time to work on a team, in cooperation with others, or behind the scenes.

# Make the Moon Your Daily Planner

The moon is a powerful tool to divine the mood of the moment. You can work with the moon in two ways. Plan by the *sign* the moon is in; plan by the *phase* of the moon. The sign will tell you the kind of activities that suit the moon's mood. The phase will tell you the best time to start or finish a certain activity.

Working with the phases of the moon is as easy as looking up at the night sky. During the new moon, when both the sun and moon are in the same sign, begin new ventures—especially activities that are favored by that sign. Then you'll utilize the powerful energies pulling you in the same direction. You'll be focused outward, toward action, and in a doing mode. Postpone breaking off, terminating, deliberating, or reflecting—activities that require introspection and passive work. These are better suited to a later moon phase.

Get your project under way during the first quarter. Then go public at the full moon, a time of high intensity, when feelings come out into the open. This is your time to shine—to express yourself. Be aware, however, that because pressures are being released, other people will also be letting off steam. Since confrontations are possible, take advantage of this time either to air grievances or to avoid arguments. Traditionally, astrologers often advise against surgery at this time, which could produce heavier bleeding.

About three days after the full moon comes the disseminating phase, a time when the energy of the cycle begins to wind down. From the last quarter of the moon to the next new moon, it's a time to cut off unproductive relationships, do serious thinking, and focus on inward-directed activities.

You'll feel some new and full moons more strongly than others, especially those new moons that fall in your sun sign and full moons in your opposite sign. Because that full moon happens at your low-energy time of year, it is likely to be an especially stressful time in a relationship, when any hidden problems or unexpressed emotions could surface.

# Full and New Moons in 2004

All dates are calculated for Eastern Standard Time and Eastern Daylight Time.

Full Moon—January 7 in Cancer
New Moon—January 21 in Aquarius

Full Moon—February 6 in Leo
New Moon—February 20 in Pisces

Full Moon—March 6 in Virgo
New Moon—March 20 in Aries

Full Moon—April 5 in Libra
New Moon—April 19 in Aries

Full Moon—May 4 in Scorpio
New Moon—May 18 in Taurus

Full Moon—June 3 in Sagittarius
New Moon—June 17 in Gemini

Full Moon—July 2 in Capricorn
New Moon—July 17 in Cancer
Full Moon—July 31 in Aquarius

13

New Moon—August 15 in Leo
Full Moon—August 29 in Pisces

New Moon—September 14 in Scorpio
Full Moon—September 28 in Aries

New Moon—October 13 in Libra
Full Moon—October 27 in Taurus

New Moon—November 12 in Scorpio
Full Moon—November 26 in Gemini

New Moon—December 11 in Sagittarius
Full Moon—December 26 in Cancer

# Moon Sign Timing

To forecast the daily emotional "weather," to determine your monthly high and low days, or to synchronize your activities with the cycles of the moon, take note of the moon's sign under your daily forecast at the end of the book. Here are some of the activities favored and the moods you are likely to encounter under each moon sign.

## Moon in Aries

Get moving! The new moon in Aries is an ideal time to start new projects. Everyone is pushy, raring to go, rather impatient, and short-tempered. Leave details and follow-up for later. Competitive sports or martial arts are great ways to let off steam. Quiet types could use some assertiveness, but it's a great day for dynamos. Be careful not to step on too many toes.

## Moon in Taurus

It's time to lay the foundations for success. Do solid, methodical tasks like follow-through or backup work.

14

Make investments, buy real estate, do appraisals, do some hard bargaining. Attend to your property. Get out in the country or spend some time in your garden. Enjoy creature comforts, music, a good dinner, sensual love-making. Forget starting a diet—this is a day when you'll feel self-indulgent.

## Moon in Gemini

Talk means action today. Telephone, write letters, fax! Make new contacts, stay in touch with steady customers. You can juggle lots of tasks today. It's a great time for mental activity of any kind. Don't try to pin people down—they, too, are feeling restless. Keep it light. Flirtations and socializing are good. Watch gossip—and don't give away secrets.

## Moon in Cancer

This is a moody, sensitive, emotional time. People respond to personal attention, to mothering. Stay at home, have a family dinner, call your mother. Nostalgia, memories, and psychic powers are heightened. You'll want to hang on to people and things (don't clean out your closets now). You could have shrewd insights into what others really need and want. Pay attention to dreams, intuition, and gut reactions.

## Moon in Leo

Everybody is in a much more confident, warm, generous mood. It's a good day to ask for a raise, show what you can do, dress like a star. People will respond to flattery, enjoy a bit of drama and theater. You may be extravagant, treat yourself royally, and show off a bit—don't break the bank! Be careful you don't promise more than you can deliver.

## Moon in Virgo

Do practical down-to-earth chores. Review your budget, make repairs, be an efficiency expert. Not a day to ask for a raise. Tend to personal care and maintenance. Have a health checkup, go on a diet, buy vitamins or health food. Make your home spotless. Take care of details and piled-up chores. Reorganize your work and life so they run more smoothly and efficiently. Save money. Be prepared for others to be in a critical, faultfinding mood.

## Moon in Libra

Attend to legal matters. Negotiate contracts. Arbitrate. Do things with your favorite partner. Socialize. Be romantic. Buy a special gift, a beautiful object. Decorate yourself or your surroundings. Buy new clothes. Throw a party. Have an elegant, romantic evening. Smooth over any ruffled feathers. Avoid confrontations. Stick to civilized discussions.

## Moon in Scorpio

This is a day to do things with passion. You'll have excellent concentration and focus. Try not to get too intense emotionally. Avoid sharp exchanges with loved ones. Others may tend to go to extremes, get jealous, overreact. Great for troubleshooting, problem solving, research, scientific work—and making love. Pay attention to those psychic vibes.

## Moon in Sagittarius

A great time for travel, philosophical discussions, setting long-range career goals. Work out, do sports, buy athletic equipment. Others will be feeling upbeat, exuberant, and adventurous. Risk taking is favored. You may feel like taking a gamble, betting on the horses, visiting a local casino, buying a lottery ticket. Teaching, writing, and spiritual activities also get the green light. Relax outdoors. Take care of animals.

## Moon in Capricorn

You can accomplish a lot now, so get on the ball! Attend to business. Issues concerning your basic responsibilities, duties, family, and elderly parents could crop up. You'll be expected to deliver on promises. Weed out the deadwood from your life. Get a dental checkup. Not a good day for gambling or taking risks.

## Moon in Aquarius

A great day for doing things with groups—clubs, meetings, outings, politics, parties. Campaign for your candidate. Work for a worthy cause. Deal with larger issues that affect humanity—the environment and metaphysical questions. Buy a computer or electronic gadget. Watch TV. Wear something outrageous. Try something you've never done before. Present an original idea. Don't stick to a rigid schedule—go with the flow. Take a class in meditation, mind control, yoga.

## Moon in Pisces

This can be a very creative day, so let your imagination work overtime. Film, theater, music, ballet could inspire you. Spend some time alone, resting and reflecting, reading or writing poetry. Daydreams can also be profitable. Help those less fortunate. Lend a listening ear to someone who may be feeling blue. Don't overindulge in self-pity or escapism, however. People are especially vulnerable to substance abuse now. Turn your thoughts to romance and someone special.

# How to Handle Eclipses

One of the most amazing phenomena, which many of us take for granted, is the spatial relationship between the sun and moon. How many of us have ever noticed or marveled that, relative to our viewpoint here on earth, both the largest source of energy (the sun) and the smallest (the moon) appear to be almost exactly the same size? Or wondered what would happen if the moon's orbit became closer to earth or farther away?

This fascinating relationship is most evident to us at the time of the solar eclipse, when the moon is directly aligned with the sun and so nearly covers it that scientists use the moment of eclipse to study solar flares. The darkening of the sun has been used in history and mythology to indicate dire happenings ahead. In some parts of the world, people hide in their homes during the darkening of the sun. When the two most powerful forces in astrology—the sun and moon—are lined up, we're sure to feel the effects both in world events and in our personal lives. Both solar and lunar eclipses are times when our natural rhythms are changed, depending on where the eclipse falls in your horoscope. If the eclipse falls on or close to your birthday, you're going to have important changes in your life, perhaps a turning point.

## Lunar Eclipses

*Lunar eclipse: A momentary "turnoff" that could help us turn our lives around.*

A lunar eclipse happens during a full moon when the earth moves exactly between the sun and moon, breaking their natural monthly opposition. Normally, the earth is not on a level plane; otherwise, eclipses would occur every month. During a lunar eclipse, the earth "short-circuits" the connection between the sun and moon. The effect on us can be either confusion or clarity. Our subconscious lunar energies, which normally respond to the rhythmic cycle of opposing sun and moon, are momentarily turned off. This could cause a bewildering disorientation that intensifies our insecurities. On the other hand, this moment of clarity might give us insights that could help change destructive emotional patterns such as addictions.

## Solar Eclipses

*Solar eclipse: Deep feelings come to the surface.*

The solar eclipse occurs during the new moon. This time, the moon blocks the sun's energies as it passes exactly between the sun and the earth. In astrological interpretation, the moon darkens the objective, conscious force, represented by the sun, allowing subconscious lunar forces, which activate our deepest emotions, to dominate. Emotional truths can be revealed or emotions can run wild, as our solar objectivity is cut off. If your sign is affected, you may find yourself beginning a period of work on a deep inner level. And you may have psychic experiences or deep feelings that come to the surface.

You'll start feeling the energies of an upcoming eclipse a few days after the previous new or full moon. The energy continues to intensify until the actual eclipse, then disperses for three or four days. So plan ahead at least a week or more before an eclipse, then allow several days afterward for the natural rhythms to return. Try not to make major moves during this period. (It's not a great time to get married, change jobs, or buy a home, for instance.)

## Eclipses in 2004

There are four eclipses this year.
    New Moon and Solar Eclipse—April 19 in Aries
    Full Moon and Lunar Eclipse—May 4 in Scorpio
    New Moon and Solar Eclipse—October 13 in Libra
    Full Moon and Lunar Eclipse—October 27 in Taurus

# Retrogrades: When the Planets Seem to Backstep

All the planets, except for the sun and moon, have times when they appear to move backward—or retrograde—as it seems from our point of view on earth. At these times, planets do not work as they normally do. So it's best to "take a break" from that planet's energies in our life and to do some work on an inner level.

## Mercury Retrograde: The Key Is in "Re"

Mercury goes retrograde most often, and its effects can be especially irritating. When it reaches a short distance ahead of the sun several times a year, it seems to move backward from our point of view. Astrologers often compare retrograde motion to the optical illusion that occurs when we ride on a train that passes another train traveling at a different speed—the second train appears to be moving in reverse.

What this means to you is that the Mercury-ruled areas of your life—analytical thought processes, communications, scheduling—are subject to all kinds of confusion. Be prepared. Communications equipment can break down. Schedules may be changed on short notice. People are late for appointments or don't show up at all. Traffic is terrible. Major purchases malfunction, don't work out, or get delivered in the wrong color. Letters don't arrive or are delivered to the wrong address. Employees will make errors that have to be corrected later. Contracts don't work out or must be renegotiated.

Since most of us can't put our lives on "hold" during Mercury retrogrades, we should learn to tame the trickster and make it work for us. The key is in the prefix *re-*. This is the time to go back over things in your life, *re*flect on what you've done during the previous months. Now you can get deeper insights, spot errors you've missed. So take time to *re*view and *re*evaluate what has happened. *R*est and *re*ward yourself—it's a good time to take a vacation, especially if you *re*visit a favorite place. *Re*organize your work and finish up projects that are backed up. Clean out your desk and closets. Throw away what you can't *re*cycle. If you must sign contracts or agreements, do so with a contingency clause that lets you *re*evaluate the terms later.

Postpone major purchases or commitments for the time being. Don't get married (unless you're *re*marrying the same person). Try not to *re*ly on other people keeping appointments, contracts, or agreements to the letter; have several alternatives. Double-check and *re*ad between the lines. Don't buy anything connected with communications or transportation (if you must, be sure to cover yourself).

Mercury retrograding through your sun sign will intensify its effect on your life.

If Mercury was retrograde when you were born, you may be one of the lucky people who don't suffer the frustrations of this period. If so, your mind probably works in a very intuitive, insightful way.

The sign in which Mercury is retrograding can give you an idea of what's in store—as well as the sun signs that will be especially challenged.

# MERCURY RETROGRADES IN 2004

Mercury has four retrograde periods this year.
    December 17, 2003 to January 6, 2004 from Scorpio to Sagittarius
    April 6 to April 30 from Taurus to Aries
    August 9 to September 2 from Virgo to Leo
    November 30 to December 20 in Sagittarius

# Venus Retrograde: Relationship Alert!

Retrograding Venus can cause your relationships to take a backward step, or it can make you extravagant and impractical. Shopping till you drop and buying what you cannot afford are trip-ups at this time. It's *not* a good time to redecorate—you'll hate the color of the walls later. Postpone getting a new hairstyle. Try not to fall in love either. But if you wish to make amends in an already troubled relationship, make peaceful overtures at this time.

## VENUS RETROGRADES IN 2004

Venus has one retrograde period this year: May 17 to June 29 in Gemini.

## Mars Moves: When to Step on the Gas

Mars shows how and when to get where you want to go. Timing your moves with Mars on your side can give you a big push. On the other hand, pushing Mars the wrong way can guarantee that you'll run into frustrations in every corner. Your best times to forge ahead are during the weeks when Mars is traveling through your sun sign or your Mars sign (look these up at the end of chapter 4 on the planets). Also consider times when Mars is in a compatible sign (fire with air signs, or earth with water signs). You'll be sure to have planetary power on your side.

## MARS RETROGRADES IN 2004

There is no Mars retrograde period in 2004.

## When Other Planets Retrograde

The slower-moving planets stay retrograde for months at a time (Jupiter, Saturn, Neptune, Uranus, and Pluto).

When Saturn is retrograde, it's an uphill battle with self-discipline. You may not be in the mood for work. You may feel more like hanging out at the beach than getting things done.

Neptune retrograde promotes a dreamy escapism from

reality, when you may feel you're in a fog (Pisces will feel this, especially).

Uranus retrograde may mean setbacks in areas where there have been sudden changes, when you may be forced to regroup or reevaluate the situation.

Pluto retrograde is a time to work on establishing proportion and balance in areas where there have been recent dramatic transformations.

When the planets move forward again, there's a shift in the atmosphere. Activities connected with each planet start moving ahead, plans that were stalled get rolling. Make a special note of those days on your calendar and proceed accordingly.

## OTHER RETROGRADES IN 2004

The five slower-moving planets all go retrograde in 2004.

Jupiter retrogrades from January 3 to May 4 in Virgo.

Saturn retrogrades from October 25, 2003 to March 7, 2004 in Cancer, then turns retrograde again on November 8, also in Cancer, for the duration of the year.

Uranus retrogrades from June 10 to November 11 in Pisces.

Neptune retrogrades from May 17 to October 24 in Aquarius.

Pluto retrogrades from March 24 to August 30 in Sagittarius.

# CHAPTER 3

# Introduction to Astrology

The basic principles of astrology are easy to learn. Once you know the basics, you can penetrate beyond the realm of your sun sign into the deeper areas of this fascinating subject, which combines science, art, spirituality, and psychology. You'll find the more you know, the more you'll want to know. So let's get started.

## Signs and Constellations: What's the Difference?

First, let's get our "sign language" straight because, for most readers, that's the starting point of astrology.

*Signs* are actually a type of celestial real estate, located on the *zodiac,* an imaginary 360-degree belt circling the earth. This belt is divided into twelve equal 30-degree portions, and these are the signs. There's confusion about the difference between the *signs* and the *constellations* of the zodiac. Constellations are patterns of stars that originally marked the twelve divisions, like signposts. Though a sign is named after the constellation that once marked the same area, the constellations are no longer in the same place relative to the earth they were centuries ago. Over hundreds of years, the earth's orbit has shifted, so that from our point of view here on earth the constellations moved. However, the signs remain in place. Most Western astrologers use the twelve-equal-part division of the zodiac. However, there are some methods of astrology that do still use the constellations instead of the signs.

Most people think of themselves in terms of their *sun sign*. A sun sign refers to the sign the sun is orbiting through at a given moment (from our point of view here on earth). For instance "I'm an Aries" means that the sun was passing through Aries when that person was born. However, there are nine other planets (plus asteroids, fixed stars, and sensitive points) that also form our total astrological personality, and some or many of these will be located in other signs. No one is completely "Aries," with all their astrological components in one sign! (Please note that, in astrology, the sun and moon are usually referred to as "planets," though of course they're not.)

As mentioned before, the sun signs are areas on the zodiac. They do not *do* anything (planets are the doers). However, they are associated with many things, depending on their location.

# Why Is a Sign Defined a Certain Way?

What makes Aries the sign of go-getters, Taurus savvy with money, Gemini talk a blue streak, and Sagittarius footloose? Definitions of the signs are not accidental. They are derived from different combinations of four concepts: a sign's *element, quality (modality*, or the way it operates), polarity, and *place (order)* in the zodiac lineup.

Take the element of fire: it's hot, passionate. Then add the active cardinal mode. Give it a jolt of positive energy, and place it first in line. And doesn't that sound like the active, me-first, driving, hotheaded, energetic Aries?

Then take the element of earth: it's practical, sensual, where things grow. Add the fixed, stable mode. Give it energy that reacts to its surroundings, that settles in. Put it after Aries. Now you've got a good idea of how sensual, earthy Taurus operates.

25

Another way to grasp the idea is to pretend you're doing a magical puzzle based on the numbers that can divide into twelve (the number of signs): 4, 3, and 2. There are four "building blocks" or elements, three ways a sign operates (qualities), and two polarities. These alternate in turn around the zodiac, with a different combination coming up for each sign.

## The Four Elements

First, consider the four elements that describe the physical concept of the sign. Is it *fiery* (dynamic), *earthy* (practical), *airy* (mental), *watery* (emotional)? Therefore, there are three zodiac signs of each of the four elements: *fire* (Aries, Leo, Sagittarius); *earth* (Taurus, Virgo, Capricorn); *air* (Gemini, Libra, Aquarius); *water* (Cancer, Scorpio, Pisces). These are the same elements that make up our planet: earth, air, fire, and water. But astrology uses the elements as *symbols* that link our body and psyche to the rhythms of the planets.

Fire signs spread warmth and enthusiasm. They are able to fire up or motivate others. They have hot tempers. These are people who make ideas catch fire and spring into existence. Earth signs are the builders of the zodiac who follow through after the initiative of fire signs to make things happen. These people are solid, practical realists who enjoy material things and sensual pleasures. They are interested in ideas that can be used to achieve concrete results. Air signs are mental people, great communicators. Following the consolidating earth signs, they'll reach out to inspire others through the use of words, social contacts, discussion, and debate. Water signs complete each four-sign series adding the ingredients of emotion, compassion, and imagination. Water sign people are nonverbal communicators who attune themselves to their surroundings and react through the medium of feelings.

## The Three Qualities

The second consideration when defining a sign is how it will operate. Will it take the initiative, or move slowly and deliberately, or adapt easily? It's *quality* (or modality) will tell. There are three qualities and four signs of each quality: cardinal, fixed, and mutable.

*Cardinal signs* are the start-up signs that begin each season (Aries, Cancer, Libra, Capricorn). These people love to be active, involved in projects. They are usually on the fast track to success, impatient to get things under way. *Fixed signs* (Taurus, Leo, Scorpio, Aquarius) move steadily, always in control. They happen in the middle of a season, after the initial character of the season is established. Fixed signs are naturally more centered. They tend to move more deliberately, do things more slowly but thoroughly. They govern parts of your horoscope where you take root and integrate your experiences. *Mutable signs* (Gemini, Virgo, Sagittarius, Pisces) embody the principle of distribution. These are the signs that break up the cycle, then prepare the way for a change by distributing the energy to the next group. Mutables are flexible, adaptable, communicative. They can move in many directions easily, darting around obstacles.

# The Two Polarities

In addition to an element and a quality, each sign has a *polarity,* either a positive or a negative electrical charge that generates energy around the zodiac, like a giant battery. Polarity refers to opposites, which you could also define as masculine/feminine, yin/yang, active/reactive. Alternating around the zodiac, the six fire and air signs are positive, active, masculine, and yang in polarity. These signs are open, expanding outward. The six earth and water signs are reactive, negative, and yin in polarity. They are nurturing and receptive, which allows the energy to develop and take shape. All positive energy would be like a car without brakes. All negative energy would be like a stalled vehicle, going nowhere. Both polarities are needed in balanced proportion.

# The Order of the Signs: Their Place

Finally we must consider the *order* of the signs—that is the *place* each sign occupies in the zodiac. This consideration is vital to the balance of the zodiac and the transmission of energy throughout the zodiac. Each sign is quite different from its neighbors on either side. Yet each seems to grow out of its predecessor like links in a chain. And each transmits a synthesis of energy gathered along the chain to the following sign—beginning with the fiery, active, positive, cardinal sign of Aries and ending with the watery, mutable, reactive Pisces.

The table shows how the signs shape up according to the four characteristics discussed.

### How the Signs Add Up

| Sign | Element | Quality | Polarity | Place |
| --- | --- | --- | --- | --- |
| Aries | fire | cardinal | masculine | first |
| Taurus | earth | fixed | feminine | second |
| Gemini | air | mutable | masculine | third |
| Cancer | water | cardinal | feminine | fourth |
| Leo | fire | fixed | masculine | fifth |
| Virgo | earth | mutable | feminine | sixth |
| Libra | air | cardinal | masculine | seventh |
| Scorpio | water | fixed | feminine | cighth |
| Sagittarius | fire | mutable | masculine | ninth |
| Capricorn | earth | cardinal | feminine | tenth |
| Aquarius | air | fixed | masculine | eleventh |
| Pisces | water | mutable | feminine | twelfth |

# The Houses and the Horoscope Chart

A horoscope chart is a map of the heavens at a given moment in time. It looks somewhat like a wheel divided with twelve spokes. In between each of the "spokes" is a section called a *house.*

Each house deals with a different area of life and is influenced by a special sign and a planet. In addition, the house is governed by the sign passing over the spoke (or cusp of the house) at that particular moment. For example, the first house is naturally associated with Aries and Mars. However, if Capricorn was the sign passing over the house cusp at the time the chart was cast, that house would have a Capricorn influence as well.

The houses start at the left center spoke (the number 9 position if you were reading a clock) and are read *counterclockwise* around the chart.

Astrologers look at the houses to tell in what area of a subject's life an event is happening or about to happen in the subject's career, finances, health, or other area designated by the house.

## The First House: Home of Aries and Mars

The sign passing over the first house at the time of your birth is known as your *ascendant,* or *rising sign.* The first house is the house of "firsts"—the first impression you make, how you initiate matters, the image you choose to project. This is where you advertise yourself, where you project your personality. Planets that fall here will intensify the way you come across to others. Often the first house will project an entirely different type of personality than the sun sign. For instance, a Capricorn with Leo in the first house will come across as much more flamboyant than the average Capricorn.

## The Second House: Home of Taurus and Venus

This house is where you experience the material world—what you value. Here are your attitudes about money, possessions, finances, whatever belongs to you, and what you own, as well as your earning and spending capacity. On a deeper level, this house reveals your sense of self-worth, the inner values that draw wealth in various forms.

## The Third House: Home of Gemini and Mercury

This house describes how you communicate with others, how you reach out to others nearby, and how you interact with the immediate environment. It shows how your thinking process works and the way you express your thoughts. Are you articulate or tongue-tied? Can you think on your feet? This house also shows your first relationships, your experiences with brothers and sisters, and how you deal with people close to you such as your neighbors or pals. It's where you take short trips, write letters, or use the telephone. It shows how your mind works in terms of left-brain logical and analytical functions.

## The Fourth House: Home of Cancer and the Moon

The fourth house shows the foundation of life, the psychological underpinnings. At the bottom of the chart, this house shows how you are nurtured and made to feel secure—your roots! It shows your early home environment and the circumstances at the end of your life (your final "home") as well as the place you call home now. Astrologers look here for information about the parental nurturers in your life.

# The Fifth House: Home of Leo and the Sun

The fifth house is where the creative potential develops. Here you express yourself and procreate in the sense that children are outgrowths of your creative ability. But this house most represents your inner childlike self who delights in play. If your inner security has been established by the time you reach this house, you are now free to have fun, romance, and love affairs and to give of yourself. This is also the place astrologers look for playful love affairs, flirtations, and brief romantic encounters (rather than long-term commitments).

# The Sixth House: Home of Virgo and Mercury

The sixth house has been called the "repair and maintenance" department. This house shows how you take care of your body and organize yourself to perform efficiently in the world. Here is where you get things done, where you look after others, and fulfill service duties such as taking care of pets. Here is what you do to survive on a day-to-day basis. The sixth house demands order in your life; otherwise there would be chaos. This house is your "job" (as opposed to your career, which is the domain of the tenth house), your diet, and your health and fitness regimens.

# The Seventh House: Home of Libra and Venus

This house shows your attitude toward partners and those with whom you enter commitments, contracts, or agreements. Here is the way you relate to others, as well as your close, intimate, one-on-one relationships (including open enemies—those you "face off" with). Open hostilities, lawsuits, divorces, and marriages happen here. If the first house represents the "I," the seventh or opposite house is the "not-I"—the complementary partner you attract by the way you come across. If you are having trouble with partnerships, consider what you are attracting by the energies of your first and seventh house.

## The Eighth House: Home of Scorpio and Pluto (also Mars)

The eighth house refers to how you merge with something or someone, and how you handle power and control. This is one of the most mysterious and powerful houses, where your energy transforms itself from "I" to "we." As you give up power and control by uniting with something or someone, two kinds of energies merge and become something greater, leading to a regeneration of the self on a higher level. Here are your attitudes toward sex, shared resources, taxes (what you share with the government). Because this house involves what belongs to others, you face issues of control and power struggles, or undergo a deep psychological transformation as you bond with another. Here you transcend yourself with dreams, drugs, and occult or psychic experiences that reflect the collective unconscious.

## The Ninth House: Home of Sagittarius and Jupiter

The ninth house shows your search for wisdom and higher knowledge—your belief system. As the third house represents the "lower mind," its opposite on the wheel, the ninth house, is the "higher mind"—the abstract, intuitive, spiritual mind that asks "big" questions like "Why are we here?" After the third house has explored what was close at hand, the ninth stretches out to broaden you mentally with higher education and travel. Here you stretch spiritually with religious activity. Since you are concerned with how everything is related, you tend to push boundaries, take risks. Here is where you express your ideas in a book or thesis, where you pontificate, philosophize, or preach.

# The Tenth House: Home of Capricorn and Saturn

The tenth house is associated with your public life and high-profile activities. Located directly overhead at the "high noon" position on the horoscope wheel, this is the most "visible" house in the chart, the one where the world sees you. It deals with your career (but not your routine "job") and your reputation. Here is where you go public, take on responsibilities (as opposed to the fourth house, where you stay home). This will affect the career you choose and your "public relations." This house is also associated with your father figure or the main authority figure in your life.

# The Eleventh House: Home of Aquarius and Uranus

The eleventh house is where you extend yourself to a group, a goal, or a belief system. This house is where you define what you really want, the kinds of friends you have, your political affiliations, and the kind of groups you identify with as an equal. Here is where you become concerned with "what other people think" or where you rebel against social conventions. Here is where you could become a socially conscious humanitarian or a partygoing social butterfly. It's where you look to others to stimulate you and discover your kinship to the rest of humanity. The sign on this house can help you understand what you gain and lose from friendships.

# The Twelfth House: Home of Pisces and Neptune

The twelfth house is where the boundaries between yourself and others become blurred, and you become selfless. Old-fashioned astrologers used to put a rather negative spin on this house, calling it the "house of self-undoing." When we "undo ourselves," we surrender control, boundaries, limits, and rules. But instead of being self-undoing, the twelfth house can be a place of great creativity and talent. It is the place where you can tap into the collective unconscious, where your imagination is limitless.

In your trip around the zodiac, you've gone from the "I" of self-assertion in the first house to the final house symbolizing the dissolution that happens before rebirth. It's where accumulated experiences are processed in the unconscious.

Spiritually oriented astrologers look to this house for evidence of past lives and karma. Places where we go for solitude or to do spiritual or reparatory work such as retreats, religious institutions, and hospitals belong to the twelfth house. Here is also where we withdraw from society voluntarily or involuntarily, put to prison because of antisocial activity. Selfless giving through charitable acts is part of this house, as is helpless receiving or dependence on charity.

In your daily life, the twelfth house reveals your deepest intimacies, your best-kept secrets, especially those you hide from yourself and keep repressed deep in the unconscious. It is where we surrender a sense of a separate self to a deep feeling of wholeness, such as selfless service in religion or any activity that involves merging with the greater whole. Many sports stars have important planets in the twelfth house that enable them to lay in the "zone," finding an inner, almost mystical, strength that transcends their limits.

# Who's Home in Your Houses?

Houses are stronger or weaker depending on how many planets are inhabiting them. If there are many planets in a given house, it follows that the activities of that house will be especially important in your life. If the planet that rules the house is also located there, this also adds power to the house.

In the next chapter we will visit the planets.

# CHAPTER 4

# Know Your Planets

When you know a person's sun sign, you already know some very useful generic qualities about that person. But when you know the placement of all ten planets, that person becomes an astrological individual with a unique horoscope. Therefore, you have a much more accurate profile of the person. And, with the full planetary picture of the horoscope, you'll be much more capable of predicting how that individual will act in a given situation.

Your horoscope includes nine other planets besides the sun—the moon is regarded as a "planet," too. Each planet represents a basic force in life. The planets are the actors of the horoscope chart. The sign and house where the planet is located in the chart represents how and where this force will manifest.

The importance of a planet in your horoscope depends on its position. A planet that's close to your rising sign will be highlighted in your chart. If two or more planets are grouped together in one sign, they usually operate like a team, playing off each other rather than expressing their energy singularly. A planet that stands alone, away from the others, is usually outstanding and often calls the shots.

Each planet has two signs where it is especially at home. These are called its *dignities*. The most favorable place for a planet is in the sign or signs it rules; the next best place is in a sign where it is *exalted*, or especially harmonious. On the other hand, there are places in the horoscope where a planet has to work harder to play its role. These places are called the planets *detriment* and *fall*. The sign opposite a planet's rulership, which embodies the opposite area of life, is its *detriment*. The sign opposite its exaltation is its *fall*. Though these terms may suggest unfortunate circumstances for the planet, that is not always true. In fact, a planet that is debilitated can actually be more complete because it must stretch itself to meet the challenges of living in a more difficult sign. Like world leaders who've had to struggle for greatness, this planet may actually develop great strength and character.

Here's a list of the best places for each planet to be. Note that, as new planets were discovered, they replaced the traditional rulers of signs which best complemented their energies.

ARIES—Mars

TAURUS—Venus, in its most sensual form

GEMINI—Mercury, in its communicative role

CANCER—the moon

LEO—the sun

VIRGO—also Mercury, this time in its more critical capacity

LIBRA—also Venus, in its more aesthetic, judgmental form

SCORPIO—Pluto, replacing Mars, the sign's original ruler

SAGITTARIUS—Jupiter

CAPRICORN—Saturn

AQUARIUS—Uranus, replacing Saturn, its original ruler

PISCES—Neptune, replacing Jupiter, its original ruler

A person who has many planets in exalted signs is lucky indeed, for here is where the planet can accomplish the most and be its most influential and creative.

SUN—exalted in Aries, where its energy creates action

MOON—exalted in Taurus, where instincts and reactions operate on a highly creative level

MERCURY—exalted in Aquarius, where it can reach analytical heights

36

VENUS—exalted in Pisces, a sign whose sensitivity encourages love and creativity

MARS—exalted in Capricorn, a sign that puts energy to work productively

JUPITER—exalted in Cancer, where it encourages nurturing and growth

SATURN—at home in Libra, where it steadies the scales of justice and promotes balanced, responsible judgment

URANUS—powerful in Scorpio, where it promotes transformation

NEPTUNE—especially favored in Cancer, where it gains the security to transcend to a higher state

PLUTO—exalted in Pisces, where it dissolves the old cycle to make way for transition to the new

# The Sun Is Always First to Consider

Your sun sign is the part of you that shines brightest. Since the sun is always the first consideration, it is important to treat it as the star of the show. It is your conscious ego. It is always center stage, even when sharing a house or a sign with several other planets. This is why sun sign astrology works for so many people. In chart interpretations, the sun can also play the parental role.

The sun rules the sign of Leo, gaining strength through the pride, dignity, and confidence of this fixed, fiery personality. It is exalted in "me-first" Aries. In its detriment, Aquarius, the sun ego is strengthened through group participation and social consciousness rather than through self-centeredness. Note how many Aquarius people are involved in politics, social work, public life, and follow the demands of their sun sign to be spokesperson for a group. In its fall, Libra, the sun needs the strength of a partner—an "other"—to enhance balance and self-expression.

Like your sun sign, each of the other nine planet's personalities is colored by the sign it is passing through at the time. For example, Mercury, the planet that rules the way you communicate, will express itself in a dynamic, headstrong Aries way if it is passing through the sign of Aries when you were born. You would communicate in a much different way if it is passing through the slower, more patient sign of Taurus. And so on through the list.

Here's a rundown of the planets and how they behave in every sign.

# The Moon Expresses Your Inner Feelings

The moon can teach you about the inner side of yourself, your needs and secrets, as well as those of others. It is your most personal planet—the receptive, reflective, female, nurturing side of you. And it reflects who you were nurtured by—the "mother" or mother figure in your chart. In a man's chart, the moon position also describes his female, receptive, emotional side as well as the woman in his life who will have the deepest effect. (Venus reveals the kind of woman who attracts him physically.)

The sign the moon was passing through at your birth reflects your instinctive emotional nature, what appeals to you subconsciously. Since accurate moon tables are too extensive for this book, check through these descriptions to find the moon sign that feels most familiar. Or, better yet, have your chart calculated by a computer service to get your accurate moon placement.

The moon rules maternal Cancer and is exalted in Taurus—both comforting, home-loving signs where the natural emotional energies of the moon are easily and productively expressed. But when the moon is in the opposite signs—in its Capricorn detriment and its Scorpio fall—it leaves the comfortable nest and deals with emotional issues of power and achievement in the outside world. Those of you with the moon in these signs will find your emotional role more challenging in life.

## Moon in Aries

You are an idealistic, impetuous person who falls in and out of love easily. This moon placement makes you both independent and ardent. You love a challenge, but could cool once your quarry is captured. You should cultivate patience and tolerance. Otherwise, you might gravitate toward those who treat you rough, just for the sake of challenge and excitement.

## Moon in Taurus

You are a sentimental soul who is very fond of the good life. You gravitate toward solid, secure relationships. You like displays of affection and creature comforts—all the tangible trappings of a cozy, safe, calm atmosphere. You are sensual and steady emotionally, but very stubborn and determined. You can't be pushed and tend to dislike changes. You should make an effort to broaden your horizons and to take a risk sometimes.

## Moon in Gemini

You crave mental stimulation and variety in life, which you usually get through an ever-varied social life or the excitement of flirtation, or multiple professional involvements—or all of these. You may marry more than once and have a rather chaotic emotional life due to your difficulty with commitment and settling down. Be sure to find a partner who is as outgoing as you are. You will have to learn at some point to focus your energies because you tend to be somewhat fragmented—to do two things at once, to have two homes, even to have two lovers. If you can find a creative way to express your many-faceted nature, you'll be ahead of the game.

# Moon in Cancer

This is the most powerful lunar position. It is sure to make a deep imprint on your character. Your needs are very much associated with your reaction to the needs of others. You are very sensitive and self-protective, though some of you may mask this with a hard shell. This placement also gives an excellent memory, keen intuition, and an uncanny ability to perceive the needs of others. All of the lunar phases will affect you, especially full moons and eclipses, so you would do well to mark them on your calendar. Because you're happiest at home, you may work at home or turn your office into a second home where you can nurture and comfort people. (You may tend to "mother the world.") With natural psychic and intuitive ability, you might be drawn to occult work in some way. Or you may get professionally involved with providing food and shelter to others.

# Moon in Leo

This warm, passionate moon takes everything to heart. You are attracted to all that is noble, generous, and aristocratic in life (and may be a bit of a snob). You have an innate ability to take command emotionally, but you do need strong support, loyalty, and loud applause from those you love. You are possessive of your loved ones and your turf, and will roar if anyone threatens to take over your territory.

# Moon in Virgo

You are rather cool until you decide if others measure up. But once someone or something meets your ideal standards, you hold up your end of the arrangement perfectly. You may, in fact, drive yourself too hard to attain some notion of perfection. Try to be a bit easier on yourself and others. Don't always act the censor! You love to be the teacher. You are drawn to situations where you can change others for the better, but sometimes you must learn to accept others for what they are. Enjoy what you have!

## Moon in Libra

A partnership-oriented moon, you may find it difficult to be alone or to do things alone. After you have learned emotional balance by leaning on yourself first, you can have excellent relationships. It is best for you to avoid extremes, which set your scales swinging and can make your love life precarious. You thrive in a rather conservative, traditional, romantic relationship where you receive attention and flattery—but not possessiveness—from your partner. You'll be your most charming in an elegant, harmonious atmosphere.

## Moon in Scorpio

This is a moon that enjoys and responds to intense, passionate feelings. You may go to extremes and have a very dramatic emotional life, full of ardor, suspicion, jealousy, and obsession. It would be much healthier to channel your need for power and control into meaningful work. This is a good position for anyone in the fields of medicine, police work, research, the occult, psychoanalysis, or intuitive work, because life-and-death situations don't faze you. However, you do take personal disappointments very hard.

## Moon in Sagittarius

You take life's ups and downs with good humor and the proverbial grain of salt. You'll love 'em and leave 'em, taking off on a great adventure at a moment's notice. "Born free" could be your slogan. Attracted by the exotic, you have wanderlust mentally and physically. You may be too much in search of new mental and spiritual stimulation to ever settle down.

## Moon in Capricorn

Are you ever accused of being too cool and calculating? You have an earthy side, but you take prestige and position very seriously. Your strong drive to succeed extends to your romantic life where you will be devoted to improving your lifestyle and rising to the top. A structured situation where you can advance methodically makes you feel wonderfully secure. You may be attracted to someone older or very much younger or from a different social world. It may be difficult to look at the lighter side of emotional relationships. Though this moon is placed in the sign of its detriment, the good news is that you tend to be very dutiful and responsible to those you care for.

## Moon in Aquarius

You are a people collector with many friends of all backgrounds. You are happiest surrounded by people and may feel uneasy when left alone. Though you usually stay friends with lovers, intense emotions and demanding one-on-one relationships turn you off. You don't like anything to be too rigid or scheduled. Though tolerant and understanding, you can be emotionally unpredictable and may opt for an unconventional love life. With plenty of space, you will be able to sustain relationships with liberal, freedom-loving types.

## Moon in Pisces

You are very responsive and empathic to others, especially if they have problems or are the underdog. (Be on guard against attracting too many people with sob stories!) You'll be happiest if you can express your creative imagination in the arts or in the spiritual or healing professions. Because you may tend to escape in fantasies or overreact to the moods of others, you need an emotional anchor to help you keep a firm foothold in reality. Steer clear of too much escapism (especially in alcohol) or re-clusiveness. Places near water soothe your moods. Working in a field that gives you emotional variety will also help you be productive.

# The Personal Planets: Mercury, Venus, and Mars

These planets work in your immediate personal life.

Mercury affects how you communicate and how your mental processes work. Are you a quick study who grasps information rapidly? Or do you learn more slowly and thoroughly? How is your concentration? Can you express yourself easily? Are you a good writer? All these questions can be answered by your Mercury placement.

Venus shows what you react to. What turns you on? What appeals to you aesthetically? Are you charming to others? Are you attractive to look at? Your taste, your refinement, your sense of balance and proportion are all Venus-ruled.

Mars is your outgoing energy, your drive and ambition. Do you reach out for new adventures? Are you assertive? Are you motivated? Self-confident? Hot-tempered? How you channel your energy and drive is revealed by your Mars placement.

# Mercury Is the Mental Planet

Since Mercury never travels far from the sun, read Mercury in your sun sign, then the sign preceding and following it. Then decide which reflects the way your mind works.

## Mercury in Aries

Your mind is very active and assertive. You never hesitate to say what you think, never shy away from a battle.

**43**

In fact, you may relish a verbal confrontation. Tact is not your strong point, so you may have to learn not to trip over your tongue.

## Mercury in Taurus

Though you may be a slow learner, you have good concentration and mental stamina. You want to make your ideas really happen. You'll attack a problem methodically and consider every angle thoroughly, never jumping to conclusions. You'll stick with a subject until you master it.

## Mercury in Gemini

You are a wonderful communicator with great facility for expressing yourself both verbally and in writing. You love gathering all kinds of information. You probably finish other people's sentences, and express yourself with eloquent hand gestures. You can talk to anybody anytime . . . and probably have phone and e-mail bills to prove it. You read anything from sci-fi to Shakespeare, and might need an extra room just for your book collection. Though you learn fast, you may lack focus and discipline. Watch a tendency to jump from subject to subject.

## Mercury in Cancer

You rely on intuition more than logic. Your mental processes are usually colored by your emotions, so you may seem shy or hesitant to voice your opinions. However, this placement gives you the advantage of great imagination and empathy in the way you communicate with others.

## Mercury in Leo

You are enthusiastic and very dramatic in the way you express yourself. You like to hold the attention of groups, and could be a great public speaker. Your mind thinks big, so you prefer to deal with the overall picture rather than with the details.

## Mercury in Virgo

This is one of the best places for Mercury. It should give you critical ability, attention to details, and thorough analysis. Your mind focuses on the practical side of things. This type of thinking is very well suited to being a teacher or editor.

## Mercury in Libra

You're either a born diplomat who smoothes over ruffled feathers or a talented debater. Many lawyers have this placement. However, since you're forever weighing the pros and cons of a situation, you may vacillate when making decisions.

## Mercury in Scorpio

This is an investigative mind that stops at nothing to get the answers. You may have a sarcastic, stinging wit or a gift for the cutting remark. There's always a grain of truth to your verbal sallies, thanks to your penetrating insight.

## Mercury in Sagittarius

You are a supersalesman with a tendency to expound. Though you are very broad-minded, you can be dogmatic when it comes to telling others what's good for them. You won't hesitate to tell the truth as you see it, so watch a tendency toward tactlessness. On the plus side, you have a great sense of humor. This position of Mercury is often considered by astrologers to be at a disadvantage because Sagittarius opposes Gemini, the sign Mercury rules, and squares off with Virgo, another

Mercury-ruled sign. What often happens is that Mercury in Sagittarius oversteps its bounds and loses sight of the facts in a situation. Do a reality check before making promises you may not be able to deliver.

## Mercury in Capricorn

This placement endows good mental discipline. You have a love of learning and a very orderly approach to your subjects. You will patiently plod through the facts and figures until you have mastered the tasks. You grasp structured situations easily, but may be short on creativity.

## Mercury in Aquarius

An independent, original thinker, you'll have more cutting-edge ideas than the average person. You will be quick to check out any unusual opportunities. Your opinions are so well-researched and grounded that once your mind is made up, it is difficult to change.

## Mercury in Pisces

You have the psychic and intuitive mind of a natural poet. Learn to make use of your creative imagination. You may think in terms of helping others, but check a tendency to be vague and forgetful of details.

# Venus Relates

Venus tells how you relate to others and to your environment. It shows where you receive pleasure, what you love to do. Find your Venus placement from the charts at the end of this chapter (pages 78–85) by looking for the year of your birth in the left-hand column. Then follow the line of that year across the page until you reach the time period of your birthday. The sign heading that column will be your Venus. If you were born on a day when Venus was changing signs, check the signs preceding or following that day to determine if that sign feels more like your Venus nature.

## Venus in Aries

You can't stand to be bored, confined, or ordered around. But a good challenge, maybe even a rousing row, turns you on. Confess—don't you pick a fight now and then just to get someone stirred up? You're attracted by the chase, not the catch, which could cause some problems in your love life if the object of your affection becomes too attainable. You like to wear red, and you can spot a trend before anyone else.

## Venus in Taurus

All your senses work in high gear. You love to be surrounded by glorious tastes, smells, textures, sounds, and visuals. Austerity is not for you! Neither is being rushed. You like time to enjoy your pleasures. Soothing surroundings with plenty of creature comforts are your cup of tea. You like to feel secure in your nest, with no sudden jolts or surprises. You like familiar objects—in fact, you may hate to let anything or anyone go.

## Venus in Gemini

You are a lively, sparkling personality who thrives in a situation that affords a constant variety and a frequent change of scenery. A varied social life is important to you, with plenty of stimulation and a chance to engage in some light flirtation. Commitment may be difficult, because playing the field is so much fun.

## Venus in Cancer

An atmosphere where you feel protected, coddled, and mothered is best for you. You love to be surrounded by children in a cozy, homelike situation. You are attracted to those who are tender and nurturing, who make you feel secure and well provided for. You may be quite secretive about your emotional life, or attracted to clandestine relationships.

## Venus in Leo

First-class attention in large doses turns you on, and so does the glitter of real gold and the flash of mirrors. You like to feel like a star at all times, surrounded by your admiring audience. The side effect is that you may be attracted to flatterers and tinsel, while the real gold requires some digging.

## Venus in Virgo

Everything neatly in its place? On the surface, you are attracted to an atmosphere where everything is in perfect order, but underneath are some basic, earthy urges. You are attracted to those who appeal to your need to teach, to be of service, or to play out a Pygmalion fantasy. You are at your best when you are busy doing something useful.

## Venus in Libra

Elegance and harmony are your key words. You can't abide an atmosphere of contention. Your taste tends toward the classic, with light harmonies of color—nothing clashing, trendy, or outrageous. You love doing things with a partner, and should be careful to pick one who is decisive but patient enough to let you weigh the pros and cons. And steer clear of argumentative types!

## Venus in Scorpio

Hidden mysteries intrigue you. In fact, anything that is too open and aboveboard is a bit of a bore. You surely have a stack of whodunits by the bed, along with an erotic magazine or two. You like to solve puzzles, and may also be fascinated with the occult, crime, or scientific research. Intense, all-or-nothing situations add spice to your life, and you love to ferret out the secrets of others. But you could get burned by your flair for living dangerously. The color black, spicy food, dark wood furniture, and heady perfume all get you in the right mood.

## Venus in Sagittarius

If you are not actually a world traveler, your surroundings are sure to reflect your love of faraway places. You like a casual outdoor atmosphere and a dog or two to pet. There should be plenty of room for athletic equipment and suitcases. You're attracted to kindred souls who love to travel and who share your freedom-loving philosophy of life. Athletics and spiritual or New Age pursuits could be other interests.

## Venus in Capricorn

No fly-by-night relationships for you! You want substance in life, and you are attracted to whatever will help you get where you are going. Status objects turn you on. And so do those who have a serious, responsible, businesslike approach as well as those who remind you of a beloved parent. It is characteristic of this placement to be attracted to someone of a different generation. Antiques, traditional clothing, and dignified behavior are becoming to you.

## Venus in Aquarius

This Venus wants to make friends, to be "cool." You like to be in a group, particularly one pushing a worthy cause. You feel quite at home surrounded by people, and could even court fame. Yet all the while you remain detached from any intense commitment. Original ideas and unpredictable people fascinate you. You don't like everything to be planned out in advance, preferring spontaneity and delightful surprises.

## Venus in Pisces

This Venus loves to give of yourself, and you find plenty of takers. Stray animals and people appeal to your heart and your pocketbook, but be careful to look at their motives realistically once in a while. You are extremely vulnerable to sob stories of all kinds. Fantasy, the arts (especially film, dance, and theater), and psychic or spiritual activities also speak to you.

# Mars Creates Action

Mars is the mover and shaker in your life. It shows how you pursue your goals, whether you have energy to burn or proceed in a slow, steady pace. It will also show how you get angry. Do you explode or do a slow burn or hold everything inside, then get revenge later?

To find your Mars, turn to the charts on pages 86–94. Then find your birth year in the left-hand column and trace the line across horizontally until you come to the column headed by the month of your birth. There you will find an abbreviation of your Mars sign. If the description of your Mars sign doesn't ring true, read the description of the sign preceding and following it. You may have been born on a day when Mars was changing signs, in which case your Mars might be in the adjacent sign.

## Mars in Aries

In the sign it rules, Mars shows its brilliant fiery nature. You have an explosive temper and can be quite impa-

50

tient. On the other hand, you have tremendous courage, energy, and drive. You'll let nothing stand in your way as you race to be first! Obstacles are met head-on and broken through by force. However, those that require patience and persistence can have you exploding in rage. You're a great starter, but not necessarily around for the finish.

## Mars in Taurus

Slow, steady, concentrated energy gives you staying power to last until the finish line. You have great stamina, and you never give up. Your tactic is to wear away obstacles with your persistence. Often you come out a winner because you've had the patience to hang in there. When angered, you do a slow burn.

## Mars in Gemini

You can't sit still for long. This Mars craves variety. You often have two or more things going on at once—it's all an amusing game to you. Your life can get very complicated, but that only adds spice and stimulation. What drives you into a nervous, hyper state? Boredom, sameness, routine, and confinement. You can do wonderful things with your hands, and you have a way with words.

## Mars in Cancer

You rarely attack head-on. Instead, you'll keep things to yourself, make plans in secret, and always cover your actions. This might be interpreted by some as manipulative, but you are only being self-protective. You get furious when anyone knows too much about you. But you do like to know all about others. Your mothering and feeding instincts can be put to good use if you work in the food, hotel, or child-care businesses. You may have to overcome your fragile sense of security, which prompts you not to take risks and to get physically upset when criticized. Don't take things so personally!

## Mars in Leo

You have a very dominant personality that takes center stage. Modesty is not one of your traits, nor is taking a backseat. You prefer giving the orders, and have been known to make a dramatic scene if they are not obeyed. Properly used, this Mars confers leadership ability, endurance, and courage.

## Mars in Virgo

You are the faultfinder of the zodiac. You notice every detail. Mistakes of any kind make you very nervous. You may worry, even if everything is going smoothly. You may not express your anger directly, but you sure can nag. You have definite likes and dislikes, and you are sure you can do the job better than anyone else. You are certainly more industrious and detail-oriented than other signs. Your Mars energy is often most positively expressed in some kind of teaching role.

## Mars in Libra

This Mars will have a passion for beauty, justice, and art. Generally, you will avoid confrontations at all costs. You prefer to spend your energy finding diplomatic solutions or weighing pros and cons. Your other techniques are passive aggression or exercising your well-known charm to get people to do what you want.

## Mars in Scorpio

This is a powerful placement, so intense that it demands careful channeling into worthwhile activities. Otherwise, you could become obsessed with your sexuality or might use your need for power and control to manipulate others. You are strong-willed, shrewd, and very private about your affairs, and you'll usually have a secret agenda behind your actions. Your great stamina, focus, and discipline would be excellent assets for careers in the military or medical fields, especially research or surgery. When angry, you don't get mad—you get even!

## Mars in Sagittarius

This expansive Mars often propels people into sales, travel, athletics, or philosophy. Your energies function well when you are on the move. You have a hot temper, and are inclined to say what you think before you consider the consequences. You shoot for high goals—and talk endlessly about them—but you may be weak on groundwork. This Mars needs a solid foundation. Watch a tendency to take unnecessary risks.

## Mars in Capricorn

This is an ambitious Mars with an excellent sense of timing. You have an eye for those who can be of use to you, and you may dismiss people ruthlessly when you're angry. But you drive yourself hard and deliver full value. This is a good placement for an executive. You'll aim for status and a high material position in life, and you'll keep climbing despite the odds. A great Mars to have!

## Mars in Aquarius

This is the most rebellious Mars. You seem to have a drive to assert yourself against the status quo. You may enjoy provoking people, shocking them out of traditional views. Or this placement could express itself in an offbeat sex life. Somehow you often find yourself in unconventional situations. You enjoy being a leader of an active group, which pursues forward-looking studies, politics, or goals.

## Mars in Pisces

This Mars is a good actor who knows just how to appeal to the sympathies of others. You create and project wonderful fantasies, or you use your sensitive antennae to crusade for those less fortunate. You get what you want through creating a veil of illusion and glamour. This is a good Mars for someone in the creative and imaginative fields—a dancer, performer, photographer, actor. Many famous film stars have this placement. Watch a tendency to manipulate by making others feel sorry for you.

# Jupiter Is the Optimist

Jupiter is the planet in your horoscope that makes you want *more*. This big, bright, swirling mass of gases is associated with abundance, prosperity, and the kind of windfall you get without too much hard work. You're optimistic under Jupiter's influence, when anything seems possible. You'll travel, expand your mind with higher education, and publish to share your knowledge widely. On the other hand, Jupiter's influence is neither discriminating nor disciplined. It represents the principle of growth without judgment. Therefore, if not kept in check, it could result in extravagance, weight gain, laziness, and carelessness.

Be sure to look up your Jupiter in the tables in this book. When the current position of Jupiter is favorable, you may get that lucky break. This is a great time to try new things, take risks, travel, or get more education. Opportunities seem to open up easily, so take advantage of them.

Once a year, Jupiter changes signs. That means you are due for an expansive time every twelve years, when Jupiter travels through your sun sign. You'll also have "up" periods every four years, when Jupiter is in the same element as your sun sign.

# Jupiter in Aries

You are the soul of enthusiasm and optimism. Your luckiest times are when you are getting started on an exciting project or selling an idea that you really believe in. You may have to watch a tendency to be arrogant with those who do not share your enthusiasm. You follow your impulses, often ignoring budget or other commonsense limitations. To produce real, solid benefits, you'll need patience and follow-through wherever this Jupiter falls in your horoscope.

# Jupiter in Taurus

You'll spend on beautiful material things, especially those that come from nature—items made of rare woods, natural fabrics, or precious gems, for instance. You can't have too much comfort or too many sensual pleasures. Watch a tendency to overindulge in good food, or to overpamper yourself with nothing but the best. Spartan living is not for you! You may be especially lucky in matters of real estate.

# Jupiter in Gemini

You are the great talker of the zodiac, and you may be a great writer, too. But restlessness could be your weak point. You jump around, talk too much, and could be a jack-of-all-trades. Keeping a secret is especially difficult, so you'll also have to watch a tendency to spill the beans. Since you love to be at the center of a beehive of activity, you'll have a vibrant social life. Your best opportunities will come through your talent for language—speaking, writing, communicating, and selling.

# Jupiter in Cancer

You are luckiest in situations where you can find emotional closeness or deal with basic security needs such as food, nurturing, or shelter. You may be a great collector. Or you may simply love to accumulate things—you are the one who stashes things away for a rainy day. You probably have a very good memory and love children. In fact, you may have many children to care for. The food, hotel, child-care, and shipping businesses hold good opportunities for you.

## Jupiter in Leo

You are a natural showman who loves to live in a larger-than-life way. Yours is a personality full of color that always finds its way into the limelight. You can't have too much attention or applause. Showbiz is a natural place for you, and so is any area where you can play to a crowd. Exercising your flair for drama, your natural playfulness, and your romantic nature brings you good fortune. But watch a tendency to be overly extravagant or to monopolize center stage.

## Jupiter in Virgo

You actually love those minute details others find boring. To you, they make all the difference between the perfect and the ordinary. You are the fine craftsman who spots every flaw. You expand your awareness by finding the most efficient methods and by being of service to others. Many of you will be drawn to medical or teaching fields. You'll also have luck in publishing, crafts, nutrition, and service professions. Watch out for a tendency to overwork.

## Jupiter in Libra

This is an other-directed Jupiter that develops best with a partner. The stimulation of others helps you grow. You are also most comfortable in harmonious, beautiful situations, and you work well with artistic people. You have a great sense of fair play and an ability to evaluate the pros and cons of a situation. You usually prefer to play the role of diplomat rather than adversary.

## Jupiter in Scorpio

You love the feeling of power and control, of taking things to their limit. You can't resist a mystery. Your shrewd, penetrating mind sees right through to the heart of most situations and people. You have luck in work that provides for solutions to matters of life and death. You may be drawn to undercover work, behind-the-scenes intrigue, psychotherapy, the occult, and sex-related ventures. Your challenge will be to develop a sense of moderation and tolerance for other beliefs. This Jupiter can be fanatical. You may have luck in handling other people's money—insurance, taxes, and inheritance can bring you a windfall.

## Jupiter in Sagittarius

Independent, outgoing, and idealistic, you'll shoot for the stars. This Jupiter compels you to travel far and wide, both physically and mentally, via higher education. You may have luck while traveling in an exotic place. You also have luck with outdoor ventures, exercise, and animals, particularly horses. Since you tend to be very open about your opinions, watch a tendency to be tactless and to exaggerate. Instead, use your wonderful sense of humor to make your point.

## Jupiter in Capricorn

Jupiter is much more restrained in Capricorn, the sign of rules and authority. Here, Jupiter can make you overwork and heighten any ambition or sense of duty you may have. You'll expand in areas that advance your position, putting you farther up the social or corporate ladder. You are lucky working within the establishment in a very structured situation where you can show off your ability to organize and reap rewards for your hard work.

## Jupiter in Aquarius

This is another freedom-loving Jupiter, with great tolerance and originality. You are at your best when you are working for a humanitarian cause and in the company of many supporters. This is a good Jupiter for a political career. You'll relate to all kinds of people on all social levels. You have an abundance of original ideas, but you are best off away from routine and any situation that imposes rigid rules. You need mental stimulation!

## Jupiter in Pisces

You are a giver whose feelings and pocketbook are easily touched by others, so choose your companions with care. You could be the original sucker for a hard-luck story. Better find a worthy hospital or a charity that will appreciate your selfless support. You have a great creative imagination. You may attract good fortune in fields related to oil, perfume, pharmaceuticals, petroleum, dance, footwear, and alcohol. But beware of overindulgence in alcohol—focus on a creative outlet instead.

# Saturn Puts on the Brakes

Jupiter speeds you up with *lucky breaks,* then along comes Saturn to slow you down with the *disciplinary brakes.* Saturn has unfairly been called a malefic planet, one of the bad guys of the zodiac. On the contrary, Saturn is one of our best friends, the kind who tells you what you need to hear even if it's not good news. Under a Saturn transit, we grow up, take responsibility for our lives, and emerge from whatever test this planet has in store as far wiser, more capable, and mature human beings. It is when we are under pressure that we grow stronger.

When Saturn hits a critical point in your horoscope, you can count on an experience that will make you slow up, pull back, and reexamine your life. It is a call to eliminate what is not working and to shape up. By the end of its twenty-eight-year trip around the zodiac, Saturn will have tested you in all areas of your life. The major tests happen in seven-year cycles, when Saturn passes over the *angles* of your chart—your rising sign, midheaven, descendant, and nadir. This is when the real life-changing experiences happen. But you are also in for a testing period whenever Saturn passes a *planet* in your chart or stresses that planet from a distance. Therefore, it is useful to check your planetary positions with the timetable of Saturn to prepare in advance, or at least to brace yourself.

When Saturn returns to its location at the time of your birth, at approximately age twenty-eight, you'll have your first Saturn return. At this time, a person usually takes stock or settles down to find his or her mission in life and assumes full adult duties and responsibilities.

Another way Saturn helps us is to reveal the karmic lessons from previous lives and to give us the chance to overcome them. So look at Saturn's challenges as much-needed opportunities for self-improvement. Under a Jupiter influence, you'll have more fun. But Saturn gives you solid, long-lasting results.

Look up your natal Saturn in the tables in this book for clues on where you need work.


## Saturn in Aries

Saturn here puts the brakes on Aries natural drive and enthusiasm. There is often an angry side to this placement. You don't let anyone push you around, and you know what's best for yourself. Following orders is not your strong point, and neither is diplomacy. You tend to be quick to go on the offensive in relationships, attacking

59

first, before anyone attacks you. Because no one quite lives up to your standards, you often wind up doing everything yourself. You'll have to learn to cooperate and tone down self-centeredness. Both Pat Buchanan and Saddam Hussein have this Saturn.

## Saturn in Taurus

A big issue is getting control of the cash flow. There will be lean periods that can be frightening, but you have the patience and endurance to stick them out and the methodical drive to prosper in the end. Learn to take a philosophical attitude, like Ben Franklin who also had this placement and who said, "A penny saved is a penny earned."

## Saturn in Gemini

You are a serious student of life, but you may have difficulty communicating or sharing your knowledge. You may be shy, speak slowly, or have fears about communicating, like Eleanor Roosevelt. You dwell in the realms of science, theory, or abstract analysis—even when you are dealing with the emotions, like Sigmund Freud who also had this placement.

## Saturn in Cancer

Your tests come with establishing a secure emotional base. In doing so, you may have to deal with some very basic fears centering on your early home environment. Most of your Saturn tests will have emotional roots in those early childhood experiences. You may have difficulty remaining objective in terms of what you try to achieve. So it will be especially important for you to deal with negative feelings such as guilt, paranoia, jealousy, resentment, and suspicion. Galileo and Michelangelo also navigated these murky waters.

## Saturn in Leo

This is an authoritarian Saturn—a strict, demanding parent who may deny the pleasure principle in your zeal to see that rules are followed. Though you may feel guilty about taking the spotlight, you are very ambitious and loyal. You have to watch a tendency toward rigidity, also toward overwork and holding back affection. Joseph Kennedy and Billy Graham share this placement.

## Saturn in Virgo

This is a cautious, exacting Saturn. You are intensely hard on yourself. Most of all, you give yourself the roughest time with your constant worries about every little detail, often making yourself sick. You may have difficulties setting priorities and getting the job done. Your tests will come in learning tolerance and understanding of others. Charles de Gaulle, Mae West, and Nathaniel Hawthorne had this meticulous Saturn.

## Saturn in Libra

Saturn is exalted here, which makes this planet an ally. You may choose very serious, older partners in life, perhaps stemming from a fear of dependency. You need to learn to stand solidly on your own before you commit to another. You are extremely cautious as you deliberate every involvement—with good reason. It is best that you find an occupation that makes good use of your sense of duty and honor. Steer clear of fly-by-night situations. Both Khrushchev and Mao Tse-tung had this placement.

## Saturn in Scorpio

You have great staying power. This Saturn tests you in situations involving the control of others. You may feel drawn to some kind of intrigue or undercover work, like J. Edgar Hoover. Or there may be an air of mystery surrounding your life and death, like Marilyn Monroe and Robert Kennedy who both had this placement. There are lessons to be learned from your sexual involvements. Often sex is used for manipulation or is somehow out of the ordinary. The Roman emperor Caligula and the transvestite Christine Jorgensen are extreme cases.

## Saturn in Sagittarius

Your challenges and lessons will come from tests of your spiritual and philosophical values, as happened to Martin Luther King and Gandhi. You are high-minded and sincere with this reflective, moral placement. Uncompromising in your ethical standards, you could become a benevolent despot.

## Saturn in Capricorn

With the help of Saturn at maximum strength, your judgment will improve with age. And like Spencer Tracy's screen image, you'll be the gray-haired hero with a strong sense of responsibility. You advance in life slowly but steadily, always with a strong hand at the helm and an eye for the advantageous situation. Like Pat Robertson, you're likely to stand for conservative values. Negatively, you may be a loner, prone to periods of melancholy.

## Saturn in Aquarius

Your tests come from relationships with groups. Do you care too much about what others think? Do you feel like an outsider, like Greta Garbo? You may fear being different from others and therefore slight your own unique, forward-looking gifts. Or like Lord Byron and Howard Hughes, you may take the opposite tack and rebel in the extreme. You can apply discipline to accomplish great humanitarian goals, as Albert Schweitzer did.

## Saturn in Pisces

Your fear of the unknown and the irrational may lead you to the safety and protection of an institution. You may go on the run like Jesse James, who had this placement, to avoid looking too deeply inside. Or you might go in the opposite, more positive direction and develop a disciplined psychoanalytic approach, which puts you more in control of your feelings. Some of you will take refuge in work with hospitals, charities, or religious institutions. Queen Victoria, who had this placement, symbolized an era when institutions of all kinds were sustained. Discipline applied to artistic work, especially poetry and dance, or to spiritual work, such as yoga or meditation, might be helpful.

# How Uranus, Neptune, and Pluto Influence Your Generation

These three planets remain in signs such a long time that a whole generation bears the imprint of the sign. Mass movements, great sweeping changes, fads that characterize a generation, even the issues of the conflicts and wars of the time are influenced by these "outer three" planets. When one of these distant planets changes signs, there is a definite shift in the atmosphere, the feeling of the end of an era.

Since these planets are so far away from the sun—too distant to be seen by the naked eye—they pick up signals from the universe at large. These planetary receivers literally link the sun with distant energies, and then perform a similar function in your horoscope by linking your central character with intuitive, spiritual, transformative forces from the cosmos. Each planet has a special domain, and will reflect this in the area of your chart where it falls.

# Uranus: The Great Awakener

There is nothing ordinary about this quirky green planet that seems to be traveling on its side, surrounded by a swarm of moons. Is it any wonder that astrologers assigned it to Aquarius, the most eccentric and gregarious sign? Uranus seems to wend its way around the sun, marching to its own tune.

Significantly, Uranus follows Saturn, the planet of limitations and structures. Often we get caught up in the structures we have created to give ourselves a sense of security. However, if we lose contact with our spiritual roots, then Uranus is likely to jolt us out of our comfortable rut and wake us up.

Uranus energy is electrical, happening in sudden flashes. It is not influenced by karma or past events, nor does it regard tradition, sex, or sentiment. The Uranus key words are surprise and awakening. Suddenly, there's that flash of inspiration, that bright idea, that totally new approach to revolutionize whatever scheme you were undertaking. A Uranus event takes you by surprise; it happens from out of the blue, for better or for worse. The Uranus place in your life is where you awaken and become your own person, leaving the structures of Saturn behind. And it is probably the most unconventional place in your chart.

Look up the sign of Uranus at the time of your birth and see where you follow your own tune.

## Uranus in Aries

Birth Dates:
  March 31, 1927–November 4, 1927
  January 13, 1928–June 6, 1934
  October 10, 1934–March 28, 1935

Your generation is original, creative, pioneering. It developed the computer, the airplane, and the cyclotron. You let nothing hold you back from exploring the unknown, and you have a powerful mixture of fire and electricity behind you. Women of your generation were among the first to be liberated. You were the unforgettable style-setters. You have a surprise in store for everyone. Like Yoko Ono, Grace Kelly, and Jacqueline Onassis, your life may be jolted by sudden and violent changes.

## Uranus in Taurus

Birth Dates:
    June 6, 1934–October 10, 1934
    March 28, 1935–August 7, 1941
    October 5, 1941–May 15, 1942

The great territorial shake of World War II began during your generation. You are independent, probably self-employed or would like to be. You have original ideas about making money, and you brace yourself for sudden changes of fortune. This Uranus can cause shakeups, particularly in finances, but it can also make you a born entrepreneur.

## Uranus in Gemini

Birth Dates:
    August 7, 1941–October 5, 1941
    May 15, 1942–August 30, 1948
    November 12, 1948–June 10, 1949

You were the first children to be influenced by television. Now, in your adult years, your generation stocks up on answering machines, cell phones, computers, and fax machines—any new way you can communicate. You have an inquiring mind, but your interests may be rather short-lived. This Uranus can be easily fragmented if there is no structure and focus.

# Uranus in Cancer

Birth Dates:
   August 30, 1948–November 12, 1948
   June 10, 1949–August 24, 1955
   January 28, 1956–June 10, 1956

This generation came at a time when divorce was becoming commonplace, so your home image is unconventional. You may have an unusual relationship with your parents; you may have come from a broken home or an unconventional one. You'll have unorthodox ideas about parenting, intimacy, food, and shelter. You may also be interested in dreams, psychic phenomena, and memory work.

# Uranus in Leo

Birth Dates:
   August 24, 1955–January 28, 1956
   June 10, 1956–November 1, 1961
   January 10, 1962–August 10, 1962

This generation understood how to use electronic media. Many of your group are now leaders in the high-tech industries, and you also understand how to use the new media to promote yourself. Like Isadora Duncan, you may have a very eccentric kind of charisma and a life that is sparked by unusual love affairs. Your children, too, may have traits that are out of the ordinary. Where this planet falls in your chart, you'll have a love of freedom, be a bit of an egomaniac, and show the full force of your personality in a unique way, like tennis great Martina Navratilova.

# Uranus in Virgo

Birth Dates:
   November 1, 1961–January 10, 1962

August 10, 1962–September 28, 1968
May 20, 1969–June 24, 1969

You'll have highly individual work methods. Many of you will be finding newer, more practical ways to use computers. Like Einstein, who had this placement, you'll break the rules brilliantly. Your generation came at a time of student rebellions, the civil rights movement, and the general acceptance of health foods. Chances are, you're concerned about pollution and cleaning up the environment. You may also be involved with nontraditional healing methods. Heavyweight champ Mike Tyson has this placement.

## Uranus in Libra

Birth Dates:
  September 28, 1968–May 20, 1969
  June 24, 1969–November 21, 1974
  May 1, 1975–September 8, 1975

Your generation will be always changing partners. Born during the era of women's liberation, you may have come from a broken home and have no clear image of what a marriage entails. There will be many sudden splits and experiments before you settle down. Your generation will be much involved in legal and political reforms and in changing artistic and fashion looks.

## Uranus in Scorpio

Birth Dates:
  November 21, 1974–May 1, 1975
  September 8, 1975–February 17, 1981
  March 20, 1981–November 16, 1981

Interest in transformation, meditation, and life after death signaled the beginning of New Age consciousness. Your generation recognizes no boundaries, no limits, and no external controls. You'll have new attitudes toward death and dying, psychic phenomena, and the occult. Like Mae West and Casanova, you'll shock 'em sexually, too.

## Uranus in Sagittarius

Birth Dates:
  February 17, 1981–March 20, 1981
  November 16, 1981–February 15, 1988
  May 27, 1988–December 2, 1988

Could this generation be the first to travel in outer space? An earlier generation with this placement included Charles Lindbergh and a time when the first zeppelins and the Wright Brothers were conquering the skies. Uranus here forecasts great discoveries, mind expansion, and long-distance travel. Like Galileo and Martin Luther, those born in these years will generate new theories about the cosmos and mankind's relation to it.

## Uranus in Capricorn

Birth Dates:
  December 20, 1904–January 30, 1912
  September 4, 1912–November 12, 1912
  February 15, 1988–May 27, 1988
  December 2, 1988–April 1, 1995
  June 9, 1995–January 12, 1996

This generation, now growing up, will challenge traditions with the help of electronic gadgets. In these years, we got organized with the help of technology put to practical use. The Internet was born following the great economic boom of the 1990s. Great leaders, who were movers and shakers of history, like Julius Caesar and Henry VIII, were born under this placement.

# Uranus in Aquarius

Birth Dates:
  January 30, 1912–September 4, 1912
  November 12, 1912–April 1, 1919
  August 16, 1919–January 22, 1920
  April 1, 1995–June 9, 1995
  January 12, 1996–March 10, 2003
  September 15, 2003–December 30, 2003

The last generation with this placement produced great innovative minds such as Leonard Bernstein and Orson Welles. The next will become another radical breakthrough generation, much concerned with global issues that involve all humanity. Already this is a time of high-tech experimentation on every level, when home computers are becoming as ubiquitous as television. It is also a time of globalization, of surprise attacks (9/11), and of "wake-up" calls, as underdeveloped countries demand attention.

# Uranus in Pisces

Birth Dates:
  April 1, 1919–August 16, 1919
  January 22, 1920–March 31, 1927
  November 4, 1927–January 12, 1928
  March 10, 2003–September 15, 2003
  December 20, 2003–May 28, 2010

Uranus moved into Pisces last year, ushering in a new generation that will surely spark new intuitions, innovations, and creativity in the arts as well as in the sciences. In the past century, Uranus in Pisces focused attention on the rise of such electronic entertainment as radio and the cinema as well as on the secretiveness of Prohibition. This produced a generation of idealists exemplified by Judy Garland's theme, "Somewhere Over the Rainbow." Uranus in Pisces hints at stealth activities, at hospital and prison reform, at high-tech drugs and medical experiments.

# Neptune Takes You Beyond Reality

Neptune is often called the planet of dissolution. It is the "dissolver" of reality. It is often maligned as the planet of illusions, drugs, and alcohol where you escape the real world. Under Neptune's influence, you see what you want to see. But Neptune also encourages you to create, to let your imagination run free. Neptune embodies the energy of glamour, subtlety, mystery, and mysticism. It governs anything that takes you beyond the mundane world, including out-of-body experiences.

Neptune acts to break through and transcend your ordinary perceptions to take you to another level of reality where you experience either confusion or ecstasy. Neptune's force can pull you off course, but only if you allow this to happen. Those who use Neptune wisely can translate their daydreams into poetry, theater, design, or inspired moves in the business world, avoiding the tricky "con artist" side of this planet.

Find your Neptune listed below.

## Neptune in Cancer

Birth Dates:
   July 19, 1901–December 25, 1901
   May 21, 1902–September 23, 1914
   December 14, 1914–July 19, 1915
   March 19, 1916–May 2, 1916

Dreams of the homeland, idealistic patriotism, and glamorization of the nurturing assets of women characterized this time. You who were born here have unusual psychic ability and deep insights into basic needs of others.

# Neptune in Leo

Birth Dates:
   September 23, 1914–December 14, 1914
   July 19, 1915–March 19, 1916
   May 2, 1916–September 21, 1928
   February 19, 1929–July 24, 1929

Neptune in Leo brought us the glamour and high living of the 1920s and the big spenders of that time. The Neptune temptations of gambling, seduction, theater, and lavish entertaining distracted from the realities of the age. Those born in that generation also made great advances in the arts.

# Neptune in Virgo

Birth Dates:
   September 21, 1928–February 19, 1929
   July 24, 1929–October 3, 1942
   April 17, 1943–August 2, 1943

Neptune in Virgo encompassed the 1930s, the Great Depression, and the beginning of World War II, when a new order was born. There was a time of facing "what doesn't work." Many were unemployed and found solace at the movies, watching the great Virgo star Greta Garbo or the escapist dance films of Busby Berkeley. New public services were born. Those with Neptune in Virgo later spread the gospel of health and fitness. This generation's devotion to spending hours at the office inspired the term "workaholic."

# Neptune in Libra

Birth Dates:
   October 3, 1942–April 17, 1943
   August 2, 1943–December 24, 1955
   March 12, 1956–October 19, 1956
   June 15, 1957–August 6, 1957

This was the time of World War II and the postwar period, when the world regained balance and returned to relative stability. Neptune in Libra was the romantic generation who would later be concerned with relating. As this generation matured, there was a new trend toward marriage and commitment. Racial and sexual equality became important issues, as they redesigned traditional roles to suit modern times.

## Neptune in Scorpio

Birth Dates:
   December 24, 1955–March 12, 1956
   October 19, 1956–June 15, 1957
   August 6, 1957–January 4, 1970
   May 3, 1970–November 6, 1970

Neptune in Scorpio brought in a generation that would become interested in transformative power. Born in an era that glamorized sex, drugs, rock and roll, and Eastern religion, they matured in a more sobering time of AIDS, cocaine abuse, and New Age spirituality. As they evolve, they will become active in healing the planet from the results of the abuse of power.

## Neptune in Sagittarius

Birth Dates:
   January 4, 1970–May 3, 1970
   November 6, 1970–January 19, 1984
   June 23, 1984–November 21, 1984

Neptune in Sagittarius was the time when space and astronaut travel became a reality. The Neptune influence glamorized new approaches to mysticism, religion, and mind expansion. This generation will take a new approach to spiritual life, with emphasis on visions, mysticism, and clairvoyance.

## Neptune in Capricorn

Birth Dates:
   January 19, 1984–June 23, 1984
   November 21, 1984–January 29, 1998

Neptune in Capricorn brought a time when delusions about material power were glamorized in the mid-1980s and 1990s. There was a boom in the stock market, and the Internet era spawned young tycoons who later lost it all. It was also a time when the psychic and occult worlds spawned a new category of business enterprise, and sold services on television.

## Neptune in Aquarius

Birth Dates:
   January 29, 1998–April 4, 2111

This should continue to be a time of breakthroughs. Here the creative influence of Neptune reaches a universal audience. This is a time of dissolving barriers, of globalization—when we truly become one world.

# Pluto: The Power Planet

Pluto is a mysterious little planet with a strange elliptical orbit that occasionally runs inside the orbit of its neighbor Neptune. Because of its eccentric path, the length of time Pluto stays in any given sign can vary from thirteen to thirty-two years. It covered only seven signs in the last century. Though it is a tiny planet, its influence is great. When Pluto zaps a strategic point in your horoscope, your life changes dramatically.

   This little planet is the power behind the scenes. It affects you at deep levels of consciousness, causing events to come to the surface that will transform you and your generation. Nothing escapes, or is sacred, with this probing planet. Its purpose is to wipe out the past so something new can happen. The Pluto place in your horoscope is where you have invisible power (Mars governs the visible power)—where you can transform, heal, and affect the unconscious needs of the masses. Pluto tells lots about how your generation projects power, what makes it seem "cool" to others. And when Pluto changes signs, there's a whole new concept of what's "cool."

## Pluto in Gemini

Birth Dates:
   Late 1800s–May 28, 1914

This was a time of mass suggestion and breakthroughs in communications, a time when many brilliant writers such as Ernest Hemingway and F. Scott Fitzgerald were born. Henry Miller, D. H. Lawrence, and James Joyce scandalized society by using explicit sexual images and language in their literature. "Muckraking" journalists exposed corruption. Pluto-ruled Scorpio President Theodore Roosevelt said, "Speak softly, but carry a big stick." This generation had an intense need to communicate and made major breakthroughs in knowledge. A compulsive restlessness and a thirst for a variety of experiences characterized many of this generation.

## Pluto in Cancer

Birth Dates:
   May 26, 1914–June 14, 1939

Dictators and mass media arose to wield emotional power over the masses. Women's rights was a popular issue. Deep sentimental feelings, acquisitiveness, and possessiveness characterized these times and people. Most of the great stars of the Hollywood era that embodied the American image were born during this period:

Grace Kelly, Esther Williams, Frank Sinatra, Lana Turner, to name a few.

## Pluto in Leo

Birth Dates:
  June 14, 1939–August 19, 1957

The performing arts played on the emotions of the masses. Mick Jagger, John Lennon, and rock and roll were born at this time. So were "baby boomers" like Bill and Hillary Clinton. Those born here tend to be self-centered, powerful, and boisterous. This generation does its own thing, for better or for worse.

## Pluto in Virgo

Birth Dates:
  August 19, 1957–October 5, 1971
  April 17, 1972–July 30, 1972

This is the "yuppie" generation that sparked a mass movement toward fitness, health, and career. It is a much more sober, serious, driven generation than the fun-loving Pluto in Leo. During this time, machines were invented to process detail work efficiently. Inventions took a practical turn with answering machines, fax machines, car phones, and home office equipment—all making the workplace far more efficient.

## Pluto in Libra

Birth Dates:
  October 5, 1971–April 17, 1972
  July 30, 1972–November 5, 1983
  May 18, 1984–August 27, 1984

A mellower generation, people born at this time are concerned with partnerships, working together, and finding diplomatic solutions to problems. Marriage is important to this generation, and they will redefine it by combining traditional values with equal partnership. This was a time of women's liberation, gay rights, ERA, and legal battles over abortion, all of which transformed our ideas about relationships.

## Pluto in Scorpio

Birth Dates:
    November 5, 1983–May 18, 1984
    August 27, 1984–January 17, 1995

Pluto was in the sign it rules for a comparatively short period of time. In 1989, it was at its perihelion, or closest point to the sun and earth. We have all felt the transforming power somewhere in our lives. This was a time of record achievements, destructive sexually transmitted diseases, nuclear power controversies, and explosive political issues. Pluto destroys in order to create new understanding—the phoenix rising from the ashes—which should be some consolation for those of you who felt Pluto's force before 1995. Sexual shockers were par for the course during these intense years when black clothing, transvestites, body piercing, tattoos, and sexually explicit advertising pushed the boundaries of good taste.

## Pluto in Sagittarius

Birth Dates:
    January 17, 1995–April 20, 1995
    November 10, 1995–January 27, 2008

During our current Pluto transit, we are being pushed to expand our horizons, to find deeper spiritual meaning in life. Pluto's opposition with Saturn in 2001 brought an enormous conflict between traditional societies and the forces of change. It signals a time when religious convictions will exert more power in our political life as well.

Since Sagittarius is the sign that rules travel, there's a good possibility that Pluto, the planet of extremes, will make space travel a reality for some of us. Already, we are seeing wealthy adventurers paying for the privilege of travel on space shuttles. Discovery of life-forms on other planets could transform our ideas about where we came from.

New dimensions in electronic publishing, concern with animal rights and the environment, and an increasing emphasis on extreme forms of religion are other signs of these times. Look for charismatic religious leaders to arise now. We'll also be developing far-reaching philosophies designed to elevate our lives with a new sense of purpose.

# VENUS SIGNS 1901–2004

| | Aries | Taurus | Gemini | Cancer | Leo | Virgo |
|---|---|---|---|---|---|---|
| **1901** | 3/29–4/22 | 4/22–5/17 | 5/17–6/10 | 6/10–7/5 | 7/5–7/29 | 7/29–8/23 |
| **1902** | 5/7–6/3 | 6/3–6/30 | 6/30–7/25 | 7/25–8/19 | 8/19–9/13 | 9/13–10/7 |
| **1903** | 2/28–3/24 | 3/24–4/18 | 4/18–5/13 | 5/13–6/9 | 6/9–7/7 | 7/7–8/17 |
| | | | | | | 9/6–11/8 |
| **1904** | 3/13–5/7 | 5/7–6/1 | 6/1–6/25 | 6/25–7/19 | 7/19–8/13 | 8/13–9/6 |
| **1905** | 2/3–3/6 | 3/6–4/9 | 7/8–8/6 | 8/6–9/1 | 9/1–9/27 | 9/27–10/21 |
| | 4/9–5/28 | 5/28–7/8 | | | | |
| **1906** | 3/1–4/7 | 4/7–5/2 | 5/2–5/26 | 5/26–6/20 | 6/20–7/16 | 7/16–8/11 |
| **1907** | 4/27–5/22 | 5/22–6/16 | 6/16–7/11 | 7/11–8/4 | 8/4–8/29 | 8/29–9/22 |
| **1908** | 2/14–3/10 | 3/10–4/5 | 4/5–5/5 | 5/5–9/8 | 9/8–10/8 | 10/8–11/3 |
| **1909** | 3/29–4/22 | 4/22–5/16 | 5/16–6/10 | 6/10–7/4 | 7/4–7/29 | 7/29–8/23 |
| **1910** | 5/7–6/3 | 6/4–6/29 | 6/30–7/24 | 7/25–8/18 | 8/19–9/12 | 9/13–10/6 |
| **1911** | 2/28–3/23 | 3/24–4/17 | 4/18–5/12 | 5/13–6/8 | 6/9–7/7 | 7/8–11/8 |
| **1912** | 4/13–5/6 | 5/7–5/31 | 6/1–6/24 | 6/24–7/18 | 7/19–8/12 | 8/13–9/5 |
| **1913** | 2/3–3/6 | 3/7–5/1 | 7/8–8/5 | 8/6–8/31 | 9/1–9/26 | 9/27–10/20 |
| | 5/2–5/30 | 5/31–7/7 | | | | |
| **1914** | 3/14–4/6 | 4/7–5/1 | 5/2–5/25 | 5/26–6/19 | 6/20–7/15 | 7/16–8/10 |
| **1915** | 4/27–5/21 | 5/22–6/15 | 6/16–7/10 | 7/11–8/3 | 8/4–8/28 | 8/29–9/21 |
| **1916** | 2/14–3/9 | 3/10–4/5 | 4/6–5/5 | 5/6–9/8 | 9/9–10/7 | 10/8–11/2 |
| **1917** | 3/29–4/21 | 4/22–5/15 | 5/16–6/9 | 6/10–7/3 | 7/4–7/28 | 7/29–8/21 |
| **1918** | 5/7–6/2 | 6/3–6/28 | 6/29–7/24 | 7/25–8/18 | 8/19–9/11 | 9/12–10/5 |
| **1919** | 2/27–3/22 | 3/23–4/16 | 4/17–5/12 | 5/13–6/7 | 6/8–7/7 | 7/8–11/8 |
| **1920** | 4/12–5/6 | 5/7–5/30 | 5/31–6/23 | 6/24–7/18 | 7/19–8/11 | 8/12–9/4 |
| **1921** | 2/3–3/6 | 3/7–4/25 | 7/8–8/5 | 8/6–8/31 | 9/1–9/25 | 9/26–10/20 |
| | 4/26–6/1 | 6/2–7/7 | | | | |
| **1922** | 3/13–4/6 | 4/7–4/30 | 5/1–5/25 | 5/26–6/19 | 6/20–7/14 | 7/15 8/0 |
| **1923** | 4/27–5/21 | 5/22–6/14 | 6/15–7/9 | 7/10–8/3 | 8/4–8/27 | 8/28–9/20 |
| **1924** | 2/13–3/8 | 3/9–4/4 | 4/5–5/5 | 5/6–9/8 | 9/9–10/7 | 10/8–11/12 |
| **1925** | 3/28–4/20 | 4/21–5/15 | 5/16–6/8 | 6/9–7/3 | 7/4–7/27 | 7/28–8/21 |

| Libra | Scorpio | Sagittarius | Capricorn | Aquarius | Pisces |
|---|---|---|---|---|---|
| 8/23–9/17 | 9/17–10/12 | 10/12–1/16 | 1/16–2/9<br>11/7–12/5 | 2/9–3/5<br>12/5–1/11 | 3/5–3/29 |
| 10/7–10/31 | 10/31–11/24 | 11/24–12/18 | 12/18–1/11 | 2/6–4/4 | 1/11–2/6<br>4/4–5/7 |
| 8/17–9/6<br>11/8–12/9 | 12/9–1/5 | | | 1/11–2/4 | 2/4–2/28 |
| 9/6–9/30 | 9/30–10/25 | 1/5–1/30<br>10/25–11/18 | 1/30–2/24<br>11/18–12/13 | 2/24–3/19<br>12/13–1/7 | 3/19–4/13 |
| 10/21–11/14 | 11/14–12/8 | 12/8–1/1/06 | | | 1/7–2/3 |
| 8/11–9/7 | 9/7–10/9<br>12/15–12/25 | 10/9–12/15<br>12/25–2/6 | 1/1–1/25 | 1/25–2/18 | 2/18–3/14 |
| 9/22–10/16 | 10/16–11/9 | 11/9–12/3 | 2/6–3/6<br>12/3–12/27 | 3/6–4/2<br>12/27–1/20 | 4/2–4/27 |
| 11/3–11/28 | 11/28–12/22 | 12/22–1/15 | | | 1/20–2/4 |
| 8/23–9/17 | 9/17–10/12 | 10/12–11/17 | 1/15–2/9<br>11/17–12/5 | 2/9–3/5<br>12/5–1/15 | 3/5–3/29 |
| 10/7–10/30 | 10/31–11/23 | 11/24–12/17 | 12/18–12/31 | 1/1–1/15<br>1/29–4/4 | 1/16–1/28<br>4/5–5/6 |
| 11/19–12/8 | 12/9–12/31 | | 1/1–1/10 | 1/11–2/2 | 2/3–2/27 |
| 9/6–9/30 | 1/1–1/4<br>10/1–10/24 | 1/5–1/29<br>10/25–11/17 | 1/30–2/23<br>11/18–12/12 | 2/24–3/18<br>12/13–12/31 | 3/19–4/12 |
| 10/21–11/13 | 11/14–12/7 | 12/8–12/31 | | 1/1–1/6 | 1/7–2/2 |
| 8/11–9/6 | 9/7–10/9<br>12/6–12/30 | 10/10–12/5<br>12/31 | 1/1–1/24 | 1/25–2/17 | 2/18–3/13 |
| 9/22–10/15 | 10/16–11/8 | 1/1–2/6<br>11/9–12/2 | 2/7–3/6<br>12/3–12/26 | 3/7–4/1<br>12/27–12/31 | 4/2–4/26 |
| 11/3–11/27 | 11/28–12/21 | 12/22–12/31 | | 1/1–1/19 | 1/20–2/13 |
| 8/22–9/16 | 9/17–10/11 | 1/1–1/14<br>10/12–11/6 | 1/15–2/7<br>11/7–12/5 | 2/8–3/4<br>12/6–12/31 | 3/5–3/28 |
| 10/6–10/29 | 10/30–11/22 | 11/23–12/16 | 12/17–12/31 | 1/1–4/5 | 4/6–5/6 |
| 11/9–12/8 | 12/9–12/31 | | 1/1–1/9 | 1/10–2/2 | 2/3–2/26 |
| 9/5–9/30 | 1/1–1/3<br>9/31–10/23 | 1/4–1/28<br>10/24–11/17 | 1/29–2/22<br>11/18–12/11 | 2/23–3/18<br>12/12–12/31 | 3/19–4/11 |
| 10/21–11/13 | 11/14–12/7 | 12/8–12/31 | | 1/1–1/6 | 1/7–2/2 |
| 8/10–9/6 | 9/7–10/10<br>11/29–12/31 | 10/11–11/28 | 1/1–1/24 | 1/25–2/16 | 2/17–3/12 |
| 9/21–10/14 | 1/1<br>10/15–11/7 | 1/2–2/6<br>11/8–12/1 | 2/7–3/5<br>12/2–12/25 | 3/6–3/31<br>12/26–12/31 | 4/1–4/26 |
| 11/13–11/26 | 11/27–12/21 | 12/22–12/31 | | 1/1–1/19 | 1/20–2/12 |
| 8/22–9/15 | 9/16–10/11 | 1/1–1/14<br>10/12–11/6 | 1/15–2/7<br>11/7–12/5 | 2/8–3/3<br>12/6–12/31 | 3/4–3/27 |

# VENUS SIGNS 1901–2004

| | Aries | Taurus | Gemini | Cancer | Leo | Virgo |
|---|---|---|---|---|---|---|
| 1926 | 5/7–6/2 | 6/3–6/28 | 6/29–7/23 | 7/24–8/17 | 8/18–9/11 | 9/12–10/5 |
| 1927 | 2/27–3/22 | 3/23–4/16 | 4/17–5/11 | 5/12–6/7 | 6/8–7/7 | 7/8–11/9 |
| 1928 | 4/12–5/5 | 5/6–5/29 | 5/30–6/23 | 6/24–7/17 | 7/18–8/11 | 8/12–9/4 |
| 1929 | 2/3–3/7 | 3/8–4/19 | 7/8–8/4 | 8/5–8/30 | 8/31–9/25 | 9/26–10/19 |
| | 4/20–6/2 | 6/3–7/7 | | | | |
| 1930 | 3/13–4/5 | 4/6–4/30 | 5/1–5/24 | 5/25–6/18 | 6/19–7/14 | 7/15–8/9 |
| 1931 | 4/26–5/20 | 5/21–6/13 | 6/14–7/8 | 7/9–8/2 | 8/3–8/26 | 8/27–9/19 |
| 1932 | 2/12–3/8 | 3/9–4/3 | 4/4–5/5 | 5/6–7/12 | 9/9–10/6 | 10/7–11/1 |
| | | | 7/13–7/27 | 7/28–9/8 | | |
| 1933 | 3/27–4/19 | 4/20–5/28 | 5/29–6/8 | 6/9–7/2 | 7/3–7/26 | 7/27–8/20 |
| 1934 | 5/6–6/1 | 6/2–6/27 | 6/28–7/22 | 7/23–8/16 | 8/17–9/10 | 9/11–10/4 |
| 1935 | 2/26–3/21 | 3/22–4/15 | 4/16–5/10 | 5/11–6/6 | 6/7–7/6 | 7/7–11/8 |
| 1936 | 4/11–5/4 | 5/5–5/28 | 5/29–6/22 | 6/23–7/16 | 7/17–8/10 | 8/11–9/4 |
| 1937 | 2/2–3/8 | 3/9–4/13 | 7/7–8/3 | 8/4–8/29 | 8/30–9/24 | 9/25–10/18 |
| | 4/14–6/3 | 6/4–7/6 | | | | |
| 1938 | 3/12–4/4 | 4/5–4/28 | 4/29–5/23 | 5/24–6/18 | 6/19–7/13 | 7/14–8/8 |
| 1939 | 4/25–5/19 | 5/20–6/13 | 6/14–7/8 | 7/9–8/1 | 8/2–8/25 | 8/26–9/19 |
| 1940 | 2/12–3/7 | 3/8–4/3 | 4/4–5/5 | 5/6–7/4 | 9/9–10/5 | 10/6–10/31 |
| | | | 7/5–7/31 | 8/1–9/8 | | |
| 1941 | 3/27–4/19 | 4/20–5/13 | 5/14–6/6 | 6/7–7/1 | 7/2–7/26 | 7/27–8/20 |
| 1942 | 5/6–6/1 | 6/2–6/26 | 6/27–7/22 | 7/23–8/16 | 8/17–9/9 | 9/10–10/3 |
| 1943 | 2/25–3/20 | 3/21–4/14 | 4/15–5/10 | 5/11–6/6 | 6/7–7/6 | 7/7–11/8 |
| 1944 | 4/10–5/3 | 5/4–5/28 | 5/29–6/21 | 6/22–7/16 | 7/17–8/9 | 8/10–9/2 |
| 1945 | 2/2–3/10 | 3/11–4/6 | 7/7–8/3 | 8/4–8/29 | 8/30–9/23 | 9/24–10/18 |
| | 4/7–6/3 | 6/4–7/6 | | | | |
| 1946 | 3/11–4/4 | 4/5–4/28 | 4/29–5/23 | 5/24–6/17 | 6/18–7/12 | 7/13–8/8 |
| 1947 | 4/25–5/19 | 5/20–6/12 | 6/13–7/7 | 7/8–8/1 | 8/2–8/25 | 8/26–9/18 |
| 1948 | 2/11–3/7 | 3/8–4/3 | 4/4–5/6 | 5/7–6/28 | 9/8–10/5 | 10/6–10/31 |
| | | | 6/29–8/2 | 8/3–9/7 | | |
| 1949 | 3/26–4/19 | 4/20–5/13 | 5/14–6/6 | 6/7–6/30 | 7/1–7/25 | 7/26–8/19 |
| 1950 | 5/5–5/31 | 6/1–6/26 | 6/27–7/21 | 7/22–8/15 | 8/16–9/9 | 9/10–10/3 |
| 1951 | 2/25–3/21 | 3/22–4/15 | 4/16–5/10 | 5/11–6/6 | 6/7–7/7 | 7/8–11/9 |

| Libra | Scorpio | Sagittarius | Capricorn | Aquarius | Pisces |
|---|---|---|---|---|---|
| 10/6-10/29 | 10/30-11/22 | 11/23-12/16 | 12/17-12/31 | 1/1-4/5 | 4/6-5/6 |
| 11/10-12/8 | 12/9-12/31 | 1/1-1/7 | 1/8 | 1/9-2/1 | 2/2-2/26 |
| 9/5-9/28 | 1/1-1/3 | 1/4-1/28 | 1/29-2/22 | 2/23-3/17 | 3/18-4/11 |
| | 9/29-10/23 | 10/24-11/16 | 11/17-12/11 | 12/12-12/31 | |
| 10/20-11/12 | 11/13-12/6 | 12/7-12/30 | 12/31 | 1/1-1/5 | 1/6-2/2 |
| 8/10-9/6 | 9/7-10/11 | 10/12-11/21 | 1/1-1/23 | 1/24-2/16 | 2/17-3/12 |
| | 11/22-12/31 | | | | |
| 9/20-10/13 | 1/1-1/3 | 1/4-2/6 | 2/7-3/4 | 3/5-3/31 | 4/1-4/25 |
| | 10/14-11/6 | 11/7-11/30 | 12/1-12/24 | 12/25-12/31 | |
| 11/2-11/25 | 11/26-12/20 | 12/21-12/31 | | 1/1-1/18 | 1/19-2/11 |
| | | | | | |
| 8/21-9/14 | 9/15-10/10 | 1/1-1/13 | 1/14-2/6 | 2/7-3/2 | 3/3-3/26 |
| | | 10/11-11/5 | 11/6-12/4 | 12/5-12/31 | |
| 10/5-10/28 | 10/29-11/21 | 11/22-12/15 | 12/16-12/31 | 1/1-4/5 | 4/6-5/5 |
| 11/9-12/7 | 12/8-12/31 | | 1/1-1/7 | 1/8-1/31 | 2/1-2/25 |
| 9/5-9/27 | 1/1-1/2 | 1/3-1/27 | 1/28-2/21 | 2/22-3/16 | 3/17-4/10 |
| | 9/28-10/22 | 10/23-11/15 | 11/16-12/10 | 12/11-12/31 | |
| 10/19-11/11 | 11/12-12/5 | 12/6-12/29 | 12/30-12/31 | 1/1-1/5 | 1/6-2/1 |
| | | | | | |
| 8/9-9/6 | 9/7-10/13 | 10/14-11/14 | 1/1-1/22 | 1/23-2/15 | 2/16-3/11 |
| | 11/15-12/31 | | | | |
| 9/20-10/13 | 1/1-1/3 | 1/4-2/5 | 2/6-3/4 | 3/5-3/30 | 3/31-4/24 |
| | 10/14-11/6 | 11/7-11/30 | 12/1-12/24 | 12/25-12/31 | |
| 11/1-11/25 | 11/26-12/19 | 12/20-12/31 | | 1/1-1/18 | 1/19-2/11 |
| | | | | | |
| 8/21-9/14 | 9/15-10/9 | 1/1-1/12 | 1/13-2/5 | 2/6-3/1 | 3/2-3/26 |
| | | 10/10-11/5 | 11/6-12/4 | 12/5-12/31 | |
| 10/4-10/27 | 10/28-11/20 | 11/21-12/14 | 12/15-12/31 | 1/1-4/5 | 4/6-5/5 |
| 11/9-12/7 | 12/8-12/31 | | 1/1-1/7 | 1/8-1/31 | 2/1-2/24 |
| 9/3-9/27 | 1/1-1/2 | 1/3-1/27 | 1/28-2/20 | 2/21-3/16 | 3/17-4/9 |
| | 9/28-10/21 | 10/22-11/15 | 11/16-12/10 | 12/11-12/31 | |
| 10/19-11/11 | 11/12-12/5 | 12/6-12/29 | 12/30-12/31 | 1/1-1/4 | 1/5-2/1 |
| | | | | | |
| 8/9-9/6 | 9/7-10/15 | 10/16-11/7 | 1/1-1/21 | 1/22-2/14 | 2/15-3/10 |
| | 11/8-12/31 | | | | |
| 9/19-10/12 | 1/1-1/4 | 1/5-2/5 | 2/6-3/4 | 3/5-3/29 | 3/30-4/24 |
| | 10/13-11/5 | 11/6-11/29 | 11/30-12/23 | 12/24-12/31 | |
| 11/1-11/25 | 11/26-12/19 | 12/20-12/31 | | 1/1-1/17 | 1/18-2/10 |
| | | | | | |
| 8/20-9/14 | 9/15-10/9 | 1/1-1/12 | 1/13-2/5 | 2/6-3/1 | 3/2-3/25 |
| | | 10/10-11/5 | 11/6-12/5 | 12/6-12/31 | |
| 10/4-10/27 | 10/28-11/20 | 11/21-12/13 | 12/14-12/31 | 1/1-4/5 | 4/6-5/4 |
| 11/10-12/7 | 12/8-12/31 | | 1/1-1/7 | 1/8-1/31 | 2/1-2/24 |

## VENUS SIGNS 1901–2004

|  | Aries | Taurus | Gemini | Cancer | Leo | Virgo |
|---|---|---|---|---|---|---|
| 1952 | 4/10–5/4 | 5/5–5/28 | 5/29–6/21 | 6/22–7/16 | 7/17–8/9 | 8/10–9/3 |
| 1953 | 2/2–3/3 | 3/4–3/31 | 7/8–8/3 | 8/4–8/29 | 8/30–9/24 | 9/25–10/18 |
|  | 4/1–6/5 | 6/6–7/7 |  |  |  |  |
| 1954 | 3/12–4/4 | 4/5–4/28 | 4/29–5/23 | 5/24–6/17 | 6/18–7/13 | 7/14–8/8 |
| 1955 | 4/25–5/19 | 5/20–6/13 | 6/14–7/7 | 7/8–8/1 | 8/2–8/25 | 8/26–9/18 |
| 1956 | 2/12–3/7 | 3/8–4/4 | 4/5–5/7 | 5/8–6/23 | 9/9–10/5 | 10/6–10/31 |
|  |  |  | 6/24–8/4 | 8/5–9/8 |  |  |
| 1957 | 3/26–4/19 | 4/20–5/13 | 5/14–6/6 | 6/7–7/1 | 7/2–7/26 | 7/27–8/19 |
| 1958 | 5/6–5/31 | 6/1–6/26 | 6/27–7/22 | 7/23–8/15 | 8/16–9/9 | 9/10–10/3 |
| 1959 | 2/25–3/20 | 3/21–4/14 | 4/15–5/10 | 5/11–6/6 | 6/7–7/8 | 7/9–9/20 |
|  |  |  |  |  | 9/21–9/24 | 9/25–11/9 |
| 1960 | 4/10–5/3 | 5/4–5/28 | 5/29–6/21 | 6/22–7/15 | 7/16–8/9 | 8/10–9/2 |
| 1961 | 2/3–6/5 | 6/6–7/7 | 7/8–8/3 | 8/4–8/29 | 8/30–9/23 | 9/24–10/17 |
| 1962 | 3/11–4/3 | 4/4–4/28 | 4/29–5/22 | 5/23–6/17 | 6/18–7/12 | 7/13–8/8 |
| 1963 | 4/24–5/18 | 5/19–6/12 | 6/13–7/7 | 7/8–7/31 | 8/1–8/25 | 8/26–9/18 |
| 1964 | 2/11–3/7 | 3/8–4/4 | 4/5–5/9 | 5/10–6/17 | 9/9–10/5 | 10/6–10/31 |
|  |  |  | 6/18–8/5 | 8/6–9/8 |  |  |
| 1965 | 3/26–4/18 | 4/19–5/12 | 5/13–6/6 | 6/7–6/30 | 7/1–7/25 | 7/26–8/19 |
| 1966 | 5/6–6/31 | 6/1–6/26 | 6/27–7/21 | 7/22–8/15 | 8/16–9/8 | 9/9–10/2 |
| 1967 | 2/24–3/20 | 3/21–4/14 | 4/15–5/10 | 5/11–6/6 | 6/7–7/8 | 7/9–9/9 |
|  |  |  |  |  | 9/10–10/1 | 10/2–11/9 |
| 1968 | 4/9–5/3 | 5/4–5/27 | 5/28–6/20 | 6/21–7/15 | 7/16–8/8 | 8/9–9/2 |
| 1969 | 2/3–6/6 | 6/7–7/6 | 7/7–8/3 | 8/4–8/28 | 8/29–9/22 | 9/23–10/17 |
| 1970 | 3/11–4/3 | 4/4–4/27 | 4/28–5/22 | 5/23–6/16 | 6/17–7/12 | 7/13–8/8 |
| 1971 | 4/24–5/18 | 5/19–6/12 | 6/13–7/6 | 7/7–7/31 | 8/1–8/24 | 8/25–9/17 |
| 1972 | 2/11–3/7 | 3/8–4/3 | 4/4–5/10 | 5/11–6/11 |  |  |
|  |  |  | 6/12–8/6 | 8/7–9/8 | 9/9–10/5 | 10/6–10/30 |
| 1973 | 3/25–4/18 | 4/18–5/12 | 5/13–6/5 | 6/6–6/29 | 7/1–7/25 | 7/26–8/19 |
| 1974 | 5/5–5/31 | 6/1–6/25 | 6/26–7/21 | 7/22–8/14 | 8/15–9/8 | 9/9–10/2 |
| 1975 | 2/24–3/20 | 3/21–4/13 | 4/14–5/9 | 5/10–6/6 | 6/7–7/9 | 7/10–9/2 |
|  |  |  |  |  | 9/3–10/4 | 10/5–11/9 |

| Libra | Scorpio | Sagittarius | Capricorn | Aquarius | Pisces |
|---|---|---|---|---|---|
| 9/4–9/27 | 1/1–1/2 | 1/3–1/27 | 1/28–2/20 | 2/21–3/16 | 3/17–4/9 |
|  | 9/28–10/21 | 10/22–11/15 | 11/16–12/10 | 12/11–12/31 |  |
| 10/19–11/11 | 11/12–12/5 | 12/6–12/29 | 12/30–12/31 | 1/1–1/5 | 1/6–2/1 |
|  |  |  |  |  |  |
| 8/9–9/6 | 9/7–10/22 | 10/23–10/27 | 1/1–1/22 | 1/23–2/15 | 2/16–3/11 |
|  | 10/28–12/31 |  |  |  |  |
| 9/19–10/13 | 1/1–1/6 | 1/7–2/5 | 2/6–3/4 | 3/5–3/30 | 3/31–4/24 |
|  | 10/14–11/5 | 11/6–11/30 | 12/1–12/24 | 12/25–12/31 |  |
| 11/1–11/25 | 11/26–12/19 | 12/20–12/31 |  | 1/1–1/17 | 1/18–2/11 |
|  |  |  |  |  |  |
| 8/20–9/14 | 9/15–10/9 | 1/1–1/12 | 1/13–2/5 | 2/6–3/1 | 3/2–3/25 |
|  |  | 10/10–11/5 | 11/6–12/6 | 12/7–12/31 |  |
| 10/4–10/27 | 10/28–11/20 | 11/21–12/14 | 12/15–12/31 | 1/1–4/6 | 4/7–5/5 |
|  |  |  |  |  |  |
| 11/10–12/7 | 12/8–12/31 |  | 1/1–1/7 | 1/8–1/31 | 2/1–2/24 |
| 9/3–9/26 | 1/1–1/2 | 1/3–1/27 | 1/28–2/20 | 2/21–3/15 | 3/16–4/9 |
|  | 9/27–10/21 | 10/22–11/15 | 11/16–12/10 | 12/11–12/31 |  |
| 10/18–11/11 | 11/12–12/4 | 12/5–12/28 | 12/29–12/31 | 1/1–1/5 | 1/6–2/2 |
| 8/9–9/6 | 9/7–12/31 |  | 1/1–1/21 | 1/22–2/14 | 2/15–3/10 |
| 9/19–10/12 | 1/1–1/6 | 1/7–2/5 | 2/6–3/4 | 3/5–3/29 | 3/30–4/23 |
|  | 10/13–11/5 | 11/6–11/29 | 11/30–12/23 | 12/24–12/31 |  |
| 11/1–11/24 | 11/25–12/19 | 12/20–12/31 |  | 1/1–1/16 | 1/17–2/10 |
|  |  |  |  |  |  |
| 8/20–9/13 | 9/14–10/9 | 1/1–1/12 | 1/13–2/5 | 2/6–3/1 | 3/2–3/25 |
|  |  | 10/10–11/5 | 11/6–12/7 | 12/8–12/31 |  |
| 10/3–10/26 | 10/27–11/19 | 11/20–12/13 | 2/7–2/25 | 1/1–2/6 | 4/7–5/5 |
|  |  |  | 12/14–12/31 | 2/26–4/6 |  |
|  |  |  |  |  |  |
| 11/10–12/7 | 12/8–12/31 |  | 1/1–1/6 | 1/7–1/30 | 1/31–2/23 |
| 9/3–9/26 | 1/1 | 1/2–1/26 | 1/27–2/20 | 2/21–3/15 | 3/16–4/8 |
|  | 9/27–10/21 | 10/22–11/14 | 12/29–12/31 | 12/10–12/31 |  |
| 10/18–11/10 | 11/11–12/4 | 12/5–12/28 | 12/29–12/31 | 1/1–1/4 | 1/5–2/2 |
| 8/9–9/7 | 9/8–12/31 |  | 1/1–1/21 | 1/22–2/14 | 2/15–3/10 |
| 9/18–10/11 | 1/1–1/7 | 1/8–2/5 | 2/6–3/4 | 3/5–3/29 | 3/30–4/23 |
|  | 10/12–11/5 | 11/6–11/29 | 11/30–12/23 | 12/24–12/31 |  |
|  | 11/25–12/18 | 12/19–12/31 |  | 1/1–1/16 | 1/17–2/10 |
| 10/31–11/24 |  |  |  |  |  |
| 8/20–9/13 | 9/14–10/8 | 1/1–1/12 | 1/13–2/4 | 2/5–2/28 | 3/1–3/24 |
|  |  | 10/9–11/5 | 11/6–12/7 | 12/8–12/31 |  |
|  |  |  | 1/30–2/28 | 1/1–1/29 |  |
| 10/3–10/26 | 10/27–11/19 | 11/20–12/13 | 12/14–12/31 | 3/1–4/6 | 4/7–5/4 |
|  |  |  | 1/1–1/6 | 1/7–1/30 | 1/31–2/23 |
| 11/10–12/7 | 12/8–12/31 |  |  |  |  |

## VENUS SIGNS 1901–2004

| | Aries | Taurus | Gemini | Cancer | Leo | Virgo |
|---|---|---|---|---|---|---|
| 1976 | 4/8–5/2 | 5/2–5/27 | 5/27—6/20 | 6/20–7/14 | 7/14–8/8 | 8/8–9/1 |
| 1977 | 2/2–6/6 | 6/6–7/6 | 7/6–8/2 | 8/2–8/28 | 8/28–9/22 | 9/22–10/17 |
| 1978 | 3/9–4/2 | 4/2–4/27 | 4/27–5/22 | 5/22–6/16 | 6/16–7/12 | 7/12–8/6 |
| 1979 | 4/23–5/18 | 5/18–6/11 | 6/11–7/6 | 7/6–7/30 | 7/30–8/24 | 8/24–9/17 |
| 1980 | 2/9–3/6 | 3/6–4/3 | 4/3–5/12 | 5/12–6/5 | 9/7–10/4 | 10/4–10/30 |
| | | | | 6/5–8/6 | 8/6–9/7 | |
| 1981 | 3/24–4/17 | 4/17–5/11 | 5/11–6/5 | 6/5–6/29 | 6/29–7/24 | 7/24–8/18 |
| 1982 | 5/4–5/30 | 5/30–6/25 | 6/25–7/20 | 7/20–8/14 | 8/14–9/7 | 9/7–10/2 |
| 1983 | 2/22–3/19 | 3/19–4/13 | 4/13–5/9 | 5/9–6/6 | 6/6–7/10 | 7/10–8/27 |
| | | | | | 8/27–10/5 | 10/5–11/9 |
| 1984 | 4/7–5/2 | 5/2–5/26 | 5/26–6/20 | 6/20–7/14 | 7/14–8/7 | 8/7–9/1 |
| 1985 | 2/2–6/6 | 6/7–7/6 | 7/6–8/2 | 8/2–8/28 | 8/28–9/22 | 9/22–10/16 |
| 1986 | 3/9–4/2 | 4/2–4/26 | 4/26–5/21 | 5/21–6/15 | 6/15–7/11 | 7/11–8/7 |
| 1987 | 4/22–5/17 | 5/17–6/11 | 6/11–7/5 | 7/5–7/30 | 7/30–8/23 | 8/23–9/16 |
| 1988 | 2/9–3/6 | 3/6–4/3 | 4/3–5/17 | 5/17–5/27 | 9/7–10/4 | 10/4–10/29 |
| | | | 5/27–8/6 | 8/28–9/22 | 9/22–10/16 | |
| 1989 | 3/23–4/16 | 4/16–5/11 | 5/11–6/4 | 6/4–6/29 | 6/29–7/24 | 7/24–8/18 |
| 1990 | 5/4–5/30 | 5/30–6/25 | 6/25–7/20 | 7/20–8/13 | 8/13–9/7 | 9/7–10/1 |
| 1991 | 2/22–3/18 | 3/18–4/13 | 4/13–5/9 | 5/9–6/6 | 6/6–7/11 | 7/11–8/21 |
| | | | | | 8/21–10/6 | 10/6–11/9 |
| 1992 | 4/7–5/1 | 5/1–5/26 | 5/26–6/19 | 6/19–7/13 | 7/13–8/7 | 8/7–8/31 |
| 1993 | 2/2–6/6 | 6/6–7/6 | 7/6–8/1 | 8/1–8/27 | 8/27–9/21 | 9/21–10/16 |
| 1994 | 3/8–4/1 | 4/1–4/26 | 4/26–5/21 | 5/21–6/15 | 6/15–7/11 | 7/11–8/7 |
| 1995 | 4/22–5/16 | 5/16–6/10 | 6/10–7/5 | 7/5–7/29 | 7/29–8/23 | 8/23–9/16 |
| 1996 | 2/9–3/6 | 3/6–4/3 | 4/3–8/7 | 8/7–9/7 | 9/7–10/4 | 10/4–10/29 |
| 1997 | 3/23–4/16 | 4/16–5/10 | 5/10–6/4 | 6/4–6/28 | 6/28–7/23 | 7/23–8/17 |
| 1998 | 5/3–5/29 | 5/29–6/24 | 6/24–7/19 | 7/19–8/13 | 8/13–9/6 | 9/6–9/30 |
| 1999 | 2/21–3/18 | 3/18–4/12 | 4/12–5/8 | 5/8–6/5 | 6/5–7/12 | 7/12–8/15 |
| | | | | | 8/15–10/7 | 10/7–11/9 |
| 2000 | 4/6–5/1 | 5/1–5/25 | 5/25–6/13 | 6/13–7/13 | 7/13–8/6 | 8/6–8/31 |
| 2001 | 2/2–6/6 | 6/6–7/5 | 7/5–8/1 | 8/1–8/26 | 8/26–9/20 | 9/20–10/15 |
| 2002 | 3/7–4/1 | 4/1–4/25 | 4/25–5/20 | 5/20–6/14 | 6/14–7/10 | 7/10–8/7 |
| 2003 | 4/21–5/16 | 5/16–6/9 | 6/9–7/4 | 7/4–7/29 | 7/29–8/22 | 8/22–9/15 |
| 2004 | 2/8–3/5 | 3/5–4/3 | 4/3–8/7 | 8/7–9/6 | 9/6–10/3 | 10/3–10/28 |

| Libra | Scorpio | Sagittarius | Capricorn | Aquarius | Pisces |
|---|---|---|---|---|---|
| 9/1–9/26 | 9/26–10/20 | 1/1–1/26 | 1/26–2/19 | 2/19–3/15 | 3/15–4/8 |
| 10/17-11/10 | 11/10-12/4 | 12/4-12/27 | 12/27-1/20/78 | | 1/4-2/2 |
| 8/6–9/7 | 9/7–1/7 | | | 1/20–2/13 | 2/13–3/9 |
| 9/17–10/11 | 10/11–11/4 | 1/7–2/5 | 2/5–3/3 | 3/3–3/29 | 3/29–4/23 |
| | | 11/4–11/28 | 11/28–12/22 | 12/22–1/16/80 | |
| 10/30–11/24 | 11/24–12/18 | 12/18–1/11/81 | | | 1/16–2/9 |
| | | | | | |
| 8/18–9/12 | 9/12–10/9 | 10/9–11/5 | 1/11–2/4 | 2/4–2/28 | 2/28–3/24 |
| | | | 11/5–12/8 | 12/8–1/23/82 | |
| 10/2–10/26 | 10/26–11/18 | 11/18–12/12 | 1/23–3/2 | 3/2–4/6 | 4/6–5/4 |
| | | | 12/12–1/5/83 | | |
| 11/9–12/6 | 12/6–1/1/84 | | | 1/5–1/29 | 1/29–2/22 |
| | | | | | |
| 9/1–9/25 | 9/25–10/20 | 1/1–1/25 | 1/25–2/19 | 2/19–3/14 | 3/14–4/7 |
| | | 10/20–11/13 | 11/13–12/9 | 12/10–1/4 | |
| 10/16–11/9 | 11/9–12/3 | 12/3–12/27 | 12/28–1/19 | | 1/4–2/2 |
| 8/7–9/7 | 9/7–1/7 | | | 1/20–2/13 | 2/13–3/9 |
| 9/16–10/10 | 10/10–11/3 | 1/7–2/5 | 2/5–3/3 | 3/3–3/28 | 3/28–4/22 |
| | | 11/3–11/28 | 11/28–12/22 | 12/22–1/15 | |
| 10/29–11/23 | 11/23–12/17 | 12/17–1/10 | | | 1/15–2/9 |
| | | | | | |
| 8/18–9/12 | 9/12–10/8 | 10/8–11/5 | 1/10–2/3 | 2/3–2/27 | 2/27–3/23 |
| | | | 11/5–12/10 | 12/10–1/16/90 | |
| 10/1–10/25 | 10/25–11/18 | 11/18–12/12 | 1/16–3/3 | 3/3–4/6 | 4/6–5/4 |
| | | | 12/12–1/5 | | |
| 11/9–12/6 | 12/6–12/31 | 12/31–1/25/92 | | 1/5–1/29 | 1/29–2/22 |
| | | | | | |
| 8/31–9/25 | 9/25–10/19 | 10/19–11/13 | 1/25–2/18 | 2/18–3/13 | 3/13–4/7 |
| | | | 11/13–12/8 | 12/8–1/3/93 | |
| 10/16–11/9 | 11/9–12/2 | 12/2–12/26 | 12/26–1/19 | | 1/3–2/2 |
| 8/7–9/7 | 9/7–1/7 | | | 1/19–2/12 | 2/12–3/8 |
| 9/16–10/10 | 10/10–11/13 | 1/7–2/4 | 2/4–3/2 | 3/2–3/28 | 3/28–4/22 |
| | | 11/3–11/27 | 11/27–12/21 | 12/21–1/15 | |
| 10/29–11/23 | 11/23–12/17 | 12/17–1/10/97 | | | 1/15–2/9 |
| 8/17–9/12 | 9/12–10/8 | 10/8–11/5 | 1/10–2/3 | 2/3–2/27 | 2/27–3/23 |
| | | | 11/5–12/12 | 12/12–1/9 | |
| 9/30–10/24 | 10/24–11/17 | 11/17–12/11 | 1/9–3/4 | 3/4–4/6 | 4/6–5/3 |
| 11/9–12/5 | 12/5–12/31 | 12/31–1/24 | | 1/4–1/28 | 1/28–2/21 |
| | | | | | |
| 8/31–9/24 | 9/24–10/19 | 10/19–11/13 | 1/24–2/18 | 2/18–3/12 | 3/13–4/6 |
| | | | 11/13–12/8 | 12/8 | |
| 10/15–11/8 | 11/8–12/2 | 12/2–12/26 | 12/26/01–1/18/02 | 12/8/00–1/3/01 | 1/3–2/2 |
| 8/7–9/7 | 9/7–1/7/03 | | 12/26/01–1/18 | 1/18–2/11 | 2/11–3/7 |
| 9/15–10/9 | 10/9–11/2 | 1/7–2/4 | 2/4–3/2 | 3/2–3/27 | 3/27–4/21 |
| | | 11/2–11/26 | 11/26–12/21 | 12/21–1/14/04 | |
| 10/28–11/22 | 11/22–12/16 | 12/16–1/9/05 | | 1/1–1/14 | 1/14–2/8 |

# How to Use the Mars, Jupiter, and Saturn Tables

Find the year of your birth on the left side of each column. The dates when the planet entered each sign are listed on the right side of each column. (Signs are abbreviated to three letters.) Your birthday should fall on or between each date listed, and your planetary placement should correspond to the earlier sign of that period.

## MARS SIGNS 1901–2004

| | | | | | | | |
|---|---|---|---|---|---|---|---|
| 1901 | MAR | 1 | Leo | 1905 | JAN | 13 | Scp |
| | MAY | 11 | Vir | | AUG | 21 | Sag |
| | JUL | 13 | Lib | | OCT | 8 | Cap |
| | AUG | 31 | Scp | | NOV | 18 | Aqu |
| | OCT | 14 | Sag | | DEC | 27 | Pic |
| | NOV | 24 | Cap | 1906 | FEB | 4 | Ari |
| 1902 | JAN | 1 | Aqu | | MAR | 17 | Tau |
| | FEB | 8 | Pic | | APR | 28 | Gem |
| | MAR | 19 | Ari | | JUN | 11 | Can |
| | APR | 27 | Tau | | JUL | 27 | Leo |
| | JUN | 7 | Gem | | SEP | 12 | Vir |
| | JUL | 20 | Can | | OCT | 30 | Lib |
| | SEP | 4 | Leo | | DEC | 17 | Scp |
| | OCT | 23 | Vir | 1907 | FEB | 5 | Sag |
| | DEC | 20 | Lib | | APR | 1 | Cap |
| 1903 | APR | 19 | Vir | | OCT | 13 | Aqu |
| | MAY | 30 | Lib | | NOV | 29 | Pic |
| | AUG | 6 | Scp | 1908 | JAN | 11 | Ari |
| | SEP | 22 | Sag | | FEB | 23 | Tau |
| | NOV | 3 | Cap | | APR | 7 | Gem |
| | DEC | 12 | Aqu | | MAY | 22 | Can |
| 1904 | JAN | 19 | Pic | | JUL | 8 | Leo |
| | FEB | 27 | Ari | | AUG | 24 | Vir |
| | APR | 6 | Tau | | OCT | 10 | Lib |
| | MAY | 18 | Gem | | NOV | 25 | Scp |
| | JUN | 30 | Can | 1909 | JAN | 10 | Sag |
| | AUG | 15 | Leo | | FEB | 24 | Cap |
| | OCT | 1 | Vir | | APR | 9 | Aqu |
| | NOV | 20 | Lib | | MAY | 25 | Pic |

| | | | | | | |
|---|---|---|---|---|---|---|
| | JUL | 21 | Ari | AUG | 19 | Can |
| | SEP | 26 | Pic | OCT | 7 | Leo |
| | NOV | 20 | Ari | 1916 MAY | 28 | Vir |
| 1910 | JAN | 23 | Tau | JUL | 23 | Lib |
| | MAR | 14 | Gem | SEP | 8 | Scp |
| | MAY | 1 | Can | OCT | 22 | Sag |
| | JUN | 19 | Leo | DEC | 1 | Cap |
| | AUG | 6 | Vir | 1917 JAN | 9 | Aqu |
| | SEP | 22 | Lib | FEB | 16 | Pic |
| | NOV | 6 | Scp | MAR | 26 | Ari |
| | DEC | 20 | Sag | MAY | 4 | Tau |
| 1911 | JAN | 31 | Cap | JUN | 14 | Gem |
| | MAR | 14 | Aqu | JUL | 28 | Can |
| | APR | 23 | Pic | SEP | 12 | Leo |
| | JUN | 2 | Ari | NOV | 2 | Vir |
| | JUL | 15 | Tau | 1918 JAN | 11 | Lib |
| | SEP | 5 | Gem | FEB | 25 | Vir |
| | NOV | 30 | Tau | JUN | 23 | Lib |
| 1912 | JAN | 30 | Gem | AUG | 17 | Scp |
| | APR | 5 | Can | OCT | 1 | Sag |
| | MAY | 28 | Leo | NOV | 11 | Cap |
| | JUL | 17 | Vir | DEC | 20 | Aqu |
| | SEP | 2 | Lib | 1919 JAN | 27 | Pic |
| | OCT | 18 | Scp | MAR | 6 | Ari |
| | NOV | 30 | Sag | APR | 15 | Tau |
| 1913 | JAN | 10 | Cap | MAY | 26 | Gem |
| | FEB | 19 | Aqu | JUL | 8 | Can |
| | MAR | 30 | Pic | AUG | 23 | Leo |
| | MAY | 8 | Ari | OCT | 10 | Vir |
| | JUN | 17 | Tau | NOV | 30 | Lib |
| | JUL | 29 | Gem | 1920 JAN | 31 | Scp |
| | SEP | 15 | Can | APR | 23 | Lib |
| 1914 | MAY | 1 | Leo | JUL | 10 | Scp |
| | JUN | 26 | Vir | SEP | 4 | Sag |
| | AUG | 14 | Lib | OCT | 18 | Cap |
| | SEP | 29 | Scp | NOV | 27 | Aqu |
| | NOV | 11 | Sag | 1921 JAN | 5 | Pic |
| | DEC | 22 | Cap | FEB | 13 | Ari |
| 1915 | JAN | 30 | Aqu | MAR | 25 | Tau |
| | MAR | 9 | Pic | MAY | 6 | Gem |
| | APR | 16 | Ari | JUN | 18 | Can |
| | MAY | 26 | Tau | AUG | 3 | Leo |
| | JUL | 6 | Gem | SEP | 19 | Vir |

|      |     |    |     |      |     |    |     |
|------|-----|----|-----|------|-----|----|-----|
|      | NOV | 6  | Lib |      | APR | 7  | Pic |
|      | DEC | 26 | Scp |      | MAY | 16 | Ari |
| 1922 | FEB | 18 | Sag |      | JUN | 26 | Tau |
|      | SEP | 13 | Cap |      | AUG | 9  | Gem |
|      | OCT | 30 | Aqu |      | OCT | 3  | Can |
|      | DEC | 11 | Pic |      | DEC | 20 | Gem |
| 1923 | JAN | 21 | Ari | 1929 | MAR | 10 | Can |
|      | MAR | 4  | Tau |      | MAY | 13 | Leo |
|      | APR | 16 | Gem |      | JUL | 4  | Vir |
|      | MAY | 30 | Can |      | AUG | 21 | Lib |
|      | JUL | 16 | Leo |      | OCT | 6  | Scp |
|      | SEP | 1  | Vir |      | NOV | 18 | Sag |
|      | OCT | 18 | Lib |      | DEC | 29 | Cap |
|      | DEC | 4  | Scp | 1930 | FEB | 6  | Aqu |
| 1924 | JAN | 19 | Sag |      | MAR | 17 | Pic |
|      | MAR | 6  | Cap |      | APR | 24 | Ari |
|      | APR | 24 | Aqu |      | JUN | 3  | Tau |
|      | JUN | 24 | Pic |      | JUL | 14 | Gem |
|      | AUG | 24 | Aqu |      | AUG | 28 | Can |
|      | OCT | 19 | Pic |      | OCT | 20 | Leo |
|      | DEC | 19 | Ari | 1931 | FEB | 16 | Can |
| 1925 | FEB | 5  | Tau |      | MAR | 30 | Leo |
|      | MAR | 24 | Gem |      | JUN | 10 | Vir |
|      | MAY | 9  | Can |      | AUG | 1  | Lib |
|      | JUN | 26 | Leo |      | SEP | 17 | Scp |
|      | AUG | 12 | Vir |      | OCT | 30 | Sag |
|      | SEP | 28 | Lib |      | DEC | 10 | Cap |
|      | NOV | 13 | Scp | 1932 | JAN | 18 | Aqu |
|      | DEC | 28 | Sag |      | FEB | 25 | Pic |
| 1926 | FEB | 9  | Cap |      | APR | 3  | Ari |
|      | MAR | 23 | Aqu |      | MAY | 12 | Tau |
|      | MAY | 3  | Pic |      | JUN | 22 | Gem |
|      | JUN | 15 | Ari |      | AUG | 4  | Can |
|      | AUG | 1  | Tau |      | SEP | 20 | Leo |
| 1927 | FEB | 22 | Gem |      | NOV | 13 | Vir |
|      | APR | 17 | Can | 1933 | JUL | 6  | Lib |
|      | JUN | 6  | Leo |      | AUG | 26 | Scp |
|      | JUL | 25 | Vir |      | OCT | 9  | Sag |
|      | SEP | 10 | Lib |      | NOV | 19 | Cap |
|      | OCT | 26 | Scp |      | DEC | 28 | Aqu |
|      | DEC | 8  | Sag | 1934 | FEB | 4  | Pic |
| 1928 | JAN | 19 | Cap |      | MAR | 14 | Ari |
|      | FEB | 28 | Aqu |      | APR | 22 | Tau |

| | | | | | | |
|---|---|---|---|---|---|---|
| | JUN | 2 | Gem | | AUG | 19 | Vir |
| | JUL | 15 | Can | | OCT | 5 | Lib |
| | AUG | 30 | Leo | | NOV | 20 | Scp |
| | OCT | 18 | Vir | 1941 | JAN | 4 | Sag |
| | DEC | 11 | Lib | | FEB | 17 | Cap |
| 1935 | JUL | 29 | Scp | | APR | 2 | Aqu |
| | SEP | 16 | Sag | | MAY | 16 | Pic |
| | OCT | 28 | Cap | | JUL | 2 | Ari |
| | DEC | 7 | Aqu | 1942 | JAN | 11 | Tau |
| 1936 | JAN | 14 | Pic | | MAR | 7 | Gem |
| | FEB | 22 | Ari | | APR | 26 | Can |
| | APR | 1 | Tau | | JUN | 14 | Leo |
| | MAY | 13 | Gem | | AUG | 1 | Vir |
| | JUN | 25 | Can | | SEP | 17 | Lib |
| | AUG | 10 | Leo | | NOV | 1 | Scp |
| | SEP | 26 | Vir | | DEC | 15 | Sag |
| | NOV | 14 | Lib | 1943 | JAN | 26 | Cap |
| 1937 | JAN | 5 | Scp | | MAR | 8 | Aqu |
| | MAR | 13 | Sag | | APR | 17 | Pic |
| | MAY | 14 | Scp | | MAY | 27 | Ari |
| | AUG | 8 | Sag | | JUL | 7 | Tau |
| | SEP | 30 | Cap | | AUG | 23 | Gem |
| | NOV | 11 | Aqu | 1944 | MAR | 28 | Can |
| | DEC | 21 | Pic | | MAY | 22 | Leo |
| 1938 | JAN | 30 | Ari | | JUL | 12 | Vir |
| | MAR | 12 | Tau | | AUG | 29 | Lib |
| | APR | 23 | Gem | | OCT | 13 | Scp |
| | JUN | 7 | Can | | NOV | 25 | Sag |
| | JUL | 22 | Leo | 1945 | JAN | 5 | Cap |
| | SEP | 7 | Vir | | FEB | 14 | Aqu |
| | OCT | 25 | Lib | | MAR | 25 | Pic |
| | DEC | 11 | Scp | | MAY | 2 | Ari |
| 1939 | JAN | 29 | Sag | | JUN | 11 | Tau |
| | MAR | 21 | Cap | | JUL | 23 | Gem |
| | MAY | 25 | Aqu | | SEP | 7 | Can |
| | JUL | 21 | Cap | | NOV | 11 | Leo |
| | SEP | 24 | Aqu | | DEC | 26 | Can |
| | NOV | 19 | Pic | 1946 | APR | 22 | Leo |
| 1940 | JAN | 4 | Ari | | JUN | 20 | Vir |
| | FEB | 17 | Tau | | AUG | 9 | Lib |
| | APR | 1 | Gem | | SEP | 24 | Scp |
| | MAY | 17 | Can | | NOV | 6 | Sag |
| | JUL | 3 | Leo | | DEC | 17 | Cap |

| 1947 | JAN | 25 | Aqu |      |     | MAR | 20 | Tau |
|       | MAR | 4  | Pic |      |     | MAY | 1  | Gem |
|       | APR | 11 | Ari |      |     | JUN | 14 | Can |
|       | MAY | 21 | Tau |      |     | JUL | 29 | Leo |
|       | JUL | 1  | Gem |      |     | SEP | 14 | Vir |
|       | AUG | 13 | Can |      |     | NOV | 1  | Lib |
|       | OCT | 1  | Leo |      |     | DEC | 20 | Scp |
|       | DEC | 1  | Vir | 1954 | FEB | 9  | Sag |
| 1948 | FEB | 12 | Leo |      |     | APR | 12 | Cap |
|       | MAY | 18 | Vir |      |     | JUL | 3  | Sag |
|       | JUL | 17 | Lib |      |     | AUG | 24 | Cap |
|       | SEP | 3  | Scp |      |     | OCT | 21 | Aqu |
|       | OCT | 17 | Sag |      |     | DEC | 4  | Pic |
|       | NOV | 26 | Cap | 1955 | JAN | 15 | Ari |
| 1949 | JAN | 4  | Aqu |      |     | FEB | 26 | Tau |
|       | FEB | 11 | Pic |      |     | APR | 10 | Gem |
|       | MAR | 21 | Ari |      |     | MAY | 26 | Can |
|       | APR | 30 | Tau |      |     | JUL | 11 | Leo |
|       | JUN | 10 | Gem |      |     | AUG | 27 | Vir |
|       | JUL | 23 | Can |      |     | OCT | 13 | Lib |
|       | SEP | 7  | Leo |      |     | NOV | 29 | Scp |
|       | OCT | 27 | Vir | 1956 | JAN | 14 | Sag |
|       | DEC | 26 | Lib |      |     | FEB | 28 | Cap |
| 1950 | MAR | 28 | Vir |      |     | APR | 14 | Aqu |
|       | JUN | 11 | Lib |      |     | JUN | 3  | Pic |
|       | AUG | 10 | Scp |      |     | DEC | 6  | Ari |
|       | SEP | 25 | Sag | 1957 | JAN | 28 | Tau |
|       | NOV | 6  | Cap |      |     | MAR | 17 | Gem |
|       | DEC | 15 | Aqu |      |     | MAY | 4  | Can |
| 1951 | JAN | 22 | Pic |      |     | JUN | 21 | Leo |
|       | MAR | 1  | Ari |      |     | AUG | 8  | Vir |
|       | APR | 10 | Tau |      |     | SEP | 24 | Lib |
|       | MAY | 21 | Gem |      |     | NOV | 8  | Scp |
|       | JUL | 3  | Can |      |     | DEC | 23 | Sag |
|       | AUG | 18 | Leo | 1958 | FEB | 3  | Cap |
|       | OCT | 5  | Vir |      |     | MAR | 17 | Aqu |
|       | NOV | 24 | Lib |      |     | APR | 27 | Pic |
| 1952 | JAN | 20 | Scp |      |     | JUN | 7  | Ari |
|       | AUG | 27 | Sag |      |     | JUL | 21 | Tau |
|       | OCT | 12 | Cap |      |     | SEP | 21 | Gem |
|       | NOV | 21 | Aqu |      |     | OCT | 29 | Tau |
|       | DEC | 30 | Pic | 1959 | FEB | 10 | Gem |
| 1953 | FEB | 8  | Ari |      |     | APR | 10 | Can |

| | | | | | | |
|---|---|---|---|---|---|---|
| | JUN | 1 | Leo | | NOV | 14 | Cap |

| Year | Month | Day | Sign | Year | Month | Day | Sign |
|---|---|---|---|---|---|---|---|
| | JUN | 1 | Leo | | NOV | 14 | Cap |
| | JUL | 20 | Vir | | DEC | 23 | Aqu |
| | SEP | 5 | Lib | 1966 | JAN | 30 | Pic |
| | OCT | 21 | Scp | | MAR | 9 | Ari |
| | DEC | 3 | Sag | | APR | 17 | Tau |
| 1960 | JAN | 14 | Cap | | MAY | 28 | Gem |
| | FEB | 23 | Aqu | | JUL | 11 | Can |
| | APR | 2 | Pic | | AUG | 25 | Leo |
| | MAY | 11 | Ari | | OCT | 12 | Vir |
| | JUN | 20 | Tau | | DEC | 4 | Lib |
| | AUG | 2 | Gem | 1967 | FEB | 12 | Scp |
| | SEP | 21 | Can | | MAR | 31 | Lib |
| 1961 | FEB | 5 | Gem | | JUL | 19 | Scp |
| | FEB | 7 | Can | | SEP | 10 | Sag |
| | MAY | 6 | Leo | | OCT | 23 | Cap |
| | JUN | 28 | Vir | | DEC | 1 | Aqu |
| | AUG | 17 | Lib | 1968 | JAN | 9 | Pic |
| | OCT | 1 | Scp | | FEB | 17 | Ari |
| | NOV | 13 | Sag | | MAR | 27 | Tau |
| | DEC | 24 | Cap | | MAY | 8 | Gem |
| 1962 | FEB | 1 | Aqu | | JUN | 21 | Can |
| | MAR | 12 | Pic | | AUG | 5 | Leo |
| | APR | 19 | Ari | | SEP | 21 | Vir |
| | MAY | 28 | Tau | | NOV | 9 | Lib |
| | JUL | 9 | Gem | | DEC | 29 | Scp |
| | AUG | 22 | Can | 1969 | FEB | 25 | Sag |
| | OCT | 11 | Leo | | SEP | 21 | Cap |
| 1963 | JUN | 3 | Vir | | NOV | 4 | Aqu |
| | JUL | 27 | Lib | | DEC | 15 | Pic |
| | SEP | 12 | Scp | 1970 | JAN | 24 | Ari |
| | OCT | 25 | Sag | | MAR | 7 | Tau |
| | DEC | 5 | Cap | | APR | 18 | Gem |
| 1964 | JAN | 13 | Aqu | | JUN | 2 | Can |
| | FEB | 20 | Plc | | JUL | 18 | Leo |
| | MAR | 29 | Ari | | SEP | 3 | Vir |
| | MAY | 7 | Tau | | OCT | 20 | Lib |
| | JUN | 17 | Gem | | DEC | 6 | Scp |
| | JUL | 30 | Can | 1971 | JAN | 23 | Sag |
| | SEP | 15 | Leo | | MAR | 12 | Cap |
| | NOV | 6 | Vir | | MAY | 3 | Aqu |
| 1965 | JUN | 29 | Lib | | NOV | 6 | Pic |
| | AUG | 20 | Scp | | DEC | 26 | Ari |
| | OCT | 4 | Sag | 1972 | FEB | 10 | Tau |

| Year | Month | Day | Sign | | Year | Month | Day | Sign |
|---|---|---|---|---|---|---|---|---|
| | MAR | 27 | Gem | | 1978 | JAN | 26 | Can |
| | MAY | 12 | Can | | | APR | 10 | Leo |
| | JUN | 28 | Leo | | | JUN | 14 | Vir |
| | AUG | 15 | Vir | | | AUG | 4 | Lib |
| | SEP | 30 | Lib | | | SEP | 19 | Scp |
| | NOV | 15 | Scp | | | NOV | 2 | Sag |
| | DEC | 30 | Sag | | | DEC | 12 | Cap |
| 1973 | FEB | 12 | Cap | | 1979 | JAN | 20 | Aqu |
| | MAR | 26 | Aqu | | | FEB | 27 | Pic |
| | MAY | 8 | Pic | | | APR | 7 | Ari |
| | JUN | 20 | Ari | | | MAY | 16 | Tau |
| | AUG | 12 | Tau | | | JUN | 26 | Gem |
| | OCT | 29 | Ari | | | AUG | 8 | Can |
| | DEC | 24 | Tau | | | SEP | 24 | Leo |
| 1974 | FEB | 27 | Gem | | | NOV | 19 | Vir |
| | APR | 20 | Can | | 1980 | MAR | 11 | Leo |
| | JUN | 9 | Leo | | | MAY | 4 | Vir |
| | JUL | 27 | Vir | | | JUL | 10 | Lib |
| | SEP | 12 | Lib | | | AUG | 29 | Scp |
| | OCT | 28 | Scp | | | OCT | 12 | Sag |
| | DEC | 10 | Sag | | | NOV | 22 | Cap |
| 1975 | JAN | 21 | Cap | | | DEC | 30 | Aqu |
| | MAR | 3 | Aqu | | 1981 | FEB | 6 | Pic |
| | APR | 11 | Pic | | | MAR | 17 | Ari |
| | MAY | 21 | Ari | | | APR | 25 | Tau |
| | JUL | 1 | Tau | | | JUN | 5 | Gem |
| | AUG | 14 | Gem | | | JUL | 18 | Can |
| | OCT | 17 | Can | | | SEP | 2 | Leo |
| | NOV | 25 | Gem | | | OCT | 21 | Vir |
| 1976 | MAR | 18 | Can | | | DEC | 16 | Lib |
| | MAY | 16 | Leo | | 1982 | AUG | 3 | Scp |
| | JUL | 6 | Vir | | | SEP | 20 | Sag |
| | AUG | 24 | Lib | | | OCT | 31 | Cap |
| | OCT | 8 | Scp | | | DEC | 10 | Aqu |
| | NOV | 20 | Sag | | 1983 | JAN | 17 | Pic |
| 1977 | JAN | 1 | Cap | | | FEB | 25 | Ari |
| | FEB | 9 | Aqu | | | APR | 5 | Tau |
| | MAR | 20 | Pic | | | MAY | 16 | Gem |
| | APR | 27 | Ari | | | JUN | 29 | Can |
| | JUN | 6 | Tau | | | AUG | 13 | Leo |
| | JUL | 17 | Gem | | | SEP | 30 | Vir |
| | SEP | 1 | Can | | | NOV | 18 | Lib |
| | OCT | 26 | Leo | | 1984 | JAN | 11 | Scp |

| | | | | | | |
|---|---|---|---|---|---|---|
| | AUG | 17 | Sag | | JUL | 12 | Tau |
| | OCT | 5 | Cap | | AUG | 31 | Gem |
| | NOV | 15 | Aqu | | DEC | 14 | Tau |
| | DEC | 25 | Pic | 1991 | JAN | 21 | Gem |
| 1985 | FEB | 2 | Ari | | APR | 3 | Can |
| | MAR | 15 | Tau | | MAY | 26 | Leo |
| | APR | 26 | Gem | | JUL | 15 | Vir |
| | JUN | 9 | Can | | SEP | 1 | Lib |
| | JUL | 25 | Leo | | OCT | 16 | Scp |
| | SEP | 10 | Vir | | NOV | 29 | Sag |
| | OCT | 27 | Lib | 1992 | JAN | 9 | Cap |
| | DEC | 14 | Scp | | FEB | 18 | Aqu |
| 1986 | FEB | 2 | Sag | | MAR | 28 | Pic |
| | MAR | 28 | Cap | | MAY | 5 | Ari |
| | OCT | 9 | Aqu | | JUN | 14 | Tau |
| | NOV | 26 | Pic | | JUL | 26 | Gem |
| 1987 | JAN | 8 | Ari | | SEP | 12 | Can |
| | FEB | 20 | Tau | 1993 | APR | 27 | Leo |
| | APR | 5 | Gem | | JUN | 23 | Vir |
| | MAY | 21 | Can | | AUG | 12 | Lib |
| | JUL | 6 | Leo | | SEP | 27 | Scp |
| | AUG | 22 | Vir | | NOV | 9 | Sag |
| | OCT | 8 | Lib | | DEC | 20 | Cap |
| | NOV | 24 | Scp | 1994 | JAN | 28 | Aqu |
| 1988 | JAN | 8 | Sag | | MAR | 7 | Pic |
| | FEB | 22 | Cap | | APR | 14 | Ari |
| | APR | 6 | Aqu | | MAY | 23 | Tau |
| | MAY | 22 | Pic | | JUL | 3 | Gem |
| | JUL | 13 | Ari | | AUG | 16 | Can |
| | OCT | 23 | Pic | | OCT | 4 | Leo |
| | NOV | 1 | Ari | | DEC | 12 | Vir |
| 1989 | JAN | 19 | Tau | 1995 | JAN | 22 | Leo |
| | MAR | 11 | Gem | | MAY | 25 | Vir |
| | APR | 29 | Can | | JUL | 21 | Lib |
| | JUN | 16 | Leo | | SEP | 7 | Scp |
| | AUG | 3 | Vir | | OCT | 20 | Sag |
| | SEP | 19 | Lib | | NOV | 30 | Cap |
| | NOV | 4 | Scp | 1996 | JAN | 8 | Aqu |
| | DEC | 18 | Sag | | FEB | 15 | Pic |
| 1990 | JAN | 29 | Cap | | MAR | 24 | Ari |
| | MAR | 11 | Aqu | | MAY | 2 | Tau |
| | APR | 20 | Pic | | JUN | 12 | Gem |
| | MAY | 31 | Ari | | JUL | 25 | Can |

| | | | | | | |
|---|---|---|---|---|---|---|
| | SEP | 9 | Leo | | SEP | 17 | Vir |
| | OCT | 30 | Vir | | NOV | 4 | Lib |
| 1997 | JAN | 3 | Lib | | DEC | 23 | Scp |
| | MAR | 8 | Vir | 2001 | FEB | 14 | Sag |
| | JUN | 19 | Lib | | SEP | 8 | Cap |
| | AUG | 14 | Scp | | OCT | 27 | Aqu |
| | SEP | 28 | Sag | | DEC | 8 | Pic |
| | NOV | 9 | Cap | 2002 | JAN | 18 | Ari |
| | DEC | 18 | Aqu | | MAR | 1 | Tau |
| 1998 | JAN | 25 | Pic | | APR | 13 | Gem |
| | MAR | 4 | Ari | | MAY | 28 | Can |
| | APR | 13 | Tau | | JUL | 13 | Leo |
| | MAY | 24 | Gem | | AUG | 29 | Vir |
| | JUL | 6 | Can | | OCT | 15 | Lib |
| | AUG | 20 | Leo | | DEC | 1 | Scp |
| | OCT | 7 | Vir | 2003 | JAN | 17 | Sag |
| | NOV | 27 | Lib | | MAR | 4 | Cap |
| 1999 | JAN | 26 | Scp | | APR | 21 | Aqu |
| | MAY | 5 | Lib | | JUN | 17 | Pic |
| | JUL | 5 | Scp | | DEC | 16 | Ari |
| | SEP | 2 | Sag | 2004 | FEB | 3 | Tau |
| | OCT | 17 | Cap | | MAR | 21 | Gem |
| | NOV | 26 | Aqu | | MAY | 7 | Can |
| 2000 | JAN | 4 | Pic | | JUN | 23 | Leo |
| | FEB | 12 | Ari | | AUG | 10 | Vir |
| | MAR | 23 | Tau | | SEP | 26 | Lib |
| | MAY | 3 | Gem | | NOV | 11 | Sep |
| | JUN | 16 | Can | | DEC | 25 | Sag |
| | AUG | 1 | Leo | | | | |

## JUPITER SIGNS 1901–2004

| | | | | | | | |
|---|---|---|---|---|---|---|---|
| 1901 | JAN | 19 | Cap | | JUL | 30 | Can |
| 1902 | FEB | 6 | Aqu | 1907 | AUG | 18 | Leo |
| 1903 | FEB | 20 | Pic | 1908 | SEP | 12 | Vir |
| 1904 | MAR | 1 | Ari | 1909 | OCT | 11 | Lib |
| | AUG | 8 | Tau | 1910 | NOV | 11 | Scp |
| | AUG | 31 | Ari | 1911 | DEC | 10 | Sag |
| 1905 | MAR | 7 | Tau | 1913 | JAN | 2 | Cap |
| | JUL | 21 | Gem | 1914 | JAN | 21 | Aqu |
| | DEC | 4 | Tau | 1915 | FEB | 4 | Pic |
| 1906 | MAR | 9 | Gem | 1916 | FEB | 12 | Ari |

|      | JUN | 26 | Tau | 1949 | APR | 12 | Aqu |
|------|-----|----|-----|------|-----|----|-----|
|      | OCT | 26 | Ari |      | JUN | 27 | Cap |
| 1917 | FEB | 12 | Tau |      | NOV | 30 | Aqu |
|      | JUN | 29 | Gem | 1950 | APR | 15 | Pic |
| 1918 | JUL | 13 | Can |      | SEP | 15 | Aqu |
| 1919 | AUG | 2  | Leo |      | DEC | 1  | Pic |
| 1920 | AUG | 27 | Vir | 1951 | APR | 21 | Ari |
| 1921 | SEP | 25 | Lib | 1952 | APR | 28 | Tau |
| 1922 | OCT | 26 | Scp | 1953 | MAY | 9  | Gem |
| 1923 | NOV | 24 | Sag | 1954 | MAY | 24 | Can |
| 1924 | DEC | 18 | Cap | 1955 | JUN | 13 | Leo |
| 1926 | JAN | 6  | Aqu |      | NOV | 17 | Vir |
| 1927 | JAN | 18 | Pic | 1956 | JAN | 18 | Leo |
|      | JUN | 6  | Ari |      | JUL | 7  | Vir |
|      | SEP | 11 | Pic |      | DEC | 13 | Lib |
| 1928 | JAN | 23 | Ari | 1957 | FEB | 19 | Vir |
|      | JUN | 4  | Tau |      | AUG | 7  | Lib |
| 1929 | JUN | 12 | Gem | 1958 | JAN | 13 | Scp |
| 1930 | JUN | 26 | Can |      | MAR | 20 | Lib |
| 1931 | JUL | 17 | Leo |      | SEP | 7  | Scp |
| 1932 | AUG | 11 | Vir | 1959 | FEB | 10 | Sag |
| 1933 | SEP | 10 | Lib |      | APR | 24 | Scp |
| 1934 | OCT | 11 | Scp |      | OCT | 5  | Sag |
| 1935 | NOV | 9  | Sag | 1960 | MAR | 1  | Cap |
| 1936 | DEC | 2  | Cap |      | JUN | 10 | Sag |
| 1937 | DEC | 20 | Aqu |      | OCT | 26 | Cap |
| 1938 | MAY | 14 | Pic | 1961 | MAR | 15 | Aqu |
|      | JUL | 30 | Aqu |      | AUG | 12 | Cap |
|      | DEC | 29 | Pic |      | NOV | 4  | Aqu |
| 1939 | MAY | 11 | Ari | 1962 | MAR | 25 | Pic |
|      | OCT | 30 | Pic | 1963 | APR | 4  | Ari |
|      | DEC | 20 | Ari | 1964 | APR | 12 | Tau |
| 1940 | MAY | 16 | Tau | 1965 | APR | 22 | Gem |
| 1941 | MAY | 26 | Gem |      | SEP | 21 | Can |
| 1942 | JUN | 10 | Can |      | NOV | 17 | Gem |
| 1943 | JUN | 30 | Leo | 1966 | MAY | 5  | Can |
| 1944 | JUL | 26 | Vir |      | SEP | 27 | Leo |
| 1945 | AUG | 25 | Lib | 1967 | JAN | 16 | Can |
| 1946 | SEP | 25 | Scp |      | MAY | 23 | Leo |
| 1947 | OCT | 24 | Sag |      | OCT | 19 | Vir |
| 1948 | NOV | 15 | Cap | 1968 | FEB | 27 | Leo |

| | | | | | | |
|---|---|---|---|---|---|---|
| | JUN | 15 | Vir | 1981 | NOV | 27 | Scp |
| | NOV | 15 | Lib | 1982 | DEC | 26 | Sag |
| 1969 | MAR | 30 | Vir | 1984 | JAN | 19 | Cap |
| | JUL | 15 | Lib | 1985 | FEB | 6 | Aqu |
| | DEC | 16 | Scp | 1986 | FEB | 20 | Pic |
| 1970 | APR | 30 | Lib | 1987 | MAR | 2 | Ari |
| | AUG | 15 | Scp | 1988 | MAR | 8 | Tau |
| 1971 | JAN | 14 | Sag | | JUL | 22 | Gem |
| | JUN | 5 | Scp | | NOV | 30 | Tau |
| | SEP | 11 | Sag | 1989 | MAR | 11 | Gem |
| 1972 | FEB | 6 | Cap | | JUL | 30 | Can |
| | JUL | 24 | Sag | 1990 | AUG | 18 | Leo |
| | SEP | 25 | Cap | 1991 | SEP | 12 | Vir |
| 1973 | FEB | 23 | Aqu | 1992 | OCT | 10 | Lib |
| 1974 | MAR | 8 | Pic | 1993 | NOV | 10 | Scp |
| 1975 | MAR | 18 | Ari | 1994 | DEC | 9 | Sag |
| 1976 | MAR | 26 | Tau | 1996 | JAN | 3 | Cap |
| | AUG | 23 | Gem | 1997 | JAN | 21 | Aqu |
| | OCT | 16 | Tau | 1998 | FEB | 4 | Pic |
| 1977 | APR | 3 | Gem | 1999 | FEB | 13 | Ari |
| | AUG | 20 | Can | | JUN | 28 | Tau |
| | DEC | 30 | Gem | | OCT | 23 | Ari |
| 1978 | APR | 12 | Can | 2000 | FEB | 14 | Tau |
| | SEP | 5 | Leo | | JUN | 30 | Gem |
| 1979 | FEB | 28 | Can | 2001 | JUL | 14 | Can |
| | APR | 20 | Leo | 2002 | AUG | 1 | Leo |
| | SEP | 29 | Vir | 2003 | AUG | 27 | Vir |
| 1980 | OCT | 27 | Lib | 2004 | SEP | 24 | Lib |

## SATURN SIGNS 1903–2004

| | | | | | | |
|---|---|---|---|---|---|---|
| 1903 | JAN | 19 | Aqu | 1912 | JUL | 7 | Gem |
| 1905 | APR | 13 | Pic | | NOV | 30 | Tau |
| | AUG | 17 | Aqu | 1913 | MAR | 26 | Gem |
| 1906 | JAN | 8 | Pic | 1914 | AUG | 24 | Can |
| 1908 | MAR | 19 | Ari | | DEC | 7 | Gem |
| 1910 | MAY | 17 | Tau | 1915 | MAY | 11 | Can |
| | DEC | 14 | Ari | 1916 | OCT | 17 | Leo |
| 1911 | JAN | 20 | Tau | | DEC | 7 | Can |

| Year | Month | Day | Sign | | Year | Month | Day | Sign |
|---|---|---|---|---|---|---|---|---|
| 1917 | JUN | 24 | Leo | | | SEP | 16 | Aqu |
| 1919 | AUG | 12 | Vir | | | DEC | 16 | Pic |
| 1921 | OCT | 7 | Lib | | 1967 | MAR | 3 | Ari |
| 1923 | DEC | 20 | Scp | | 1969 | APR | 29 | Tau |
| 1924 | APR | 6 | Lib | | 1971 | JUN | 18 | Gem |
| | SEP | 13 | Scp | | 1972 | JAN | 10 | Tau |
| 1926 | DEC | 2 | Sag | | | FEB | 21 | Gem |
| 1929 | MAR | 15 | Cap | | 1973 | AUG | 1 | Can |
| | MAY | 5 | Sag | | 1974 | JAN | 7 | Gem |
| | NOV | 30 | Cap | | | APR | 18 | Can |
| 1932 | FEB | 24 | Aqu | | 1975 | SEP | 17 | Leo |
| | AUG | 13 | Cap | | 1976 | JAN | 14 | Can |
| | NOV | 20 | Aqu | | | JUN | 5 | Leo |
| 1935 | FEB | 14 | Pic | | 1977 | NOV | 17 | Vir |
| 1937 | APR | 25 | Ari | | 1978 | JAN | 5 | Leo |
| | OCT | 18 | Pic | | | JUL | 26 | Vir |
| 1938 | JAN | 14 | Ari | | 1980 | SEP | 21 | Lib |
| 1939 | JUL | 6 | Tau | | 1982 | NOV | 29 | Scp |
| | SEP | 22 | Ari | | 1983 | MAY | 6 | Lib |
| 1940 | MAR | 20 | Tau | | | AUG | 24 | Scp |
| 1942 | MAY | 8 | Gem | | 1985 | NOV | 17 | Sag |
| 1944 | JUN | 20 | Can | | 1988 | FEB | 13 | Cap |
| 1946 | AUG | 2 | Leo | | | JUN | 10 | Sag |
| 1948 | SEP | 19 | Vir | | | NOV | 12 | Cap |
| 1949 | APR | 3 | Leo | | 1991 | FEB | 6 | Aqu |
| | MAY | 29 | Vir | | 1993 | MAY | 21 | Pic |
| 1950 | NOV | 20 | Lib | | | JUN | 30 | Aqu |
| 1951 | MAR | 7 | Vir | | 1994 | JAN | 28 | Pic |
| | AUG | 13 | Lib | | 1996 | APR | 7 | Ari |
| 1953 | OCT | 22 | Scp | | 1998 | JUN | 9 | Tau |
| 1956 | JAN | 12 | Sag | | | OCT | 25 | Ari |
| | MAY | 14 | Scp | | 1999 | MAR | 1 | Tau |
| | OCT | 10 | Sag | | 2000 | AUG | 10 | Gem |
| 1959 | JAN | 5 | Cap | | | OCT | 16 | Tau |
| 1962 | JAN | 3 | Aqu | | 2001 | APR | 21 | Gem |
| 1964 | MAR | 24 | Pic | | 2003 | JUN | 3 | Can |

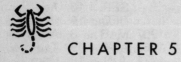

## CHAPTER 5

# How to Read the Symbols on Your Chart

Looking at an astrology chart for the first time, you will see symbols that seem as mysterious as ancient runes and cave drawings. These symbols, called *glyphs,* are used by astrologers worldwide and by computer astrology programs. In order to understand a horoscope chart or to use one of the popular astrology programs on your PC, you must learn to read the glyphs.

Each glyph contains clues to the meaning of the signs and the planets. Since there are only twelve signs and ten planets (not counting a few asteroids and other space creatures some astrologers use), it's a lot easier than learning to read a foreign language.

Here's a code cracker for the glyphs, beginning with the glyphs for the planets. To those who already know their glyphs, don't just skim over the chapter. These familiar graphics have hidden meanings you will discover!

## The Glyphs for the Planets

The glyphs for the planets are easy to learn. They're simple combinations of the most basic visual elements: the circle, the semicircle or arc, and the cross. However, each component of a glyph has a special meaning in relation to the other parts of the symbol.

The circle, which has no beginning or end, is one of the oldest symbols of spirit or spiritual forces. All of the early diagrams of the heavens—spiritual territory—are shown in circular form. The never-ending line of the circle is the perfect symbol for eternity. The semicircle or arc is an incomplete circle, symbolizing the receptive, finite soul, which contains spiritual potential in the curving line.

The vertical line of the cross symbolizes movement from heaven to earth. The horizontal line describes temporal movement, here and now, in time and space. Combined in a cross, the vertical and horizontal planes symbolize manifestation in the material world.

## The Sun Glyph ☉

The sun is always shown by this powerful solar symbol, a circle with a point in the center. The center point is you, your spiritual center, and the symbol represents your infinite personality incarnating (the point) into the finite cycles of birth and death.

The sun has been represented by a circle or disk since ancient Egyptian times when the solar disk represented the Sun god, Ra. Some archaeologists believe the great stone circles found in England were centers of sun worship. This particular version of the symbol was brought into common use in the sixteenth century after German occultist and scholar Cornelius Agrippa (1486–1535) wrote a book called *Die Occulta Philosophia,* which became accepted as the authority in its field. Agrippa collected many medieval astrological and magical symbols in this book, which have been used by astrologers since then.

## The Moon Glyph ☽

The moon glyph is the most recognizable symbol on a chart, a left-facing arc stylized into the crescent moon. As part of a circle, the arc symbolizes the potential fulfillment of the entire circle, the life force that is still incomplete. Therefore, it is the ideal representation of the reactive, receptive, emotional nature of the moon.

## The Mercury Glyph ☿

Mercury contains all three elemental symbols: the crescent, the circle, and the cross in vertical order. This is the "Venus with a hat" glyph (compare with the symbol of Venus). With another stretch of the imagination, can't you see the winged cap of Mercury the messenger? Think of the upturned crescent as antennae that tune in and transmit messages from the sun, reminding you that Mercury is the way you communicate, the way your mind works. The upturned arc is receiving energy into the spirit or solar circle, which will later be translated into action on the material plane, symbolized by the cross. All the elements are equally sized because Mercury is neutral; it doesn't play favorites! This planet symbolizes objective, detached, unemotional thinking.

## The Venus Glyph ♀

Here the relationship is between two components: the circle of spirit and the cross of matter. Spirit is elevated over matter, pulling it upward. Venus asks, "What is beautiful? What do you like best? What do you love to have done to you?" Consequently, Venus determines both your ideal of beauty and what feels good sensually. It governs your own allure and power to attract, as well as what attracts and pleases you.

## The Mars Glyph ♂

In this glyph, the cross of matter is stylized into an arrowhead pointed up and outward, propelled by the circle of spirit. With a little imagination, you can visualize it as the shield and spear of Mars, the ancient god of war. You can deduce that Mars embodies your spiritual energy projected into the outer world. It's your assertiveness, your initiative, your aggressive drive, what you like to do to others, your temper. If you know someone's Mars, you know whether they'll blow up when angry or do a slow burn. Your task is to use your outgoing Mars energy wisely and well.

## The Jupiter Glyph ♃

Jupiter is the basic cross of matter, with a large stylized crescent perched on the left side of the horizontal, temporal plane. You might think of the crescent as an open hand, because one meaning of Jupiter is "luck," what's handed to you. You don't have to work for what you get from Jupiter; it comes to you, if you're open to it.

The Jupiter glyph might also remind you of a jumbo jet plane, with a huge tail fin, about to take off. This is the planet of travel, mental and spiritual, of expanding your horizons via new ideas, new spiritual dimensions, and new places. Jupiter embodies the optimism and enthusiasm of the traveler about to embark on an exciting adventure.

## The Saturn Glyph ♄

Flip Jupiter over, and you've got Saturn. This might not be immediately apparent because Saturn is usually stylized into an "h" form like the one shown here. The principle it expresses is the opposite of Jupiter's expansive tendencies. Saturn pulls you back to earth: the receptive arc is pushed down underneath the cross of matter. Before there are any rewards or expansion, the duties and obligations of the material world must be considered. Saturn says, "Stop, wait, finish your chores before you take off!"

Saturn's glyph also resembles the sickle of old "Father Time." Saturn was first known as Chronos, the Greek god of time, for time brings all matter to an end. When it was the most distant planet (before the discovery of Uranus), Saturn was believed to be the place where time stopped. After the soul departed from earth, it journeyed back to the outer reaches of the universe and finally stopped at Saturn, or at "the end of time."

## The Uranus Glyph ♅

The glyph for Uranus is often stylized to form a capital "H" after Sir William Herschel who discovered the planet. But the more esoteric version curves the two pillars of the H into crescent antennae, or "ears," like satellite disks receiving signals from space. These are perched on the horizontal material line of the cross of matter and pushed from below by the circle of the spirit. To many sci-fi fans, Uranus looks like an orbiting satellite.

Uranus channels the highest energy of all, the white electrical light of the universal spiritual force that holds the cosmos together. This pure electrical energy is gathered from all over the universe. Because Uranus energy doesn't follow any ordinary celestial drumbeat, it can't be controlled or predicted (which is also true of those who are strongly influenced by this eccentric planet). In the symbol, this energy is manifested through the balance of polarities (the two opposite arms of the glyph) like the two polarized wires of a lightbulb.

## The Neptune Glyph ♆

Neptune's glyph is usually stylized to look like a trident, the weapon of the Roman god Neptune. However, on a more esoteric level, it shows the large upturned crescent of the soul pierced through by the cross of matter. Neptune nails down, or materializes, soul energy, bringing impulses from the soul level into manifestation. That is why Neptune is associated with imagination or "imagining in," making an image of the soul. Neptune works through feeling, sensitivity, and mystical capacity to bring the divine into the earthly realm.

# The Pluto Glyph ♀

Pluto is written two ways. One is a composite of the letters "PL," the first two letters of the word Pluto and coincidentally the initials of Percival Lowell, one of the planet's discoverers. The other, more esoteric symbol is a small circle above a large open crescent that surmounts the cross of matter. This depicts Pluto's power to regenerate. Imagine a new little spirit emerging from the sheltering cup of the soul. Pluto rules the forces of life and death. After this planet has passed a sensitive point in your chart, you are transformed, reborn in some way.

Sci-fi fans might visualize this glyph as a small satellite (the circle) being launched. It was shortly after Pluto's discovery that we learned how to harness the nuclear forces that made space exploration possible. Pluto rules the transformative power of atomic energy, which totally changed our lives and from which there is no turning back.

# The Glyphs for the Signs

On an astrology chart, the glyph for the sign will appear after that of the planet. For example, when you see the moon glyph followed first by a number and then by another glyph representing the sign, this means that the moon was passing over a certain degree of that astrological sign at the time of the chart. On the dividing lines between the houses on your chart, you'll find the symbol for the sign that rules the house.

Because sun sign symbols do not contain the same basic geometric components of the planetary glyphs, we must look elsewhere for clues to their meanings. Many have been passed down from ancient Egyptian and Chaldean civilizations with few modifications. Others have been adapted over the centuries.

In deciphering many of the glyphs, you'll often find that the symbols reveal a dual nature of the sign, which is not always apparent in the usual sun sign descriptions. For instance, the Gemini glyph is similar to the Roman numeral for two, and reveals this sign's longing to discover a twin soul. The Cancer glyph may be interpreted as resembling either the nurturing breasts or the self-protective claws of a crab, both symbols associated with the contrasting qualities of this sign. Libra's glyph embodies the duality of the spirit balanced with material reality. The Sagittarius glyph shows that the aspirant must also carry along the earthly animal nature in his quest. The Capricorn sea goat is another symbol with dual emphasis. The goat climbs high, yet is always pulled back by the deep waters of the unconscious. Aquarius embodies the double waves of mental detachment, balanced by the desire for connection with others in a friendly way. Finally, the two fishes of Pisces, which are forever tied together, show the duality of the soul and the spirit that must be reconciled.

## The Aries Glyph ♈

Since the symbol for Aries is the Ram, this glyph is obviously associated with a ram's horns, which characterize one aspect of the Aries personality—an aggressive, me-first, leaping-headfirst attitude. But the symbol can be interpreted in other ways as well. Some astrologers liken it to a fountain of energy, which Aries people also embody. The first sign of the zodiac bursts on the scene eagerly, ready to go. Another analogy is to the eyebrows and nose of the human head, which Aries rules, and the thinking power that is initiated by the brain.

One theory of this symbol links it to the Egyptian god Amun, represented by a ram in ancient times. As Amun-Ra, this god was believed to embody the creator of the universe, the leader of all the other gods. This relates easily to the position of Aries as the leader (or first sign) of the zodiac, which begins at the spring equinox, a time of the year when nature is renewed.

# The Taurus Glyph ♉

This is another easy glyph to draw and identify. It takes little imagination to decipher the bull's head with long curving horns. Like its symbol the Bull, the archetypal Taurus is slow to anger but ferocious when provoked, as well as stubborn, steady, and sensual. Another association is the larynx (and thyroid) of the throat area (ruled by Taurus) and the eustachian tubes running up to the ears, which coincides with the relationship of Taurus to the voice, song, and music. Many famous singers, musicians, and composers have prominent Taurus influences.

Many ancient religions involved a bull as the central figure in fertility rites or initiations, usually symbolizing the victory of man over his animal nature. Another possible origin is in the sacred bull of Egypt, who embodied the incarnate form of Osiris, god of death and resurrection. In early Christian imagery, the Taurus Bull represented St. Luke.

# The Gemini Glyph ♊

The standard glyph immediately calls to mind the Roman numeral for two (II) and the Twins symbol, as it is called, for Gemini. In almost all drawings and images used for this sign, the relationship between two persons is emphasized. Usually one twin will be touching the other, which signifies communication, human contact, the desire to share.

The top line of the Gemini glyph indicates mental communication, while the bottom line indicates shared physical space.

The most famous Gemini legend is that of the twin sons, Castor and Pollux, one of whom had a mortal father while the other was the son of Zeus, king of the gods. When it came time for the mortal twin to die, his grief-stricken brother pleaded with Zeus, who agreed to let them spend half the year on earth in mortal form and half in immortal life, with the gods on Mt. Olympus. This reflects a basic duality of humankind, which possesses an immortal soul yet is also subject to the limits of mortality.

## The Cancer Glyph ♋

Two convenient images relate to the Cancer glyph. It is easiest to decode the curving claws of the Cancer symbol, the Crab. Like the crab, Cancer's element is water. This sensitive sign also has a hard protective shell to protect its tender interior. The crab must be wily to escape predators, scampering sideways and hiding under rocks. The crab also responds to the cycles of the moon, as do all shellfish. The other image is that of two female breasts, which Cancer rules, showing that this is a sign that nurtures and protects others as well as itself.

In ancient Egypt, Cancer was also represented by the scarab beetle, a symbol of regeneration and eternal life.

## The Leo Glyph ♌

Notice that the Leo glyph seems to be an extension of Cancer's glyph, with a significant difference. In the Cancer glyph, the lines curve inward protectively. The Leo glyph expresses energy outwardly. And there is no duality in the symbol, the Lion, or in Leo, the sign.

Lions have belonged to the sign of Leo since earliest times. It is not difficult to imagine the king of beasts with his sweeping mane and curling tail from this glyph. The upward sweep of the glyph easily describes the positive energy of Leo: the flourishing tail, their flamboyant qualities. Another analogy, perhaps a stretch of the imagination, is that of a heart leaping up with joy and enthusiasm, also very typical of Leo, which also rules the heart. In early Christian imagery, the Leo Lion represented St. Mark.

## The Virgo Glyph ♍

You can read much into this mysterious glyph. For instance, it could represent the initials of "Mary Virgin," or a young woman holding a staff of wheat, or stylized female genitalia, all common interpretations. The "M" shape might also remind you that Virgo is ruled by Mercury. The cross beneath the symbol reveals the grounded, practical nature of this earth sign.

The earliest zodiacs link Virgo with the Egyptian goddess Isis who gave birth to the god Horus, after her husband Osiris had been killed, in the archetype of a miraculous conception. There are many ancient statues of Isis nursing her baby son, which are reminiscent of medieval Virgin and Child motifs. This sign has also been associated with the image of the Holy Grail, when the Virgo symbol was substituted with a chalice.

## The Libra Glyph ♎

It is not difficult to read the standard image for Libra, the Scales, into this glyph. There is another meaning, however, that is equally relevant: the setting sun as it descends over the horizon. Libra's natural position on the zodiac wheel is the descendant, or sunset position (as the Aries natural position is the ascendant, or rising sign). Both images relate to Libra's personality. Libra is always weighing pros and cons for a balanced decision. In the sunset image, the sun (male) hovers over the horizontal earth (female) before setting. Libra is the space between these lines, harmonizing yin and yang, spiritual and material, male and female, ideal and real worlds. The glyph has also been linked to the kidneys, which are ruled by Libra.

## The Scorpio Glyph ♏

With its barbed tail, this glyph is easy to identify as the Scorpion for the sign of Scorpio. It also represents the male sexual parts, over which the sign rules. From the arrowhead, you can draw the conclusion that Mars was once its ruler. Some earlier Egyptian glyphs for Scorpio represent it as an erect serpent, so the Serpent is an alternate symbol.

Another symbol for Scorpio, which is not identifiable in this glyph, is the Eagle. Scorpios can go to extremes, either in soaring like the eagle or self-destructing like the scorpion. In early Christian imagery, which often used zodiacal symbols, the Scorpio Eagle was chosen to symbolize the intense apostle St. John the Evangelist.

## The Sagittarius Glyph ♐

This is one of the easiest to spot and draw: an upward pointing arrow lifting up a cross. The arrow is pointing skyward, while the cross represents the four elements of the material world, which the arrow must convey. Elevating materiality into spirituality is an important Sagittarius quality, which explains why this sign is associated with higher learning, religion, philosophy, travel—the aspiring professions. Sagittarius can also send barbed arrows of frankness in the pursuit of truth, so the Archer symbol for Sagittarius is apt. (Sagittarius is also the sign of the supersalesman.)

Sagittarius is symbolically represented by the centaur, a mythological creature who is half man, half horse, aiming his arrow toward the skies. Though Sagittarius is motivated by spiritual aspiration, it also must balance the powerful appetites of the animal nature. The centaur Chiron, a figure in Greek mythology, became a wise teacher who, after many adventures and world travels, was killed by a poisoned arrow.

## The Capricorn Glyph ♑

One of the most difficult symbols to draw, this glyph may take some practice. It is a representation of the sea goat: a mythical animal that is a goat with a curving fish's tail. The goat part of Capricorn wants to leave the waters of the emotions and climb to the elevated areas of life. But the fish tail is the unconscious, the deep chaotic psychic level that draws the goat back. Capricorn is often trying to escape the deep, feeling part of life by submerging himself in work, steadily ascending to the top. To some people, the glyph represents a seated figure with a bent knee, a reminder that Capricorn governs the knee area of the body.

An interesting aspect of this glyph is the contrast of the sharp pointed horns—which represent the penetrating, shrewd, conscious side of Capricorn—with the swishing tail—which represents its serpentine, unconscious, emotional force. One Capricorn legend, which dates from Roman times, tells of the earthy fertility god, Pan, who tried to save himself from uncontrollable sexual desires by jumping into the Nile. His upper body then turned into a goat, while the lower part became a fish. Later, Jupiter gave him a safe haven as a constellation in the skies.

## The Aquarius Glyph ♒

This ancient water symbol can be traced back to an Egyptian hieroglyph representing streams of life force. Symbolized by the Water Bearer, Aquarius is distributor of the waters of life—the magic liquid of regeneration. The two waves can also be linked to the positive and negative charges of the electrical energy that Aquarius rules, a sort of universal wavelength. Aquarius is tuned in intuitively to higher forces via this electrical force. The duality of the glyph could also refer to the dual nature of Aquarius, a sign that runs hot and cold and that is friendly but also detached in the mental world of air signs.

In Greek legends, Aquarius is represented by Ganymede, who was carried to heaven by an eagle in order to become the cupbearer of Zeus and to supervise the annual flooding of the Nile. The sign later became associated with aviation and notions of flight.

# The Pisces Glyph ♓

Here is an abstraction of the familiar image of Pisces, two Fishes swimming in opposite directions yet bound together by a cord. The Fishes represent the spirit—which yearns for the freedom of heaven—and the soul—which remains attached to the desires of the temporal world. During life on earth, the spirit and the soul are bound together. When they complement each other, instead of pulling in opposite directions, they facilitate the Pisces creativity. The ancient version of this glyph, taken from the Egyptians, had no connecting line, which was added in the fourteenth century.

In another interpretation, it is said that the left fish indicates the direction of involution or the beginning of a cycle, while the right fish signifies the direction of evolution, the way to completion of a cycle. It's an appropriate grand finale for Pisces, the last sign of the zodiac.

# CHAPTER 6

# What Is Your Rising Sign?

Your rising sign, also called the *ascendant,* is the sign of
the zodiac passing over the eastern horizon at the very
moment you were born. The rising sign is one of the
most important factors in your horoscope. The rising sign
determines the way your chart is set up and the location
of planets within the chart.

As the earth turns, a different sign rises over the horizon every two hours. This explains why other babies who
were born in the same place, but later or earlier in the
same day, would have a different chart. Even though the
planets would be in the same signs, the rising sign would
be earlier or later. Therefore, the planets would be in
another place, or "house," in their horoscopes, emphasizing different areas of their lives.

If you have read the description of the "houses" in
chapter 3 of this book, you'll know that the houses are
twelve stationary divisions of the horoscope, which represent areas of life. The sign moving over the boundary
(cusp) of each house describes that area of life.

The rising sign rules the first house, which is the physical body, your outward appearance, your style, tastes,
health, and physical environment (where you are most
comfortable working and living). After the rising sign is
determined, then each of the next eleven houses in the
chart will be influenced by the signs following in
sequence.

When we know the rising sign of a chart, then we know
where to put each planet. Without a valid rising sign, your
collection of planets would have no "homes."

Once the rising sign is established, it becomes possible

to analyze a chart accurately because the astrologer knows in which house or area of life the planets will operate. For instance, if Mars is in Gemini and your rising sign is in Taurus, then Mars will most likely be active in the second house, the house of finances, of your chart. If you were born later in the day and your rising sign is Virgo, then Mars will be positioned at the top of your chart, energizing your tenth house, the house of career.

Many astrologers insist on knowing the exact time of a client's birth before they will analyze a chart. The more exact your birth time, the more accurately an astrologer can position the planets in your chart.

Your rising sign has an important relationship with your sun sign. Some will complement the sun sign; others hide it under a totally different mask, as if playing an entirely different role, making it difficult to guess the person's sun sign from outer appearances. This may be the reason why you might not look or act like your sun sign's archetype. For example, a Leo with a conservative Capricorn ascendant would come across as much more serious than a Leo with a fiery Aries or Sagittarius ascendant.

It is usually the rising sign that creates the first impression you make. However, if the sun sign is accompanied by other planets in the same sign, this might overpower the impression of the rising sign. For instance, a Leo sun plus a Leo Venus and Leo Jupiter would counteract the more conservative image that would otherwise be conveyed by the person's Capricorn ascendant.

Rising signs change every two hours with the earth's rotation. Those born early in the morning when the sun was on the horizon will be most likely to project the image of their sun sign. These people are often called a "double Aries" or a "double Virgo" because the same sun sign and ascendant reinforce each other.

Look up your rising sign from the chart at the end of this chapter. Since rising signs change every two hours, it is important to know your birth time as close to the minute as possible. Even a few minutes' difference could change the rising sign and therefore the setup of your chart. If you are unsure about the exact time, but know within a few hours, check the following descriptions to see which is most like the personality you project.

## Aries Rising: High Energy

You are the most aggressive version of your sun sign, with boundless energy that can be used productively if it's channeled in the right direction. Watch a tendency to overreact emotionally and blow your top. You come across as openly competitive, a positive asset in business or sports. Be on guard against impatience, which could lead to head injuries. Your walk and bearing could have the telltale head-forward Aries posture. You may wear more bright colors, especially red, than others of your sign. You may also have a tendency to drive your car faster.

## Taurus Rising: Earthbound

You're slow-moving, with a beautiful (or distinctive) speaking or singing voice that can be especially soothing or melodious. You probably surround yourself with comfort, good food, luxurious surroundings, and other sensual pleasures. You prefer welcoming others into your home to gadding about. You may have a talent for business, especially in trading, appraising, and real estate. A Taurus ascendant gives a well-padded physique that gains weight easily. This ascendant can also endow females with a curvaceous beauty.

## Gemini Rising: The Communicator

You're naturally sociable, with lighter, more ethereal mannerisms than others of your sign, especially if you're female. You love to communicate with people, and express your ideas and feelings easily. You may have a talent for writing or public speaking. You thrive on variety, a constantly changing scene, and a lively social life. However, you may relate to others at a deeper level than might be suspected. And you will be far more sympathetic and caring than you project. You will probably travel widely, changing partners and jobs several times (or juggle two at once). Physically, your nerves are quite sensitive. Occasionally, you would benefit from a calm, tranquil atmosphere away from your usual social scene.

## Cancer Rising: Nurturing

You are naturally acquisitive, possessive, private, a moneymaker. You easily pick up others' needs and feelings— a great gift in business, the arts, and personal relationships. But you must guard against overreacting or taking things too personally, especially during full moon periods. Find creative outlets for your natural nurturing gifts, such as helping the less fortunate, particularly children. Your insights would be helpful in psychology. Your desire to feed and care for others would be useful in the restaurant, hotel, or child-care industries. You may be especially fond of wearing romantic old clothes, collecting antiques, and, of course, dining on exquisite food. Since your body may retain fluids, pay attention to your diet. To relax, escape to places near water.

## Leo Rising: Scene Player

You may come across as more poised than you really feel. However, you play it to the hilt, projecting a proud royal presence. A Leo ascendant gives you a natural flair for drama, and you might be accused of stealing the spotlight. You'll also project a much more outgoing, optimistic, sunny personality than others of your sign. You take care to please your public by always projecting your best star quality, probably tossing a luxuriant mane of hair, sporting a striking hairstyle, or dressing to impress. Females often dazzle with spectacular jewelry. Since you may have a strong parental nature, you could well be the regal family matriarch or patriarch.

# Virgo Rising: Discriminating

Virgo rising masks your inner nature with a practical, analytical outer image. You seem neat, orderly, more particular than others of your sign. Others in your life may feel they must live up to your high standards. Though at times you may be openly critical, this masks a well-meaning desire to have only the best for loved ones. Your sharp eye for details could be used in the financial world, or your literary skills could draw you to teaching or publishing. The healing arts, health care, and service-oriented professions attract many with a Virgo ascendant. You're likely to take good care of yourself, with great attention to health, diet, and exercise. Physically, you may have a very sensitive digestive system.

# Libra Rising: Charming and Social

Libra rising gives you a charming, social, public persona. You tend to avoid confrontations in relationships, preferring to smooth the way or negotiate diplomatically rather than give in to an emotional reaction. Because you are interested in all aspects of a situation, you may be slow to reach decisions. Physically, you'll have good proportions and physical symmetry. You will move with natural grace and balance. You're likely to have pleasing, if not beautiful, facial features, with a winning smile. You'll show natural good taste and harmony in your clothes and home decor. Legal, diplomatic, or public relations professions could draw your interest.

# Scorpio Rising: Mysterious Charisma

You project an intriguing air of mystery with this ascendant, as the Scorpio secretiveness and sense of underlying power combines with your sun sign. There's more to you than meets the eye. You seem like someone who is always in control and who can move comfortably in the world of power. Your physical look comes across as intense. Many of you have remarkable eyes, with a direct, penetrating gaze. But you'll never reveal your private agenda, and you tend to keep your true feelings under wraps (watch a tendency toward paranoia). You may have an interesting romantic history with secret love affairs. Many of you heighten your air of mystery by wearing black. You're happiest near water and should provide yourself with a seaside retreat.

# Sagittarius Rising: The Wanderer

You travel with this ascendant. You may also be a more outdoor, sportive type, with an athletic, casual, outgoing air. Your moods are camouflaged with cheerful optimism or a philosophical attitude. Though you don't hesitate to speak your mind, you can also laugh at your troubles or crack a joke more easily than others of your sign. A Sagittarius ascendant can also draw you to the field of higher education or to spiritual life. You'll seem to have less attachment to things and people, and may travel widely. Your strong, fast legs are a physical bonus.

# Capricorn Rising: Serious Business

This rising sign makes you come across as serious, goal-oriented, disciplined, and careful with cash. You are not one of the zodiac's big spenders, though you might splurge occasionally on items with good investment value. You're the traditional, conservative type in dress and environment, and you might come across as quite formal and businesslike. You'll function well in a structured or corporate environment where you can climb to the top. (You are always aware of who's the boss.) In your personal life, you could be a loner or a single parent who is "father and mother" to your children.

## Aquarius Rising: One of a Kind

You come across as less concerned about what others think and could even be a bit eccentric. Your appearance is sure to be unique and memorable. You're more at ease with groups of people than others in your sign, and you may be attracted to public life. Your appearance may be unique, either unconventional or unimportant to you. Those of you whose sun is in a water sign (Cancer, Scorpio, Pisces) may exercise your nurturing qualities with a large group, an extended family, or a day-care or community center.

## Pisces Rising: Romantic Roles

Your creative, nurturing talents are heightened and so is your ability to project emotional drama. And your dreamy eyes and poetic air bring out the protective instinct in others. You could be attracted to the arts, especially theater, dance, film, and photography, or to psychology, spiritual practice, and charity work. You are happiest when you are using your creative ability to help others. Since you are vulnerable to mood swings, it is especially important for you to find interesting, creative work where you can express your talents and heighten your self-esteem. Accentuate the positive. Be wary of escapist tendencies, particularly involving alcohol or drugs to which you are supersensitive.

# RISING SIGNS—A.M. BIRTHS

| | 1 AM | 2 AM | 3 AM | 4 AM | 5 AM | 6 AM | 7 AM | 8 AM | 9 AM | 10 AM | 11 AM | 12 NOON |
|---|---|---|---|---|---|---|---|---|---|---|---|---|
| Jan 1 | Lib | Sc | Sc | Sc | Sag | Sag | Cap | Cap | Aq | Aq | Pis | Ar |
| Jan 9 | Lib | Sc | Sc | Sag | Sag | Sag | Cap | Cap | Aq | Pis | Ar | Tau |
| Jan 17 | Sc | Sc | Sc | Sag | Sag | Cap | Cap | Aq | Aq | Pis | Ar | Tau |
| Jan 25 | Sc | Sc | Sag | Sag | Sag | Cap | Cap | Aq | Pis | Ar | Tau | Tau |
| Feb 2 | Sc | Sc | Sag | Sag | Cap | Cap | Aq | Pis | Pis | Ar | Tau | Gem |
| Feb 10 | Sc | Sag | Sag | Sag | Cap | Cap | Aq | Pis | Ar | Tau | Tau | Gem |
| Feb 18 | Sc | Sag | Sag | Cap | Cap | Aq | Pis | Pis | Ar | Tau | Gem | Gem |
| Feb 26 | Sag | Sag | Sag | Cap | Aq | Aq | Pis | Ar | Tau | Tau | Gem | Gem |
| Mar 6 | Sag | Sag | Cap | Cap | Aq | Pis | Pis | Ar | Tau | Gem | Gem | Can |
| Mar 14 | Sag | Cap | Cap | Aq | Aq | Pis | Ar | Tau | Tau | Gem | Gem | Can |
| Mar 22 | Sag | Cap | Cap | Aq | Pis | Ar | Ar | Tau | Gem | Gem | Can | Can |
| Mar 30 | Cap | Cap | Aq | Pis | Pis | Ar | Tau | Tau | Gem | Can | Can | Can |
| Apr 7 | Cap | Cap | Aq | Pis | Ar | Ar | Tau | Gem | Gem | Can | Can | Leo |
| Apr 14 | Cap | Aq | Aq | Pis | Ar | Tau | Tau | Gem | Gem | Can | Can | Leo |
| Apr 22 | Cap | Aq | Pis | Ar | Ar | Tau | Gem | Gem | Gem | Can | Leo | Leo |
| Apr 30 | Aq | Aq | Pis | Ar | Tau | Tau | Gem | Can | Can | Can | Leo | Leo |
| May 8 | Aq | Pis | Ar | Ar | Tau | Gem | Gem | Can | Can | Leo | Leo | Leo |
| May 16 | Aq | Pis | Ar | Tau | Gem | Gem | Can | Can | Can | Leo | Leo | Vir |
| May 24 | Pis | Ar | Ar | Tau | Gem | Gem | Can | Can | Leo | Leo | Leo | Vir |
| June 1 | Pis | Ar | Tau | Gem | Gem | Can | Can | Can | Leo | Leo | Vir | Vir |
| June 9 | Ar | Ar | Tau | Gem | Gem | Can | Can | Leo | Leo | Leo | Vir | Vir |
| June 17 | Ar | Tau | Gem | Gem | Can | Can | Can | Leo | Leo | Vir | Vir | Vir |
| June 25 | Tau | Tau | Gem | Gem | Can | Can | Leo | Leo | Leo | Vir | Vir | Lib |
| July 3 | Tau | Gem | Gem | Can | Can | Can | Leo | Leo | Vir | Vir | Vir | Lib |
| July 11 | Tau | Gem | Gem | Can | Can | Leo | Leo | Leo | Vir | Vir | Lib | Lib |
| July 18 | Gem | Gem | Can | Can | Can | Leo | Leo | Vir | Vir | Vir | Lib | Lib |
| July 26 | Gem | Gem | Can | Can | Leo | Leo | Vir | Vir | Vir | Lib | Lib | Lib |
| Aug 3 | Gem | Can | Can | Can | Leo | Leo | Vir | Vir | Vir | Lib | Lib | Sc |
| Aug 11 | Gem | Can | Can | Leo | Leo | Leo | Vir | Vir | Lib | Lib | Lib | Sc |
| Aug 18 | Can | Can | Can | Leo | Leo | Vir | Vir | Vir | Lib | Lib | Sc | Sc |
| Aug 27 | Can | Can | Leo | Leo | Leo | Vir | Vir | Lib | Lib | Lib | Sc | Sc |
| Sept 4 | Can | Can | Leo | Leo | Leo | Vir | Vir | Vir | Lib | Lib | Sc | Sc |
| Sept 12 | Can | Leo | Leo | Leo | Vir | Vir | Lib | Lib | Lib | Sc | Sc | Sag |
| Sept 20 | Leo | Leo | Leo | Vir | Vir | Vir | Lib | Lib | Sc | Sc | Sc | Sag |
| Sept 28 | Leo | Leo | Leo | Vir | Vir | Lib | Lib | Lib | Sc | Sc | Sag | Sag |
| Oct 6 | Leo | Leo | Vir | Vir | Vir | Lib | Lib | Sc | Sc | Sc | Sag | Sag |
| Oct 14 | Leo | Vir | Vir | Vir | Lib | Lib | Lib | Sc | Sc | Sag | Sag | Cap |
| Oct 22 | Leo | Vir | Vir | Lib | Lib | Lib | Sc | Sc | Sc | Sag | Sag | Cap |
| Oct 30 | Vir | Vir | Vir | Lib | Lib | Sc | Sc | Sc | Sag | Sag | Cap | Cap |
| Nov 7 | Vir | Vir | Lib | Lib | Lib | Sc | Sc | Sc | Sag | Sag | Cap | Cap |
| Nov 15 | Vir | Vir | Lib | Lib | Sc | Sc | Sc | Sag | Sag | Cap | Cap | Aq |
| Nov 23 | Vir | Lib | Lib | Lib | Sc | Sc | Sag | Sag | Sag | Cap | Cap | Aq |
| Dec 1 | Vir | Lib | Lib | Sc | Sc | Sc | Sag | Sag | Cap | Cap | Aq | Aq |
| Dec 9 | Lib | Lib | Lib | Sc | Sc | Sc | Sag | Sag | Cap | Cap | Aq | Pis |
| Dec 18 | Lib | Lib | Sc | Sc | Sc | Sag | Sag | Cap | Cap | Aq | Aq | Pis |
| Dec 28 | Lib | Lib | Sc | Sc | Sag | Sag | Sag | Cap | Aq | Aq | Pis | Ar |

# RISING SIGNS—P.M. BIRTHS

| | 1 PM | 2 PM | 3 PM | 4 PM | 5 PM | 6 PM | 7 PM | 8 PM | 9 PM | 10 PM | 11 PM | 12 MID-NIGHT |
|---|---|---|---|---|---|---|---|---|---|---|---|---|
| Jan 1 | Tau | Gem | Gem | Can | Can | Can | Leo | Leo | Vir | Vir | Vir | Lib |
| Jan 9 | Tau | Gem | Gem | Can | Can | Leo | Leo | Leo | Vir | Vir | Vir | Lib |
| Jan 17 | Gem | Gem | Can | Can | Can | Leo | Leo | Vir | Vir | Lib | Lib | Lib |
| Jan 25 | Gem | Gem | Can | Can | Leo | Leo | Leo | Vir | Vir | Lib | Lib | Lib |
| Feb 2 | Gem | Can | Can | Can | Leo | Leo | Vir | Vir | Vir | Lib | Lib | Sc |
| Feb 10 | Gem | Can | Can | Leo | Leo | Leo | Vir | Vir | Lib | Lib | Lib | Sc |
| Feb 18 | Can | Can | Can | Leo | Leo | Vir | Vir | Vir | Lib | Lib | Sc | Sc |
| Feb 26 | Can | Can | Leo | Leo | Leo | Vir | Vir | Lib | Lib | Lib | Sc | Sc |
| Mar 6 | Can | Can | Leo | Leo | Leo | Vir | Vir | Vir | Lib | Sc | Sc | Sc |
| Mar 14 | Can | Leo | Leo | Vir | Vir | Vir | Lib | Lib | Lib | Sc | Sc | Sag |
| Mar 22 | Leo | Leo | Leo | Vir | Vir | Lib | Lib | Lib | Sc | Sc | Sc | Sag |
| Mar 30 | Leo | Leo | Vir | Vir | Vir | Lib | Lib | Sc | Sc | Sc | Sag | Sag |
| Apr 7 | Leo | Leo | Vir | Vir | Lib | Lib | Lib | Sc | Sc | Sc | Sag | Sag |
| Apr 14 | Leo | Vir | Vir | Vir | Lib | Lib | Sc | Sc | Sc | Sag | Sag | Cap |
| Apr 22 | Leo | Vir | Vir | Lib | Lib | Lib | Sc | Sc | Sc | Sag | Sag | Cap |
| Apr 30 | Vir | Vir | Vir | Lib | Lib | Sc | Sc | Sc | Sag | Sag | Cap | Cap |
| May 8 | Vir | Vir | Lib | Lib | Lib | Sc | Sc | Sag | Sag | Sag | Cap | Cap |
| May 16 | Vir | Vir | Lib | Lib | Sc | Sc | Sc | Sag | Sag | Cap | Cap | Aq |
| May 24 | Vir | Lib | Lib | Lib | Sc | Sc | Sag | Sag | Sag | Cap | Cap | Aq |
| June 1 | Vir | Lib | Lib | Sc | Sc | Sc | Sag | Sag | Cap | Cap | Aq | Aq |
| June 9 | Lib | Lib | Lib | Sc | Sc | Sag | Sag | Sag | Cap | Cap | Aq | Pis |
| June 17 | Lib | Lib | Sc | Sc | Sc | Sag | Sag | Cap | Cap | Aq | Aq | Pis |
| June 25 | Lib | Lib | Sc | Sc | Sag | Sag | Sag | Cap | Cap | Aq | Pis | Ar |
| July 3 | Lib | Sc | Sc | Sc | Sag | Sag | Cap | Cap | Aq | Aq | Pis | Ar |
| July 11 | Lib | Sc | Sc | Sag | Sag | Sag | Cap | Cap | Aq | Pis | Ar | Tau |
| July 18 | Sc | Sc | Sc | Sag | Sag | Cap | Cap | Aq | Aq | Pis | Ar | Tau |
| July 26 | Sc | Sc | Sag | Sag | Sag | Cap | Cap | Aq | Pis | Ar | Tau | Tau |
| Aug 3 | Sc | Sc | Sag | Sag | Cap | Cap | Aq | Aq | Pis | Ar | Tau | Gem |
| Aug 11 | Sc | Sag | Sag | Sag | Cap | Cap | Aq | Pis | Ar | Tau | Tau | Gem |
| Aug 18 | Sc | Sag | Sag | Cap | Cap | Aq | Pis | Pis | Ar | Tau | Gem | Gem |
| Aug 27 | Sag | Sag | Sag | Cap | Cap | Aq | Pis | Ar | Tau | Tau | Gem | Gem |
| Sept 4 | Sag | Sag | Cap | Cap | Aq | Pis | Pis | Ar | Tau | Gem | Gem | Can |
| Sept 12 | Sag | Sag | Cap | Aq | Aq | Pis | Ar | Tau | Tau | Gem | Gem | Can |
| Sept 20 | Sag | Cap | Cap | Aq | Pis | Pis | Ar | Tau | Gem | Gem | Can | Can |
| Sept 28 | Cap | Cap | Aq | Aq | Pis | Ar | Tau | Tau | Gem | Gem | Can | Can |
| Oct 6 | Cap | Cap | Aq | Pis | Ar | Ar | Tau | Gem | Gem | Can | Can | Leo |
| Oct 14 | Cap | Aq | Aq | Pis | Ar | Tau | Tau | Gem | Gem | Can | Can | Leo |
| Oct 22 | Cap | Aq | Pis | Ar | Ar | Tau | Gem | Gem | Can | Can | Leo | Leo |
| Oct 30 | Aq | Aq | Pis | Ar | Tau | Tau | Gem | Can | Can | Can | Leo | Leo |
| Nov 7 | Aq | Aq | Pis | Ar | Tau | Tau | Gem | Can | Can | Can | Leo | Leo |
| Nov 15 | Aq | Pis | Ar | Tau | Gem | Gem | Can | Can | Can | Leo | Leo | Vir |
| Nov 23 | Pis | Ar | Ar | Tau | Gem | Gem | Can | Can | Leo | Leo | Leo | Vir |
| Dec 1 | Pis | Ar | Tau | Gem | Gem | Can | Can | Can | Leo | Leo | Vir | Vir |
| Dec 9 | Ar | Tau | Tau | Gem | Gem | Can | Can | Leo | Leo | Leo | Vir | Vir |
| Dec 18 | Ar | Tau | Gem | Gem | Can | Can | Can | Leo | Leo | Vir | Vir | Vir |
| Dec 28 | Tau | Tau | Gem | Gem | Can | Can | Leo | Leo | Vir | Vir | Vir | Lib |

119

# CHAPTER 7

# Astrology Around the Worldwide Web

If you're connected to the Internet, you've got the gateway to a world of information about astrology. Thousands of astrological sites offer you everything from chart services to chat rooms to individual readings. Even better are the freebies! You'll find *free* software, *free* charts, *free* articles to download. You can get an education in astrology from your computer screen, share your insights with new astrology-minded pals in a chat room or on a mailing list, then later meet them in person at one of the hundreds of conferences around the world. You can even see how your face compares to others of your sign. Is there a "family resemblance" among Virgos?

If you're curious to see a copy of your chart (or someone else's), want to study astrology in depth, or chat with another astrology fan, please take our guided tour. The following sites were chosen for general interest and are ideal places to start your "surfing" adventures. Many are hubs of information with their own selection of links to other sites. One caveat: Though these sites were selected with longevity in mind, the Internet is a volatile place where sites can disappear or change without notice. Therefore, some of our sites may have changed addresses, names, or content by the time this book is published.

## Free Charts

Astrolabe Software at *www.alabe.com* distributes some of the most creative and user-friendly programs now available; Solar Fire is a favorite of top astrologers. Visitors to the site are greeted with a chart of the time you log on. You can get your chart calculated, with a free mini-interpretation e-mailed to you.

Don't miss this fabulous site, one of our favorites. Go to *www.astro.com* and check into Astrodienst, an international site that has long been one of the best astrology sites on the Internet. Its world atlas will give you the accurate longitude and latitude of your birthplace for setting up your horoscope. Then you can print out your chart in a range of easy-to-read formats. One handy feature for beginners: The planetary placement is listed in words alongside the chart (a real help for those who haven't yet learned to read the astrology glyphs).

There are many other attractions at this site, such as a list of your astro-twins (famous people born on your birth date). The site even sorts the "twins" to feature those who also have your identical rising sign. You can then click on their names and get an instant chart of your famous signmates.

How about some astrological vacation planning? Let Astrodienst help you choose where on earth you'll be happiest, where you'll fall in love, or where you're in for a "heavy" time. First pull up an astro-map at Astro-click Travel, another clever feature on the Astrodienst site. On the interactive chart that appears, you can view your astrological chart projected on a map of the earth. The lines on the chart that track each of the planets indicate what type of experience you might expect at that location. Click on a line, and up pops an explanation. So click before you travel!

# Free Software

Try before you buy. Software manufacturers on the Web are generous with free downloads of demo versions of their software. You may then calculate charts using their data. Before you invest serious money in astrology software, you can see how the program works for your needs. You can preview Astrolabe Software programs favored by many professional astrologers at *www.alabe. com*. Check out the latest demo of Solar Fire, one of the most user-friendly astrology programs available—you'll be impressed.

Matrix Software, another source of terrific astrology software, also offers free demo disks. Address: *www.astrologysoftware.com*

## A Free Fully Functional Astrology Program

If you're computer-savvy, you can't go wrong with Walter Pullen's amazingly complete Astrolog program, which is offered absolutely free at the site. Address: *www.magitech.com/~cruiser1/astrolog.htm*

Astrolog is an ultrasophisticated program with all the features of much more expensive programs. It comes in versions for all formats—DOS, Windows, MAC, UNIX—and has some cool features such as a revolving globe and a constellation map. A "must" for those who want to get involved with astrology without paying big bucks for a professional-caliber program. Or for those who want to add Astrolog's unique features to their astrology software library. This program has it all!

## Another Free Program!

Surf to *www.astroscan.ca* for a free program called Astroscan. Stunning graphics and ease of use make this basic program a winner. Astroscan has a fun list of celebrity charts you can call up with a few clicks.

## A Super Shareware Program

Check out Halloran Software's site at *www.halloran.com*. There are several levels of Windows astrology software from which to choose. Of interest to beginners is the Astrology for Windows shareware program, which is available in unregistered demo form as a free download and in registered form for $26.50 (at this writing). The calculations in this program may be all that an astrology hobbyist needs. The price for the full-service program is certainly reasonable.

## Free Oracle Readings

Got a decision to make? Get a cosmic consensus at the Matrix site; you may consult the stars, the I Ching, the runes, the tarot, even fortune cookies. Here's where to connect with news groups and on-line discussions. Their almanac helps you schedule the best day to sign on the dotted line, ask for a raise, or plant your rosebush. Address: *www.thenewage.com*

# On-line Astrology Course

Schedule a long visit to *www.panplanet.com* where you will find the Canopus Academy of Astrology, a site loaded with goodies. For the experienced astrologer, there is a collection of articles from top astrologers. They've done the work for you when it comes to picking the best astrology links on the Web, so be sure to check out those bestowed with the Canopus Award of Excellence.

Astrologer Linda Reid, an accomplished astrology teacher and author, offers a complete on-line curriculum for all levels of astrology study plus individual tutoring. To get your feet wet, Linda is offering an excellent beginners' course at this site, a terrific way to get off and running in astrology.

# Top Astrologers Comment on Current Events

Find out how top astrologers view the latest headlines at the "must-see" StarIQ site. Many of the best minds in astrology comment on the latest news, stock market ups and downs, political contenders. You can sign up to receive e-mail forecasts at the most important times keyed to your individual chart. This is one of the best of the on-line forecasts. Address: *www.stariq.com*

# Astrology Lite

For lighter entertainment, go to Astronet, *www.astrology.com/astronet*, for the Internet's equivalent of an astrology mall. Astronet offers interactive fun for everyone. At this writing, there's a special area for teenage astrology fans, advice to the lovelorn, plus a grab bag of horoscopes, a shopping area for books, reports, and software as well as links to all the popular fashion magazine astrology columns.

*Swoon.com* is another mall-like site aimed at dating, mating, and relating. It has fun features to spark up your love life and plenty of advice for lovers. Address: *www.swoon.com*

# Find an Astrologer Here

## The A.F.A. Web site

This is the interesting Web site of the prestigious American Federation of Astrologers. The A.F.A. has a directory of astrologers restricted to those who meet their stringent requirements. Check out their correspondence course if you would like to study astrology in depth. Address: *www.astrologers.com*

## The NCGR Web site

The Web site of the National Council for Geocosmic Research (NCGR), a leading astrology organization that places great emphasis on education, has a list of accredited astrologers nationwide on their site. Address: *www.geocosmic.org*

# Tools Every Astrologer Needs Are On-line

## Internet Atlas

Find the geographic longitude and latitude and the correct time zone for any city worldwide. You'll need this information to calculate a chart. Address: *www.astro. com/atlas*

## The Exact Time Anywhere in the World

A fun site with fascinating graphics that give you the exact time anywhere in the world. Click on the world map, and the correct time and zone for that place light up. Address: *www.timeticker.com*

## Check the Weather Forecast

More accurate than your local TV forecast is the Weathersage, who uses astrology to predict snowstorms and hurricanes. Get your long-range forecast at this super site. Other attractions here are charts and interpretations of people in the news as well as techniques of business forecasting to help us understand these changing times. Address: *www.weathersage.com*

## Celebrate the Queen's Birthday

A great jumping off place for an astrology tour of the Internet, this site has a veritable Burke's Peerage of royal birthdays. There's a good selection of articles, tools such as a U.S. and World Atlas, information on conferences, software, tapes, and groups. The links at this site will send you off in the right direction. Information about the latest Palm Pilot astrology software is also available here. Address: *www.zodiacal.com*

## Astrology Worldwide

Interested in astrology in Europe? Deborah Houlding, one of the U.K.'s top astrologers, has gathered some of the finest European talent on this super Web site, as well as a comprehensive list of links and conferences. Tour the world of astrology here. Address: *www.astrology-world.com*

## Astrology Alive

Barbara Schermer has one of the most innovative and holistic approaches to astrology. She was one of the first astrologers to go on-line, so there's always a "cutting edge" to this site and a great list of links. Barbara is always on top of what's happening now in astrology. Address: *www.astrologyalive.com*

## National Council for Geocosmic Research (NCGR)

A key stop on any astrological tour of the Net. Here's where you can find local chapters in your area, get information on the NCGR testing and certification programs, get a conference schedule. There is a list of certified astrologers for those who want readings. Order lecture tapes from their nationwide conferences, or get complete lists of conference topics to study at home. Good links to resources. Address: *www.geocosmic.org*

# Where to Find Charts of the Famous

When the news is breaking, you can bet Lois Rodden will be the first to get accurate birthdays of the headline-makers, and put up their charts on her Web site: *www.astrodatabank.com*. Rodden's meticulous research is astrology's most reliable source for data of the famous and infamous. Her Web site specializes in birthdays and charts of current newsmakers, political figures, and international celebrities. You can also participate in an analysis of the charts and see what other astrologers have to say about them. The AstroDatabank program, which you can purchase at the site, provides thousands of birthdays sorted into categories. It's an excellent research tool.

Go to *www.imdb.com* for a comprehensive list of film celebrities including bios, plus lists of famous couples from today and yesteryear. Look under "biographies."

The Matrix software site maintains a list of 30,000 celebrities at: *www.astrologysoftware.com/resources*

Yet another good source for celebrity birth dates is the humorous Metamaze site: *www.metamaze.com/bdays*. You can find some interesting offbeat newsmakers here.


# For Astrology Books

## National Clearinghouse for Astrology Books

A wide selection of books on all aspects of astrology, from the basics to advanced, is available at this on-line bookstore. Also, many hard-to-find and recycled books. Address: *www.astroamerica.com*

The Heart Center Library site is an excellent resource if you are searching for a particular book or researching a specific aspect of astrology. Address: *www.thenew age.com*

The following addresses also have a good selection of astrology books for sale, some of which are unique to the site.

*www.panplanet.com*
*www.astrocom.com*

Browse the huge astrology list of on-line bookstore Amazon.com at *www.amazon.com*.

# Astrology Tapes for At-Home Study

You can study at home with world-famous astrologers via audiocassette recordings from Pegasus Tapes. There's an extensive selection taped from conferences, classes, lectures, and seminars. An especially good source for astrologers who emphasize psychological and mythological themes. Address: *www.pegasustape.com*

# For History and Mythology Buffs

Be sure to visit the astrology section of this gorgeous site, dedicated to the history and mythology of many traditions. One of the most beautifully designed sites we've seen. Address: *www.elore.com*

The leading authority on the history of astrology, Robert Hand, has an excellent site that features his cutting-edge research. See what one of astrology's great teachers has to offer. Address: *www.robhand.com*

The Project Hindsight group of scholarly astrologers is devoted to restoring the astrology of the Hellenistic period, the primary source for all later Western astrology. There are fascinating articles for astrology fans on this site. Address: *www.projecthindsight.com*

Readers interested in mythology should also check out *www.pantheon.org* for stories of gods and goddesses.

# Astrology Magazine

## The Mountain Astrologer

A favorite magazine of astrology fans, *The Mountain Astrologer* has an interesting Web site featuring the latest news from an astrological point of view, plus feature articles from the magazine. Address: *www.mountain astrologer.com*

# Financial Astrology

Curious about how astrologers play the market? Financial astrology is a hot specialty, with many tipsters, players, and theorists. There are on-line columns, newsletters, specialized financial astrology software, and mutual funds run by astrology seers. One of the most respected financial astrologers is Ray Merriman, whose column on *www.stariq.com* is a "must read" for those following the bulls and bears.

Go to *www.afund.com* or *www.alphee.com* for tips and forecasts from two other top financial astrologers.

# See an Image of the Newest Planet: Qua Wha?

As if we didn't have enough planets to interpret, NASA's Hubble Space Telescope has found a new one. Astronomers have measured the largest object in the solar system ever since the discovery of Pluto 72 years ago. Approximately half the size of Pluto, the new baby has been christened "Quaoar" (pronounced *kwa-whar*). Like Pluto, Quaoar dwells in the Kuiper belt, an icy belt of cometlike bodies extending 7 billion miles beyond Neptune's orbit.

View the new baby at the Hubble Web site address: *oposite.stsci.edu/pubinfo/pr/2002/17/index.html*

# Do You Look Like Others of Your Sign?

Is there a "family resemblance" among Leos? Among Virgos? Find out at this fascinating site, which compares faces of people with the same sun, moon, and ascendant signs. Great fun! Then you can add a picture of your own face to the show. Address: *www.habarbadi.com/astrofaces*

# CHAPTER 8

# Astrology Resources

Would you like to delve deeper into astrology and meet other astrology fans? The astrology community welcomes you! You'll soon discover that there's no end to the fascinating techniques and aspects of our age-old art. What's more, you can connect with local astrologers at club meetings and conferences. There's always something new to learn, a lively debate to join, some information to share.

Here are the resources you need to find the right astrology software for your computer, to attend meetings and conferences, to study advanced techniques, or to buy books and tapes.

Whether you'd like to know more about such specialties as financial astrology or techniques for timing events, or if you'd prefer the psychological or mythological approach, you'll meet the top astrologers at conferences sponsored by the National Council for Geocosmic Research. NCGR is dedicated to providing quality education, bringing astrologers and astrology fans together at conferences, and promoting fellowship. Their course structure provides a systematized study of the many facets of astrology.

You can explore astrology via your computer no matter what your level of expertise. Even if you are using an older model, there are still calculation and interpretation programs available. They may not have all the bells and whistles or the exciting graphics, but they'll get the job done!

Newcomers to astrology should learn some of the basics, including the glyphs, before you invest in a computer program. Use chapter 5 in this book to help you learn the symbols easily; then you'll be able to read the charts without consulting the "help" section of your software every time. Several programs such as Astrolabe's Solar Fire have pop-up definitions to help you decipher the meanings of planets and aspects. Just click your mouse on a glyph or an icon on the screen, and a window with an instant definition appears.

You don't have to spend a fortune to get a perfectly adequate astrology program. In fact, if you are connected to the Internet, you can download one free. Astrology software is available at all price levels, from a sophisticated free application like Astrolog, which you can download from the Web site, to inexpensive programs for under $100 such as Winstar Express, to the more expensive astrology programs such as Winstar Plus, Solar Fire, or Io (for the Mac), which are used by serious students and professionals. Before you make an investment, it's a good idea to download a sample, which is usually available on the company's Web site, or to order a demo disk.

If you're baffled by the variety of software available, most of the companies on our list will be happy to help you find the right application for your needs.

Students of astrology who live in out-of-the-way places or are unable to fit classes into your schedule have several options. There are online courses offered at astrology Web sites, such as *www.panplanet.com*, the NCGR and A.F.A. Web sites. Some astrology teachers will send you a series of audiotapes, or you can order audiotaped seminars of recent conferences. Other teachers offer correspondence courses that use their workbooks or computer printouts.

# Nationwide Astrology Organizations and Conferences

Contact these organizations for information on conferences, workshops, local meetings, conference tapes, referrals.

# National Council for Geocosmic Research (NCGR)

Educational workshops, tapes, conferences, and a directory of professional astrologers are available from this nationwide organization devoted to promoting astrological education. For a $35 annual membership fee, you get their excellent publications and newsletters, plus the opportunity to network with other astrology buffs at local chapter events (there are chapters in 20 states).

To join NCGR, contact the current membership director (as of this writing):

Linda Fei, Membership Director
NCGR
1359 Sargent Ave.
St. Paul, MN 55105

For the latest information about NCGR, consult their Web site: *www.geocosmic.org*.

## American Federation of Astrologers (A.F.A.)

This is one of the oldest astrological organizations in the United States, established 1938. They offer conferences, conventions, and a thorough correspondence course. If you are looking for a reading, the Web site will refer you to an accredited A.F.A. astrologer.

A.F.A.
P.O. Box 22040
Tempe, AZ 85285-2040
Phone: (888) 301-7630 or (480) 838-1751
Fax: (480) 838-8293
Web site: *www.astrologers.com*

## Association for Astrological Networking (A.F.A.N.)

Did you know that astrologers are still being harassed for practicing astrology? A.F.A.N. provides support and legal information, and works toward improving the public image of astrology. A.F.A.N.'s network of local astrologers links with the international astrological community. Here are the people who will go to bat for astrology when it is attacked in the media. Everyone who cares about astrology should join!

A.F.A.N.
8306 Wilshire Blvd.
PMB 537
Beverly Hills, CA 90211
Phone: (800) 578-2326
E-mail: *info@afan.org*
Web site: *www.afan.org*

## Astrology Conferences on Tape

Would you like to hear top astrology lectures on tape? Pegasus has a wonderful selection of tapes from conferences, featuring world-famous astrologers.

Pegasus Tapes
P.O. Box 419
Santa Ysabel, CA 92070
Phone: (800) 288-PEGASUS

## International Society for Astrology Research (ISAR)

An international organization of professional astrologers dedicated to encouraging the highest standards of quality in the field of astrology with an emphasis on research. Among ISAR's benefits are a quarterly journal, a weekly e-mail newsletter, and a free biennial membership directory.

ISAR
P.O. Box 38613
Los Angeles, CA 90038

Web site: *www.isarastrology.com*
Fax: (800) 933-0301

# Astrology Software

## Astrolabe

One of the top astrology software resources. Check out the latest version of their powerful Solar Fire software for Windows. It's a breeze to use and will grow with your increasing knowledge of astrology to the most sophisticated levels. This company also markets a variety of programs for all levels of expertise and a wide selection of computer-generated astrology readings. A good resource for innovative software as well as applications for older computers.

Astrolabe
Box 1750-R
Brewster, MA 02631
Phone: (800) 843-6682
Web site: *www.alabe.com*

## Matrix Software

A wide variety of software in all price ranges, demo disks, student and advanced levels, lots of interesting readings. Check out Winstar Express, a powerful but reasonably priced program suitable for all skill levels.

Matrix Software
407 N. State Street
Big Rapids, MI 49307
Phone: (800) 416-3924
Web site: *www.astrologysoftware.com*

# Astro Communications Services (ACS)

Books, software for MAC and IBM compatibles, individual charts, and telephone readings are offered by this California company. Find technical astrology materials here such as The American Ephemeris and PC atlases. ACS will calculate and send charts to you, a valuable service if you do not have a computer.

ACS Publications
5521 Ruffin Road
San Diego, CA 92123
Phone: (800) 888-9983
Fax: (858) 492-9917
Web site: *www.astrocom.com*

# Air Software

Here you'll find powerful, creative astrology software, like Star Trax 2000. For beginners, check out Father Time, which finds your best days. Check out Nostradamus, which answers all your questions. Financial astrology programs for stock market traders are a specialty.

Air Software
115 Caya Avenue
West Hartford, CT 06110
Phone: (800) 659-1247
Web site: *www.alphee.com*

# Time Cycles Research: For MAC Users

Here's where MAC users can find astrology software that's as sophisticated as it gets. If you have a MAC, you'll love their beautiful graphic IO Series programs.

Time Cycles Research
375 Willets Avenue
Waterford, CT 06385

Fax: (860) 442-0625
Web site: *www.timecycles.com*

# Astrology Magazines

In addition to articles by top astrologers, most have listings of astrology conferences, events, and local happenings.

*American Astrology*
Dept. 4
P.O. Box 2021
Marion, OH 43306-8121

*Dell Horoscope*
P.O. Box 54097
Boulder, CO 80322-4097

*The Mountain Astrologer*
P.O. Box 970
Cedar Ridge, CA 95924
Web site: *www.mountainastrologer.com*

# Astrology College

An accredited college dedicated to astrology is here at last! Check out the Kepler College listed below.

## Kepler College of Astrological Arts and Sciences

A degree-granting college, which is also a center of astrology, has long been the dream of the astrological community and is a giant step forward in providing credibility to the profession.

Therefore, the opening of Kepler College in 2000 was a historical event for astrology. It is the only college in the western hemisphere authorized to issue B.A. and M.A. degrees in Astrological Studies. The entire curriculum is based on astrology.

For more information, contact:

Kepler College of Astrological Arts and Sciences
4630 200th Street SW
Suite P
Lynnwood, WA 98036
Voice: (425) 673-4292
Fax: (425) 673-4983
Web site: *www.kepler.edu*

# CHAPTER 9

# How About a Personal Reading?

If you are interested in astrology, at some point you'll consider having a personal reading. For instance, an important date is coming up, perhaps a wedding or the start of a new business, and you're wondering if an astrologically picked date could influence the outcome. You've fallen in love and must know if it will last forever. Your partnership is not going well, and you're not sure if you can continue to work together. You're in a downslide when problems seem insurmountable. Or you simply want to have your chart interpreted by an expert.

But what kind of reading should you have? There are so many options for readings that sorting through them can be a daunting task. Besides individual one-on-one readings with a professional astrologer, there are telephone readings, Internet readings, tapes, computer-generated reports, and celebrity-sponsored readings. Here's what to look for and some cautionary notes.

Done by a qualified astrologer, the personal reading can be an empowering experience if you want to reach your full potential, size up a lover or business situation, or find out what the future has in store. There are astrologers who are specialists in certain areas such as finance or medical astrology. And, unfortunately, there are many questionable practitioners who range from streetwise gypsy fortune-tellers to unscrupulous scam artists.

The following basic guidelines can help you sort out your options to find the reading that's right for you.

# One-on-One Consultations with a Professional Astrologer

Nothing compares to a one-on-one consultation with a professional astrologer who has analyzed thousands of charts and can pinpoint the potential in yours. During your reading, you can get your specific questions answered. For instance, how to get along better with your mate or coworker. There are many astrologers who now combine their skills with training in psychology and are well-suited to help you examine your alternatives.

To give you an accurate reading, an astrologer needs certain information from you: the date, time, and place where you were born. (A horoscope can be cast about anyone or anything that has a specific time and place.) Most astrologers will then enter this information into a computer, which will calculate a chart in seconds. From the resulting chart, the astrologer will do an interpretation.

If you don't know your exact birth time, you can usually locate it at the Bureau of Vital Statistics at the city hall or county seat of the state where you were born. If you still have no success in getting your time of birth, some astrologers can estimate an approximate birth time by using past events in your life to determine the chart. This technique is called *rectification*.

# How to Find an Astrologer

Choose your astrologer with the same care as any trusted adviser such as a doctor, lawyer, or banker. Unfortunately, anyone can claim to be an astrologer—to date, there is no licensing of astrologers or universally established professional criteria. However, there are nationwide organizations of serious, committed astrologers that can help you in your search.

Good places to start your investigation are organizations such as the American Federation of Astrologers (A.F.A.) or the National Council for Geocosmic Research (NCGR), which offer a program of study and certification. If you live near a major city, there is sure to be an active NCGR chapter or astrology club in your area; many are listed in astrology magazines available at your local newsstand. In response to many requests for referrals, both the A.F.A. and the NCGR have directories of professional astrologers listed on their Web sites; these directories include a glossary of terms and an explanation of specialties within the astrological field. Contact the NCGR and A.F.A. headquarters (see also chapter 7 and chapter 8 in this book) for information.

# Warning Signals

As a potentially lucrative freelance business, astrology has always attracted self-styled experts who may not have the knowledge or the counseling experience to give a helpful reading. These astrologers can range from the well-meaning amateur to the charlatan or street-corner gypsy who has for many years given astrology a bad name. Be very wary of astrologers who claim to have occult powers or who make pretentious claims of celebrated clients or miraculous achievements. You can often tell from the initial phone conversation if the astrologer is legitimate. He or she should ask for your birthday time and place, then conduct the conversation in a professional manner. Any astrologer who gives a reading based only on your sun sign is highly suspect.

When you arrive at the reading, the astrologer should be prepared. The consultation should be conducted in a private, quiet place. The astrologer should be interested in your problems of the moment. A good reading involves feedback on your part. So if the reading is not relating to your concerns, you should let the astrologer know. You should feel free to ask questions and get clarifications of technical terms. The more you actively participate, rather than expecting the astrologer to carry the reading or come forth with oracular predictions, the more meaningful your experience will be. An astrologer should help you validate your current experience and be frank about possible negative happenings, but also suggest a positive course of action.

In their approach to a reading, some astrologers may be more literal, others more intuitive. Those who have had counseling training may take a more psychological approach. Though some astrologers may seem to have an almost psychic ability, extrasensory perception or any other parapsychological talent is not essential. A very accurate picture can be drawn from the data in your horoscope chart.

An astrologer may do several charts for each client, including one for the time of birth and a "progressed chart," showing the evolution from birth to the present time. According to your individual needs, there are many other possibilities, such as a chart for a different location if you are contemplating a change of place. Relationships between any two people, things, or events can be interpreted with a chart that compares one partner's horoscope with the other's. A composite chart, which uses the midpoint between planets in two individual charts to describe the relationship, is another commonly used device.

An astrologer will be particularly interested in transits, those times when cycling planets activate the planets or sensitive points in your birth chart. These indicate important events in your life.

Many astrologers offer tape-recorded readings, another option to consider, especially if the astrologer you choose lives at a distance. In this case, you'll be mailed a taped reading based on your birth chart. This type of reading is more personal than a computer printout and can give you valuable insights, though it is not equivalent to a live dialogue with the astrologer when you can discuss your specific interests and issues of the moment.

# The Telephone Reading

Telephone readings come in two varieties: a dial-in taped reading, usually recorded in advance by an astrologer, or a live consultation with an "astrologer" on the other end of the line. The taped readings are general daily or weekly forecasts, applied to all members of your sign and charged by the minute. The quality depends on the astrologer. One caution: Be aware that these readings can run up quite a telephone bill, especially if you get into the habit of calling every day. Be sure that you are aware of the per-minute cost of each call beforehand.

Live telephone readings also vary with the expertise of the astrologer. Ideally, the astrologer at the other end of the line enters your birth data into a computer, which then quickly calculates your chart. This chart will be referred to during the consultation. The advantage of a live telephone reading is that your individual chart is used and you can ask about a specific problem. However, before you invest in any reading, be sure that your astrologer is qualified and that you fully understand in advance how much you will be charged. There should be no unpleasant financial surprises later.

# Computer-Generated Reports

Companies that offer computer programs (such as ACS, Matrix, Astrolabe) also offer a variety of computer-generated horoscope readings. These can be quite comprehensive, offering a beautiful printout of the chart plus many pages of detailed information about each planet and aspect of the chart. You can then study it at your convenience. Of course, the interpretations will be general, since there is no personal input from you, and may not cover your immediate concerns. Since computer-generated horoscopes are much lower in cost than live consultations, you might consider them as either a supplement or a preparation for an eventual live reading. You'll then be more familiar with your chart and able to plan specific questions in advance. They also make a terrific gift for astrology fans. There are several companies, listed in chapters 7 and 8, that offer computerized readings prepared by reputable astrologers.

Whichever option you decide to pursue, may your reading be an empowering one!

## CHAPTER 10

# Are You Having a Midlife Crisis? Signposts from the Stars

The stereotype is all too familiar. A middle-aged man divorces his wife and marries a younger woman, buys a red convertible and a snazzy new wardrobe, begins to diet and work out, and updates his hairstyle. Women are less dramatic. Perhaps she'll start a new career or take up activities outside the home, have plastic surgery, join a gym, and stock up on antiaging creams. She might break out of her normal routine by having an affair with a younger man or someone unlike her husband. Confirmed singles may finally marry or settle down with a partner. These signs all point to a midlife crisis.

As a milestone birthday or high school reunion approaches, we start to evaluate our lives. We look at our declining physical shape. We assess our accomplishments, or lack of them. And often we must face the fact that we're not the success we expected to be back then. (And we're certainly not the hot young thing we were in our twenties and thirties!)

To astrologers, the midlife crisis period is predictable and understandable. It's part of a natural process that affects individuals between the approximate ages of 37 to 47. This process involves major transits of the slow-moving outer planets, Neptune, Uranus, and Pluto, and also a phase in the transit of Saturn.

Neptune, Uranus, Pluto, and Saturn are the planets that cause profound and dramatic changes in our lives. These planets challenge the status quo, forcing us to evaluate where we've been and where we're going. If we are unhappy, then we will be strongly pushed to make changes, some of which will happen suddenly and dramatically. In the long view, this process is preparing us for the latter part of our lives, for accepting maturity.

# Who's Likely to Have a Midlife Crisis This Year?

## The Pluto Phase

This year, the Pluto phase of the midlife crisis will affect those born from 1967 to 1969 (those who would be age 37 to 39). During 2004, Pluto in Sagittarius will form a 90 degree ("square") angle to the Pluto in Virgo position in the individual's chart. This is considered a tense aspect, because the square angle falls in signs of the same quality (way of operating) but of different elements. This year, it will be the mutable (changeable) sign of the fire element Sagittarius and the mutable (changeable) sign of the earth element Virgo. Fire igniting earth can produce a volcanic eruption—or transform clay into beautiful ceramics!

Pluto is the planet of transformation, causing unconscious feelings to surface from deep inside us. It is a time when we face issues of power, control, and sexuality—when we ask ourselves who we really are. "Are you expressing your real self or one that has been programmed by parents and society?" This process could lead to great uncertainty. The challenge is to get past our fears, to eventually come to terms with ourselves, developing a better understanding of our true persona. Needless to say, this is a great time to do deep inner psychological work.

## The Neptune Phase

During the Neptune phase this year, transiting Neptune in Aquarius will square the natal Neptune in Scorpio of those born from 1962 to 1964 (now age 42 to 44). At this phase of midlife, we are asked to go with the flow. But you may experience a lack of direction as you navigate this foggy Neptune transit. The past no longer provides security, yet the future is not clear.

This Neptune phase can be a very frustrating, confusing time when all is not as it seems. A tendency to escape, especially via Neptune-ruled drugs or alcohol, may be a strong temptation—a temptation to be avoided. Although nothing is certain, this transit can be used positively for inner development, for spiritual work, for projects that stretch the imagination.

## The Uranus Phase

The Uranus phase is often the most dramatic, rattling the structure of your life. Uranus is the planet that shakes you up with a bolt from out of the blue. This year, Uranus in Pisces opposes Uranus in Virgo in the charts of those born from 1962 to 1964 (age 42 to 44). It's a double whammy for these midlifers, as they are going through the Neptune phase at the same time.

Uranus can prompt very sudden changes, breaking up patterns that are no longer working for you. It can make you feel as rebellious as an adolescent, if you've felt tied down for too long. The desire is intense to do something that will change your life, to break away from restrictions of any kind. Perhaps a divorce, adopting or having a child, changing your career, moving to another country will be options. There may be a feeling that this is your last chance, so you must do it now.

With Uranus opposite Uranus, you can act very radically and impulsively. So it might serve you well to ask beforehand what part of life is holding you back. Where do you need a chance to breathe? It may be possible to add some excitement to your life and to make changes without shaking up everyone else.

# The Saturn Phase

The Saturn phase of this cycle happens when Saturn opposes an individual's natal Saturn. This year, Saturn in Cancer opposes the natal Saturn in Capricorn of those born from December 1959 to March 1961 (those now age 43 to 45).

Saturn is the testing planet that gives you a reality check. If you have been out of sync and need to rethink your situation, Saturn will make you do it. However, if you have cleared away outworn patterns during the previous transits, you may accept your newfound maturity and move on. Saturn will help you build for a fulfilling future.

# Astrological Tips for Utilizing the Transits

The midlife crisis transits can be very uncomfortable. You may experience a wide range of feelings and often deep insecurity while you go through changes. You may baffle others. You may no longer feel satisfied with a lifestyle that seemed so stable for so long, which often happens during the Uranus phase. You may question the meaning of life, then develop your spiritual side during the Neptune phase. The Saturn and Pluto phases sometimes bring significant loss or change, such as the death of a parent, a divorce, or the loss of a job.

It is important to remember that these transits signal a natural process we all go through. Understanding the process from an astrological point of view can help you see ahead more clearly and avoid making impulsive decisions that you may later regret.

One way to utilize these transits is to ask what the experiences are revealing about your inner needs. If you haven't accomplished what you would like to do, you may be inspired to create a life that is more satisfying. Once you get over the bumpy parts of these transits, you may find that your midlife years are the most fulfilling ever.

# CHAPTER 11

# Sex and the Stars: A Leap Year Guide to Heating Up Your Love Life

Want to charm a Capricorn? Hook a Pisces? Corral a Taurus? Here are sun sign seduction tips guaranteed to keep your lover begging for more.

## How to Love Every Sign

### Aries: Daredevil Lover

This highly physical sign is walking dynamite with a brief attention span. Don't be too easy to get, ladies. A little challenge, a lively debate, a merry chase only heats them up. They want to see what you're made of. Once you've lured them into your lair, be a challenge, a bit of a daredevil, pull out your X-rated tricks. Don't give your all—let them know there's more where that came from.

Make it exciting, show you're up for adventure. Wear bright red somewhere interesting. Since Aries rules the head and face, be sure to focus on these areas in your lovemaking. Use your lips, tongue, breath (even your eyelashes) to the max. Practice scalp massages, deep kissing techniques.

Aries won't wait. So when you make your move, be sure you're ready to follow through. No head games or teasing!

To keep *you* happy: You've got to voice your own

needs. This lover will be focused on his. Teach him how to please, or this could be a one-sided adventure.

## Taurus: Sweet Treats

Taurus wins as the most sensual sign, with the most sexual stamina. Taurus is earthy and lusty in bed, can go on all night. This is not a sign to tease. Like the Bull, they'll see red—not bed. So make them comfortable. Then bombard all their senses.

Good food gets Taurus in the mood. The right music (learn their preferences), fragrance, touchy-feely clothes and bed linens turn them on. Give them a massage with delicious smelling and tasting oils; focus on the neck area. Once that's relaxed, work downward.

Taurus is associated with the throat and neck area. They tend to favor oral techniques and are the best kissers! They hate interruptions, so turn off the phone. Since they can be very vocal lovers, choose a setting where you won't be disturbed. And don't ever rush them. Enjoy a long, slow, delicious encounter.

## Gemini: Playtime

Playful Gemini loves games, so make your seduction fun and playful. Be their lost twin soul, their confidante. Share deep secrets, live out fantasies. This sign adores variety. Nothing bores Gemini more than making love the same way all the time, or bringing on the heavy emotions. So trot out all the roles you've been longing to play—here's the perfect partner. But remember to keep it light and fun.

Gemini's turn-on zone is the hands, and this sign gives the best massages. Let Gemini wrap you around their little fingers—literally. Gadgets that can be turned on with a touch are Gemini amusers. Gemini is great at doing two things at once, like making love while watching an erotic film. Do turn the cell phone off, however, unless you want company. On the other hand, Gemini is your sign for superhot phone sex.

Gemini loves a change of scene. So experiment on the floor, in the shower, on the kitchen table. Borrow a friend's apartment or rent a room in a hotel for variety.

## Cancer: In the Mood

The key to Cancer is to get this Moon Child in the mood. Consult the moon—full moon is best. Wining, dining, old-fashioned courtship, breakfast in bed are turn-ons. Whatever makes your Cancer feel secure will promote shedding inhibitions in the sack. (Don't try any of your Aries daredevil techniques here!) Cancer prefers familiar, comfortable, homey surroundings.

Cancer's turn-on zone is the breasts. Cancer women often have naturally inflated chests. Cancer men may fantasize about a well-endowed playmate. If your breasts are enhanced, show them off. Cancer will want to know all your deepest secrets, so invent a few good ones. But lots of luck delving into their innermost thoughts!

A sure thing: Take your Cancer near water. The sight and sound of the sea can be their aphrodisiac. A moonlit beach, deserted swimming pool, Jacuzzi, or a bubble bath are good seduction spots. Listen to the rain patter on the roof in a mountain cabin.

## Leo: The Royal Treatment

Leo must be The Best and hear it from you often. In return, they'll perform for you, telling you just what you want to hear (true or not). They like a lover with style and endurance, to be swept off their feet and into bed.

Leos like to go first-class all the way, so build them up with lots of attention, wining and dining, special gifts. Never mention other lovers or make them feel like second best. A sure signal for Leo to look elsewhere is a competitive spouse.

Leos take great pride in their body, so you should pour

on the admiration. A few well placed mirrors could inspire them. So would a striptease of beautiful lingerie, expensive fragrance on the sheets, and, if female, an occasional luxury hotel room, with champagne and caviar delivered by room service. Leo's erogenous zone is the lower back, so a massage with expensive oils would make your lion purr with pleasure.

## Virgo: Pedestal Perfect

Virgo's standards are so sky-high that you may feel intimidated at first. The key to pleasing fussy Virgo lovers is to look for the hot fantasy beneath their cool surface. Secret tip: They're really looking for someone to make-over. So let Virgo play teacher and you play willing student; the doctor–patient routine works as well. Be Eliza Doolittle to his Henry Higgins.

Let Virgo help you improve your life, quit smoking, learn French, diet. Read an erotic book together, then practice the techniques. Or study the esoteric, erotic exercises from the Far East.

The Virgo erogenous zone is the tummy area, which should be your base of operations. Virgo likes things pristine and clean. Fall into crisp, immaculate white sheets. Wear a sheer, virginal white nightie. Smell shower-fresh with no heavy perfume. Be sure your surroundings pass the hospital test. A shower together afterward (with great-smelling soap) could get the ball rolling again.

## Libra: The Beauty Lover

Libra must be turned on aesthetically. Make sure you look as beautiful as possible, and are wearing something stylishly seductive but never vulgar. Have a mental affair first, as you flirt and flatter this sign. Then proceed to the physical. Approach Libra like a dance partner, ready to waltz or tango.

Libra must be in the mood for love; otherwise, forget

it. Any kind of ugliness is a turnoff. Provide the right atmosphere, elegant and harmonious. No loud noise, clashing colors, or uncomfortable beds.

Libra is not an especially spontaneous lover, so it is best to spend time warming them up. Libra's back is his erogenous zone, your cue to provide backrubs with scented potions. Once in bed, you can be a bit aggressive sexually. Libra loves strong, decisive moves. Set the scene, know what you want, and let Libra be happy to provide it.

## Scorpio: Sex in the Raw

Scorpio is legendary in bed, often called the "sex sign of the zodiac." But seducing them is often a power game. Scorpio likes to be in control—even the quiet, unassuming ones. Scorpio loves a mystery, so don't tell all. Keep them guessing about you, offering tantalizing hints along the way. The hint of danger often turns Scorpio on, so you'll find members of this sign experimenting with the exotic and highly erotic forms of sex. Sadomasochism, bondage, anything that tests the limits of power could be a turn-on for Scorpio.

Invest in some sexy black leather, some powerful music (depending on your tastes). Clothes that lace, buckle, or zip tempt Scorpio to untie you. Present yourself as a mysterious package just waiting to be unwrapped.

Once in bed, there are no holds barred with Scorpio. They'll find your most pleasurable pressure points, touch you as you've never been touched before. They are quickly aroused (the genital area belongs to this sign) and willing to try anything. But they can be possessive. Don't expect your Scorpio to share you with anyone. It's all or nothing for them.

## Sagittarius: The Sexual Athletes

Sagittarius men are the Don Juans of the zodiac, love 'em and leave 'em types who are difficult to pin down.

Your seduction strategy is to join them in their many pursuits, then hook them with love on the road.

Sagittarius enjoys sex in venues that suggest movement—planes, SUVs, boats. But a favorite turn-on place is outdoors, in nature. A deserted hiking path, a field of tall grass, a remote woodland glade all give the Centaur sexy ideas. Athletic Sagittarius might go for some personal training in an empty gym. Join your Sagittarius for amorous aerobics, meditate together, explore the tantric forms of sex. Lovemaking after hiking and skiing would be healthy fun.

Sagittarius enjoys lovers from exotic ethnic backgrounds, lovers met in spiritual pursuits or on college campuses. Sagittarius are great cheerleaders and motivators, and will enjoy feeling that they have inspired you to "be all that you can be."

There may be a canine or feline companion sharing your Sagittarius lover's bed with you, so check your allergies. And bring Fido or Felix a toy to keep them occupied.


## Capricorn: Animal Instincts

The great news about Capricorn lovers is that they improve with age. They are probably the sexiest seniors. So stick around, if you have a young one. They're lusty in bed (it's not the sign of the Goat for nothing), and can be quite raunchy and turned on by X-rated words and deeds. If this is not your thing, let them know. The Capricorn erogenous zone is the knees. Some discreet fondling in public places could be your opener.

Capricorn tends to think of sex as part of a game plan for the future. They are well-organized, and might regard lovemaking as relaxation after a long day's work. This sign often combines business with pleasure. So look for a Capricorn where there's a convention, trade show, or work-related conference.

Getting Capricorn's mind off his agenda and onto yours could take some doing. Separate him from his buddies by whispering sexy secrets in his ear. Then convince him you're an asset to his image and a boon to his health. Though he may seem uptight at first, you'll soon discover he's a love animal who makes a wonderful and permanent pet.

## Aquarius: Far-out Lover

This sign really does not want an all-consuming passion or an all-or-nothing relationship. Aquarius need space. But once they feel free to experiment with a spontaneous and exciting partner, Aquarius can give you a far-out sexual adventure.

Passion begins in the mind, so a good mental buildup is key. Aquarius is an inventive sign who believes love is a playground without rules. Plan surprise, unpredictable encounters in unusual places. Find ways to make love transcendental, an extraordinary and unique experience. Be ready to try anything Aquarius suggests—if only once. Calves and ankles are the special Aquarius erogenous zone, so perfect your legwork.

Be careful not to be too possessive. Your Aquarius needs lots of space, tolerance for friends (including old lovers), and their many outside interests.

## Pisces: Fantasy Time

Pisces is the sign of fantasy and imagination. This sign has great theatrical talent. Pisces looks for lovers who will take care of them. Pisces will return the favor! Here is someone who can psych out your deepest desires without mentioning them.

Pisces falls for sob stories and is always ready to empathize. It wouldn't hurt to have a small problem for Pisces to help you overcome. It might help if you cry on his shoulder, for this sign needs to be needed.

Use your imagination when setting the scene for love. A dramatic setting brings out Pisces theatrical talents. Or creatively use the element of water. Rain on the roof, waterfalls, showers, beach houses, waterbeds, and Jacuzzis could turn up the heat. Experiment with pulsating jets of water. Take midnight skinny dips in deserted pools.

The Pisces erogenous zone is the feet. This is your cue to play footsie. Learn to give a sensuous foot massage using scented lotions. Let him paint your toes. Beautiful toenails in sexy sandals are a special turn-on.

## Your Hot Planets: Mars and Venus Tango Together

Here's a tip for finding your hottest love match. If your lover's Mars sign makes favorable aspects to your Venus—is in the same element (earth, air, fire, water) or is in the same sign—your lover will do what you want done! Mars influences how we act when we make love, while Venus shows what we like done to us.

Sometimes fighting and making up is the sexiest fun of all. If you're the type who needs a spark to keep lust alive (you know who you are!), then look for Mars and Venus in different signs of the same quality (fixed or cardinal or mutable). For instance, a fixed sign (Taurus, Leo, Scorpio, Aquarius) paired with another fixed sign can have a sexy standoff, a hot tug of war before you finally surrender. Two cardinal signs (Aries, Cancer, Libra, Capricorn) set off passionate fireworks when they clash. Mutable signs (Gemini, Virgo, Sagittarius, Pisces) play a fascinating game of cat and mouse, never quite catching each other.

## The Best Time for Love

The best time for love is when Venus is in your sign, making you the most desirable sign in the zodiac. This only lasts about three weeks (unless Venus is retrograde), so don't waste time! And find out the time this year when Venus is in your sign by consulting the Venus chart at the end of chapter 4.

## Who's the Sexiest Sign of the Zodiac?

It depends on what sign *you* are. Astrology has traditionally given this honor to Scorpio, the sign associated with the sex organs. However, we are all a combination of different signs (and turn-ons). Gemini's communicating ability and manual dexterity could deliver the magic touch. Cancer's tenderness and understanding could bring out your passion more than regal Leo.

## Who'll Be Faithful?

The earth signs of Capricorn, Taurus, and Virgo are usually the most faithful. They tend to be more home-oriented and family-oriented, and they are usually choosy about their mates. It's impractical, inconvenient, and probably expensive to play around—so they think.

## Who's Most Likely to Cheat?

The mutable signs of Gemini, Pisces, and Sagittarius win the playboy or playgirl sweepstakes. These signs tend to be changeable, fickle, and easily bored. But they're so much fun!

# CHAPTER 12

# Can Astrology Help You Get Rich? Financial Portents in the Stars

What financial portents are in the stars? What can you do about them? And what do solar flares signal about market investments?

Like many tyrants, kings, and tycoons you, too, can benefit from astrology's insights in predicting current growth trends. (The financial tycoon J. P. Morgan is rumored to have consulted an astrologer.) So find out where your best opportunities lie and what stage of the wheel of success you're on, then make savvy decisions to play the market or stay on the sidelines.

Using the trends in this chapter, you can formulate your strategy for building wealth in 2004.

## Solar Flares Bring out the Bears

Some business astrologers swear by the solar flare. Whenever there is a dramatic fiery ejection from the sun, there seems to be a drop in the stock market. Unfortunately, there seems to be no reliable advance notice to enable us to time major solar flares. However, you can see some cool photos of the latest ones on-line at *www.spacewatcher.com*.

# Pisces Issues Come Forward

The movements of the planet Uranus are big factors in the stability of the financial picture. After Uranus moved into Pisces last year, all things relating to Pisces are major issues for the next seven years. While in Aquarius, the sign of high technology, Uranus sent the stock of dotcoms and Internet startups soaring. Now watch what it does for Pisces businesses. Scientific medicine should have spectacular success. Look for new advances in pharmaceuticals, especially antibiotics (inspired by bioterrorism), in embryonic research, and in genetics. Hospitals should become more focused on treating each person as an individual, perhaps based on a personal genetic profile. There should be terrific investment opportunities in these areas.

Petroleum is associated with Pisces, so it's no surprise that oil issues will remain in the headlines. Our huge appetite for oil may remain one of America's most vulnerable points. This year, expect major changes in our energy policy and consumption. Redesigned fuel-efficient or electrical cars are possibilities. So are nonfossil sources of energy.

Offshore oil exploration and development of oceanic energy reserves may be accelerated, as well as development of hydroelectric power companies, as we tap oceans and rivers for power sources. Look for investment opportunities in power-saving devices of all kinds.

Pisces is associated with all things aquatic, of course. Fish farms, water purifying systems, swimming pools, ocean studies, shipping, sea plants as food, ocean exploration, submarine travel, and naval supplies are investment possibilities.

Creative areas have historically done well, as Uranus in Pisces stimulates avant-garde artists. New music, computer-generated art and entertainment, and the dance world (especially ballet) should thrive. Other Pisces areas include film, footwear, cosmetics, podiatry, fountains, gases, dance, alcohol and other intoxicants, any business involving fantasy and creativity, religion-oriented businesses, yoga and other spiritual practices, retreats, charities, and any institutions that help the underdog.

# The Jupiter Factor

Good fortune and big money are always associated with Jupiter, which embodies the principle of expansion. Jupiter has a twelve-year cycle, staying in each sign for approximately one year. When Jupiter enters a sign, the fields influenced by that sign seem new and profitable, and they usually provide excellent investment opportunities. Areas of speculation governed by the sign Jupiter is passing through will have the hottest market potential—they're the ones that currently arouse excitement and enthusiasm.

This year Jupiter finishes its transit of Virgo, then moves into Libra in late September. The areas these signs influence should have expansive opportunities. Those born in earth signs (Virgo, Capricorn, Taurus) should take advantage of Jupiter's beneficial rays during the first half of the year. Those born in air signs (Libra, Aquarius, Gemini) should look for growth opportunities from October on.

## Jupiter-Favored Growth Areas

All that is health-promoting, detail-oriented, and educational should get a big boost from Jupiter in Virgo. Watch efficient Virgo-related areas for growth opportunities: organizers, accountants, administrators, haute cuisine, public health, the medical and health industries, medicinal herbs, grain production, education, the service business, sanitation, sewing and tailoring, personal trainers, health clubs.

In Libra, Jupiter will promote harmony, justice, the arts, the legal profession, diplomacy, social life, and all the peripheral businesses associated with social events. With Jupiter in the "marriage sign," this should be a boom time for weddings and the wedding business. It should be an excellent time for the fashion business, interior design, and all the design-related fields. Perhaps we'll be wearing more pink, a Libra color. Look for opportunities in health fields that stress balance: diet, yoga, aerobics, dancing, skating.

# In Your Personal Life

Find the house where Jupiter in Virgo and Jupiter in Libra will fall in your chart to indicate where you'll have the most expansive potential this year. Just look up your rising sign from the chart in this book (pp. 118–119) and check the following list. (Those who know their exact birth time and place, and who have access to the Internet, can get an accurate chart on-line from one of the sources recommended in the Internet chapter in this book.)

### ARIES RISING: DETAILS, DETAILS
This is the time when you may seem bogged down in details, in learning the operation of the company from the ground up, or in taking care of the mundane aspects that make a business operate efficiently. But remember, it is only through creating a smooth working operation that fortunes can be made in the long haul. You have only to read the financial section of your newspaper to see how many promising companies get swept away by poor management. This is also an excellent time to take care of yourself. Set up a diet and exercise regime. Get your body in good shape. In the latter months of the year, consider joining a partner to get ahead faster.

### TAURUS RISING: A CREATIVE BONANZA
For creative Taurus, this is bonanza time—the inspiration flows! Put some fun into your life and help others to do so for profit. Your best ideas will come when you play

at your job (don't they always?), finding more creative ways to get the work done. The only danger here is too much fun—you may be more interested in pleasure than profit. Love affairs, fun times, and recreation can impose on work time. You may find it difficult to stick to any routines. Since this placement also rules children, you may find yourself involved with them in some way—or you may become a parent.

## GEMINI RISING: LUCK BEGINS AT HOME
Your success potential is tied to your domestic life. This is often a time of moving or relocating, as you try to arrange your personal lifestyle for the next twelve years. This is the time to establish your personal space, strengthen family ties, and give yourself a solid base of operations. You can now create the much-needed balance between your private life and the outside world that will shore you up for the next twelve years. Aim for greater family harmony and inner strength. Opportunities to invest in real estate could be winners.

## CANCER RISING: COMMUNICATIONS
You will overflow with ideas, so record them for future reference. Write up a storm! Sign up for a course that interests you—it could pay off in the future. Your social life is buzzing, as the phone rings off the hook. Make new business contacts in your local area. You may also find a lucky financial venture that involves your friends or siblings. In the fall, home life takes priority. This is the time to redecorate, renovate, expand, or buy a new home.

## LEO RISING: INCREASE YOUR SECURITY
Be a saver, not a spender, this year. Now is the time to use those contacts you made last year to consolidate your financial security. You may find that your cash flow increases, as there is generally more money available for big splurges. Watch this tendency! It might be a better idea to use this time of opportunity to protect yourself

with backup funds for a more secure future. This is a time to develop good money management habits!

## VIRGO RISING: THE IMAGE THAT SELLS
For most of the year, you hold the luckiest cards. With Jupiter energizing your ascendant, you look like a winner without even trying. Use this time to kick off the next twelve-year cycle in the most advantageous way. Circulate among influential people, make personal contacts, sell yourself. Push yourself out in the public eye, even if you're the shy type. This is the time to be your most social self! One cautionary note: Jupiter means expansion, and this position rules your physical body—so watch your diet. You'll tend to put on weight easily. The latter half of the year, focus on making a budget and savings plan that you can live with. If you've been caught up in an extravagant lifestyle, do a reality check.

## LIBRA RISING: WARM-UP FOR THE BIG TIME
You've come to the end of a twelve-year Jupiter cycle, and late September will start another cycle when Jupiter enters your sign of Libra. Use the first half of the year to review what you've learned in the last twelve years, to experiment with new ventures. Proceed slowly, as you will be bringing many matters that have occupied you over the past dozen years to a close. It's also a good time to get centered spiritually, to line up your ducks in a row, so you'll be ready to seize the moment when opportunities arise late September with Jupiter entering Libra. Then go for it in October when you'll hold the best cards in the deck.

## SCORPIO RISING: THE BIG LEAGUE
Jupiter brings you group connections this year. Others will be looking to you for inspiration. Since you can now win the support of the movers and shakers in your field and are ready to lead the pack, put some of the ideas formulated in previous cycles into action. This is the time when you make the team, come to the aid of your party,

or find a new audience for your talents. In the fall, you may be ready for some solitude! This is a good time to rest, regroup, do some solitary creative work, or fund-raise for your favorite hospital or charity.

## SAGITTARIUS RISING: BUILD YOUR PRESTIGE

It's a great time to promote yourself, be highly visible, and build up your professional image. This cycle favors public activities rather than domestic life. It's a great time to deal with VIPs and top brass. You should be feeling superconfident, and it will show. You may be starting a new career or making a stronger commitment to the one you're in. Follow up with social contacts, and exercise your leadership skill in the fall.

## CAPRICORN RISING: AIM HIGH

This is the ideal time to get higher education, develop your philosophy of life, and formulate new directions for the future. Aim high, look at the big overall picture. Publish your book, get a college or graduate degree, travel abroad. Expand your mind and horizons. Take a calculated risk. You may feel like changing your life around and trying something completely new. The ideas you get early in the year and the interesting people you meet will enhance your reputation and career.

## AQUARIUS RISING: WATCH THE CASH FLOW

You'll have opportunities to use credit and to deal with banks, loan companies, and the IRS. Be very careful with your credit cards during this period. There could be a strong temptation to overextend. You may find others more than willing to lend you money at high interest. If you're a risk taker, you may have to keep a strict eye on expenditures—Jupiter encourages gambling! You might also find yourself managing money for others and getting involved in joint ventures.

## PISCES RISING: MAKING COMMITMENTS

Commitments can be fortunate for you this year. Many

people marry at this time. However, this is not a good time for solo ventures. You are best off working in tandem and letting your partner share the spotlight. You may have to submerge your own agenda for a while in order to take full advantage of this period. So think "togetherness." You can use others to your advantage, but don't try to take over. Since this is the area of open enemies, you could learn much about your adversaries and gain the advantage in the future. In the latter months, the focus shifts to joint finances.

## CHAPTER 13

# The Generation of 2004: Astrological Portraits of Children Born This Year

Children born this year belong to one of the most spiritual generations in history. The three outer planets, Uranus, Neptune, and Pluto, which stay in a sign for at least seven years, are the ones that most affect each generation. Now moving through Pisces, Aquarius, and Sagittarius respectively, the three most visionary signs, these planets are sure to imprint the children of 2004.

As Uranus moved into Pisces last year, it ushered in a new atmosphere. In the past century, Uranus in Pisces coincided with enormous creativity, which should impact this year's children. Neptune in Aquarius and Pluto in Sagittarius are continuing their transits, bringing a time of dissolving barriers, of globalization, of interest in religion and spirituality—breaking away from the materialism of the last century. In contrast, this generation will truly be "children of the world," searching for deeper meanings to existence.

Astrology can be an especially helpful tool. It can be used to design an environment that will enhance and encourage each child's positive qualities. Some parents start from before conception, planning the birth of their child in order to harmonize with the signs of other family members. However, each baby has its own schedule. If yours arrives a week early or late, or elects a different sign from the one you planned, recognize that the "new" sign may be more in line with the mission your child is meant to accomplish. In other words, if you were hoping for a Libra child and he or she arrives during Virgo, that Virgo energy may be just what is needed to stimulate or complement your family.

Remember, there are many astrological elements besides the sun sign that indicate strong family ties. Usually each child will share a particular planetary placement, an emphasis on a particular sign or house, or a certain chart configuration with the parents and other family members. Often there is a significant planetary angle that will define the parent-child relationship, such as family sun signs that form a T-square or a triangle.

One important thing you can do is to be sure the exact moment of birth is recorded. This will be essential in calculating an accurate astrological chart, if you should wish to have one drawn up in the future.

The following descriptions can be applied to the sun sign or to the moon sign (if known) of a child. The sun sign will describe basic personality, and the moon sign will indicate the child's emotional needs.

# The Aries Child

Baby Aries is quite a handful! This energetic child will walk—and run—as soon as possible, and will perform daring feats of exploration. Caregivers should be vigilant. Little Aries seems to know no fear, and is especially vulnerable to head injuries. Many Aries children, in their rush to get on with life, seem hyperactive; they are easily frustrated when they can't get their own way. Violent temper tantrums and dramatic physical displays are par for the course with this child.

The very young Aries should be monitored carefully, since they are prone to take risks and may injure themselves. Aries love to take things apart and may break toys easily. But with encouragement, the child will develop formidable coordination. Aries bossy tendencies should be molded into leadership qualities rather than bullying techniques. Otherwise, the "me-first" Aries will have many clashes with other strong-willed youngsters.

Encourage this child to take out aggressions and frustrations in active, competitive sports, where they usually excel. When young Aries learns to focus energies long enough to master a subject and learns consideration for others, the indomitable Aries spirit will rise to the head of the class.

Aries born in 2004 will have both the sun and Saturn in active cardinal signs. This child will be a do-er, a real achiever. Look out, world!

# The Taurus Child

Taurus is a cuddly, affectionate child who eagerly explores the world of the senses, especially the sense of taste and touch. The Taurus child can be a big eater and will put on weight easily if not encouraged to exercise. Since this child likes comfort and gravitates to beauty, try coaxing little Taurus to exercise to music. Or take him or her outdoors on hikes or long walks in a local park or woodland. Though Taurus may be a slow learner, this sign has an excellent retentive memory and generally masters a subject thoroughly. Taurus is interested in results and will see each project patiently through to completion, continuing long after others have given up.

Choose Taurus toys carefully to help develop innate talents. Construction toys, such as blocks or erector sets, appeal to their love of building. Paints or crayons develop their sense of color. Many Taurus have musical talent and love to sing, which is apparent at a young age.

Taurus will usually want a pet or two, and a few plants of his or her own. Give little Taurus a mini-garden and watch the natural green thumb develop. This child has a strong sense of acquisition and an early grasp of material value. After filling a piggy bank, Taurus graduates to a savings account—before other children have even started to learn the value of money.

This year's Taurus baby will benefit from lucky Jupiter in Virgo and sensible Saturn in Cancer. These placements give the little Bull super financial savvy. Start that savings account early!

# The Gemini Child

Little Gemini will talk as soon as possible, filling the air with questions and chatter. This is a friendly child who enjoys social contact, seems to require company, and adapts quickly to different surroundings. Geminis have quick minds that easily grasp the use of words, books, and telephones, and will probably learn to talk and read at an earlier age than most.

Though they are fast learners, Gemini may have a short attention span, darting from subject to subject. Projects and games that help focus the mind could be used to help them concentrate. Musical instruments, typewriters, and computers help older Gemini children combine mental with manual dexterity.

Geminis should be encouraged to finish what they start before they go on to another project. Otherwise, they can become jack-of-all-trades types who have trouble completing anything they do. Their disposition is usually cheerful and witty, making these children popular with their peers and delightful company at home.

This year's Gemini baby should go to the head of the class! Jupiter in Virgo endows an extra dose of mental smarts. Uranus in Pisces could inspire Gemini to make an unusual career choice, perhaps in a high-tech field.

# The Cancer Child

The emotional, sensitive Cancer child is especially influenced by patterns set in early life. Young Cancers cling to their first memories as well as their childhood possessions. They thrive in calm emotional waters, with a loving, protective mother, and usually remain close to her (even if their relationship with her was difficult) throughout their lives.

Divorce, death—anything that disturbs the safe family unit—is devastating to Cancers, who may need extra support and reassurance during a family crisis.

Cancers sometimes need a firm hand to push the positive, creative side of their personality and to discourage them from getting swept away by emotional moods or resorting to emotional manipulation to get their way. If this child is praised and encouraged to find creative expression, Cancers will be able to express their positive side consistently on a firm, secure foundation.

Saturn in Cancer makes the little Moon Child born in 2004 become a serious and responsible citizen who can accomplish much. Jupiter in Virgo will provide supportive friends and loving relatives.

# The Leo Child

Leo children love the limelight and will plot to get the lion's share of attention. These children assert themselves with flair and drama, and can behave like tiny tyrants to get their way. But in general they have a sunny, positive disposition, and are rarely subject to blue moods.

At school, Leo is the type voted most popular, head cheerleader, homecoming queen. Leo is sure to be noticed for personality, if not for stunning looks or academic work; the homely Leo will be a class clown; the unhappy Leo can be the class bully.

Above all, a Leo child cannot tolerate being ignored for long. Drama or performing arts classes, sports, and school politics are healthy ways for Leo to be a star. But Leos must learn to take lesser roles occasionally, or they will have some painful put-downs in store. Usually, Leo popularity is well earned; they are hard workers who try to measure up to their own high standards—and usually succeed.

The Leo born in 2004 balances star quality with caring concern for others, thanks to Saturn in nurturing Cancer. Mercury in Virgo and Jupiter in Virgo give the Leo child practical smarts and tycoon potential.

## The Virgo Child

The young Virgo can be a quiet, serious child, with a quick, intelligent mind. Early on, little Virgo shows far more attention to detail and concern with small things than other children. Little Virgo has a built-in sense of order and a fascination of how things work. It is important for these children to have a place of their own, which they can order as they wish and where they can read or busy themselves with crafts and hobbies.

This child's personality can be very sensitive. Little Virgo may get "hyper" and overreact to seemingly small irritations, which can take the form of stomach upsets or delicate digestive systems. But this child will flourish where there is mental stimulation and a sense of order.

Virgos thrive in school, especially in writing or language skills, and seem truly happy when buried in books. Chances are, young Virgo will learn to read ahead of classmates. Hobbies that involve detail work or that develop fine craftsmanship are especially suited to young Virgos.

This is the best year to be a Virgo! A planetary bonanza of Mars in Virgo and Jupiter in Virgo will give the Virgo-born child a double dose of luck. With benevolent rays from Saturn in Cancer, this child has a winning hand.

## The Libra Child

The Libra child learns early about the power of charm and good looks. Libra is often a very physically appealing child with an enchanting dimpled smile, who is naturally sociable and enjoys the company of both children and adults. It is a rare Libra child who is a discipline problem. But when their behavior is unacceptable, they respond better to calm discussion than displays of emotion, especially if the discussion revolves around fairness.

Because young Libras without a strong direction tend to drift with the mood of the group, these children should be encouraged to develop their unique talents and powers of discrimination so they can later stand on their own.

In school, this child is usually popular and will often have to choose between social invitations and studies. In the teen years, social pressures mount as the young Libra begins to look for a partner. This is the sign of "best friends," so Libra's choice of companions can have a strong effect on his or her future direction. Beautiful Libra girls may be tempted to go steady or have an unwise early marriage. Chances are, both sexes will fall in and out of love several times in their search for the ideal partner.

Lucky Libra! Jupiter moves into Libra in 2004, making this year one of the sign's luckiest years. Mars in Libra endows the child with energy. And if the child is born between September 28 and October 16, Mercury in Libra will give a lively intelligence. Here is another winner in the zodiac sweepstakes!

# The Scorpio Child

The Scorpio child may seem quiet and shy on the surface, but will surprise others with intensity of feelings and force of willpower. Scorpio children are single-minded when they want something and intensely passionate about whatever they do. One of a caregiver's tasks is to teach this child to balance activities and emotions, yet at the same time to make the most of their great concentration and intense commitment.

Since young Scorpios do not show their depth of feelings easily, parents will have to learn to read almost imperceptible signs that troubles are brewing beneath the surface. Both Scorpio boys and girls enjoy games of power and control on or off the playground. She may take an early interest in the opposite sex, masquerading as a tomboy, while he may be intensely competitive and something of a loner.

When their powerful energies are directed into work, sports, or challenging studies, Scorpio is a superachiever thoroughly focused on a goal. With trusted friends, young Scorpio is devoted and caring—the proverbial friend "through thick and thin," loyal for life.

This year's Scorpio child could be quieter than others, with a lot going on beneath the surface. There's plenty of imagination and creativity to be developed in this visionary child.

# The Sagittarius Child

The restless, athletic Sagittarius child will be out of the playpen and off on explorative adventures as soon as possible. Little Sagittarius is remarkably well coordinated, attempting daredevil feats on any wheeled vehicle from scooters to skateboards. These natural athletes need little encouragement to channel their energies into sports. The cheerful, friendly dispositions of Sagittarius youngsters earn them popularity in school. Once they have found a subject where their talent and imagination can soar, they will do well academically. They love animals, especially horses, and will be sure to have a pet or two, if not a home zoo. When they are old enough to take care of themselves, they'll clamor to be off on adventures of their own, away from home if possible.

This is a child who loves to travel, will not get homesick at summer camp, and may sign up to be a foreign exchange student or spend summers abroad. Outdoor adventure appeals to little Sagittarius, especially if it involves an active sport, such as skiing, cycling, or mountain climbing. Give them enough space and encouragement, and their fiery spirit will propel them to achieve high goals.

The Sagittarius born in 2004 has charisma and power, thanks to potent Pluto in Sagittarius. Jupiter in Libra endows a sense of fairness and love of beauty. What a beautiful mind!

# The Capricorn Child

The purposeful, goal-oriented Capricorn child will work to capacity if he or she feels this will bring results. They're not ones who enjoy work for its own sake—there must be an end in sight. Authority figures can do much to motivate this child. But once set on an upward path, young Capricorn will mobilize his or her energy and talent and will work harder, and with more perseverance, than any other sign. Capricorn has built-in self-discipline that can achieve remarkable results, even if lacking the flashy personality, quick brainpower, or penetrating insight of others. Once involved, young Capricorn will stick to a task until it is mastered. This child also knows how to use others to advantage, and may well become the team captain or class president.

A wise parent will set realistic goals for the Capricorn child, paving the way for the early thrill of achievement. Youngsters should be encouraged to express their caring, feeling side to others, as well as their natural aptitude for leadership.

Capricorn children may be especially fond of grandparents and older relatives, and will enjoy spending time with them and learning from them. It is not uncommon for young Capricorns to have an older mentor or teacher who guides them. With their great respect for authority, Capricorn children will take this influence very much to heart.

The Capricorn born in 2004 will have serious and responsible partnerships, thanks to Saturn in the opposite sign of Cancer. Jupiter promises a stellar career, with high earning power.

# The Aquarius Child

The Aquarius child has an innovative, well-focused mind that often streaks so far ahead of peers that this child seems like an "oddball." Routine studies never hold the restless youngster for long; he or she will look for another, more experimental place to try out their ideas and to develop their inventions. Life is a laboratory to the inquiring Aquarius mind.

School politics, sports, science, and the arts offer scope for this child's talents. But if there is no room for expression within approved social limits, Aquarius is sure to rebel.

Questioning institutions and religions comes naturally, so these children may find an outlet elsewhere, becoming "rebels with a cause." It is better not to force this child to conform. Instead, channel forward-thinking young minds into constructive group activities.

Aquarius children born this year will have far-out glamour as well as charisma, thanks to their planetary ruler, Uranus, in a friendly bond with planet Neptune. This child could become a rock star, a statesman, a scientist. It's the most creative Aquarius ever!

# The Pisces Child

Give young Pisces praise, applause, and a gentle but firm push in the right direction. Lovable Pisces children may be abundantly talented. But they may be hesitant to express themselves because they are quite sensitive and easily hurt. It is a parent's challenge to help them gain self-esteem and self-confidence. However, this same sensitivity makes them trusted friends who'll have many confidants as they develop socially. It also endows many Pisces with spectacular creative talent.

Pisces adores drama and theatrics of all sorts. Encourage them to channel their creativity into art forms rather than indulging in emotional dramas. As they develop their creative ideas, they may need more solitude than other children. But though daydreaming can be creative, it is important that these natural dreamers not dwell too long in the world of fantasy. Teach them practical coping skills for the real world.

Since Pisces are sensitive physically, parents should help them build strong bodies with proper diet and regular exercise. Young Pisces may gravitate to individual sports, such as swimming, sailing, and skiing, rather than to team sports. Or they may prefer artistic physical activities like dance or ice skating.

Born "givers," these children are often drawn to the underdog (they fall quickly for sob stories) and attract those who might take advantage of their empathic nature. Teach them to choose friends wisely and to set boundaries in relationships, to protect their emotional vulnerability—invaluable lessons in later life.

With the planet Uranus now in Pisces, this generation of Pisces will be movers and shakers. This child may have a rebellious streak that rattles the status quo. Saturn in Cancer is a stabilizing force, while Jupiter in Virgo could bring luck in love.

## CHAPTER 14

# The Scorpio Personality

In the northern hemisphere, Scorpio occurs after crops have been harvested, the leaves have fallen, and preparations for winter have begun. Like its ruling planet, Pluto, Scorpio is concerned with the mysterious cycle of death and transformation. Scorpio is the sign of sex, of power, of procreation. The eighth sign of the zodiac, Scorpio is further defined by the element of water; by its ruling planet, Pluto; by its feminine, reactive, yin polarity; and by its fixed modality (the way it operates), as steady and penetrating as a laser beam.

Your personal blend of planets and rising sign, based on your moment of birth, adds another set of colors to your horoscope. Otherwise, all Scorpios would be alike. Key planets in solid, practical earth signs could quiet your Scorpio personality down. An emphasis on fire signs might make you more flamboyant than the usual Scorpio. However, the more planets in Scorpio you have, the more you'll recognize yourself in the following descriptions.

# The Scorpio Man: Man of Mystery

Yours is known as the sex sign of the zodiac. But if the truth be known, you're much more interested in issues of power and control. You're challenged by unsolved problems and mysteries of any kind. You're a natural detective who won't stop until you know what makes things and people tick. In spite of your aloof manner, you're always aware of what is going on (especially of who is running the show), and you're remarkably perceptive about people's true motives.

Beneath your deliberately cool surface, you may be far less secure. One of the most sensitive signs of the zodiac, you keep your vulnerability a dark secret to seal yourself off from rejection. When you do fall for someone, nothing less than total possession will do. Scorpio feels he should own the woman he loves (though he's also able to enjoy pure sex for its own sake elsewhere). Yours is the most possessive sign, with no toleration for disloyalty.

You are single-minded in pursuit of what you want, be it a job, a prize, or a person. It was with good reason that Scorpio fashion designer Calvin Klein named his first fragrance "Obsession." Your great concentration, intensity, and stamina make you a formidable competitor. But your love of power can degenerate into manipulation, bullying, and even violence if you are frustrated. You harbor a grudge and seek revenge when injured. As Teddy Roosevelt said, "Speak softly, but carry a big stick."

## In a Relationship

When Scorpio falls in love, you are so single-minded about the object of your affection that, if you lose that love for any reason, you are devastated. Often this is the one experience that can teach Scorpio about healthy detachment and the wisdom of getting to know someone slowly and gradually for longevity's sake.

After issues of power and control are settled within the relationship, you become a loyal and devoted mate. But first you may go through a period of testing in which you are not above using emotional manipulation to gain the upper hand. You need a partner who will provide rational balance and perspective when you go to extremes and who will help you look on the lighter, brighter side of life.

# The Scorpio Woman: Still Waters Run Deep

Like your male counterpart, the mysterious, mesmerizing Scorpio woman hides intense emotions under a cool, controlled facade. But inside you are passionate, determined, and totally committed to everything you do. This makes you seem very stable and somewhat predictable. You're not one for surprises or spontaneous moves; there is usually a strategy behind every step you take. All your formidable energy is zeroed in on your goal. The Scorpio woman is rarely plagued by self-doubt. You know exactly where you are going and rarely waver from your path. Once committed, you remain loyal and dedicated, and you will patiently see your projects through to completion. Hillary Clinton embodies these typical Scorpio traits.

Scorpio is the "heaviest" sign of the zodiac, so let those who skim the surface of life be forewarned. You delve deep and demand total commitment—anything less is not worthwhile. Since you are extremely vulnerable beneath your cool controlled surface, you are deeply hurt by betrayal. When disappointed, you can strike back with lethal accuracy.

The good girl/bad girl extremes of Scorpio are reflected in the sex-charged and power-charged roles Scorpio actresses have played in recent years, starting with Vivien Leigh as Scarlett O'Hara in Gone With the Wind. Jodie Foster and Julia Roberts both gained fame playing sexually charged roles in *Taxi Driver, The Accused,* and *Pretty Woman.* Scorpios Jodie Foster and Goldie Hawn have braved the Hollywood establishment by producing and directing their own projects.

178

Unfortunately, Scorpio intensity frightens away many who are not ready to commit to a bond that reaches to the soul level. The Scorpio woman considers this kind of fright a weakness, and so she blocks out many potentially interesting relationships. It is only after a period of tempering that you learn tolerance for a more balanced and rational relationship—and learn to give your partner space to be his own person.

A Scorpio woman is not one to play around with or take lightly. Though you may seem very sweet and naïve, you can quickly see through deception. An excellent detective, you sense immediately when something is hidden, yet you yourself are never completely open about your own motives. This secretiveness can cause suspicion and mistrust. Others wonder what is lurking beneath that unruffled surface.

Anger brings out your venomous side. Scorpio has a suspicious streak and often overreacts to imaginary slights. You tend to see things in black and white, and you go to extremes when you're upset. Then it is very difficult to coax you out of a black mood. You are more likely to get revenge than to forgive and forget.

## In a Relationship

Much maligned as a femme fatale, the typical Scorpio is a one-man (at a time) woman, intensely loyal and devoted to your mate. Though you may experiment before settling down, as a Scorpio you are looking for total commitment. After marriage, you're so completely involved with your husband that you can be devastated if the marriage fails. However, once committed, your intense involvement could backfire if you become overly demanding, possessive, and jealous. Then you will smother a more freedom-loving partner. You must learn not to give in to those negative suspicions, which can escalate into destructive paranoia.

You reach your full potential as a mate once you have learned to share yourself with your partner rather than try to control the relationship. On the plus side, as a Scorpio you will stay with your true mate after he earns your trust, even through the most difficult times, as Hillary Clinton demonstrated. You are someone he can count on to support him, no matter what the sacrifice. And, in the long run, you can transform his life for the better.

# Scorpio in the Family

## The Scorpio Parent

Scorpios are committed to everything they do, especially to being a good parent. Though you may not express your feelings openly, you are able to convey to your children a feeling of being deeply loved. It is this strong foundation of emotional security that gives your children confidence. Trust and loyalty are unspoken givens. You'll defend your children to the maximum, and you'll provide them with the ways and means to live up to your high hopes. But you are a strict parent who insists on control and discipline, which could create problems with an equally strong-willed child. You may have to learn lessons of flexibility and tolerance from your children. And you will also have to learn when to let go, to allow your children to follow their own interests in the outside world. However, your children always know you will be there for them, ready to provide a life raft in the roughest waters.

## The Scorpio Stepparent

In marriage, Scorpios can be intensely possessive of a mate. It is especially important that you and your step-children get along before the marriage, and that you are sincerely willing to reach out to them. Otherwise, power struggles can develop. It would also help to discuss problems openly as they occur rather than let anger, hurt feelings, or misunderstandings build up. Be flexible enough to allow your mate time with the children, apart from you. Have some outside activities to help diffuse your energy, so it is not overly concentrated on the family.

## The Scorpio Grandparent

Grandchildren can provide some of the most liberating, joyful experiences of your life. At last you can show your playful childlike side, with a fun-loving little playmate who demands nothing of you. You're free from the disciplining responsibilities of parenthood and the intense emotional commitment. You're no longer involved in power struggles or overworked, so you're free to spend happy times with the children. Grandchildren can also bring out the generosity in Scorpio, particularly when providing for their future security. You'll make a lasting impression on the youngest generation, and they'll make you feel born again!

CHAPTER 15

# Scorpio Style: Fashion, Home, and Healthy Living Tips Especially for You!

Finding the lifestyle that suits you best couldn't be easier. Just follow your Scorpio solar muse! Since each sun sign resonates to certain colors, styles, places, music, you can't miss. In the following pages are cosmic tips for selecting the clothes, home environment, colors, sounds, and places that enhance your personality.

## Scorpio Home Decor

If you're a typical Scorpio, you care about your home decor very much or not at all. There's nothing wishy-washy about the ideal Scorpio atmosphere. Either it's a supersensual atmosphere, with dark woods, rich tapestry colors, sink-in upholstery, brocade walls, luxurious leather or suede coverings, and Oriental rugs. Or it's pared down to the essentials. In the latter case, rooms can be stark and minimal in one or two colors, often black and white.

Some Scorpios ignore the surroundings entirely, being focused on another agenda. This kind of Scorpio might live in a virtually unfurnished apartment or delegate the decor to someone else, simply because he or she is not involved or interested enough to decorate. For those who do care, marine motifs, voluptuous nudes, and dramatic ancient artifacts might appeal. Or you may go for the Victorian look, with carved wood furniture. You'll pay special attention to the bedroom, perhaps pulling out all the stops with satin sheets, mirrored walls and seductive lighting effects.

Scorpio enjoys transforming the environment. You are often the one to buy a crumbling house or gut a forlorn apartment. Renovating from the ground up, tearing down and rebuilding, restoring a vintage building, or bringing a dull room to life would fully engage your energy. Rather than just a surface redo, you'll get right down to the plumbing and structure, stripping the walls and floors bare. Give yourself a beautiful bathroom with top-of-the-line fixtures. Or go all out with an indoor sauna or Jacuzzi to create your personal spa. Be sure there's a secret sanctuary somewhere to restore your spirit.

## Scorpio Music

Scorpio loves intense music—thundering symphonies and dramatic operas with life-and-death themes. You also love sexy tangos, sensual cello sounds, Paul Simon, Bonnie Raitt, Joni Mitchell. Mysterious New Age music has Scorpio appeal. More avant-garde Scorpios go for powerful heavy-metal sounds with a driving beat and an undercurrent of danger. The black leather and biker paraphernalia side of the rock scene is pure Scorpio. Gospel music can also stir your soul. The new CD burners were made for Scorpio, as you love to control what you hear. Now you can make your own kind of music in whatever combination of sounds turns you on.

## Your Special Scorpio Colors

Basic black and a deep, rich burgundy are traditional Scorpio colors. But some Scorpios, particularly pale blondes, prefer off-white tones or neutrals, which are calming and offset the intense Scorpio personality. The deep blues of the ocean also resonate and bring your intensity into balance.

## The Scorpio Fashionista

Like other fixed signs, Scorpio usually sticks to a signature look: the sporty, classic style of Jodie Foster; the avant-garde trendiness of Chloe Sevigny and Bjork; the ultrafeminine gamine look of Callista Flockhart. Many Scorpio women, like Lauren Hutton, prefer man-tailored styles. Scorpio loves to wear black, particularly black velvet or black leather, and will use intense makeup or none at all to dramatize strong bone structure and mesmerizing eyes.

Indulge yourself in some sexy accessories like stiletto boots, lacy lingerie, and at least one vibrantly colored scarf—just to hint at your inner passionate nature.

Calvin Klein's fashion style is pure Scorpio, with its streamlined, uncluttered sexy look from head to toe. (Leave it to a Scorpio to put a woman in man-styled underwear and name a fragrance "Obsession.") Rae Kawaikubo of Comme des Garçons goes to the opposite extreme to make a severe avant-garde statement with stark, futuristic looks.

## The Healthy Scorpio

Though your sign usually has a strong constitution that can literally rise from the ashes of extreme illness or misfortune, resist the temptation to take this for granted or sabotage your health with self-destructive habits. Try to curb excessive tendencies in any area of your life.

Know when to quit and when to seek help—and don't hesitate to ask for help when you need it.

Your sign rules the regenerative and eliminative organs. Therefore, it follows that sexual activity can be a source of good or ill health for Scorpio. It is important to examine your attitudes about sex, to follow safe sexual practices, and to seek balance in sex—as in all other areas of your life.

Yo-yo dieting, with its extreme ups and downs, can be another Scorpio problem. Some Scorpios will go to great lengths to become thin, even resorting to surgical means. Rather than obsessing about food and diet, try to diffuse this energy into other areas of your life.

It's no accident that Scorpio's month coincides with football season, which reminds us that sports are a very healthy way to diffuse emotions. If you enjoy winter sports, be sure to prepare ahead of time for the ski slopes or the ice rinks. Be sure to warm up your muscles before you go all out. Water sports are a terrific outlet for Scorpio, so sign up for pool aerobics or competitive swimming. And be sure to treat yourself to a vacation at a spectacular tropical beach resort. Somehow, just being near a salt water environment can restore your equilibrium.

# Scorpio Getaways

Scorpios relax to the sound of the pounding surf, your best tranquilizer, and thrill to the crashing waves. Find a beach that's away from the crowd, one that feels like yours alone, such as the deserted beaches of Martha's Vineyard, the Baja Peninsula, the surfing beaches of California, or the Caribbean in off-season.

You will never go to a place because it's "in," at least not for a vacation. You prefer a place where there is a challenge or a mystical experience such as a difficult mountain to scale, great fishing or skiing, unexplored terrain, the ruins of an ancient civilization. Australia, Brazil, Morocco, Norway, and China are exotic Scorpio destinations that fill the bill. You'll enjoy exploring the classic treasures of Greece, Mexico, and Peru as well as the erotically decorated temples of India.

Scorpios can travel with minimum luggage and are usually expert packers. Invest in some leather carry-on bags so you can skip the baggage claim and avoid lost luggage. Combination locks should keep your possessions secure, though you might want to look into a hidden money belt or a waist packet to store your vital items. Take wearable waterproof containers to the beach to hold credit cards and cash. Scorpios who are truly concerned with security can find clothes hangers with secret compartments to store valuables. Hidden pockets or compartments of any kind are very much a Scorpio thing!

Credit cards are ruled by Scorpio. Before you go, be sure to check which cards are accepted and how much cash you'll need. Investigate travel insurance and any special travel deal provided by your credit card company.

# CHAPTER 16

# Scorpio at Work

Scorpios are born survivors in the competitive workplace. You usually know exactly what you want and will put in the necessary groundwork to prepare for a top position. You are capable of getting and keeping great responsibility, though others may underestimate your quiet demeanor, at first mistaking it for shyness.

Scorpio talents often work best within a structured organization rather than in a freelance situation. Large companies give you a wide scope and plenty of potential power. Higher-ups soon notice how you stay cool in a crisis and keep your job well under control. As the zodiac's supersleuth, you shine in detective, research, or troubleshooting spots. Concentration and focus help in life-or-death fields such as medicine and in high-pressure television spots where you'll be the steady anchor. (Pat Sajak, Jane Pauley, Morley Safer, Walter Cronkite, and Dick Cavett are good examples in broadcasting.) Handling other people's money can be trusted to Scorpio accountants, financial planners, investment bankers, and brokers. Your sharp perception works for you in psychology, psychotherapy, or the theater. Both the fashion world (Calvin Klein) and fine arts (Picasso) know your strong statements. Stay away from jobs that have a dead end, that are in risky fly-by-night businesses, or that require on-the-spot improvisation rather than steady discipline.

For examples of Scorpio survivors, you shouldn't go farther than Bill Gates of Microsoft or U.S. Senator Hillary Clinton. These Scorpios have weathered great storms and emerged with mega-success through shrewd career maneuvers and careful planning. Like most Scorpios in power positions, they have been able to transform the lives of others: Gates through his work combating disease in Africa, and Hillary through her career as senator from New York.

## The Scorpio Boss

You hire your staff with a keen perception of everyone's strengths and weaknesses. You are totally in command of all that happens in your domain and will rarely hand over the reins, even temporarily. Since you do not trust easily, you may be hesitant to delegate and so you take on too much responsibility yourself. Your suspiciousness could even degenerate into paranoia, where you think of others in black-and-white terms, either for you or against you. But you care intensely about your work and are generous with others who are equally dedicated. A winner of power games, you can be lethal with competition. However, you are extremely supportive of anyone who gives you the proper respect and loyalty.

## Scorpio on a Team

Since you aim for total control of your job, you will always have a motive behind your moves. You like work where there is a challenge and a chance to wield power, whether it's a weapon, a big machine, or a company checkbook. Sometimes Scorpio will work overtime to make yourself indispensable, simply for the power of being so needed! You are always aware of what is happening in the office, of who's doing what to whom. You are particularly good at assessing the weak points of others (or of the organization), and using this to your advantage. When you're interested in your work, you have unbeatable stamina—tolerating working conditions and hours that would make others rebel! You are very steady and stable on the job, rarely getting sidetracked to another profession or seduced by another organization.

# How to Succeed

Pick a job where there is a weakness you can correct or chaos you can order—and then take over! Play up your best characteristics:

- Cool control
- Stamina
- Perception
- Concentration
- Ability to handle pressure
- Steadiness
- Drive

# CHAPTER 17

# Learn from the Scorpio Famous

There's no better way to learn about the pitfalls and prizes of your sign than to study the lives of your rich and famous sign-mates. For sure you'll find the intense Scorpio drive in Ted Turner and Bill Gates. The Scorpio magnetism is in Billy Graham and Hillary Clinton. Strong women of the silver screen like Vivien Leigh and Hedy Lamarr are archetypal Scorpio sirens. Scorpios who dance to their own tune: Whoopi Goldberg, k.d. lang, Bjork, Chloe Sevigny.

Astrology can tell you more about your sun sign heroes and heroines than tabloids or magazine articles. Like what really turns them on (check their Venus). Or what makes them rattled (scope their Saturn). Compare similarities and differences between the celebrities who embody the typical Scorpio sun sign traits and those who seem untypical. Then look up the influence of other planets in the horoscope of your favorites, using the charts in this book. It's a fun way to further your education in astrology.

## Scorpio Celebrities

Sarah Bernhardt (10/23/1844)
Michael Crichton (10/23/42)
Kevin Kline (10/24/47)
Pablo Picasso (10/25/1881)
Tracy Nelson (10/25/63)

Pat Sajak (10/26/46)
Hillary Clinton (10/26/47)
Jaclyn Smith (10/26/47)
John Cleese (10/27/39)
Simon LeBon (10/27/58)
Marla Maples (10/27/63)
Evelyn Waugh (10/28/1903)
Dennis Franz (10/28/44)
Annie Potts (10/28/52)
Bill Gates (10/28/55)
Julia Roberts (10/28/67)
Richard Dreyfuss (10/29/47)
Kate Jackson (10/29/48)
Winona Ryder (10/29/48)
Louis Malle (10/30/32)
Grace Slick (10/30/39)
Dale Evans (10/31/12)
Diedre Hall (10/31/49)
Jane Pauley (10/31/50)
Harry Hamlin (10/31/51)
Lyle Lovett (11/1/57)
Jenny McCarthy (11/1/72)
Daniel Boone (11/2/1754)
Stefanie Powers (11/2/42)
k.d. lang (11/2/61)
Charles Bronson (11/3/22)
Roseanne (11/3/52)
Kate Capshaw (11/3/53)
Pauline Trigere (11/4/12)
Yanni (11/4/22)
Sean "Puffy" Combs (11/4/69)
Matthew McConaughey (11/4/69)
Roy Rogers (11/5/12)
Vivien Leigh (11/5/13)
Ike Turner (11/5/31)
Sam Shepard (11/5/43)
Tatum O'Neal (11/5/63)
Mike Nichols (11/6/31)
Maria Shriver (11/6/55)

Ethan Hawke (11/6/70)
Billy Graham (11/7/18)
Katharine Hepburn (11/8/1907)
Bonnie Raitt (11/8/49)
Hedy Lamarr (11/9/13)
Carl Sagan (11/9/34)
Richard Burton (11/10/25)
Roy Scheider (11/10/32)
Demi Moore (11/11/62)
Calista Flockhart (11/11/64)
Leonardo DiCaprio (11/11/74)
Grace Kelly (11/12/29)
Richard Mulligan (11/13/32)
Whoopi Goldberg (11/13/55)
Aaron Copland (11/14/1900)
Prince Charles (11/14/48)
Ed Asner (11/15/29)
Bo Derek (11/16/56)
Lauren Hutton (11/17/43)
Danny DeVito (11/17/44)
Linda Evans (11/18/42)
Ted Turner (11/19/38)
Ahmad Rashad (11/19/49)
Jodie Foster (11/19/62)
Sean Young (11/20/59)
Marlo Thomas (11/21/38)
Goldie Hawn (11/21/45)
Mariel Hemingway (11/21/61)
Nicolette Sheridan (11/21/63)
Bjork (11/21/65)

# CHAPTER 18

# Scorpio Relating: How You Get Along with Every Sign

Your intense Scorpio nature makes your choice of a partner especially important. Whether you're looking for a business partner or a life companion, this compatibility "cheat sheet" will help you understand each other's basic needs. Once you understand how your partner's sun sign is likely to view commitment and what each of you wants from a relationship, you'll be in a much better position to judge whether your cosmic combination has staying power.

## Scorpio/Aries

**THE PERKS:**
One of the zodiac's challenging pairs, your Mars-ruled chemistry could ignite with frequent battles of the sexes. You both love a dare! Neither of you gives in, but you'll never bore each other (though you might wear each other out). Aries direct, uncomplicated forcefulness especially intrigues Scorpio, and you are caught off guard, for once.

**THE CHALLENGES:**
You both could play so hard to get that you never really connect! Aries never quite trusts secretive Scorpio, while

Scorpio intrigues and power plays can fizzle under direct Aries fire. You are both jealous and controlling, but this dynamic duo can work if you focus on high ideals and mutual respect.

# Scorpio/Taurus

**THE PERKS:**
Many marriages happen when these opposites attract. Taurus has a calming effect on Scorpio innate paranoia. And Taurus responds to Scorpio intensity and fascinating air of mystery. Together, these signs have the perfect complement of sensuality and sexuality.

**THE CHALLENGES:**
Problems of control are inevitable when you both want to run the show. Avoid long and bitter battles or silent stand-offs by drawing territorial lines from the start.

# Scorpio/Gemini

**THE PERKS:**
You're a fascinating mystery to each other. Gemini is immune from Scorpio paranoia, laughs away dark moods, and matches wits in power games. Scorpio intensity, focus, and sexual magnetism draw scattered Gemini like a moth to a flame.

**THE CHALLENGES:**
Scorpio can get "heavy," possessive, and jealous—intense feelings that Gemini doesn't take seriously. To make this one last, Gemini needs to treat Scorpio like the one and only, while Scorpio must use a light touch, and learn not to take Gemini flirtations to heart.

# Scorpio/Cancer

**THE PERKS:**
Cancer actually enjoys Scorpio intensity and possessiveness—it shows how much they care! And, like Scorpio Prince Charles and Cancer Camilla Parker Bowles (also Princess Diana, another Cancer), this pair cares deeply about those they love. Strong emotions are a great bond that can survive heavy storms.

**THE CHALLENGES:**
Your Scorpio mysterious and melancholy moods can leave Cancer feeling isolated and insecure. And the more Cancer clings, the more Scorpio withdraws. Outside interests can lighten the mood—or provide a means of escape.

# Scorpio/Leo

**THE PERKS:**
Scorpio innate power with Leo confidence and authority can make a fascinating high-profile combination like Scorpio Hillary and Leo Bill Clinton. There is great mutual respect and loyalty here, as well as sexual dynamite. You two magnetic, unconquerable heroes offer each other enough challenges to keep the sparks flying.

**THE CHALLENGES:**
Scorpio natural secretiveness and Leo openness could conflict, especially if Scorpio reveals a powerful will and need for control from under a deceptively quiet facade. And Leo is often surprised by the sheer intensity of your Scorpio drive and willpower. Though as a Scorpio you won't fight for the spotlight, you will often exercise con-

trol from behind the scenes. When these two intense, stubborn, demanding signs collide, it's a no-win situation.

# Scorpio/Virgo

**THE PERKS:**
With Scorpio, Virgo encounters intense feelings too powerful to intellectualize or analyze. This could be a grand passion, especially when Scorpio is challenged to uncover the Virgo earthy, sensual side. Your penetrating minds are simpatico, and so is your dedication to meaningful work (here is a fellow healer). Virgo provides the stability and structure that keep Scorpio on the right track.

**THE CHALLENGES:**
Virgo may cool off if Scorpio goes to extremes or plays manipulative games. Scorpio could find Virgo perfectionism irritating and the Virgo approach to sex too limited.

# Scorpio/Libra

**THE PERKS:**
The interplay of Scorpio intensity and Libra objectivity makes an exciting cat-and-mouse game. Libra intellect and flair balance your powerful Scorpio charisma. Scorpio adds warmth and substance to the cool Libra demeanor.

**THE CHALLENGES:**
Libra must learn to handle your sensitive Scorpio feelings with velvet gloves. When not taken seriously, Scorpio retaliates with a force that could send the Libra scales swinging way off balance. On the other hand, Scorpio

must give Libra room to exercise his or her mental and social skills.

# Scorpio/Scorpio

**THE PERKS:**
The list of legendary Scorpio-Scorpio couples reads like a historical who's who—Abigail and John Adams, Marie and Pierre Curie, Dale Evans and Roy Rogers. You'll match each other's intensity and commitment, knowing instinctively where to tread with caution.

**THE CHALLENGES:**
Since you both like to be in control, power struggles are always on the menu. Share some of your secrets. Air your grievances immediately rather than letting them fester.

# Scorpio/Sagittarius

**THE PERKS:**
Sagittarius sees an erotic adventure in Scorpio—and doesn't mind playing with fire. Scorpio is impressed with Sagittarius high ideals, energy, and competitive spirit. Sagittarius humor diffuses Scorpio intensity, while Scorpio provides the focus for Sagittarius to reach those goals.

**THE CHALLENGES:**
Scorpio sees through schemes and won't fall for a sales pitch unless it has substance. Sagittarius may object to your Scorpio drive for power rather than for higher goals. Sagittarius will flee from Scorpio possessiveness or heavy-handed controlling tactics.

# Scorpio/Capricorn

**THE PERKS:**
Sexy Scorpio takes the Capricorn mind off business. Though you could get wrapped up in each other, you are also turned on by power and position. You'll join forces to scale the heights.

**THE CHALLENGES:**
Capricorn has no patience for intrigue or hidden agendas. Scorpio will find this sign supremely focused on his or her own goals. Capricorn won't be easily diverted, even if this means leaving your Scorpio emotional needs—and ego—in the backseat.

# Scorpio/Aquarius

**THE PERKS:**
Both of you respect each other's uncompromising position and mental focus. You will probably have an unconventional relationship—spiced up by sexual experimentation and the element of surprise.

**THE CHALLENGES:**
Scorpio could feel that Aquarius is a loose cannon who is likely to sink the ship. Or both of these fixed signs could come to a stubborn stand-off. Aquarius tunes out Scorpio possessiveness. Scorpio looks elsewhere for intimacy and intensity.

# Scorpio/Pisces

**THE PERKS:**
When these two signs click, nothing gets in their way. The Pisces desire to merge completely with a beloved is

just the all-or-nothing message Scorpio has been waiting for. These two will play it to the hilt, often shedding previous spouses or bucking public opinion (like Liz Taylor and Richard Burton once did).

## THE CHALLENGES:
Both signs are possessive, yet neither likes to be possessed. Scorpio could easily mistake Pisces vulnerability for weakness—a big mistake. Both signs fuel each other's escapist tendencies when dark moods hit. Learning to merge without submerging one's identity is an important lesson for this couple.

# CHAPTER 19

# Astrological Outlook for Scorpio in 2004

During 2004, you will be active, creative, and involved with romance. Your intellectual curiosity will stir. You'll obtain the story behind the story. You will delve into "social problems." Many will rely upon you for their emotional and financial welfare.

Saturn in the sign of Cancer all year places pressure on your ninth house. This relates to travel and concern with how people live in foreign lands. The focus is also on writing, advertising, and publishing. These are areas in which doors open—follow through on these "rare opportunities."

Your Scorpio passion will be appreciated. Many will look to you for inspiration.

March and December will be your most memorable months.

Key numbers: 5, 4, 2.

Gemini, Virgo, and Sagittarius will play active roles in your life this year.

With Gemini, it will be your Pluto and the Gemini Mercury. There is plenty of physical attraction here. The relationship could be "explosive." Your eighth house will be emphasized. This means that, with Gemini, much will be unknown. The key is not to fear the unknown. You will take steps in a new direction.

With Virgo, many of your hopes and wishes could be fulfilled. Once again, it is your Pluto and the Virgo Mercury. Ideas and concepts will be original and controversial. Your eleventh house will be highlighted. You will be lucky with Virgo. You discover what you really want and how to obtain it. There will be a tendency in this relationship to "gamble with security."

With Sagittarius, your Pluto combines with the Jupiter of Sagittarius. In this relationship, there is "financial pressure." On the positive side, you will be rewarded for hard work. On the negative side, you become avaricious. Deception is likely to be involved. By trying to do too much and to seek perfection, the relationship could fall apart. In the long run, however, you will earn more money and you will learn more about money and how it gets that way.

In the following pages, you will find your diary in advance forecasted daily. You will have lucky numbers that include racetrack predictions. You will also have valuable hints about love, money, and health.

Start reading for the adventure into your day-by-day future.

# CHAPTER 20

# Eighteen Months of Day-by-Day Predictions—July 2003 to December 2004

*Moon sign times are calculated for Eastern Standard Time and Eastern Daylight Time. Please adjust for your local time zone.*

## JULY 2003

***Tuesday, July 1 (Moon in Cancer to Leo 9:11 a.m.)*** On this first day of July, your creative juices stir. You'll be especially attractive. There could be a reason for celebration. Your popularity is on the rise. People want to be with you and vie to see if they can wine and dine you. Sagittarius is involved.

***Wednesday, July 2 (Moon in Leo)*** Revise, review, rebuild. Someone in a position of authority is on your side, and a promotion is due as a result. Taurus, Leo, and another Scorpio play key roles and could have these letters or initials in their names: D, M, V. Have luck with number 4.

***Thursday, July 3 (Moon in Leo to Virgo 4:15 p.m.)*** At the track: post position special—number 1 p.p. in the fifth race. Hot daily doubles: 1 and 5, 3 and

2, 4 and 1. Away from the track, a secret is revealed; you'll be asked to "write about it." A flirtation is serious, but maintain your emotional equilibrium.

*Friday, July 4 (Moon in Virgo)*     Attention revolves around your home, repairs, decorating, and remodeling. Celebrate this holiday by recalling the American Revolution and talking about the significance of the Declaration of Independence. Taurus, Libra, and another Scorpio will play prominent roles.

*Saturday, July 5 (Moon in Virgo to Libra 9:19 p.m.)*     What appears to be a defeat will be transformed into a rousing victory. The lunar position emphasizes your ability to make wishes come true. Avoid self-deception; see people and places as they are, not merely as you wish they could be.

*Sunday, July 6 (Moon in Libra)*     On this Sunday, hold tight to what you recently gained. Someone wants to take from you something of value while giving nothing in return. Be on guard. Maintain your balance. Realize your own worth. A Cancer is involved.

*Monday, July 7 (Moon in Libra)*     This could mark the beginning or the ending of a romance or major project. Look behind the scenes. A secret arrangement is being made behind your back. You are not being neurotic, merely protecting your interests. A Pisces figures prominently.

*Tuesday, July 8 (Moon in Libra to Scorpio 12:42 a.m.)* Provide enlightenment. Encourage someone temporarily confined to home or hospital. Don't fear the unknown. Take the initiative! Be a role model for those who are reticent. Display the courage of your convictions. Let it be known you are not afraid and do not intend to "go away."

**Wednesday, July 9 (Moon in Scorpio)**    Lucky lottery: 2, 8, 12, 16, 33, 4. Make a fresh start. Your lunar cycle is high, so you will be at the right place at a special moment where the action occurs. The emphasis is also on your home, marital status, direction, and motivation. Capricorn is represented.

**Thursday, July 10 (Moon in Scorpio to Sagittarius 2:47 a.m.)**    Your cycle continues high. Take the initiative; don't follow others. There will be a reason for celebrating. You emit personal magnetism and sex appeal. Protect yourself in emotional clinches. Do not lower your standards. Have luck with number 3.

**Friday, July 11 (Moon in Sagittarius)**    What appeared to be an immovable object will finally cease to be a problem. This is your makeover day; dress differently, change your appearance. People comment, "You look different. You could be a movie star!" A Leo plays a dramatic role.

**Saturday, July 12 (Moon in Sagittarius to Capricorn 4:20 a.m.)**    Money is earned via the written word. Take notes; record thoughts and dreams. Good news: A lost article is located. It has sentimental value. Gemini, Virgo, and Sagittarius play instrumental roles and have these letters in their names: E, N, W. Your lucky number is 5.

**Sunday, July 13 (Moon in Capricorn)**    The full moon is in Capricorn, which is your third house. That coincides with short trips, visits, entertaining guests at home. A domestic adjustment is necessary and could include a change of residence or marital status. A Libra plays the top role.

**Monday, July 14 (Moon in Capricorn to Aquarius 6:37 a.m.)**    Outline boundaries. Estimate your property value. What seemed a "sure thing" will turn out to be something entirely different. Focus on diversity and versatility. Expand your social horizons. Pisces and Virgo will play fantastic roles.

**Tuesday, July 15 (Moon in Aquarius)**    You'll be surprised at the amount of money invested in home or property. You will be told, "If you want it done right you will have to spend money!" Maintain your emotional equilibrium. Cancer and Capricorn will play "steadying" roles.

**Wednesday, July 16 (Moon in Aquarius to Pisces 11:14 a.m.)**    Let go of a situation that drains you financially or emotionally. You deserve more freedom of thought and of action. Someone takes you for granted and thus takes advantage. Have no more of it! Aries and Libra figure in this scenario.

**Thursday, July 17 (Moon in Pisces)**    Focus on creativity, variety, romance. Imprint your style, wear bright colors. Don't follow others—original thinking is the key to success and happiness. A romantic Leo could win your heart. Be careful. You deserve the best; make sure you get it!

**Friday, July 18 (Moon in Pisces to Aries 7:19 p.m.)**    A family member confides, "I am in love and don't know what to do about it!" Don't get caught up in a love triangle; be sympathetic, but remain neutral. An excellent dinner tonight will help heal frayed nerves. A Cancer is involved.

**Saturday, July 19 (Moon in Aries)**    What begins as an "impossible task" will turn out to be easy, even fun. Your property value is subject to change. An Aquarius plays a key role in this area. Gemini and Sagittarius will also be involved. Accept an invitation to a prestigious social affair. Your lucky number is 3.

**Sunday, July 20 (Moon in Aries)**    Start a conditioning program; keep resolutions about exercise and diet. As obstacles are overcome, spiritual values surface. Energy makes a dramatic comeback. You are going to emerge victorious despite the odds. Taurus is represented.

**Monday, July 21 (Moon in Aries to Taurus 6:47 a.m.)** Time is on your side. Refuse to be rushed into making a snap decision. Take notes, read and write, perhaps start a diary. Gemini, Virgo, and Sagittarius will play outstanding roles and have these initials in their names: E, N, W. Your lucky number is 5.

**Tuesday, July 22 (Moon in Taurus)**    Remain close to home. Repairs are required. Decorate and remodel. Today's scenario also features flowers, music, romance—your love is not unrequited. A family member needs you and says so. Libra and Taurus play mysterious roles.

**Wednesday, July 23 (Moon in Taurus to Gemini 7:41 p.m.)**    At the track: post position special—number 1 p.p. in the seventh race. Hot daily doubles: 3 and 4, 1 and 5, 6 and 2. Away from the track, see people and relationships as they are and not merely as you wish they could be. A Pisces is in this picture.

**Thursday, July 24 (Moon in Gemini)**    Money comes from a surprise source. You are involved with a financial transaction and very much involved in a relationship. You will be told in no uncertain terms: "This is your life!" Focus on distribution, promotion, and more harmonious dealings with superiors.

**Friday, July 25 (Moon in Gemini)**    Someone you care about seems suddenly to have become invisible. Be

206

patient; finish what you start. Answers are found in arcane literature. An interest in the mantic arts will increase. You will find astrology of immense help.

**Saturday, July 26 (Moon in Gemini to Cancer 7:22 a.m.)**
Lucky lottery: 1, 4, 33, 12, 18, 22. Make a new start. Exercise independence, creativity, and original thinking. A love relationship blossoms. Make an important concession here, and be ready to take a chance on romance. This applies no matter what your age.

**Sunday, July 27 (Moon in Cancer)**  Focus on your home, family, and marital status. No matter how far you go from home, you will be called back. Don't neglect details, especially plumbing. Cancer and Capricorn will play instrumental roles. Get legal papers in order.

**Monday, July 28 (Moon in Cancer to Leo 4:15 p.m.)**  Be sure your roofing can "withstand" inclement weather. The spotlight is on direction, motivation, and the need for meditation. Look beyond the immediate. Attend a social gathering where you could meet someone destined to play an important role in your life.

**Tuesday, July 29 (Moon in Leo)**  The new moon in Leo is in your tenth house; this relates to your career and dealings with authorities, perhaps governmental representatives. Stress showmanship. Let it be known that you are alive and kicking. Leo, Taurus, and another Scorpio will play astounding roles.

**Wednesday, July 30 (Moon in Leo to Virgo 10:25 p.m.)**  By writing, you gain prestige and a possible promotion. Someone of the opposite sex could be bold enough to state, "There are times when I can hardly keep my hands off you!" Don't believe everything you hear. Your lucky number is 5.

**Thursday, July 31 (Moon in Virgo)**     On this last day of July, the emphasis will be on public relations, your reputation, and legal rights. If single, you could meet your future mate. Married or single, you need to cooperate with someone familiar with rules and regulations.

## AUGUST 2003

**Friday, August 1 (Moon in Virgo)**     Despite objections by some who lack faith, you move ahead and hurdle the obstacles. Taurus, Leo, and another Scorpio become your strong allies. Read the fine print; be aware of the hidden clauses in any agreement. Display strength of your convictions.

**Saturday, August 2 (Moon in Virgo to Libra 2:46 a.m.)**     Get ready for change, travel, and a variety of sensations. A discovery is made by entering an area previously prohibited. Communicate with someone you care about who is confined to home or hospital. Written material is important, providing an outlet for your creative surge.

**Sunday, August 3 (Moon in Libra)**     Attention revolves around your home and family as well as a romantic interlude that lends spice. A family member has been keeping a secret; you will learn about it tonight. Don't fear the unknown. Stand tall, have courage. A Libra is involved.

**Monday, August 4 (Moon in Libra to Scorpio 6:11 a.m.)** Define terms. Insist on answers, not evasions. Your cycle moves up, and circumstances take a dramatic turn in your favor. Choose quality; don't accept secondhand goods. Pisces and Virgo play outstanding roles. Have luck with number 7.

*Tuesday, August 5 (Moon in Scorpio)*   You'll have things your way. So you have to ask yourself, "What is my way?" Accent your personality, make new contacts, wear bright colors. Elements of timing and luck ride with you. Don't get in your own way. A Capricorn is involved.

*Wednesday, August 6 (Moon in Scorpio to Sagittarius 9:10 a.m.)*   Lucky lottery: 9, 12, 18, 13, 33, 22. Look beyond the immediate. You have the ability to predict the future, especially your own. Steer clear of those who take you for granted. A love relationship gets warm, if you can stand the heat!

*Thursday, August 7 (Moon in Sagittarius)*   What you learned 24 hours ago will be put to use tonight. Focus on original thinking, independence, and the courage of your convictions. Leo and Aquarius play astonishing roles and have these letters or initials in their names: A, S, J. Your lucky number is 1.

*Friday, August 8 (Moon in Sagittarius to Capricorn 12:02 p.m.)*   On this Friday, the question of your marital status could loom large. The moon is in your second house, which has to do with personal possessions and locating lost articles. An opportunity will exist to increase your income. A Cancer is involved.

*Saturday, August 9 (Moon in Capricorn)*   Highlight your versatility and intellectual curiosity. Be with people who are not afraid to state their views on politics. Ignore someone who attempts to "put you down." Gemini and Sagittarius will play encouraging roles. Have luck with number 3.

*Sunday, August 10 (Moon in Capricorn to Aquarius 3:23 p.m.)*   You will be dubbed an "indispensable person." Prove your worth by attending to details overlooked by others. Taurus, Leo, and another Scorpio play major roles. A relative requests that you join in a short trip to retrieve your legal papers.

*Monday, August 11 (Moon in Aquarius)*    Get ready for the unusual! Read and write. A flirtation will lend spice. Examine claims in connection with real estate. Don't get caught up in a whirlwind of illusion. Gain is indicated by writing your experiences.

*Tuesday, August 12 (Moon in Aquarius to Pisces 8:18 p.m.)*    The full moon in Aquarius is in your fourth house, relating to where you live. A romantic involvement gets serious. If you are single, it could lead to marriage. If you are married, there could be an addition to your family quite soon. A Taurus is in this picture.

*Wednesday, August 13 (Moon in Pisces)*    At the track: post position special— number 3 p.p. in the fifth race. Hot daily doubles: 1 and 7, 3 and 5, 1 and 1. Away from the track, avoid self-deception. Maintain your emotional equilibrium. You could find yourself in the throes of a hot romance.

*Thursday, August 14 (Moon in Pisces)*    Money is involved—invest in your own capabilities. Going into business for yourself would be a good idea. Get priorities in order. Let it be known: "I am running things!" Capricorn and Cancer will play significant roles.

*Friday, August 15 (Moon in Pisces to Aries 3:59 a.m.)* Keep resolutions about health. Be friendly with a coworker who shares your basic interests. Let go of a losing proposition. Welcome the chance for a reunion with a loved one. In any color scheme, involve red. A long journey provides a way to reorganize priorities.

*Saturday, August 16 (Moon in Aries)*    The Aries moon relates to an "aggressive" coworker. Focus on creativity as well as a different kind of love. Let it be known: "I am not to be taken for granted!" Leo and Aquarius will play mysterious roles. Have luck with number 1.

*Sunday, August 17 (Moon in Aries to Taurus 2:52 a.m.)* Play the waiting game. Don't be too available. Let others play a guessing game. Focus on giving service, fulfilling basic needs. Be creatively selfish. This means raise your self-esteem. The emphasis is on cooperative efforts and proposals of partnership or marriage.

*Monday, August 18 (Moon in Taurus)* Give full play to intellectual inquiries, especially those involving legalities. The question of your marital status will loom large. Check legal rights and permissions. Social activities accelerate. Avoid scattering your forces.

*Tuesday, August 19 (Moon in Taurus)* Don't ask for more than you can handle. Details have yet to be ironed out. Focus on public relations, learning who really is your friend and otherwise. If you are single, the question of marriage could be raised yet again. A Taurus is involved.

*Wednesday, August 20 (Moon in Taurus to Gemini 3:40 a.m.)* Lucky lottery: 5, 3, 35, 18, 22, 1. The emphasis is on a variety of experiences and an ability to express yourself in writing. A flirtation lends spice, but be ready to move on. Gemini, Virgo, and Sagittarius play major roles.

*Thursday, August 21 (Moon in Gemini)* Attention revolves around the necessity for remaining on familiar ground. This is not the time for "getting away." A family member needs you and will say so. If you do go away, you will be called back. Check interest rates, and be wary concerning investments.

*Friday, August 22 (Moon in Gemini to Cancer 3:43 p.m.)*     Avoid self-deception. Someone attempts to pull the wool over your eyes. Within 24 hours, you learn about a proposed journey that could include a foreign land. Communicate via advertising and publishing. Pisces plays a significant role.

*Saturday, August 23 (Moon in Cancer)*     On this Saturday, get ready for a "lively night." A relationship intensifies and could get too hot not to cool down. The lunar aspect promotes sensuality, creativity, and romance. Capricorn and Cancer figure in this scenario. Your lucky number is 8.

*Sunday, August 24 (Moon in Cancer)*     A very hot relationship could get under way. No fooling around! If not serious, move on. The "other person" wants it to last. Aries and Libra will play substantial roles. You will know them by the initials I and R in their names. Your lucky number is 9.

*Monday, August 25 (Moon in Cancer to Leo 12:46 a.m.)*     Everything points to creativity, imprinting your own style. Don't follow others; let them follow you. Emphasize original thinking and the courage of your convictions. Your professional superior wants to consult with you. It results in promotion and more responsibility.

*Tuesday, August 26 (Moon in Leo)*     The Leo moon is in your tenth house. This relates to promotion, distribution, and taking charge of a huge operation. A family member expresses the desire to redecorate and remodel in order to make the home beautiful. Agree, if at all possible.

*Wednesday, August 27 (Moon in Leo to Virgo 6:25 a.m.)*     The new moon in Virgo relates to your eleventh house; many of your hopes and wishes can be fulfilled. You win friends and influence people. Arrange a social gathering among those who have a sense of humor and intellectual curiosity.

**Thursday, August 28 (Moon in Virgo)**     An obstacle that appeared to be immovable will move due to your efforts. You will have luck in matters of speculation by sticking with number 4. Rewrite, review, rebuild; this is your makeover day. A Taurus is in this picture.

**Friday, August 29 (Moon in Virgo to Libra 9:40 a.m.)** Within 24 hours, mysterious happenings take place. Look behind the scenes; do not fear the unknown. Read and write, express feelings, publicize charitable events. Gemini, Virgo, and Sagittarius will boost your morale.

**Saturday, August 30 (Moon in Libra)**     A secret is revealed. Follow subtle clues that could lead to riches. You require "private time" in order to meditate. What once "disappeared" will make a dramatic reappearance. Taurus and Libra figure in this scenario.

**Sunday, August 31 (Moon in Libra to Scorpio 11:59 a.m.)**     On this last day of August, see people and relationships in a realistic light. The moon in your twelfth house means temporary confinement, an aura of mystery, intrigue. People want to know everything about your personal life. Don't tell all; don't confide or confess.

# SEPTEMBER 2003

**Monday, September 1 (Moon in Scorpio)**     On this first day of the month, your cycle is high. Read, write, learn by teaching. Others find you attractive, but you could get involved in a "complicated flirtation." If only playing games, you will pay the price. Know it and respond accordingly.

*Tuesday, September 2 (Moon in Scorpio to Sagittarius 2:31 p.m.)* A domestic adjustment is featured. This could involve a possible change of residence or marital status. Almost effortlessly, you will be at the right place at a special time. Your judgment and intuition are on target. A Taurus is featured.

*Wednesday, September 3 (Moon in Sagittarius)* Lucky lottery: 6, 13, 7, 4, 14, 12. Lie low, play the waiting game. Time is on your side, so don't equate delay with defeat. Someone wants to trip you up—don't give them the satisfaction. Be sure shoes fit well; don't let your vanity cause discomfort.

*Thursday, September 4 (Moon in Sagittarius to Capricorn 5:50 p.m.)* There are ways to increase your income—you will find them! Focus on promotion, more responsibility, and ways of distribution. Someone you care about will seek advice. Give it without taking sides. Walk a fine line between being helpful and going where you don't belong.

*Friday, September 5 (Moon in Capricorn)* Be finished with someone who takes you for granted. Today's scenario highlights trips, visits, and relatives who feel they know best how to live your life. Finish what you start. Participate in an idealistic project. An Aries plays a dramatic role.

*Saturday, September 6 (Moon in Capricorn to Aquarius 10:14 p.m.)* Answer: Affirmative. It is time for a new start in a different direction. A short trip is necessary to obtain a legal document. Refuse to be held back by the lack of a "signed paper." Imprint your style; don't follow others. Have luck with number 1.

*Sunday, September 7 (Moon in Aquarius)* Within 24 hours, you locate what you have been looking for in connection with your property or home. Stick to rules and regulations. By so doing, you avoid future complications. Taurus, Leo, and another Scorpio will play featured roles.

**Monday, September 8 (Moon in Aquarius)**  Your property will look wonderful, but could be "too shaky." Spread your emotional wings, but know where and why you are flying. Don't scatter your forces. Gemini and Sagittarius will help you when most needed. Your lucky number is 3.

**Tuesday, September 9 (Moon in Aquarius to Pisces 4:06 a.m.)**  Be willing to revise, review, rewrite, and rebuild. This is your "makeover" day. Wear your hair in a different style. People will comment, "You look different. Everything about you is wonderful!" Taurus, Leo, and another Scorpio play key roles.

**Wednesday, September 10 (Moon in Pisces)**  At the track: post position special—number 3 p.p. in the second race. Hot daily doubles: 2 and 3, 5 and 5, 4 and 6. Away from the track, play with passion. The full moon in Pisces is in your fifth house, which equates to creative projects, a variety of sensations, and intense romance.

**Thursday, September 11 (Moon in Pisces to Aries 12:09 p.m.)**  During this time, you could change your residence or marital status. Focus on change, travel, and unusual experiences. Maintain creative control while you share your skill and talent. The "right people" take notice. You could be knocking on the doors of fame and fortune.

**Friday, September 12 (Moon in Aries)**  Keep resolutions about your general health. Revise work methods. Don't lose sleep over a minor problem. Define terms. Avoid self-deception. Someone you trust could mean well, but lacks financing. Maintain an aura of mystery and intrigue.

**Saturday, September 13 (Moon in Aries to Taurus 10:49 p.m.)**   You are doing it correctly! Some people, feeling they know more than they actually do, will tell you otherwise. This is your power play day. Do things your way; it will be the right way. Capricorn and Cancer will play involved roles.

**Sunday, September 14 (Moon in Taurus)**   A legal document could arrive tomorrow. Complete a project you have been working on. What you finish could have international implications. The prospect of a journey overseas is a distinct possibility. A reunion tonight is with someone you once loved.

**Monday, September 15 (Moon in Taurus)**   The emphasis is on partnership or marriage. You will be closely observed concerning legal rights and permissions. Accent original thinking. Take a chance on romance. There will be spice in your life, which will mark an end to boredom. A Leo figures prominently.

**Tuesday, September 16 (Moon in Taurus to Gemini 11:31 a.m.)**   Check your property rights. A family member is sincere, but could be sincerely misinformed. Focus on local politics, cooperative efforts, and proposals of partnership or marriage. You can afford to play the waiting game.

**Wednesday, September 17 (Moon in Gemini)**   Lucky lottery: 3, 5, 35, 22, 18, 16. Avoid trying to please everyone; that is the sure road to madness. Arrange a social gathering that includes those with definite political views. A clash of ideas will prove exciting and informative.

***Thursday, September 18 (Moon in Gemini)*** Rebuild.
Find out where financial backing can be made available.
Many answers are found by studying arcane literature.
Keep an open mind without being naive. A romantic
rendezvous is fun, but could prove expensive. Maintain
your emotional equilibrium.

***Friday, September 19 (Moon in Gemini to Cancer 12:06
a.m.)*** Someone you once loved is now becoming a
pest. Know when to say, "Enough!" A romantic interlude has run its course. If you stop now, there will be
no ill feelings and no one will be hurt. Your Scorpio
passion surfaces; don't let go!

***Saturday, September 20 (Moon in Cancer)*** A long-
distance communication verifies your opinions. Find
someone who can represent your talent or product in a
foreign nation. Keep your plans flexible. Read and write;
learn through the process of teaching others. Your popularity rises—people want to wine and dine you.

***Sunday, September 21 (Moon in Cancer to Leo 10:00
a.m.)*** A favorable lunar aspect coincides with philosophy, psychology, and theology. A family member has
much to tell you; show that you are willing to listen. A
long journey could mark the conclusion of a search.
Pisces and Virgo play fascinating roles.

***Monday, September 22 (Moon in Leo)*** This could be
your lucky day, especially if you stick with number 8.
Focus on promotion, distribution, and added recognition.
On a personal level, you might become involved in a
relationship that goes all the way, including marriage. A
Capricorn is represented.

***Tuesday, September 23 (Moon in Leo to Virgo 4:03
p.m.)*** A chance exists for international recognition as
well as participation in a humanitarian project. Look be-

yond the immediate. Advertise and publish. A relationship begins or ends. By tonight, the answers become crystal clear.

**Wednesday, September 24 (Moon in Virgo)**    At the track: post position special—number 7 p.p. in the first race. Hot daily doubles: 6 and 3, 1 and 7, 3 and 5. Away from the track, wear bright colors so that people know you are alive and kicking. A new kind of love requires that you maintain your emotional equilibrium.

**Thursday, September 25 (Moon in Virgo to Libra 6:48 p.m.)**    Refuse to be limited by those who lack talent or faith. Look beyond the immediate. You can perceive the future and make it come true. Analyze published material, which could provide the answer to a dilemma. A Cancer is involved.

**Friday, September 26 (Moon in Libra)**    Give full play to your intellectual curiosity. Late last night's new moon in Libra represents your twelfth house. This relates to theaters, hospitals, institutions, and secrets. You gain a new way of looking at people and places; what was previously hidden is revealed. A Gemini is involved.

**Saturday, September 27 (Moon in Libra to Scorpio 7:51 p.m.)**    Don't let details elude you. What was held back will be released; there are flaws not previously detected. Let others know that you are "in the know." Once this is established, you could gain access to pertinent data. A Taurus is involved.

**Sunday, September 28 (Moon in Scorpio)**    Keep your mind open to ideas concerning theology. Your lunar cycle is high. You live and learn, and find there is spice in your life. Write your thoughts; take note of dreams. Tonight's dream, properly interpreted, could be a guidepost to the future.

*Monday, September 29 (Moon in Scorpio to Sagittarius 8:56 p.m.)*    On this Monday, a domestic adjustment is necessary. Make intelligent concessions, without abandoning your principles. The moon in your sign emphasizes your personality and sex appeal. Don't break any hearts. The heart you break could be your own. A Libra is involved.

*Tuesday, September 30 (Moon in Sagittarius)*    On this last day of September, be sure to visit someone temporarily confined to home or hospital. Define terms. Get commitments in writing. A money promise will be paid following a delay. There is a "hidden matter" you can learn about tonight.

# OCTOBER 2003

*Wednesday, October 1 (Moon in Sagittarius to Capricorn 11:21 p.m.)*    Money that had been held back will be released. Yes, you waited and won. A domestic adjustment could include an actual change of residence or marital status. You should be dealing with or corresponding with people in distant cities and foreign lands.

*Thursday, October 2 (Moon in Capricorn)*    Within 24 hours, you will feel: "I have the right to enjoy success!" Focus on exclusivity, without making yourself too available. Maintain your aura of mystery, of intrigue. Be selective; choose top quality. A Virgo is involved.

*Friday, October 3 (Moon in Capricorn)*    This can be your power play day, if you so permit. The waiting game is over. Get your fair share, and let others know you mean business. On a personal level, a relationship is hot and heavy. A short trip involves a relative who needs your cooperation.

*Saturday, October 4 (Moon in Capricorn to Aquarius 3:45 a.m.)* Keep plans flexible. You could get a sudden notice that travel is imminent. Look beyond the immediate, but finish what you start. A romantic involvement lends spice. Refuse to give up something of value for nothing. Your lucky number is 9.

*Sunday, October 5 (Moon in Aquarius)* You are on more solid ground, so let go of preconceived notions. Create, invent! Give and receive love. You will be with talented, temperamental people—maintain your own emotional equilibrium. Make personal appearances.

*Monday, October 6 (Moon in Aquarius to Pisces 10:20 a.m.)* Focus on where you live and the need to decorate or remodel. The feeling of being confined is only temporary. You get solid backing. Your family will be on your side. The emphasis is on proposals that include partnership or marriage.

*Tuesday, October 7 (Moon in Pisces)* The emphasis is on social activity and creative projects. You will be flattered by a special member of the opposite sex. You will entertain and be entertained. Today's scenario highlights the excitement of change, travel, and variety. Have luck with number 3.

*Wednesday, October 8 (Moon in Pisces to Aries 7:07 p.m.)* Lucky lottery: 4, 7, 12, 17, 6, 26. Be willing to revise, review, rewrite; this could be your "makeover" day. The moon in Pisces represents your fifth house, which relates to children and a variety of sensations. A Taurus is in the picture.

*Thursday, October 9 (Moon in Aries)* Keep resolutions about diet and exercise. Your energy level will soar, if you so permit. The employment picture will be clarified. Let things run at home as well as at work. Gemini, Virgo, and Sagittarius will play featured roles.

*Friday, October 10 (Moon in Aries)* Focus on beauty, art, music, and the ability to make your home attractive. The full moon in Aries represents your sixth house, which relates to your ability to persevere in the job at hand. Someone who shares your interests will pay a meaningful compliment.

*Saturday, October 11 (Moon in Aries to Taurus 6:04 a.m.)* Don't get emotionally involved with one who takes you for granted and would like to "take you." Define terms. Know when to say, "Enough!" An aura of deception exists, deliberate or otherwise. Pisces and Virgo figure in this scenario.

*Sunday, October 12 (Moon in Taurus)* Lie low, play the waiting game. Be careful about signing a document. You do not have a clear picture now. If you wait, you will ultimately win. Don't be cajoled into making a snap decision. Cancer and Capricorn play major roles.

*Monday, October 13 (Moon in Taurus to Gemini 6:44 p.m.)* A legal agreement might be over when you thought it was just beginning. You discover hidden clauses; what appeared on the surface was not the complete story. Remember once again: "All that glitters is not gold." Aries and Libra will play outstanding roles.

*Tuesday, October 14 (Moon in Gemini)* A mystery is solved, to your advantage. You learn where the money is and how it got that way. Wipe the slate clean. Get rid of preconceived notions. Maintain creative control. It is your style and talent people want. A Leo is represented.

*Wednesday, October 15 (Moon in Gemini)* Look beyond the immediate. Decide on your future direction and

motivation. Many answers will be available, if you meditate. Focus on cooperative efforts, partnership, and marriage. Keep diet resolutions; tonight you will enjoy a
seafood dinner.

*Thursday, October 16 (Moon in Gemini to Cancer 7:39
a.m.)* Your cycle moves up. What had blocked your
way will be removed. A contact made at a recent social
gathering will prove valuable. Give full play to your intellectual curiosity. Gemini and Sagittarius play mysterious
roles. Your lucky number is 3.

*Friday, October 17 (Moon in Cancer)* Long-range
plans crystallize. Focus on advertising and publishing; be
sure your material is circulated in a foreign land. By
rewriting, you will be assured of acceptance. A Taurus
and another Scorpio figure in this scenario.

*Saturday, October 18 (Moon in Cancer to Leo 6:40
p.m.)* Written material brings recognition. On a personal level, there will be spice in your life. Someone of
the opposite sex declares, "I can hardly keep my hands
off you!" This elevates your morale, but don't believe
everything you hear. A Sagittarius is involved.

*Sunday, October 19 (Moon in Leo)* Blend your career with domestic life. Make an intelligent concession,
but don't abandon your principles. If single, you could
meet your future mate. Married or single, make your
home more comfortable and attractive. Another Scorpio
is involved.

*Monday, October 20 (Moon in Leo)* Define terms.
Insist on answers, not evasions. Someone in a position
of authority seeks a meeting. Display your knowledge of
showmanship. You will be counted on to draw a crowd,
so wear bright colors. See people and relationships in a
realistic light.

*Tuesday, October 21 (Moon in Leo to Virgo 1:59 a.m.)* You might be saying, "It seems impossible, but my wishes are being fulfilled!" Elements of timing and luck ride with you. In matters of speculation, stick with number 8. A relationship is hot and heavy. You'll be involved, more than originally expected.

*Wednesday, October 22 (Moon in Virgo)* A project will be completed according to your specifications. A romance grows. Don't make promises you cannot keep. Long-range expectations are closer to fulfillment than might be anticipated. An Aries plays a spectacular role.

*Thursday, October 23 (Moon in Virgo to Libra 5:26 a.m.)* The answer to a question: Yes, this is the time to try something new. Emphasize innovativeness—your ability to invent, to create. Wear bright colors, including yellow and gold. Let others know you are alive and kicking. Leo and Aquarius figure in this scenario.

*Friday, October 24 (Moon in Libra)* What had been hidden will be revealed. This could relate to where you live and with whom. The focus is on your partnership or marital status. Keep health resolutions, especially in connection with your diet. Cancer and Capricorn will play amazing roles.

*Saturday, October 25 (Moon in Libra to Scorpio 6:07 a.m.)* The new moon in your sign emphasizes the possibility of a "new love." Circumstances are turning in your favor, even as you read these lines. Diversify! Highlight versatility and intellectual curiosity. Lucky lottery: 3, 12, 2, 20, 14, 17.

*Sunday, October 26—Daylight Saving Time Ends (Moon in Scorpio)* On this Sunday you will know that your love is not unrequited. Details relating to responsibility will become crystal clear. Check your plumbing and electricity. Be willing to rebuild, to rewrite, to make this your makeover day.

*Monday, October 27 (Moon in Scorpio to Sagittarius 4:54 a.m.)*    You receive a written notice that you have additional funds coming to you. It is important to budget assets. Your cycle continues high. You will be at the right place at a special moment. A Sagittarius will prove of immense help. Your lucky number is 5.

*Tuesday, October 28 (Moon in Sagittarius)*    At the track: post position special—number 3 p.p. in the fifth race. Hot daily doubles: 3 and 7, 4 and 6, 1 and 1. Away from the track, make a domestic adjustment that includes beautifying your surroundings. A Libra plays a helpful role.

*Wednesday, October 29 (Moon in Sagittarius to Capricorn 5:36 a.m.)*    A relative could involve you in a wild-goose chase, if you so permit. Be sure of what is expected of you. Be flexible, but don't scatter your forces. Avoid self-deception; see relationships in a realistic light. Pisces is represented.

*Thursday, October 30 (Moon in Capricorn)*    You get results based on previous efforts. Take special care in traffic; people tend to be careless at the wheel during this cycle. What you thought was finished will be revived. A relationship could run its course. A Capricorn plays a key role.

*Friday, October 31 (Moon in·Capricorn to Aquarius 8:41 a.m.)*    Steer clear of a bibulous individual. No matter what the costume, you won't be able to hide who you are. Know it and have fun, but don't attempt to deceive. Get rid of preconceived notions. On this Halloween, you can predict your future.

*Saturday, November 1 (Moon in Aquarius)*    Attention revolves around real estate, especially the sale or purchase of property. See people and relationships in a realistic light. Someone may want to deceive you; protect yourself in emotional clinches. Pisces and Virgo play mysterious roles.

*Sunday, November 2 (Moon in Aquarius to Pisces 2:52 p.m.)*    A payoff day when you get results of recent efforts, which can bring a substantial payment. Capricorn and Cancer will play outstanding roles. Spiritual values surface. Heed "inner messages." Refuse to be overwhelmed by a "salesperson."

*Monday, November 3 (Moon in Pisces)*    You'll be dealing with children who are restless, creative, and demanding. Let go of a losing proposition. Set the pace. Take charge of your destiny. A reunion tonight involves a romantic interlude. A Libra plays a fantastic role.

*Tuesday, November 4 (Moon in Pisces)*    Your powers of persuasion peak. Focus on the fulfillment of desires. Be careful what you ask for—you are likely to get it. Creative juices stir. You could be in love! Leo and Aquarius will "show the way." Your lucky number is 1.

*Wednesday, November 5 (Moon in Pisces to Aries 12:02 a.m.)*    Attention revolves around your home, family, and marital status. Meditate and answers will come from within. Keep recent diet resolutions. A seafood dinner tonight will be delicious and nourishing. A Cancer is involved.

*Thursday, November 6 (Moon in Aries)*    The emphasis is on getting the job done as well as stabilizing your sleep pattern. Highlight versatility. Bring together those of opposing political views. Gemini and Sagittarius play top roles and could have these letters or initials in their names: C, L, U.

**Friday, November 7 (Moon in Aries to Taurus 11:28 a.m.)**    At the track: post position special—number 3 p.p. in the fifth race. Hot daily doubles: 2 and 5, 4 and 4, 3 and 1. Away from the track, attend to details and study the fine print. The employment picture is emphasized; you'll be told what is upcoming.

**Saturday, November 8 (Moon in Taurus)**    Lucky lottery: 5, 7, 12, 13, 18, 43. Get ready for a change of direction. Keep your options open. A flirtation gets hot and heavy; know when to say, "Enough!" Gemini, Virgo, and Sagittarius play sensational roles and have these initials in their names: E, N, W.

**Sunday, November 9 (Moon in Taurus)**    Last night's full moon and lunar eclipse fell in Taurus, your seventh house. The spotlight is on partnership or your marital status. Be sure legal affairs are in order. A verdict or judgment will be upset. Domestic adjustment could result in a change of residence as well as marriage plans.

**Monday, November 10 (Moon in Taurus to Gemini 12:13 a.m.)**    Pay attention to what you see out of the corner of your eye. You could discover deception, deliberate or otherwise. Lie low; play the waiting game. Pisces and Virgo will edge their way into this scenario.

**Tuesday, November 11 (Moon in Gemini)**    A discovery is made concerning the financial status of someone close to you. Dig deep for information. Don't fear the occult. You're in the driver's seat, so act accordingly. Capricorn and Cancer play amazing roles. Have luck with number 8.

*Wednesday, November 12 (Moon in Gemini to Cancer 1:09 p.m.)*    Unless you obtain facts, let go of a situation. Let it be known you have had enough evasions. Communication is received from a distant city or foreign land. Your views will be verified. Aries and Libra will play major roles.

*Thursday, November 13 (Moon in Cancer)*    Your lucky number is 1. Creative juices stir. Physical attraction is much in evidence. Give logic equal time. Don't be swept off your feet. Stress independence and original thinking. A "different" kind of romance is on the horizon.

*Friday, November 14 (Moon in Cancer)*    Focus on your home, marital status, and decisions concerning direction and motivation. Keep diet resolutions. Consider where you are to live and with whom. Avoid brooding; accent meditation. A gift is received from a family member who had been anything but friendly.

*Saturday, November 15 (Moon in Cancer to Leo 12:46 a.m.)*    Diversify! Give full rein to your intellectual curiosity. Participate in social activities. You will meet someone destined to play an important role in your life. Gemini and Sagittarius act in a mysterious way. Your lucky number is 3.

*Sunday, November 16 (Moon in Leo)*    Good news is received; you passed a test with flying colors. A promotion is due; you could be in a position of authority. A passionate relationship runs its course, unless you do something about it. Taurus, Leo, and another Scorpio figure in this scenario.

*Monday, November 17 (Moon in Leo to Virgo 9:34 a.m.)*    The written word is important, so get thoughts and concepts on paper. A member of the opposite sex

227

confides, "At times, I can hardly keep my hands off you!" Don't believe everything you hear. Maintain your emotional equilibrium. Virgo is represented.

*Tuesday, November 18 (Moon in Virgo)*    A wish comes true in connection with your home or marital status. Music plays; march to your own tune. Beautify your quarters, including flowers and art. Taurus and Libra will play fantastic roles. If diplomatic, you win. If you force issues, you come up empty-handed.

*Wednesday, November 19 (Moon in Virgo to Libra 2:40 p.m.)*    Lucky lottery: 6, 13, 5, 22, 18, 1. Define terms. Ask for what you need; you will receive a gift of a luxury item. Avoid self-deception. Refuse to be taken for granted. Perfect techniques and streamline procedures. A Pisces plays a role.

*Thursday, November 20 (Moon in Libra)*    A secret meeting works to your advantage. What was kept confidential will be revealed. You'll be trusted to be discreet. Don't tell all; don't confide or confess. You gain prestige and a promotion. A Capricorn figures prominently.

*Friday, November 21 (Moon in Libra to Scorpio 4:22 p.m.)*    Today's Libra moon represents your twelfth house. Focus on institutions, hospitals, the theater. Get "in touch" with one temporarily confined to home. You will receive valid counsel. A reunion with someone you once loved is scheduled tonight.

*Saturday, November 22 (Moon in Scorpio)*    Don't hesitate to express your doubts or suspicions. Insist on proof in writing. You are due for a fresh start in a new direction. Avoid heavy lifting. Leo and Aquarius play significant roles and could have these letters in their names: A, S, J. Have luck with number 1.

*Sunday, November 23 (Moon in Scorpio to Sagittarius 4:02 p.m.)*   The new moon and solar eclipse fall in your sign. A change of scene occurs. You undergo a personality transformation. A personal relationship could be upset, which might work out to your advantage. Steer clear of explosives as well as heavy-drinking individuals.

*Monday, November 24 (Moon in Sagittarius)*   A money situation is solved. A young person has much to do with it. Be independent, not arrogant. Make an appointment to see someone in authority. But don't go hat in hand. Exude confidence. Today you have an abundance of sex appeal.

*Tuesday, November 25 (Moon in Sagittarius to Capricorn 3:31 p.m.)*   Funds that had been tied up will be released. A lost article is located. Your earning power increases. A family member confides, "I will need more than I originally requested!" Taurus, Leo, and another Scorpio figure in this scenario.

*Wednesday, November 26 (Moon in Capricorn)*   A short trip is necessary. A relative is involved. A legal document has been misplaced, but will be found on a shelf. Be prepared for a variety of experiences. Don't take a flirtation too lightly! Read and write; perhaps you should start a diary.

*Thursday, November 27 (Moon in Capricorn to Aquarius 4:48 p.m.)*   Be with your family, if possible. A relative visits to share the holiday. Inject humor into the proceedings. A traditional dinner will be fine. You will receive compliments. Enjoy this Thanksgiving. Taurus and Libra play meaningful roles.

*Friday, November 28 (Moon in Aquarius)*   Attention revolves around real estate, including the sale or purchase of a home. Be aware of the fine print and attend to details that include plumbing. Someone attempts to deceive you—protect yourself at close quarters. Pisces and Virgo will play stunning roles.

**Saturday, November 29 (Moon in Aquarius to Pisces 9:26 p.m.)**    Money changes hands—you play an instrumental role. A relationship gets hot and heavy. If merely playing games, look out! The other person is serious and expects a legal commitment. Capricorn and Cancer play fascinating roles and have these letters in their names: H, Q, Z.

**Sunday, November 30 (Moon in Pisces)**    Look beyond the immediate. A new, exciting relationship is on the horizon. If you are married, the spark that brought you together reignites. If single, you fall in love with your future mate. Aries and Libra will play "prophetic" roles.

# DECEMBER 2003

**Monday, December 1 (Moon in Pisces)**    You get off to a roaring start on this first day of the month. Your creative juices are activated. Highlight original thinking as well as new ways of distribution. Capricorn and Cancer play amazing roles and have these initials in their names: H, Q, Z.

**Tuesday, December 2 (Moon in Pisces to Aries 5:55 a.m.)**    Your creative project will succeed—it could be known internationally. Look beyond the immediate in connection with a personal relationship. Don't carry someone else's burden. Refuse to be taken for granted.

**Wednesday, December 3 (Moon in Aries)**    Keep recent resolutions about your health. Be careful about your diet. Make a fresh start. Emphasize original thinking. Be independent in thought and in action. Wear bright colors, including yellow or gold. Have luck with number 1.

*Thursday, December 4 (Moon in Aries to Taurus 5:29 p.m.)* Blend work methods with domestic duties. The focus is on your home, especially emotional security with a partner. You'll be asked to cooperate in a local political situation. Proposals received include partnership or marriage. A Cancer is involved.

*Friday, December 5 (Moon in Taurus)* Accept a social invitation. You will receive news about a legal document. Be amiable, but stick to your principles. Legal affairs dominate—take nothing for granted where the law is concerned. A Sagittarius plays a role.

*Saturday, December 6 (Moon in Taurus)* Legal pitfalls are present, so be thorough and aware of hidden clauses. Someone tells you something—it is not the entire truth. See people and relationships as they actually exist. Revise, review, rewrite. Another Scorpio is involved.

*Sunday, December 7 (Moon in Taurus to Gemini 6:25 a.m.)* Be analytical. Find out why something occurred. Your marital status figures prominently. A frank discussion with someone who would be your partner is necessary. Gemini, Virgo, and Sagittarius play unusual roles and have these letters in their names: E, N, W.

*Monday, December 8 (Moon in Gemini)* The full moon in Gemini represents your eighth house. Emotions take over, and you feel you really are in love. Be careful—you could be involved in a "triangle." Maintain your emotional equilibrium. Taurus, Libra, and another Scorpio figure in this scenario.

*Tuesday, December 9 (Moon in Gemini to Cancer 7:10 p.m.)* Promised funding has not been canceled, so don't equate delay with defeat. What you need will be forthcoming. Play the waiting game. Time is on your side. Mysterious circumstances are involved—someone who attempts deception will be caught red-handed.

**Wednesday, December 10 (Moon in Cancer)**  Don't mix up fiction with fact. Dig deep for information about the financial status of someone who makes grandiose promises. An individual who wants to be your representative should show proof of capabilities. Capricorn and Cancer play astounding roles.

**Thursday, December 11 (Moon in Cancer)**  An intense relationship is featured—this could be the beginning or the end. Check your travel plans. It is not unlikely that you could be visiting a foreign nation. Participate in a humanitarian project. An Aries figures in this scenario.

**Friday, December 12 (Moon in Cancer to Leo 6:39 a.m.)**  Emphasize original thinking and independence. Insist on maintaining creative control. You are due for a new start in a different direction. Don't follow others. Create your own tradition! A romance gets too hot not to cool down. A Leo is involved.

**Saturday, December 13 (Moon in Leo)**  A Capricorn who wants to "sign you up" should be told, "Show me the money!" Keep your options open. Don't be cajoled into making a snap decision. Your marital status figures prominently; have documents at hand, including a birth certificate.

**Sunday, December 14 (Moon in Leo to Virgo 4:05 p.m.)**  Spiritual values surface. Someone you admire will return the compliment. You are on your way to "bigger things," if you so permit. Don't give up something of value for nothing. A passionate relationship puts you on edge. Strive to maintain your emotional equilibrium.

**Monday, December 15 (Moon in Virgo)**     Be willing to tear down in order to rebuild. What you "imagine" could be transformed into reality. Be analytical. Also be careful what you ask for, because you are very likely to receive it. Elements of timing and luck ride with you; stick with number 4.

**Tuesday, December 16 (Moon in Virgo to Libra 10:44 p.m.)**     At the track, choose horses and jockeys with these letters in their names: E, N, W. Post position special—number 5 p.p. in the third race. Hot daily doubles: 1 and 6, 5 and 7, 3 and 8. Away from the track, read, write, and learn through the process of teaching.

**Wednesday, December 17 (Moon in Libra)**     A family secret will be out in the open. Don't make a federal case of it. No finger-pointing, please! Be diplomatic, remain calm. Money will be replaced. Music plays, so dance to your own tune. Make your home beautiful by decorating and remodeling.

**Thursday, December 18 (Moon in Libra)**     Be discreet. Don't tell all; don't confide or confess. You will have access to classified information. Get a definition of terms; also be sure promises are in writing. Deception could be involved, deliberate or otherwise. A secret meeting occurs tonight.

**Friday, December 19 (Moon in Libra to Scorpio 2:18 a.m.)**     Get ready for a lively weekend! The lunar cycle is high, so you will be at the right place at a special moment almost effortlessly. Your personality sparkles. Others find you sexually attractive. Don't fall head over heels. Keep your balance; don't go below your station.

*Saturday, December 20 (Moon in Scorpio)*    Finish what you start. Imprint your style. Stress original thinking. A promise has not been broken; a delivery was delayed. Wear bright colors as you make personal appearances. Your cycle continues high; therefore, people want to read what you write and hear what you say.

*Sunday, December 21 (Moon in Scorpio to Sagittarius 3:14 a.m.)*    Spiritual values are much in evidence. State your beliefs, speaking from the heart. Leo and Aquarius will be very much attuned. As your creative juices stir, you could undergo a "revelation." Guard your possessions; you receive news that a lost article has been located.

*Monday, December 22 (Moon in Sagittarius)*    A special collection turns out to be worth more than you originally expected. Luck rides with you, if you stick to home base. Pay attention to a minor digestive problem; keep resolutions about your diet. A Capricorn is involved.

*Tuesday, December 23 (Moon in Sagittarius to Capricorn 2:55 a.m.)*    The new moon in Capricorn represents your third house. Take special care in traffic. Arrange a new deal with a relative. There's social activity tonight. Laugh at your own foibles so that others will also laugh at their foolishness.

*Wednesday, December 24 (Moon in Capricorn)*    On this Christmas Eve, you receive gifts that are heavy in weight. You will enjoy the holiday and recognize some of its real meaning. Taurus, Leo, and another Scorpio figure in this scenario. Puzzle pieces will fall into place.

*Thursday, December 25 (Moon in Capricorn to Aquarius 3:13 a.m.)*    Stay close to home. Celebrate the holiday with your family. Written material is important. Write and read your thoughts about the "greatest story ever told." That "heavy" gift turns out to be something you wanted but could not afford.

*Friday, December 26 (Moon in Aquarius)*     Attention revolves around your home and the ability to beautify your surroundings. Music is involved. Your voice is different. Some comment, "It is melodious." Romance figures prominently. What you yearned for will come true.

*Saturday, December 27 (Moon in Aquarius to Pisces 6:09 a.m.)*     Look beyond the immediate. Be sure it is love and not mere infatuation. Keep your options open, because instructions and directions are subject to sudden change. You undergo a variety of sensations. You will be assured that your love is not unrequited. A Pisces is involved.

*Sunday, December 28 (Moon in Pisces)*     Someone who disappointed you in the past will more than make up for it tonight. Be open-minded, but not naive. Give and receive love. Remember it is human to err, but divine to forgive. Capricorn and Cancer will play dramatic roles.

*Monday, December 29 (Moon in Pisces to Aries 1:09 p.m.)*     Get ready for New Year's Eve. You could be the life of the party, but go easy on adult beverages. Steer clear of heavy drinkers. Stay with someone who takes you seriously and would not hurt you for the world. Aries is represented.

*Tuesday, December 30 (Moon in Aries)*     Keep resolutions about your general health, exercise, and diet. Check the invitation list—don't forget someone who will arrive from out of town. A splendid celebration, if you stick to home base. Leo and Aquarius liven things and do care about you!

*Wednesday, December 31 (Moon in Aries)* The accent is on moderation. Be with family, if possible. You receive proposals that involve business and marriage. If you are married, make a resolution that you will remain together. If single, you could meet your future mate. A Cancer plays an important role.

## HAPPY NEW YEAR!

## JANUARY 2004

*Thursday, January 1 (Moon in Aries to Taurus 12:03 a.m.)* On this first day of the year, you are likely to be in a "dreamy state." Strive to define terms and to make this a day of self-revelation. Accent health: pace yourself where work is concerned. Pisces and Virgo will play memorable roles.

*Friday, January 2 (Moon in Taurus)* Be observant where contractual obligations are concerned. The lunar position highlights legal affairs, public image, and marriage. Focus also on time to be alone in order to organize your thoughts and to meditate. Capricorn and Cancer will play unorthodox roles.

*Saturday, January 3 (Moon in Taurus to Gemini 12:57 p.m.)* On this Saturday, be ready to encounter a "world traveler." It could be a romantic time, when a relationship could begin or end. Steer clear of someone who constantly takes you for granted. Look beyond the immediate. Dare to dream! Aries and Libra will play fascinating roles. Your lucky number is 9.

*Sunday, January 4 (Moon in Gemini)* Highlight inventiveness. Accent independence of thought and of action. The answer to your question: This is the time to imprint your own style and to think seriously of going into business for yourself. Those who accuse you of selfish motives are envious. Leo and Aquarius are involved.

**Monday, January 5 (Moon in Gemini)**    This could be a day during which you create "favorable memories." You learn more about where you are going and why you are here. Your philosophical concepts come into sharp, clear focus. Don't be afraid of the metaphysical or the occult. A Cancer plays a role.

**Tuesday, January 6 (Moon in Gemini to Cancer 1:39 a.m.)**    Within 24 hours, you receive an invitation to travel or to publish, or both. Your popularity increases. Your opinions will be sought concerning fashion and politics. Speak your mind. Frankness on your part will be much appreciated. Keep recent resolutions about exercise, diet, and knowledge of nutrition.

**Wednesday, January 7 (Moon in Cancer)**    The full moon in Cancer represents your ninth house. This relates to romance as well as dreams of long ago and far away. Keep an open mind without being naive. Review, rewrite, and rebuild. You have a marvelous opportunity to correct past mistakes. Another Scorpio is involved.

**Thursday, January 8 (Moon in Cancer to Leo 12:38 p.m.)**    Today's lunar aspect coincides with romance, creativity, and the ability to put ideas across via advertising and publishing. Gemini, Virgo, and Sagittarius will play "stunning" roles. These letters could be in their names: E, N, W. A flirtation could become serious.

**Friday, January 9 (Moon in Leo)**    At the track, choose number 6 post position in the sixth race. With the moon in Leo, this could be your lucky day! Focus on promotion and activity in connection with your business or career. Use your instinctive knowledge of publicity and showmanship. A Libra figures in this scenario.

**Saturday, January 10 (Moon in Leo to Virgo 9:38 p.m.)** There will be some delay, but ultimately your wish will be fulfilled. The package you have been waiting for could arrive by tonight. Make your terms crystal clear. Outline boundaries. See relationships as they are, not merely as you wish they could be. Pisces is represented.

**Sunday, January 11 (Moon in Virgo)** Within 24 hours, you could have a spectacular run of luck! Don't get in your own way. Accept goodwill and wishes in a gracious manner; avoid being obsequious. Tonight, a relationship intensifies; it could get too hot. If you don't want to handle it, make your feelings clear.

**Monday, January 12 (Moon in Virgo)** The moon is in your eleventh house. This relates to the fulfillment of hopes and wishes, especially in connection with communication and writing. You will be sought after. People want you to write resumes and references. Do what you can, but know when to say, "Enough is enough!"

**Tuesday, January 13 (Moon in Virgo to Libra 4:38 a.m.)** Take the initiative to make dreams come true. Wear brighter colors. Agree to personal appearances. The Virgo moon is on the cusp of your eleventh house. This means write letters and articles, start a diary or a book. Leo and Aquarius will play instrumental roles.

**Wednesday, January 14 (Moon in Libra)** Lucky lottery: 2, 12, 18, 22, 33, 15. Financial aid comes from an unusual source and could relate to partnership or marriage. You will feel more secure. You will love and be loved. Capricorn and Cancer figure in this dynamic scenario.

***Thursday, January 15 (Moon in Libra to Scorpio 9:33 a.m.)*** Focus on secrets. Observe the necessity for being discreet. You could be handling "classified information." Do not fall prey to false flattery. Some people want something for nothing, and you could be the prime target. Don't give them the satisfaction!

***Friday, January 16 (Moon in Scorpio)*** In your lunar cycle high, you will be at the right place at a crucial moment almost effortlessly. Highlight your personality. Realize that you exude sex appeal. Be discriminating. Don't let just anybody into your exclusive circle. Taurus, Leo, and another Scorpio will play dramatic roles.

***Saturday, January 17 (Moon in Scorpio to Sagittarius 12:19 p.m.)*** State your needs in a direct way. You get what you want by maintaining a confident attitude. Open the lines of communication. Bring up subjects usually considered "off-limits." A frank appraisal of your situation as it exists is necessary. A Virgo figures prominently.

***Sunday, January 18 (Moon in Sagittarius)*** Remain close to your family. What was lost will be recovered, including money. You receive an art object as a gift; accept this as a gesture of friendship and love. A domestic adjustment restores harmony at home. Bitterness will be erased. A family member makes a major concession.

***Monday, January 19 (Moon in Sagittarius to Capricorn 1:25 p.m.)*** Let optimism rule! You will discover that where you are is the right place for this time. You are thus relieved of an emotional burden. Refuse to give up something for nothing. Define terms—make things work your way. A Pisces figures in this scenario.

***Tuesday, January 20 (Moon in Capricorn)*** Someone you have mistrusted will prove his or her loyalty to you.

You will receive a promotion and added recognition. A relationship is too hot not to cool down. Don't play games with emotions; the heart you break could be your own. Capricorn is represented.

**Wednesday, January 21 (Moon in Capricorn to Aquarius 2:12 p.m.)** At the track, choose number 8 post position in the eighth race. Away from the track, complete a creative project. Your advice is sought concerning romance, love, and marriage. Aries and Libra will play stimulating roles. Someone you once loved will make a surprise appearance.

**Thursday, January 22 (Moon in Aquarius)** Last night's new moon in Aquarius activates your fourth house. This relates to home ground, the conclusion of a project, your family, and marriage. A new outlook is necessary. You will meet a fascinating Aquarius, but stay cool. Have luck with number 1.

**Friday, January 23 (Moon in Aquarius to Pisces 4:30 p.m.)** You will find suitable living quarters where your needs can be met. Realize it, and don't continue an unnecessary search. Sensitive feelings are involved, especially those of family members. Make intelligent concessions. This need not mean abandoning your principles.

**Saturday, January 24 (Moon in Pisces)** Accent diversity, versatility, and your intellectual curiosity. The Pisces moon relates to creativity, style, and sex appeal. Elevate your self-esteem. Do not settle for second best. A young person could accept you as a "role model." Don't disappoint others, or yourself. Your fortunate number is 3.

**Sunday, January 25 (Moon in Pisces to Aries 10:07 p.m.)** A creative endeavor will succeed despite a delay. Be aware of details, including proper measurements and fine print. Despite the odds, you will win. Taurus, Leo, and another Scorpio figure in this fascinating scenario. At the track, choose number 4 post position in the fourth race.

**Monday, January 26 (Moon in Aries)**    Get ready for change, travel, and a variety of "sensations." You will take better care of yourself, and those who care about you will help you to do so. Separate false flattery from the "real thing." Keep in mind: All that glitters is not gold!

**Tuesday, January 27 (Moon in Aries)**    Accent diplomacy. Pay more than usual attention to your family. The emphasis is on where you live and your marital status. An unassuming Taurus could win your heart, if you so permit. Libra and another Scorpio also play compelling roles and have these letters in their names: F, O, X.

**Wednesday, January 28 (Moon in Aries to Taurus 7:47 a.m.)**    Lucky lottery: 9, 19, 25, 34, 35, 36. Define terms. Keep health resolutions. Obey safety rules in connection with a unique task. Steer clear of those who take you for granted. Look behind the scenes. Someone wants to tell you something, but is too shy to approach you.

**Thursday, January 29 (Moon in Taurus)**    Lie low, get organized. Play your cards close to the chest. Don't tell all. Don't confide or confess. Keep secrets sacred; you'll be handling confidential information. Discretion truly is the better part of valor. Capricorn and Cancer figure in this scenario.

**Friday, January 30 (Moon in Taurus to Gemini 8:18 p.m.)**    The Taurus moon represents your seventh house. This relates to partnership and marriage. A legal agreement requires special attention. Don't take anything for granted! Look beyond the immediate. Dare to dream. Predict your future and make it come true. Love will play a major role.

**Saturday, January 31 (Moon in Gemini)**    On this last day of January, with the moon in Gemini, tread softly. Accent original thinking. Emphasize independence, creativity, and your pioneering spirit. At the track, choose number 1 post position in the first race. Tonight—love and laughter!

# FEBRUARY 2004

**Sunday, February 1 (Moon in Gemini)**    Although it is Sunday, your mind is filled with original, daring concepts. Communicate with someone of a metaphysical bent. Focus on organization as well as the recognition of priorities and how best to use them. Capricorn and Cancer figure in today's dynamic scenario.

**Monday, February 2 (Moon in Gemini to Cancer 9:03 a.m.)**    A relationship could begin or end. Look beyond the immediate to contemplate your future. Finish a project that could involve you in a humanitarian activity, perhaps in another land. This will certainly not be an ordinary Monday! An Aries is in the picture.

**Tuesday, February 3 (Moon in Cancer)**    What had been "abstract" will become crystal clear. A love relationship is restored. The spark that brought you together will reignite. Make a fresh start in a new direction. The answer to the question of a journey: Yes, go. You could encounter adventure and romance. Your lucky number is 1.

**Wednesday, February 4 (Moon in Cancer to Leo 7:50 p.m.)**    If single, you could meet your future mate. If you are married, there could be an addition to the family in the near future. Whether you are married or single, a decision will be made regarding the "direction of your life." Avoid a tendency to brood. Transform brooding into meditation. A Capricorn is involved.

**Thursday, February 5 (Moon in Leo)**   The answers come from within. Accent humor, versatility, and intellectual curiosity. Your popularity continues. People want to be with you, and some wish to wine and dine you. Avoid scattering your efforts. Don't attempt to please everyone. Have luck with number 3.

**Friday, February 6 (Moon in Leo)**   The full moon in Leo represents your tenth house. This relates to a career or business connected with publicity and showmanship. Tear down in order to rebuild. Present a different image of yourself. People who previously overlooked you will now ask plaintively, "Where have you been—we missed you?"

**Saturday, February 7 (Moon in Leo to Virgo 4:03 a.m.)**   A lively Saturday! Important people will seek your favor. Read and write; communicate thoughts clearly. A bold Leo states: "At times I can hardly keep my hands off you!" Indeed, this is a Saturday night live! Lucky lottery: 5, 41, 13, 18, 12, 32.

**Sunday, February 8 (Moon in Virgo)**   Your spiritual values surface. Be in close proximity to your family. A domestic adjustment restores harmony at home. A money dispute will be amicably settled. Many of your wishes come true in a surprising way. Wish for what you need as well as for luxury items and romance.

**Monday, February 9 (Moon in Virgo to Libra 10:13 a.m.)**   In matters of speculation, stick with number 7. At the track, choose number 7 post position in the seventh race. In a love relationship, you do not have the complete story. Be aware of it; avoid self-deception. Don't be taken for granted. Maintain an aura of mystery and intrigue.

***Tuesday, February 10 (Moon in Libra)***    Much happens behind the scenes. Don't be intimidated. You possess the power and authority to protect yourself in almost any situation. A secret meeting will be held. Attention could revolve around you. Capricorn and Cancer play outstanding roles.

***Wednesday, February 11 (Moon in Libra to Scorpio 2:58 p.m.)***    Someone who did not seem to take notice of you will now confide, "I am very much attracted to you!" Be careful! Don't play games with emotions. The heart you break could be your own. Focus on romance, the creative process, and the ability to complete an idealistic endeavor.

***Thursday, February 12 (Moon in Scorpio)***    Start something new! In your lunar cycle high, you will be at the right place at a crucial moment. Present original ideas to your superior. Today's scenario features romance, business, and advancement in your career. Leo and Aquarius command attention and will play dramatic roles.

***Friday, February 13 (Moon in Scorpio to Sagittarius 6:36 p.m.)***    This could be your lucky day! At the track, choose number 2 post position in the second race. Questions about partnership and marriage will loom large. Whether married or single, you are not alone. A Cancer is involved.

***Saturday, February 14 (Moon in Sagittarius)***    On this Valentine's Day, you receive "proof" that you have not been forgotten. Messages on cards received relate to romance and love. You will be verbally asked by someone who intrigues you: "Will you be my valentine?" Have luck with number 3.

**Sunday, February 15 (Moon in Sagittarius to Capricorn 9:15 p.m.)**   You will work out a mechanical defect and profit as a result. A lost article will be retrieved tonight. A love relationship reignites. If merely playing games, move on. Your emotional well-being depends on your ability to maintain balance and a sense of fair play. A Taurus is involved.

**Monday, February 16 (Moon in Capricorn)**   You will be busy in connection with relatives, trips, and favors. Be generous, not extravagant. Be helpful and forbearing, but know when to say, "Enough is enough!" An excellent day for reading, writing, and teaching. A flirtation lends spice, but could get out of hand.

**Tuesday, February 17 (Moon in Capricorn to Aquarius 11:28 p.m.)**   Practical matters dominate. A family member confides, "I need more money!" Be diplomatic and generous, but know when to draw the line. You might be asking yourself, "Is this déjà vu?" Today's scenario features familiar faces and places. Questions about finances seem to repeat: "I've heard that song before!"

**Wednesday, February 18 (Moon in Aquarius)**   Focus on real estate, land, and space. Your living quarters could be more commodious. Define terms, outline boundaries. Strive to streamline procedures and to perfect techniques. Pisces and Virgo will cooperate in a project that could bring you recognition.

**Thursday, February 19 (Moon in Aquarius)**   Your views will be vindicated. You envision future prospects in connection with the location of land. Some people regard you as a "figure of mystery." Keep it that way!

Set priorities; then proceed straight ahead. A relationship is passionate yet complicated.

***Friday, February 20 (Moon in Aquarius to Pisces 2:27 a.m.)*** The new moon in Pisces represents your fifth house. This relates to sexual attraction and the creative process. Finish what you start. Find someone to represent your talent or product in another land. Don't be taken for granted by someone who is "fantastic" when it comes to romantic whisperings.

***Saturday, February 21 (Moon in Pisces)*** Imprint your own style. Take the initiative. Do not follow others. The adventure of an "exciting romance" will be featured. Wear brighter colors when you make personal appearances. You will exude a kind of subtle appeal that is difficult to resist. A Leo will play a dramatic role. Your lucky number is 1.

***Sunday, February 22 (Moon in Pisces to Aries 7:45 a.m.)*** Questions concerning cooperative efforts, where you reside, and your marital status will loom large. You could receive proposals that include business, career, and marriage. Someone you once loved will make a surprise appearance. Maintain your emotional equilibrium!

***Monday, February 23 (Moon in Aries)*** Don't attempt to please everyone. That is a sure way to madness! Those who care about you will be pleased if you are happy. Accent diversity and versatility. Bring forth your sense of humor. What appeared to be a major problem 24 hours ago could now be a laughing matter.

***Tuesday, February 24 (Moon in Aries to Taurus 4:30 p.m.)*** Keep health resolutions including exercise, diet, and knowledge of nutrition. Someone you work with could turn out to be a "fascinating character." Don't be swept off your feet by words of flattery. Taurus, Leo, and another Scorpio will figure in this scenario.

**Wednesday, February 25 (Moon in Taurus)**  Lucky lottery: 5, 22, 6, 12, 18, 15. Get promises in writing. A charming fast-talker may not have the necessary finances to participate in a project. Be selective and discriminating. A flirtation lends spice, but could go farther than you anticipated.

**Thursday, February 26 (Moon in Taurus)**  Attention revolves around where you live and with whom. The question of income will loom large. If single, you could meet your future mate. If you are married, there could be an addition to your family sooner than anticipated. Be diplomatic, without abandoning your principles.

**Friday, February 27 (Moon in Taurus to Gemini 4:23 a.m.)**  You learn more about money and how you get it. Delve deep into the investigation of assets of one who would be your partner or mate. You could learn more than you care to know. Avoid making accusations; strive to be fair-minded. A Pisces will play an essential role.

**Saturday, February 28 (Moon in Gemini)**  This could be your power play day! Delve deep into areas previously prohibited. What had been hidden will be revealed—to your advantage. A physical attraction is involved. Don't give up something of value for a temporary thrill. Have luck with number 8.

**Sunday, February 29 (Moon in Gemini to Cancer 5:12 p.m.)**  Today's scenario will feature children, challenge, change, and a variety of sensations. Tonight, stick to familiar ground. Make an intelligent concession to your family. Aries and Libra will play outstanding roles.

**Monday, March 1 (Moon in Cancer)**    There's plenty of action and controversy today. By fighting hard, you win your way and get what you want. Strive for universal appeal; this means obtain permission to communicate with someone in a foreign land. Aries and Libra will play exciting roles.

**Tuesday, March 2 (Moon in Cancer)**    Dare to dream! Let go of preconceived notions. Accent the inventive and original thinking. Emphasize drama and showmanship. You could meet someone who fits your idea of the "perfect lover." Don't give up something of value for a temporary thrill.

**Wednesday, March 3 (Moon in Cancer to Leo 4:18 a.m.)**    Your efforts compel admiration from someone who is your professional superior. Don't hold back! Ask questions, assert your needs. Maintain your equilibrium and sense of humor. You receive favorable comments on your style of dressing. Lucky lottery: 3, 20, 22, 14, 2, 5.

**Thursday, March 4 (Moon in Leo)**    Don't be embarrassed by someone who says things that are "out of order." Overcome adversity with humor, wit, and wisdom. Laugh at your own foibles. Let others know that you are well aware of both your limitations and your potential. A Sagittarius figures in this scenario.

**Friday, March 5 (Moon in Leo to Virgo 12:19 p.m.)**    Attend to details early. Within 24 hours, you will have more responsibility, a promotion, or greater financial resources. Review and rewrite. Correct past mistakes that include proper measurements. Taurus, Leo, and another Scorpio will play memorable roles.

***Saturday, March 6 (Moon in Virgo)***     The full moon in Virgo represents your eleventh house. This relates to your hopes and wishes, speculation, and romance. Win friends and influence people. Give praise where it is deserved. Show that you are sensitive to the needs of others. They, in turn, will be aware of your needs. Your lucky number is 5.

***Sunday, March 7 (Moon in Virgo to Libra 5:32 p.m.)***     Beautify your surroundings. Hang pictures and photographs on the walls. Almost everything you do will turn out "just right." The lunar position relates to winning friends and exerting your influence. Taurus and Libra will contribute suggestions concerning your home life.

***Monday, March 8 (Moon in Libra)***     Avoid confusion based on "interference" by relatives. Be gracious, but say, "Thanks, but no, thanks!" Define terms. Perceive relationships as they are, not merely as you wish they could be. Translated, this means avoid self-deception. Virgo is represented.

***Tuesday, March 9 (Moon in Libra to Scorpio 9:04 p.m.)***     Today's scenario highlights secrecy and access to classified information. Be discreet. Do not tell all. Don't confide or confess. Maintain an aura of exclusivity. Someone who wants something for nothing will flatter you. Capricorn and Cancer play astonishing roles.

***Wednesday, March 10 (Moon in Scorpio)***     It's your lunar cycle high, so the emphasis is on timing and being at the right place. Show off your personality and sex appeal. This is no time to be modest—straight ahead! People are aware of you and want to wine and dine you. It appears that you have achieved "celebrity status."

***Thursday, March 11 (Moon in Scorpio to Sagittarius 11:58 p.m.)*** Give serious consideration to going into business for yourself. Make personal appearances; exude confidence. You will be at the right place at a crucial moment, almost effortlessly. Ride with the tide; don't get in your own way. Your lucky number is 1.

***Friday, March 12 (Moon in Sagittarius)*** Focus on direction, motivation, and the need for meditation. The question of partnership or marriage will loom large. Fix things at home. Fixtures, roofing, and plumbing could be in need of repair. You will be dealing with Capricorn and Cancer. Be suave!

***Saturday, March 13 (Moon in Sagittarius)*** Good news about finances! You will have something to celebrate. Highlight wit and wisdom, intelligence and humor. The emphasis is on your ability to be versatile without scattering your forces. Laugh at your foibles instead of brooding about them. A Sagittarius is in this picture. Your lucky number is 3.

***Sunday, March 14 (Moon in Sagittarius to Capricorn 2:52 a.m.)*** Take special care in traffic. A short trip could be necessary at the request of a relative. Accent intellectual curiosity. Explore various aspects of a proposition offered by someone who is usually trustworthy. Taurus, Leo, and another Scorpio will play amazing roles.

***Monday, March 15 (Moon in Capricorn)*** Be ready for change, travel, and a variety of "sensations." A flirtation could lead to something big. Don't play games with your emotions. The heart you break could be your own. An excellent day for reading and writing. Start a diary. You will get the drift of a complicated problem. You solve it to the satisfaction of many.

250

*Tuesday, March 16 (Moon in Capricorn to Aquarius 6:11 a.m.)* Attention revolves around your property and home. Listening to music will help alleviate tension. There was a dispute over your finances or budget; that will be resolved. Domestic harmony will be restored. A dilemma concerning marriage will be amicably settled. A Libra plays a major role.

*Wednesday, March 17 (Moon in Aquarius)* Stick close to familiar ground. Accent moderation in connection with adult beverages. You will obtain fascinating information about Saint Patrick. He supposedly drove the snakes out of Ireland; skeptics, however, insist no snakes were there in the first place. Have luck with number 7.

*Thursday, March 18 (Moon in Aquarius to Pisces 10:26 a.m.)* Within 24 hours, your vitality makes a comeback. You will exude sex appeal, so you must practice restraint. Focus on children, challenge, change, and a variety of experiences. A power play day for you! You'll be in charge of organization and lining up priorities.

*Friday, March 19 (Moon in Pisces)* Today's lunar position emphasizes freedom of thought and of action. Look beyond the immediate. You could receive an invitation to visit a foreign land. Absence from home ground and a loved one is only temporary. People who care about you will understand and encourage your activities.

*Saturday, March 20 (Moon in Pisces to Aries 4:29 p.m.)* The new moon is in Pisces, which is your fifth house. This relates to romance and creativity. Focus on affairs of the heart. If single, you could meet your future mate. Make a fresh start. Stress independence and original thinking. Lucky lottery: 1, 12, 18, 27, 28, 5.

*Sunday, March 21 (Moon in Aries)*     Attend religious services with your family. You will be asked many questions by young people. Don't be embarrassed if you don't know all of the answers. Focus on your home, partnership, and marital status. Participate in civic activities. A Cancer is on your side and will show you the way.

*Monday, March 22 (Moon in Aries)*     What had been a source of concern will turn out to be a laughing matter. You win the cooperation of an Aries who had been on the sidelines. Your versatility, humor, and enthusiasm will attract friends and increase your popularity. Keep diet resolutions.

*Tuesday, March 23 (Moon in Aries to Taurus 1:10 a.m.)*     There are obstacles, but you will overcome them. Funding will be made available. Be aware of legal restrictions; be knowledgeable about rights and permissions. The question of marriage will loom large. Taurus, Leo, and another Scorpio will figure in this scenario.

*Wednesday, March 24 (Moon in Taurus)*     Read and write. Do most of your work behind the scenes. Lie low, play the waiting game. Someone wants you to fail and makes no secret of it. Protect yourself at close quarters. Show that you can give as well as take it. Your ability to fight for what is right will surface.

*Thursday, March 25 (Moon in Taurus to Gemini 12:35 p.m.)*     Pressure will be relieved. You are doing the right thing; you will obtain legal clearance. For a time, you were doubtful. With this good news, you can celebrate with a clear conscience. A relative makes a gesture of love. Who can ask for anything more?

*Friday, March 26 (Moon in Gemini)*     You learn more about the financial status of someone who would be your partner or mate. The news may not be encouraging, but at least you will have the truth. Dig deep into areas previously prohibited. Define terms. Avoid self-deception. A Pisces figures prominently.

**Saturday, March 27 (Moon in Gemini)**  You will have power and confidence—this applies to your personal as well as professional life. A relationship intensifies. Be aware of what is happening. Do not run because you cannot hide. You'll ask, "Is this déjà vu?" The scenario features familiar faces and places. Your lucky number is 8.

**Sunday, March 28 (Moon in Gemini to Cancer 1:24 a.m.)**  Your spiritual values surface. This scenario features variety, excitement, and children. Imprint your style. Don't waver from basic objectives. Finish what you start. Advertise and publish. Aries and Libra add spice to life. Your lucky number is 9.

**Monday, March 29 (Moon in Cancer)**  Your inventive qualities will be made obvious. Don't follow others. Imprint your personal style. Create your own tradition. You will be complimented on your appearance. You will receive tempting offers relating to romance. Leo and Aquarius figure in this scenario.

**Tuesday, March 30 (Moon in Cancer to Leo 1:08 p.m.)**  Your cycle moves up. You will receive recognition long overdue. Published material will help. You earn respect, and you could get a raise in pay. Major questions relate to where you live and your marital status. The answers will be forthcoming tonight. A Cancer is involved.

**Wednesday, March 31 (Moon in Leo)**  On this last day of March, you'll recognize an opportunity and do something about it. The lunar position relates to ambition and direct action, also an intensified romantic situation. Accent diversity and versatility. Humor gets you in and out of "tight spots." Have luck with number 3.

# APRIL 2004

***Thursday, April 1 (Moon in Leo to Virgo 9:46 p.m.)***    Those who attempt to make a "fool" of you will be in for a stunning surprise! Accent independence and creativity. Realize the value of your own worth. Don't follow others. Your way is the right way for today. Leo and Aquarius play dramatic roles.

***Friday, April 2 (Moon in Virgo)***    Many of your desires in connection with home or marital status will be fulfilled. This could be the start of a "winning streak!" In matters of speculation, stick with number 2. At the track, choose number 2 post position in the second race.

***Saturday, April 3 (Moon in Virgo)***    You will have something to celebrate! The burden of a losing proposition is lifted. You will be in charge of a social gathering. Pull out all the stops for discussions. Express your views in a direct way, but don't forget humor. Gemini and Sagittarius will play featured roles.

***Sunday, April 4—Daylight Saving Time Begins (Moon in Virgo to Libra 3:53 a.m.)***    Let your spiritual values surface. Make a gesture of reconciliation to your family. A recent error should be corrected. It turns out to be no harm, no foul. Revise and review. If you do some serious rewriting, an article that had been rejected will be accepted.

***Monday, April 5 (Moon in Libra)***    The full moon in Libra represents your twelfth house. This highlights secrets, hospitals, institutions, and television production. If discreet, you could be given an assignment that elevates you above mediocrity and into the big leagues. Gemini, Virgo, and Sagittarius play fascinating roles.

*Tuesday, April 6 (Moon in Libra to Scorpio 6:25 a.m.)* At the track, choose number 6 post position in the sixth race. It's your lunar cycle high, so the element of luck rides with you. A domestic adjustment could include an actual change of residence. Beautify your surroundings, smell the flowers, and listen to the music. A Libra is in this scenario.

*Wednesday, April 7 (Moon in Scorpio)* Circumstances turn in your favor. Make a decision on what you need and how far you will go to obtain it. The key is to avoid self-deception. Know where you are going and why. Your intuitive intellect figures in a dynamic way. Lucky lottery: 25, 32, 7, 15, 16, 12.

*Thursday, April 8 (Moon in Scorpio to Sagittarius 7:51 a.m.)* The financial structure will be revised in your favor. A relationship intensifies—the "other party" expects a legal partnership or marriage. If merely playing games, move on. Set priorities; then make use of them. Capricorn and Cancer figure in your business and career activities.

*Friday, April 9 (Moon in Sagittarius)* Focus on idealism. Participate in a charitable enterprise. Open the lines of communication. Find out what is going on in another land. You could be tested and challenged. Complete a project. Do not be deterred by someone who lacks talent or faith. Your lucky number is 9.

*Saturday, April 10 (Moon in Sagittarius to Capricorn 9:34 a.m.)* Arrangements will be made for you to profit from a transaction. Take the initiative. Accent originality. Speak your mind in a refreshing, frank way. Don't be a copycat! Let others copy you, if they so desire. By tonight, meanings will be made crystal clear. A Leo is involved.

*Sunday, April 11 (Moon in Capricorn)* A relative makes a short trip and contacts you. A Cancer is involved. The subject of your conversation will be home and marriage. The focus is also on direction, motivation, and meditation. Keep plans flexible. A surprise announcement will reveal that someone once in charge has now been discharged.

*Monday, April 12 (Moon in Capricorn to Aquarius 12:33 p.m.)* Get together with people who are not afraid of a "clash of ideas." Accent humor and intelligence. Use your ability to see both sides of questions. Your "services" will be sought as an umpire. Your reply: "Thanks, but no, thanks!" Gemini and Sagittarius will play startling roles.

*Tuesday, April 13 (Moon in Aquarius)* Revise and review. Correct measurements; acknowledge past errors. The lunar position accents structure, solid material, rules, and regulations that ultimately work in your favor. Taurus, Leo, and another Scorpio figure in this fascinating scenario.

*Wednesday, April 14 (Moon in Aquarius to Pisces 5:24 p.m.)* Teach and write. The "written word" could prove to be your greatest ally. Get your thoughts and opinions on paper. Submit a different format to your superior. A flirtation is serious. It could be the start of "something big." Lucky lottery: 5, 10, 20, 13, 18, 38.

*Thursday, April 15 (Moon in Pisces)* The Pisces moon represents your fifth house. This equates to creativity and a serious romance. Don't give up something of value for a temporary thrill. Enjoy the throes of passion, but know when to say, "Enough!" A domestic adjustment will involve where you live and with whom.

*Friday, April 16 (Moon in Pisces)* What had been a puzzle will become clear. There are some missing pieces, which will be obtained within a week. Define terms. Set boundaries. Give serious thought to a real estate proposal. Pisces and Virgo will figure in today's "creative" scenario.

*Saturday, April 17 (Moon in Pisces to Aries 12:25 a.m.)* Practical matters dominate. You are in a position to help those who rely upon you for their emotional and financial well-being. Be generous, but save enough time for yourself for meditation and for attention to someone you care about. Capricorn and Cancer play "revealing" roles.

*Sunday, April 18 (Moon in Aries)* Finish what you start. Look beyond the immediate. Someone you meet during a search or other important service will play a major role in your life. Aries and Libra are due to play active roles and to stimulate your thought process.

*Monday, April 19 (Moon in Aries to Taurus 9:43 a.m.)* The new moon and solar eclipse occur in the last degree of Aries, your sixth house. Your employment picture could be in disarray. People who accepted your services with gratitude could now express a "grouchy" temperament. Today's position of planets draws attention to a greater need for proper rest and diet.

*Tuesday, April 20 (Moon in Taurus)* Caution! The lunar position puts forth this message: "Wait and see. Don't rush or force issues. The waiting game is your kind of day today, so play it!" Check invoices; review a project. The emphasis is on your home, a solid base, and workable tools.

*Wednesday, April 21 (Moon in Taurus to Gemini 9:11 p.m.)*     Keep up-to-date on fashion news and trends. Your opinions will be sought; your words will be quoted. Accent diversity, versatility, and intelligence. Give full play to your intellectual curiosity. Loosen your clothing: adapt your wearing apparel to everyday weather. Have luck with number 3.

*Thursday, April 22 (Moon in Gemini)*     Accept the challenge of a unique investigation. This could lead to the probing of financial assets relating to someone who might be your partner or mate. You discover that some facts have been kept secret. Be understanding, but refuse to be naive.

*Friday, April 23 (Moon in Gemini)*     You could be accused of playing on the grounds of the occult. You will be in areas previously prohibited. Still, this will provide excitement, mystery, and intrigue. You could also learn more than you care to know. Remember, knowledge is power!

*Saturday, April 24 (Moon in Gemini to Cancer 9:57 a.m.)*     A family member comes up with a grand idea that will turn out to be "moneymaking." This idea or concept could include household items and material required to "build a home." A domestic adjustment is featured. Optimism will replace gloom. A Taurus plays a sensational role.

*Sunday, April 25 (Moon in Cancer)*     It's your kind of day! Spiritual values dominate. This will be a day of self-revelation. Your extrasensory perception will be "working overtime." Your inner feelings will be strong enough to permit you to select the "right numbers." A Pisces plays a role in these activities.

*Monday, April 26 (Moon in Cancer to Leo 10:15 p.m.)* You have the ability to look beyond the immediate. You'll obtain necessary funding to "fulfill a dream." Set priorities. Get legal protection for your ideas and methods. You could be "sitting on a gold mine!" Now it is time to get up and into the game—the game of your life!

*Tuesday, April 27 (Moon in Leo)* Focus on contacts with people who make the world go around. Don't make excuses for success. State frankly that you enjoy succeeding and have no nostalgic feeling for failure. This message becomes crystal clear tonight. Aries and Libra will play roles in today's scenario.

*Wednesday, April 28 (Moon in Leo)* Lucky lottery: 28, 12, 18, 14, 38, 40. Use your natural instincts for showmanship. Stress originality. Participate in a pioneering project. Special note: Don't lift heavy objects; your back could be vulnerable to injury. Leo and Aquarius figure in this scenario.

*Thursday, April 29 (Moon in Leo to Virgo 8:01 a.m.)* Within 24 hours, there will be a stunning surprise for you! The lunar position indicates winning friends, influencing people, and perhaps starting a lucky streak. A major wish comes true, especially in connection with love, sex, and marriage. A Capricorn is in this picture.

*Friday, April 30 (Moon in Virgo)* The Virgo moon relates to your eleventh house. This, in turn, coincides with your popularity and "awesome" power of persuasion. You will win in games of chance and in love. Are you up to all of this good news? Ride with the tide— don't get in your own way!

259

***Saturday, May 1 (Moon in Virgo to Libra 2:03 p.m.)*** Be close to home and family, if possible. Many of your fondest hopes and desires could be fulfilled. At the track, choose number 2 post position in the second race. Attention revolves around your financial status and suitable living quarters. A Capricorn is in the picture.

***Sunday, May 2 (Moon in Libra)*** Highlight versatility. Maintain an aura of mystery, of intrigue. People want to be with you, but it is necessary to be selective. Keep recent resolutions concerning exercise and diet. Gemini and Sagittarius will play outstanding roles. Your lucky number is 3.

***Monday, May 3 (Moon in Libra to Scorpio 4:37 p.m.)*** Restrictions are lifted. You will tear down in order to rebuild on a more solid structure. Another Scorpio will figure in today's dynamic scenario. Accent your individuality. Don't follow others; let others follow you, if they so desire. A secret will be revealed.

***Tuesday, May 4 (Moon in Scorpio)*** The full moon in Scorpio in your first house indicates a high cycle. You will be at the right place at a crucial moment. People notice you and want to read what you write and hear what you say. A flirtation lends spice, but don't let it get out of hand.

***Wednesday, May 5 (Moon in Scorpio to Sagittarius 5:07 p.m.)*** Emphasize your personality. Make amends to a family member who meant no harm in uttering "unbelievable" words. Be gracious, mature, and wise. Wear bright colors, including shades of green. Focus on your ability to beautify your home, and to entertain people who mean much to you.

*Thursday, May 6 (Moon in Sagittarius)*    Good news: You reap benefits for past endeavors! Define terms. Avoid self-deception. An opportunity exists to perfect techniques and to streamline procedures. Pisces and Virgo will figure in today's colorful scenario. Your lucky number is 7.

*Friday, May 7 (Moon in Sagittarius to Capricorn 5:16 p.m.)*    You will be approached about an investment. Check past records, including dividends. Money will play a top role. You will be on top of it as the result of research. Older people and companies will flourish. Be sensitive to trends and cycles.

*Saturday, May 8 (Moon in Capricorn)*    A mission is completed. You find the answer to the question: "Was this trip necessary?" As the future unfolds, you will be capable of predicting it. Trust your inner feelings. A love relationship is on target. Proceed accordingly—you will love and be loved. A Libra is involved.

*Sunday, May 9 (Moon in Capricorn to Aquarius 6:46 p.m.)*    A new approach is necessary. Be with creative, dynamic people. Avoid those who take you for granted. Have enough self-esteem to be "creatively selfish." Don't follow others. Create your own style and tradition. A new contact with a Leo will ultimately prove fruitful.

*Monday, May 10 (Moon in Aquarius)*    The emphasis is on design, architecture, and working tools. You gain cooperation from someone you admire. This association could lead to something as important as marriage. You will be invited to dine tonight by a Cancer. The bill of fare will be seafood.

*Tuesday, May 11 (Moon in Aquarius to Pisces 10:52 p.m.)*    You will be in more commodious living quarters. Your game room will be used for fun and skill.

261

Be up-to-date on fashion news; you could be tested and challenged on the subject. Gemini and Sagittarius play remarkable roles. Your lucky number is 3.

**Wednesday, May 12 (Moon in Pisces)**   The Pisces moon is in your fifth house. This relates to children, challenge, change, and a variety of sensations. You exude sex appeal, so protect yourself at close quarters. Taurus, Leo, and another Scorpio will figure prominently. Lucky lottery: 4, 14, 22, 13, 18, 5.

**Thursday, May 13 (Moon in Pisces)**   You will be considered "alluring." People are drawn to you. At least one person will declare, "At times I can hardly keep my hands off you!" Written material is important, so get your thoughts and feelings on paper. Start a diary!

**Friday, May 14 (Moon in Pisces to Aries 6:01 a.m.)**   Go slow. Accent moderation. Your family will make concessions; you get your wish. Today's scenario features flowers, art objects, and music. Find your rhythm and dance to your own tune. Taurus, Libra, and another Scorpio play roles in this unusual scenario. Look for these letters in their names: F, O, X.

**Saturday, May 15 (Moon in Aries)**   Focus on basic issues, including home repairs. Define terms. Get obligations and commitments in writing. Deception could be involved, deliberate or otherwise. Be sure not to fool yourself! Place trust in how you feel, not how others tell you to feel. A Pisces is featured.

**Sunday, May 16 (Moon in Aries to Taurus 3:56 p.m.)**   Your confidence returns. Spiritual values surface. You know for certain that you are doing the right thing. The emphasis is on responsibility, promotion, and direction. Many rely on you for their emotional and fi-

nancial welfare. Despite doubts, you will come through
with flying colors!

**Monday, May 17 (Moon in Taurus)**     Finish one thing
before starting something else. If you complete a project,
you'll gain admiration and additional funding. Aries and
Libra will play substantial roles. Follow through on an
idea that requires further development.

**Tuesday, May 18 (Moon in Taurus)**     You learn more
about publishing rights and permissions. Also, you learn
more about how to protect your own material. Ultimately, you discover that most transactions are a two-
way street. The motives of someone you trust will be
made clear. Be open-minded, not naive.

**Wednesday, May 19 (Moon in Taurus to Gemini 3:46
a.m.)**     The new moon in Taurus is in your seventh
house. This relates to legal activities and marriage.
Within 24 hours, you could solve a mystery that will enable your cash flow to improve. Capricorn and Cancer
play roles in this scenario.

**Thursday, May 20 (Moon in Gemini)**     Discover more
than one way of achieving your goal. Highlight versatility, diversity, and intellectual curiosity. Your popularity
is on the rise. People want to be with you, and some will
wine and dine you. A Sagittarius figures in this dramatic scenario.

**Friday, May 21 (Moon in Gemini to Cancer 4:34
p.m.)**     You recently emerged from an emotional or
financial crisis. Today, you see your way clear. The missing key will be located. Encourage people to have faith
in themselves. By helping others, you will aid your own
cause. Taurus, Leo, and another Scorpio play fascinating roles.

*Saturday, May 22 (Moon in Cancer)*   Separate yourself from those who take you for granted. Highlight change, variety, and experimentation. Someone of the opposite sex finds you attractive and says so. It elevates your morale, but don't believe everything you hear! Lucky lottery: 5, 14, 23, 11, 2, 9.

*Sunday, May 23 (Moon in Cancer)*   A family member talks about philosophy and reincarnation. Purchase a luxury item as a gift for a loved one. This action will work wonders in bringing about happiness. It is a small gesture, but you will be immensely pleased by the results. A Libra is represented.

*Monday, May 24 (Moon in Cancer to Leo 5:06 a.m.)* Take the initiative in defining terms and outlining boundaries. Separate fact from illusion. Avoid wishful thinking and self-deception. You'll be dealing with temperamental people who feel inferior and attempt to cover up by speaking loudly and bluffing. A Pisces is in this picture.

*Tuesday, May 25 (Moon in Leo)*   Blend practicality with creative imagination. Take charge! Line up priorities, organize, and look to the future. Your earnings increase; you will be handsomely rewarded for your foresight. Capricorn and Cancer play meaningful roles. Your lucky number is 8.

*Wednesday, May 26 (Moon in Leo to Virgo 3:50 p.m.)*   Within 24 hours, your "dreamscape" could become a reality. Maintain your emotional equilibrium. You will do the right thing at a special moment. Your business or career competition will fade. You will be in charge, and no questions will be forthcoming.

*Thursday, May 27 (Moon in Virgo)*   Take the initiative. Elements of timing and of luck ride with you. Take charge; you proved your capability 24 hours ago. Today and tonight, it is "straight ahead." Leo and Aquarius figure prominently. There is more pressure due to added responsibility.

**Friday, May 28 (Moon in Virgo to Libra 11:20 p.m.)** Focus on a desire that will be fulfilled. The emphasis is on love, creativity, and your marital status. A decision will be made concerning the "direction of your life." It is not a dream! It actually occurs, and you are in the driver's seat.

**Saturday, May 29 (Moon in Libra)** Your popularity increases. People rely upon you for their emotional and financial security. Exude confidence. Your views will be verified. This could be your day of vindication. Gemini and Sagittarius figure in this fascinating scenario. Have luck with number 3.

**Sunday, May 30 (Moon in Libra)** This is your make-over day. Wear your clothes and hair in different styles. A check of details, including measurements, will prove you are on the right track. Someone who had been anonymous will step forward and become your valuable ally. Another Scorpio plays a memorable role.

**Monday, May 31 (Moon in Libra to Scorpio 3:06 a.m.)** You experience more freedom of thought and of action. In your lunar cycle high, circumstances take a dramatic turn in your favor. You get the proverbial "lucky break." Gemini, Virgo, and Sagittarius will play essential roles. Your lucky number is 5.

## JUNE 2004

**Tuesday, June 1 (Moon in Scorpio)** You obtain fresh material. Now you could be ready for a new adventure. Exude confidence. You will be attractive and have an abundance of sex appeal. In your lunar cycle high, let your intuition serve as a reliable guide. Have luck with number 3.

**Wednesday, June 2 (Moon in Scorpio to Sagittarius 3:51 a.m.)** Your expenses will be paid for an exploratory journey. Elements of luck ride with you; don't get in your own way. Gemini and Sagittarius will play dynamic roles and could have these letters in their names: D, M, V. Taurus and another Scorpio also figure in today's "complicated" scenario.

**Thursday, June 3 (Moon in Sagittarius)** You are hereby given permission to sing in or out of the shower! The full moon started this day in Sagittarius, your second house. This equates to your earning power and the ability to locate lost articles. You could have the best of both worlds—romance, love, and money.

**Friday, June 4 (Moon in Sagittarius to Capricorn 3:12 a.m.)** A relative makes a surprise appearance. Be gracious, but let it be known that you would appreciate "advance notice." Taurus, Libra, and another Scorpio will figure in today's dramatic scenario. Lend a hand to a loved one who throws aside false pride and asks for help.

**Saturday, June 5 (Moon in Capricorn)** On this Saturday, the emphasis is on mystery and intrigue as well as confidential methods of obtaining funding. Your security is enhanced. You'll be saying to yourself, "Life can be beautiful after all!" Pisces and Virgo will play fascinating roles. Have luck with number 7.

**Sunday, June 6 (Moon in Capricorn to Aquarius 3:10 a.m.)** Attention revolves around your home and the ability to beautify your surroundings. A gentle and generous approach brings the desired results. However, do not confuse generosity with extravagance. Protect your valuables. Insist on getting a square deal. A Cancer is involved.

**Monday, June 7 (Moon in Aquarius)**    You will meet a fascinating, creative Aquarius—this could be the start of something big! Toss aside preconceived notions. Today, you can accomplish what others consider "impossible." You could be on the precipice of fame and fortune. You will be in the news and making news.

**Tuesday, June 8 (Moon in Aquarius to Pisces 5:38 a.m.)**    The moon is in Pisces, your fifth house. This represents creativity, sexual attraction, and an outlet for pent-up feelings. Make a fresh start. Emphasize independence. You will know where you are and what to do about it. A Leo plays a dramatic role.

**Wednesday, June 9 (Moon in Pisces)**    The emphasis is on partnership, cooperative efforts, civic activities, and your marital status. What was owed to you will be paid. Work out a budget that enables you to save money and travel at the same time. Capricorn and Cancer will play "sensational" roles.

**Thursday, June 10 (Moon in Pisces to Aries 11:50 a.m.)** Keep recent health resolutions relating to exercise, diet, and nutrition. Social activities could serve as a reason for meeting someone destined to play a major role in your life. Gemini and Sagittarius figure prominently. In matters of speculation, stick with number 3.

**Friday, June 11 (Moon in Aries)**    An Aries will provide helpful hints concerning your job and health. You will be inspired, and you will also provide inspiration for others. You will learn more about starting your own business. A Taurus will play a major role.

*Saturday, June 12 (Moon in Aries to Taurus 9:36 p.m.)* This will be a lively Saturday night! Communicate via the written word. Listen while others state their views. You will be asked for "feedback." Be honest, without being brutal. You are on the precipice of a stunning adventure. Lucky lottery: 5, 47, 30, 33, 2, 12.

*Sunday, June 13 (Moon in Taurus)* You will learn as a result of gentle hints that serious negotiations are getting under way. Focus on legal affairs and proposals of partnership or marriage. Taurus, Libra, and another Scorpio will play essential roles. Home cooking is featured tonight!

*Monday, June 14 (Moon in Taurus)* Time is on your side. Play the waiting game. Focus on clearing away legal debris. You will learn more about rights and permissions, and you will greatly benefit as a result. Pisces and Virgo will play outstanding roles and could have these letters in their names: G, P, Y.

*Tuesday, June 15 (Moon in Taurus to Gemini 9:43 a.m.)* Someone who had remained anonymous will be out in the open. Grab this opportunity to thank that person for past favors. Don't permit your pride to deter progress. Genuine pride is positive; false pride is negative and hurtful. This message becomes crystal clear tonight.

*Wednesday, June 16 (Moon in Gemini)* You have lately become involved in "mysterious happenings." Tonight, you get the story as it is, not how you imagined it might be. Travel and romance could be involved. You will perhaps learn more than you care to know, but the truth will set you free.

*Thursday, June 17 (Moon in Gemini to Cancer 10:36 p.m.)* The new moon in Gemini represents your eighth house. This relates to secret sources of income, especially that of your partner or mate. Avoid heavy lifting. Dress up your product. Make use of advertising, publicity, and showmanship. Leo and Aquarius figure in this scenario.

**Friday, June 18 (Moon in Cancer)**     You could receive surprising news from someone who meant much to you in the past. The favorable lunar aspect coincides with communication from a foreign land. You could locate "just the right person" to represent your talent or product. You have plenty to offer, so don't be shy when it comes to naming your price.

**Saturday, June 19 (Moon in Cancer)**     You know somehow that life is turning in your favor. Focus on humor, intellectual curiosity, and a long-range projection into the future. You are positive that once again you are in control of your fate. A Sagittarius figures prominently. Your lucky number is 3.

**Sunday, June 20 (Moon in Cancer to Leo 11:03 a.m.)**     On this Sunday, you take care of practical matters, including home repairs. Within 24 hours, your prestige will be elevated. You will know that your work is appreciated and that you are going to be promoted. Taurus and another Scorpio will play dynamic roles.

**Monday, June 21 (Moon in Leo)**     You will be encouraged to write, to suggest how to get the job done in a more efficient way. It is important to read and write, to learn through the process of teaching. You will have more freedom of thought, of action. A Gemini figures in this scenario.

**Tuesday, June 22 (Moon in Leo to Virgo 10:08 p.m.)**     Attention revolves around restoring domestic harmony. You receive a gift, a luxury item, which helps beautify your home. You realize that you are on the right

269

track. Taurus, Libra, and another Scorpio contribute to your happiness. Have luck with number 6.

**Wednesday, June 23 (Moon in Virgo)**     Do not equate delay with defeat. Today's eleventh house moon coincides with "joyous news." A friendship that had been cool will grow warmer. Your power of persuasion is great. Once again, your popularity is on the rise. Lucky lottery: 7, 30, 33, 14, 12, 8.

**Thursday, June 24 (Moon in Virgo)**     Dreams will be transformed into realities. You will regard this as your "lucky day." At the track, choose number 8 post position in the second and ninth races. You will be reassured of progress by someone you respect. A Capricorn plays the top role.

**Friday, June 25 (Moon in Virgo to Libra 6:49 a.m.)** What had been hidden will be revealed, to your advantage. Finish a creative project. Don't be dismayed by those who lack talent or faith. A love spark reignites. Your emotional equilibrium is featured, and you will not fear the unknown. An Aries is in the picture.

**Saturday, June 26 (Moon in Libra)**     A lively Saturday night! Make a fresh start. Express yourself. Don't follow others. Give serious consideration to starting your own business. You exude sex appeal. You will be reassured that the spark of romance is indeed reignited. A Leo is featured.

**Sunday, June 27 (Moon in Libra to Scorpio 12:10 p.m.)**     Your lunar cycle moves up. Circumstances are turning in your favor. You will note that events are transpiring to bring you closer to your ultimate goal. As a result, fulfillment replaces doubt and suspicion. The question of your marital status looms large. Find out where you stand and what to do about it.

*Monday, June 28 (Moon in Scorpio)*     You will have reason to celebrate! Open the lines of communication. You will be assured that you are at the right place and time. Gemini and Sagittarius will play helpful roles. Note: Keep recent diet resolutions. Do so, and you'll be on the way to better health.

*Tuesday, June 29 (Moon in Scorpio to Sagittarius 2:14 p.m.)*     Your personality is attractive and stylish. Take the initiative and create your own tradition. Don't wait to be told what to do. Follow your intuitive intellect and your heart. At the track, choose number 4 post position in the fourth race.

*Wednesday, June 30 (Moon in Sagittarius)*     On this Wednesday, you receive a check in payment for written material. Be ready for the adventure of change and a variety of sensations. A flirtation heats up, but protect yourself in emotional clinches. Don't give up something of value for temporary satisfaction. This message becomes crystal clear tonight. A Virgo is involved.

### JULY 2004

*Thursday, July 1 (Moon in Sagittarius to Capricorn 2:00 p.m.)*     The lunar position equates to "good news" about money. You locate a lost article. Financial backing comes from a surprise source. You've been thinking about the holiday celebration. Arrange to have the Declaration of Independence read aloud.

*Friday, July 2 (Moon in Capricorn)*     The full moon is in Capricorn, which accents your third house. This represents ideas that require further development. Deal gingerly with relatives; some will be subject to temperamental outbursts. A unique relationship blends the romantic with the intellectual.

*Saturday, July 3 (Moon in Capricorn to Aquarius 1:22 p.m.)*     Attention revolves around domestic issues that could include an actual change of residence or marital status. You will receive a gift, a luxury item that brightens your surroundings. Be kind, diplomatic, and generous. However, don't confuse generosity with extravagance. A Libra is involved.

*Sunday, July 4 (Moon in Aquarius)*     Stick close to home. Remove safety hazards. Take no chances with explosives. One of your guests will volunteer to read the Declaration of Independence. Be sensitive to the feelings of others. Refuse to be taken for granted, and don't take others for granted.

*Monday, July 5 (Moon in Aquarius to Pisces 2:27 p.m.)*     A business or career enterprise should be seriously considered. A relative is sincere about obtaining financial backing. Get your priorities in order. The pressure is on due to added responsibility. You will be up to it! Capricorn plays an outstanding role.

*Tuesday, July 6 (Moon in Pisces)*     Questions concerning who pays for what will be asked. Look beyond the immediate. By giving, you also will receive. Focus on trips, visits, and dealings with relatives. The emphasis is also on creativity, children, and variety. The written word will be preserved; write with care and feeling. An Aries is involved.

*Wednesday, July 7 (Moon in Pisces to Aries 7:03 p.m.)*     Perfect techniques, streamline procedures. The moon position highlights travel and a variety of sensations. You could be dealing with children or people with "young ideas." Take the initiative in making a new start. Leo and Aquarius figure prominently. Your lucky number is 1.

*Thursday, July 8 (Moon in Aries)*     You get tasks completed in such a way that you receive a promotion. A personal relationship "sizzles." You are going places—how far will depend entirely upon your ambition. The question of marriage looms large. Answers are found behind the scenes and via meditation.

*Friday, July 9 (Moon in Aries)*     Keep plans flexible. Preserve the right to maintain creative control. Highlight diversity and versatility. Give full play to your intellectual curiosity. Ask questions; obtain answers, not evasions. Gemini and Sagittarius will play fascinating roles. Number 3 is lucky for you today.

*Saturday, July 10 (Moon in Aries to Taurus 3:50 a.m.)*     Go slow. Check details and correct measurements. Be positive concerning legal rights and permissions. Focus also on partnership and marriage. Live up to promises. You can run, but you cannot hide. Taurus, Leo, and another Scorpio will figure in today's dramatic scenario.

*Sunday, July 11 (Moon in Taurus)*     Blend intuition with reasoning power. Analyze the situations at hand as well as relationships. If you want the "situation" to last, you'll have to work at it. Avoid seeing only what you want to see. Perceive the truth of the matter, then take action. A Virgo is represented.

*Monday, July 12 (Moon in Taurus to Gemini 3:44 p.m.)*     A ship comes out of drydock; you will be on the move again. Steps will be taken to restore domestic tranquillity. Focus on comfortable living, flowers, music, and romance. If you are married, the love spark reignites. If single, you could meet your future mate.

*Tuesday, July 13 (Moon in Gemini)*     Define terms. Make meanings crystal clear. The moon in your eighth house indicates you will be dealing with life-and-death situations. Avoid brooding. Do what you know is best, and don't invent limitations. Questions will concern money and how it gets that way. A Pisces figures prominently.

**Wednesday, July 14 (Moon in Gemini)**    Once again, you will be "in charge." On the domestic front, you get organized. Make your living quarters more attractive. Where your profession and career are concerned, you'll have more responsibility. Your earning power increases. Lucky lottery: 8, 33, 35, 4, 12, 18.

**Thursday, July 15 (Moon in Gemini to Cancer 4:40 a.m.)**    At the track, choose number 8 post position in the ninth race. You have the ability today to "peer into the future." Open the lines of communication. Someone from a foreign land wants to talk to you. This person, likely an Aries, could represent your talent or product overseas.

**Friday, July 16 (Moon in Cancer)**    A favorable lunar aspect coincides with philosophy, psychology, and more knowledge of the mantic arts, including astrology. Highlight original thinking. Take the initiative, but protect yourself in emotional clinches. Leo and Aquarius will play exciting roles.

**Saturday, July 17 (Moon in Cancer to Leo 4:55 p.m.)**    The new moon is in the last degrees of Cancer. This means that within 24 hours, you will receive the package you have been waiting for. You are going to be pleasantly surprised! Questions about civic activities, partnership, and marriage will command the spotlight. A Capricorn figures in this scenario.

**Sunday, July 18 (Moon in Leo)**    Your standing in the community will be elevated. Attend religious services with someone you admire. Later, there will be reason to celebrate. This could be a day of love and laughter, if you so permit. Expand your horizons. See the "funny side of life." A Gemini plays a role.

**Monday, July 19 (Moon in Leo)**     On this Monday, you will be made aware of "new responsibilities." Rewrite and rebuild. This could be your makeover day. Wear your clothes and hair in different styles. You will receive favorable comments as a result. A Taurus and another Scorpio are involved.

**Tuesday, July 20 (Moon in Leo to Virgo 3:43 a.m.)**     The Virgo moon relates to your eleventh house. This means that through reading and writing many of your hopes and wishes could become realities. You'll be fortunate in matters of speculation by sticking with number 5. At the track, choose number 5 post position in the fifth race.

**Wednesday, July 21 (Moon in Virgo)**     Beautify your surroundings, especially at home. People who had not shown any interest in your living quarters could now be enthusiastic in helping you to make your home beautiful. Music plays. Find your rhythm and dance to your own tune. Your voice is melodious. Sing in or out of the shower.

**Thursday, July 22 (Moon in Virgo to Libra 12:37 p.m.)**     Within 24 hours, you will be involved in secrets. You'll be dealing with people who have much to hide. Be discreet. Keep some secrets sacred. You can obtain the story behind the story, if you persist. Pisces and Virgo will play instrumental roles.

**Friday, July 23 (Moon in Libra)**     The key is balance and emotional equilibrium. A Capricorn attempts to "sweep you off your feet!" Enjoy the flattery and attention, but avoid being naive. Don't give up something of value for a temporary thrill. Recent research turned up something useful; be aware of it and express confidence.

**Saturday, July 24 (Moon in Libra to Scorpio 7:07 p.m.)**     The moon in Libra represents your twelfth house. This relates to theater, clandestine activities, dealings with hospitals and institutions, and unorthodox methods of healing. People will be drawn to you. By helping others with their problems, your own will also diminish. Aries and Libra figure prominently.

**Sunday, July 25 (Moon in Scorpio)**     On this Sunday, you will be at the right place at a crucial moment, almost effortlessly. You exude personality and sex appeal. You could be in love with the "right person." Take the initiative. Toss aside preconceived notions and false pride. A Leo will play a fantastic role.

**Monday, July 26 (Moon in Scorpio to Sagittarius 10:46 p.m.)**     A decision will be reached concerning a partnership or marital status. You also learn more about the "direction of your life." Your intuitive intellect is honed to razor-sharpness. Trust a hunch; stick with number 2 in matters of speculation. A Cancer plays a dynamic role.

**Tuesday, July 27 (Moon in Sagittarius)**     Good luck! All things being equal, you could win a contest. Turn on your Scorpio charm. You draw winning numbers and "people who win." If you so permit, this could be a day of joy. I just heard you say, "Nothing is perfect!" That is true, but let me say this can be a near-perfect day.

**Wednesday, July 28 (Moon in Sagittarius to Capricorn 11:56 p.m.)**     Some things today will have a way of working out in your favor. You might be asking, "Is this déjà vu?" Today's scenario highlights familiar places and faces. Your emotional shell will shatter, which will be in your favor. Persons you care about will have a good and true look at you.

***Thursday, July 29 (Moon in Capricorn)*** Events happen at a fast pace, so keep your options open. Have notes and research at hand. Someone of the opposite sex finds you attractive and declares, "At times I can hardly keep my hands off you!" Those are words that kindle the flame in your heart. Gemini, Virgo, and Sagittarius will play dynamic roles.

***Friday, July 30 (Moon in Capricorn to Aquarius 11:54 p.m.)*** Attention revolves around where you live, design, color coordination, and architecture. You will be admired for your knowledge of the lives of composers. If you don't agree with official biographies, say so and state your reasons. Taurus, Libra, and another Scorpio figure in this memorable scenario.

***Saturday, July 31 (Moon in Aquarius)*** On this Saturday, there is a blue moon in Aquarius. That is your fourth house, representing property and real estate. You get the proverbial "second chance" in connection with a sale or purchase. Avoid self-deception. You lack complete information, so it is best to play the waiting game.

# AUGUST 2004

***Sunday, August 1 (Moon in Aquarius)*** You feel "grounded." Focus on practicality. Be willing to review and to rebuild. You get information that helps in your "spiritual growth." You will be attracted to someone who "works with words." Gemini and Virgo play instrumental roles.

***Monday, August 2 (Moon in Aquarius to Pisces 12:35 a.m.)*** You will be confronted with news of a promotion. The emphasis is on pressure and on an intensified relationship. A domestic adjustment could include a change of residence or marital status. Aries and Libra confide their thoughts and feelings to you.

***Tuesday, August 3 (Moon in Pisces)*** Be careful! Individuals drawn to you could be involved in a promotional scheme and want to use your money. Be open-minded, but not naive. Insist that information be put in writing. What had been a harmless flirtation is now ultraserious. A Pisces is involved.

***Wednesday, August 4 (Moon in Pisces to Aries 3:59 a.m.)*** Someone you admire will press for your participation in a get-rich-quick scheme. Your response: "Thanks, but no, thanks!" A romantic relationship lends spice, but could become controversial and expensive. A Capricorn figures prominently.

***Thursday, August 5 (Moon in Aries)*** Don't give up! Complete a project you started three months ago. Your services are in demand. Do what you can to help others, but also consider your own requirements. A new assignment could take you to a different city. Aries and Libra figure in this scenario.

***Friday, August 6 (Moon in Aries to Taurus 11:26 a.m.)*** Do necessary research and think seriously of beginning a business of your own. You will receive encouragement from those you respect. Do your own thing; do not follow others. Within 24 hours, a legal process will be completed. Leo and Aquarius are involved.

***Saturday, August 7 (Moon in Taurus)*** Slow your pace. Repairs are needed at home. This includes fixtures and plumbing. People are inquisitive about your marital status or a special partnership. There is no need to answer rude questions, so protect your reputation. Aquarius and Cancer are prominent in today's activities.

**Sunday, August 8 (Moon in Taurus to Gemini 10:32 p.m.)** A very lively Sunday! You could participate in sports or games of chance. You easily outdo the competition. A legal problem is solved; you'll have reason to celebrate. Someone who had ignored you may now desire to wine and dine you. A Sagittarius is involved.

**Monday, August 9 (Moon in Gemini)** This could be regarded as a "perfect Monday" for you. Be aware of details, which could have slipped your attention, including correct measurements. A relationship is troubled, but exciting, and could be rewarding. Taurus, Leo, and another Scorpio play important roles.

**Tuesday, August 10 (Moon in Gemini)** Recent records reveal that events are transpiring to bring you closer to your ultimate goal. You will enjoy more freedom of thought, of action. Focus on reading and writing, also a flirtation that could become "serious." A Sagittarius figures prominently.

**Wednesday, August 11 (Moon in Gemini to Cancer 11:19 a.m.)** A domestic adjustment takes place, which will relieve emotional and financial pressure. Be diplomatic. Remember that you do not have to win every argument. Your family is on your side; let them be so, and do not rob them of their pride. Your lucky number is 6.

**Thursday, August 12 (Moon in Cancer)** You will hear "faraway music." Find your rhythm, dance to your own tune. Discover faster ways to complete a project. Define terms and perfect techniques. Avoid self-deception. Do not attempt to please everyone. A Pisces will play a dominant role.

279

*Friday, August 13 (Moon in Cancer to Leo 11:28 p.m.)* A business venture can succeed, if you fully participate. This is not an unlucky day. Stay in control of your emotions, but give full rein to your creativity. A long-range project can come "closer." Capricorn and Cancer figure in this scenario.

*Saturday, August 14 (Moon in Leo)* A lively Saturday night! Romantic interests flourish. If it is love you seek, you could find it tonight. Don't be taken for granted, and don't take others for granted either. Aries and Libra play significant roles. Your lucky number is 9.

*Sunday, August 15 (Moon in Leo)* Let spiritual values surface. Your thoughts will be original. You will make favorable impressions on creative, successful people. Don't lift heavy objects. Your back could be vulnerable to injury. Leo and Aquarius will play featured roles.

*Monday, August 16 (Moon in Leo to Virgo 9:48 a.m.)* Last night's new moon happened in Leo, your tenth house. This relates to business, added recognition, and promotion in your career. Questions about cooperative efforts, partnership, and marriage will loom large. Meditate to decide on the "direction of your life."

*Tuesday, August 17 (Moon in Virgo)* Many of your fondest hopes and wishes could become realities. There will be reason to celebrate. Emphasize humor and versatility. You will have luck in matters of speculation, especially by sticking with number 3. A Gemini plays a dynamic role.

*Wednesday, August 18 (Moon in Virgo to Libra 6:08 p.m.)* You will be cautioned by those who care about you: "Take one step at a time!" You win friends and exert a powerful influence on people. Your popularity is on the rise. You will be wined and dined. Taurus, Leo, and another Scorpio will play "majestic" roles.

***Thursday, August 19 (Moon in Libra)***   The Libra moon represents your twelfth house, which relates to "mysterious happenings." Do not neglect a friend who is temporarily confined to home or hospital. Work behind the scenes; be thorough and "tender." Virgo and Gemini are involved.

***Friday, August 20 (Moon in Libra)***   A family secret is "up for grabs." Keep secrets sacred. Don't tell all. Don't confide or confess. You'll be dealing with institutions, hospitals, perhaps the theater. Taurus, Libra, and another Scorpio figure prominently in helping you decorate or remodel your home.

***Saturday, August 21 (Moon in Libra to Scorpio 12:35 a.m.)***   Your lunar cycle is high. Trust your own judgment. Take care of your destiny. See relationships in a realistic light. You will be at the right place at a crucial moment, almost effortlessly. Your intuitive intellect is honed to razor-sharpness. Have luck with number 7.

***Sunday, August 22 (Moon in Scorpio)***   Power play! Don't let any person get in your way—straight ahead! Focus on production, organization, and recognition of priorities. Your cycle is high for money and romance. A relationship is hot and heavy. If you are married, the love spark reignites.

***Monday, August 23 (Moon in Scorpio to Sagittarius 5:07 a.m.)***   Let go of a losing proposition. The way is cleared for winning and for participating in a profitable enterprise. On a personal level, romance dominates. Your ideals will be fulfilled. Aries and Libra will play "magnificent" roles.

*Tuesday, August 24 (Moon in Sagittarius)*     The answer to your question: This is the time to start a business or career. Exercise independence and original thinking. A love relationship intensifies. Don't play games, because the heart you break could be your own. Speak frankly. A Leo will play a dramatic role.

*Wednesday, August 25 (Moon in Sagittarius to Capricorn 7:45 a.m.)*     A short trip is necessary to attend a special occasion involving a relative. This might include an engagement party or wedding reception. Your own civic activities will be scrutinized. Take care with tax write-offs. Lucky lottery: 6, 26, 2, 20, 14, 24.

*Thursday, August 26 (Moon in Capricorn)*     At the track, choose number 3 post position in the third race. Keep plans flexible. You are going to be a winner and might want to take the night off to celebrate. Gemini and Sagittarius play significant roles and could have these letters in their names: C, L, U.

*Friday, August 27 (Moon in Capricorn to Aquarius 9:07 a.m.)*     Within 24 hours, you learn the value of your property. This information makes you feel more secure emotionally and financially. Be thorough in your research. Be positive of obtaining a fair deal. A Taurus and another Scorpio will play memorable roles. Have luck with number 4.

*Saturday, August 28 (Moon in Aquarius)*     Good news comes via the written word. An investigation turns up the solution to a problem. You exude sex appeal; be careful of whom you permit to enter your exclusive circle. Gemini, Virgo, and Sagittarius figure in this "perplexing" scenario.

*Sunday, August 29 (Moon in Aquarius to Pisces 10:33 a.m.)*     Be with your family this Sunday. If you wander far away, you will be called back. Something "interesting" is happening at home. This could involve security, basic values, and a consideration of changing your residence or names. Taurus and Libra figure in this scenario.

**Monday, August 30 (Moon in Pisces)**     The full moon was in Pisces last night, which accents your fifth house. This relates to creativity, style, and sex appeal. Don't lower your standards. You could be in love, so be sure your love is not unrequited. Pisces and Virgo figure prominently and have these letters in their names: G, P, Y.

**Tuesday, August 31 (Moon in Pisces to Aries 1:46 p.m.)**     On this last day of August, avoid the temptation to throw caution aside. Demand the best. A personal relationship intensifies and will be exciting yet controversial. You are in the driver's seat; know it, and act accordingly. A Capricorn plays a dynamic role.

# SEPTEMBER 2004

**Wednesday, September 1 (Moon in Aries)**     The moon is in Aries, your sixth house. This relates to special services, work, and health. Stay close to home, if possible. Harmony can be restored on the domestic front, if you so permit. Taurus, Libra, and another Scorpio figure prominently. Your lucky number is 6.

**Thursday, September 2 (Moon in Aries to Taurus 8:16 p.m.)**     Define terms, get promises in writing. You could be involved in a real estate transaction. Perceive people as they are, not merely as you wish they could be. Avoid self-deception. Look behind the scenes for answers. A Pisces plays an amazing role.

*Friday, September 3 (Moon in Taurus)*   A powerful Friday! A setback can be transformed into a victory; you are in the driver's seat. Accept the pressure of added responsibility. A relationship is not "comfortable," but it is exciting. Capricorn and Cancer will play illustrious roles.

*Saturday, September 4 (Moon in Taurus)*   You gain recognition due to participation in humanitarian activities. Play the waiting game. Be positive about your legal rights and permissions. The question of marriage will loom large. Aries and Libra will play instrumental roles. Have luck with number 9.

*Sunday, September 5 (Moon in Taurus to Gemini 6:24 a.m.)*   You learn more about mystery and spirituality. Make a fresh start. Be willing to enter areas previously off-limits. The financial status of one close to you will be revealed. You could learn more than you care to know. A Leo figures prominently.

*Monday, September 6 (Moon in Gemini)*   Meaningful questions arise. Some will include the mysteries of life and death. Don't shy away from what is meaningful. The more you face issues, the better it will be. Capricorn and Cancer figure in today's dynamic scenario and have these letters in their names: B, K, T.

*Tuesday, September 7 (Moon in Gemini to Cancer 6:49 p.m.)*   Within 24 hours, you experience a favorable lunar aspect. This will include communication from a "lost love." Focus on learning how the other half lives and what you can do about it. Gemini and Sagittarius could play extraordinary roles. Your lucky number is 3.

*Wednesday, September 8 (Moon in Cancer)*   This is your makeover day. Wear your hair and clothes in different styles. Rewrite and rebuild. Get repairs done at

284

home, including roofing and plumbing. You are more secure than perhaps you realize. Taurus, Leo, and another Scorpio will play meaningful roles.

***Thursday, September 9 (Moon in Cancer)*** Focus on change, travel, and a variety of "sensations." A romantic relationship lends spice, imbuing you with hope, optimism, and inspiration. Gemini, Virgo, and Sagittarius play instrumental roles and are likely to have these letters in their names: E, N, W.

***Friday, September 10 (Moon in Cancer to Leo 7:05 a.m.)*** An agreement is reached with your family concerning your business or career. You will be happier as a result. More recognition is due. Superiors will show appreciation for your work and worth. Taurus, Libra, and another Scorpio will play dramatic roles.

***Saturday, September 11 (Moon in Leo)*** At the track, choose number 7 post position in the seventh race. Use your extrasensory perception. Your intuitive intellect is honed to razor-sharpness now. Stick with the underdog, and you come out on top despite the odds. Pisces and Virgo figure prominently in activities.

***Sunday, September 12 (Moon in Leo to Virgo 5:15 p.m.)*** Within 24 hours, some of your fondest wishes will be fulfilled. You gain the cooperation tonight of someone in a position of authority. Exude confidence. Let it be known that you know what you are talking about—don't go anywhere hat in hand. A Capricorn is involved.

***Monday, September 13 (Moon in Virgo)*** You'll be rid of a losing proposition. Elements of timing and of luck ride with you. Go with the tide; don't get in your own way. During this cycle, you win friends and influence people. You could also win a contest, and money seems to appear out of nowhere.

**Tuesday, September 14 (Moon in Virgo)**  The new moon is in Virgo, your eleventh house. This relates to friends, hopes, wishes, and matters of speculation. You will be termed "one lucky person!" At the track, choose number 1 post position in the first race. Leo and Aquarius will play exciting roles in your activities today.

**Wednesday, September 15 (Moon in Virgo to Libra 12:52 a.m.)**  You could be involved in a "secret mission." Focus on cooperative efforts, your partnership, and marital status. The "mission" could involve balancing the budget, even investigating a spy network. Capricorn and Cancer will play instrumental roles. Have luck with number 2.

**Thursday, September 16 (Moon in Libra)**  Keep your plans flexible. You could be called upon to entertain a unique group. Accent humor, diversity, and intellectual curiosity. Be up-to-date on fashion news; you will be tested and perhaps challenged. Keep recent exercise and diet resolutions.

**Friday, September 17 (Moon in Libra to Scorpio 6:24 a.m.)**  Your lunar cycle is high, so circumstances are turning in your favor. Tear down in order to rebuild. Express your own ideas. Be creatively selfish. Have enough self-esteem to have things your way, because today your way is the right way. Another Scorpio is in the picture.

**Saturday, September 18 (Moon in Scorpio)**  Read and write, learn by teaching. You have the gift today of making education a pleasure. You exude an aura of sensuality and sex appeal. Be careful! Protect yourself at

286

close quarters; don't give up something of value for nothing. Lucky lottery: 5, 14, 27, 18, 2, 12.

***Sunday, September 19 (Moon in Scorpio to Sagittarius 10:28 a.m.)***     On this Sunday, almost everything works out for you. Family harmony returns. A moneymaking opportunity is available, and you can take advantage of it. Beautify your surroundings. You will soon be entertaining important people in your home. A Libra plays a top role.

***Monday, September 20 (Moon in Sagittarius)***     Don't be in too much of a rush. Some people want your money without giving anything in exchange. Get commitments in writing. Avoid self-deception. Dare to dream, but know when to say, "Enough!" Pisces and Virgo will play "stunning" roles.

***Tuesday, September 21 (Moon in Sagittarius to Capricorn 1:34 p.m.)***     It will seem as if there is money everywhere. The key is preparation, organization, and research. If you are ready, money will come your way. A relationship intensifies. Don't play games with emotions. The heart you break could be your own. Cancer and Capricorn figure prominently.

***Wednesday, September 22 (Moon in Capricorn)***     Accent universal appeal. That means invent or produce something that people the world over will desire for their own use. It's not easy, but with your Scorpio passion and enthusiasm you can do it. Capricorn and Cancer figure in "complicated" arrangements.

***Thursday, September 23 (Moon in Capricorn to Aquarius 4:09 p.m.)***     The moon in Capricorn is in your third house. This accents relatives, trips, visits, and ideas that require further development. Stress independence and original thinking. Don't wait for others. Lead the way.

Imprint your own style; wear bright colors, including yellow and gold.

*Friday, September 24 (Moon in Aquarius)*    Focus on your home, land, and the sale or purchase of property. The question of marriage looms large. After some introspection, you discern the "direction of your life." A Cancer extends a dinner invitation; waste no time in accepting. Seafood will be the main dish.

*Saturday, September 25 (Moon in Aquarius to Pisces 6:55 p.m.)*    You might wish you had more spacious living quarters when people gather for a social occasion in your home. You will entertain and be entertained. There will be much laughter and talk of political affairs. Gemini and Sagittarius play key roles. Have luck with number 3.

*Sunday, September 26 (Moon in Pisces)*    Obstacles will be removed. Spiritual values surface, along with your "creative urge." You could meet another Scorpio who talks about the mantic arts and sciences. This will help you overcome your fear of the unknown. Check for the correct measurements in a recent project.

*Monday, September 27 (Moon in Pisces to Aries 10:57 p.m.)*    Focus on a variety of interests, including children, trips, and visits. An excellent day for reading, writing, and teaching. If you have not done so already, start a diary! The written word will figure prominently. You will experience more freedom of thought and of action.

*Tuesday, September 28 (Moon in Aries)*    At the track, choose number 6 post position in the second and sixth races. The full moon in Aries represents your sixth house. This relates to special services as well as a demand for your talent or product. You might be asking, "Is it love or lust?"

*Wednesday, September 29 (Moon in Aries)*     See people and situations as they actually exist. Avoid self-deception. Enjoy romance, but know when to say, "Enough is enough!" Obtain the story behind the story. Discern motives; reject superficial responses. Lucky lottery: 7, 25, 19, 16, 42, 13.

*Thursday, September 30 (Moon in Aries to Taurus 5:23 a.m.)*     On this last day of September, you emerge from darkness and enjoy the sensation of "greater light." The emphasis is on how you keep your records; the Internal Revenue Service might express unusual interest. Capricorn and Cancer will play revelatory roles.


# OCTOBER 2004

*Friday, October 1 (Moon in Taurus)*     Review your legal rights. The spotlight is on partnership, cooperative efforts, and your marital status. Go slow, be thorough. Avoid a tendency toward self-deception. A relationship is romantic, but could lack a solid base. Be sure that both of you are free to pursue your quest.

*Saturday, October 2 (Moon in Taurus to Gemini 2:55 p.m.)*     Many might depend upon you for their emotional and financial security. Follow through on policies; don't accept second best. The question of marriage could loom large. Remember that you can run, but you cannot hide. A Capricorn is involved.

*Sunday, October 3 (Moon in Gemini)*     Let spiritual values surface. Get the job done in an efficient way. What begins as "tedious" will conclude in adventure. Don't let yourself be taken for granted. Look beyond the immediate. Take charge of your own destiny. Aries and Libra will play fascinating roles.

*Monday, October 4 (Moon in Gemini)*    Shake off previous notions. Highlight original thinking. Follow through on "invention." Avoid heavy lifting. Assess current values, and be positive about your earning power. Your love is not unrequited, so do not be afraid to take a chance on romance.

*Tuesday, October 5 (Moon in Gemini to Cancer 2:53 a.m.)*    You need the cooperation of one with whom you are emotionally involved. Speak frankly and from the heart. Questions about partnership and marriage will arise. Explain your position, and if you are sincere, the results will be gratifying. A Cancer is involved.

*Wednesday, October 6 (Moon in Cancer)*    At the track, choose number 3 post position in the third race. Check legal documents. Be sure you are getting your fair share. If married, be prepared for a possible addition to your family. If single, you could meet your future mate. Sagittarius is represented.

*Thursday, October 7 (Moon in Cancer to Leo 3:22 p.m.)*    You locate the representation needed if you are going to expand your business and career activities. Advertise and publicize. Let the world know you are alive and kicking. Participation in a humanitarian project could take you to a foreign nation.

*Friday, October 8 (Moon in Leo)*    The Leo moon is in your tenth house. This relates to promotion, career, and business acumen. The emphasis is on reading and writing, learning through the process of teaching. A relationship is serious. If you are merely playing games, move on. A Gemini figures in this scenario.

*Saturday, October 9 (Moon in Leo)*    Attention revolves around your home, family, and income potential. You could hear the sound of music. Find your rhythm and dance to your own tune. You will be questioned about art, music, and literature. Your words could be quoted; know it, and be careful what you say or write.

**Sunday, October 10 (Moon in Leo to Virgo 1:58 a.m.)**   Elements of timing and of luck ride with you. Some of your fondest hopes and wishes come true. Don't deceive yourself about someone who refuses to put promises in writing. Protect yourself in emotional clinches. Be aware of a "whispering campaign."

**Monday, October 11 (Moon in Virgo)**   A unique publication contains needed information. Know it, get busy, and find it. Generally speaking, this is a favorable day. You will remember it with a smile. A business venture could succeed if you properly "image" it. Have luck with number 8.

**Tuesday, October 12 (Moon in Virgo to Libra 9:30 a.m.)**   You get the proverbial "second chance," but it could actually be your "last chance." Highlight a degree of flippancy. Emphasize versatility and humor. Cooperate in a civic project. Finish what you start. Perceive potential beyond the immediate. Aries and Libra are involved.

**Wednesday, October 13 (Moon in Libra)**   You will be going into business for yourself almost immediately. Something dramatic happens behind the scenes, which has a direct effect on you. Leo and Aquarius play meaningful roles and could have these letters in their names: A, S, J. Your lucky number is 1.

**Thursday, October 14 (Moon in Libra to Scorpio 2:09 p.m.)**   There was a new moon and solar eclipse in Libra last night. They relate to secrets that are sacred. Steer clear of explosives. Check the exit signs in buildings you enter. What had been a clandestine relationship will be out in the open. Know it, and prepare a "covering story."

**Friday, October 15 (Moon in Scorpio)**   Keep up-to-date on fashion trends; your opinions and commentaries will be sought. Place emphasis on the newest styles, especially lack of tightness in clothing. Loose-fitting garments will be extremely popular. Your cycle is high, so elements of timing and of luck ride with you. Your fortunate number is 3.

**Saturday, October 16 (Moon in Scorpio to Sagittarius 4:57 p.m.)**   Lucky lottery: 47, 12, 2, 8, 5, 18. Your personality is overwhelming; you exude sex appeal. Upset the odds. Do things your way, because your way is the right way today. A special article will be accepted, but first requires "rewriting." Taurus is represented.

**Sunday, October 17 (Moon in Sagittarius)**   You retrieve a lost article that had great sentimental value. Focus on an engagement ring or something you cherished. Have you been careless with it? Make a resolution to take care of valuables. Do not be taken for granted by irresponsible people.

**Monday, October 18 (Moon in Sagittarius to Capricorn 7:06 p.m.)**   A dent made in your budget will be worth it, if you beautify your home and surroundings. Focus on art, especially creative projects, including painting. Be gentle and generous, but know when to say, "Enough!" Taurus, Libra, and another Scorpio figure prominently.

**Tuesday, October 19 (Moon in Capricorn)**   You could be asking, "Is this déjà vu?" Today's scenario features familiar faces and places. A relative who had been out of sight will make an appearance. Define terms. Outline boundaries. Get commitments in writing. A Pisces plays a mysterious role.

**Wednesday, October 20 (Moon in Capricorn to Aquarius 9:37 p.m.)**  A relative offers financial backing for what could be a "daring project." Keep plans flexible. Express your feelings, but mingle humor with "serious talk." Capricorn and Cancer play significant roles and have these letters in their names: H, Q, Z. Your lucky number is 8.

**Thursday, October 21 (Moon in Aquarius)**  You will be involved in a real estate or land transaction. Your role is important; be aware of it, and respond accordingly. Modesty at this time is not appropriate. Speak up! State your views with refreshing frankness. A long-distance call verifies your beliefs and elevates your morale.

**Friday, October 22 (Moon in Aquarius)**  You will be especially inventive. Close associates and neighbors will comment favorably on your appearance. If single, you could meet someone destined to play a major role in your life. If you are married, the spark that brought you together will reignite.

**Saturday, October 23 (Moon in Aquarius to Pisces 1:13 a.m.)**  At the track, choose number 2 post position in the second race. The lunar position emphasizes personality, creativity, and sex appeal. Be discriminating; do not lower your standards. A young person announces: "You are my role model!" A Cancer is involved.

**Sunday, October 24 (Moon in Pisces)**  A favorable lunar aspect coincides with the fulfillment of creative aspirations. Go all the way or not at all! Accent color coordination and showmanship. Gemini and Sagittarius will figure in today's dramatic scenario.

*Monday, October 25 (Moon in Pisces to Aries 6:24 a.m.)* On this Monday, you discover methods of getting the job done with the least effort. Rewrite, review, and rebuild. This can be your makeover day. Don't be satisfied with the status quo. Break free into new areas of thought and of action. A Taurus is in this picture.

*Tuesday, October 26 (Moon in Aries)* You will be dealing with creative, temperamental people, especially Gemini, Virgo, and Sagittarius. Put your requests in writing. You are being taken seriously—a quick response comes as a pleasant surprise. A flirtation lends spice and elevates your morale. Do not give up something of value for a temporary thrill.

*Wednesday, October 27 (Moon in Aries to Taurus 1:37 p.m.)* Medical appointments might be postponed or rescheduled at the last minute. Lucky lottery: 6, 15, 9, 27, 13, 40. Your vitality makes a comeback. A minor digestive problem can easily be resolved, if you so permit. Taurus, Libra, and another Scorpio offer helpful suggestions. Listen!

*Thursday, October 28 (Moon in Taurus)* The full moon and lunar eclipse last night occurred in Taurus, your seventh house. This represents legal affairs, marriage, partnerships, and public attention. Avoid snap decisions. They could work to your detriment. Protect your reputation, especially when dealing with persons who have proven in the past not to be friends.

*Friday, October 29 (Moon in Taurus to Gemini 11:11 p.m.)* This is your power play day! Clearly state your desires and needs. Others are willing to listen and take the appropriate action. There is no need to settle for "second best." If single, you may receive a proposal that requires more than usual consideration. Capricorn and Cancer figure in this scenario.

***Saturday, October 30 (Moon in Gemini)*** An unexpected meeting or communication could stir memories of long ago and far away. Do not allow emotions to override practicality. Someone may want something for nothing. You could be the prime target! Aries and Libra figure in this "complicated" scenario. Your lucky number is 9.

***Sunday, October 31—Daylight Saving Time Ends (Moon in Gemini)*** On this Halloween, the moon will be in Gemini, which adds up to "more tricks" than usual. Things are not what they appear to be on the surface. Masks will be innovative, and so will costumes. There will be an ongoing game of "Who am I?" Leo and Aquarius play outstanding roles.

# NOVEMBER 2004

***Monday, November 1 (Moon in Gemini to Cancer 9:53 a.m.)*** You gain financial information. Make your views known. Be direct, exude confidence. A Leo in your life will provide spice and excitement. Set priorities, then move "straight ahead." Capricorn and Cancer also play roles.

***Tuesday, November 2 (Moon in Cancer)*** Rise above petty arguments over money and how it got that way. You will attract affection, romance, and love—if you so permit. Finish rather than begin a project. Plan on an international scale. Aries and Libra figure in this scenario.

***Wednesday, November 3 (Moon in Cancer to Leo 10:32 p.m.)*** Make a fresh start. Decorate your home. Allow more light to enter the rooms. Accent originality and daring. A "great love" could be just around the corner.

Your Scorpio passion will find a constructive outlet. Have luck with number 1.

**Thursday, November 4 (Moon in Leo)** Use showmanship and knowledge of color coordination to "dress up" a product. You could be entering an area of "show business." You will be more secure in connection with your property and home. A Cancer is involved.

**Friday, November 5 (Moon in Leo)** Your standing in the community is upgraded. You could win a popularity contest. An influential person could take you "under his wing." Reserve judgment on a major business transaction. All the facts are not in. There could be a plumbing problem on your property.

**Saturday, November 6 (Moon in Leo to Virgo 10:00 a.m.)** Some pressure is relieved. In a way, you will admit to yourself that you miss the challenge of meeting deadlines. Review and rebuild. If you rewrite, material that had been rejected could now be accepted. Taurus, Leo, and another Scorpio play "fantastic" roles.

**Sunday, November 7 (Moon in Virgo)** Metaphysical questions will be asked and answered. The Virgo moon represents your eleventh house. This means that some of your fondest hopes and wishes can be fulfilled. You'll have the best of everything today; these will include romance, love, and money.

**Monday, November 8 (Moon in Virgo to Libra 6:23 p.m.)** Attention revolves around your lifestyle and the ability to win in games of chance. You will be lucky, but know when to say, "Enough is enough!" Taurus, Libra, and another Scorpio figure in today's dramatic scenario. Stick close to home, if possible. Your opinion will be sought about an environmental problem.

***Tuesday, November 9 (Moon in Libra)*** A clandestine operation comes to light. Define terms. Find out what it is you really want to know. It might be better to let things remain as they are—don't fix it, if it's not broken! Pisces and Virgo will play significant roles.

***Wednesday, November 10 (Moon in Libra to Scorpio 11:06 p.m.)*** Someone who has been doing "secret" work will ask, "What next?" Focus on organization, priorities, and the need to protect sources. Backstage maneuvers will figure prominently; much has been accomplished in recent actions. A Capricorn becomes your ally.

***Thursday, November 11 (Moon in Scorpio)*** Your lunar cycle is high, so your judgment and intuition will be on target. If you are married, the love spark reignites. If single, you could meet your future mate. Whether you are married or single, complete a project that has humanitarian aspects. An Aries will figure in this scenario.

***Friday, November 12 (Moon in Scorpio)*** Circumstances turn in your favor. You get the proverbial "lucky break." Highlight your personality. Make special appearances. Realize that you exude sex appeal. A romantic Leo confides, "At times I can hardly keep my hands off you!" Your fortunate number is 1.

***Saturday, November 13 (Moon in Scorpio to Sagittarius 12:57 a.m.)*** The financial picture brightens. A debt will be paid. Your family is involved, and you could be the direct beneficiary. Focus on direction, motivation, and the need for meditation. You will be invited to dine. A Cancer will be the chef. Lucky lottery: 2, 12, 20, 18, 45, 7.

***Sunday, November 14 (Moon in Sagittarius)*** Try to include the colors pink and purple in your clothing. You will receive many comments, most of them favorable. An opportunity you missed three days ago will again be available. Finances are involved. Don't let a major chance for success escape. A Sagittarius is involved.

**Monday, November 15 (Moon in Sagittarius to Capricorn 1:34 a.m.)**   Tie together loose ends. Someone you admire is "stretching the truth." Be understanding and sympathetic. But know when to decide, "Enough is enough!" Fun and games today, and perhaps tonight will be a time of love and laughter. A Taurus will figure prominently.

**Tuesday, November 16 (Moon in Capricorn)**   There are many trips and visits today. Do not let relatives involve you in a "harebrained" scheme. Insist on having the facts, as well as promises, in writing. A good time to submit an article for publication. The written word could bring you fame and fortune.

**Wednesday, November 17 (Moon in Capricorn to Aquarius 2:40 a.m.)**   Focus on your home, relatives, and decisions relating to partnership and marriage. The key is to be diplomatic. Don't attempt to force issues. If receptive, you get what you need. If attempting to "muscle your way," you lose. In plain words, strong-arm methods do not bring the desired results.

**Thursday, November 18 (Moon in Aquarius)**   Focus on real estate, property, and your living quarters. Define terms. Discover what you really need in contrast to needless luxury. Take note of your dreams. Properly interpreted, they could be the doorway to your future. Tonight's dream will be memorable!

**Friday, November 19 (Moon in Aquarius to Pisces 5:38 a.m.)**   Creative resources surge to the forefront. Focus on organization. Put together the pieces of a puzzle. A personal relationship could get too hot not to cool down. Children could be involved, along with a short trip and a clash of ideas with a loved one.

*Saturday, November 20 (Moon in Pisces)*     A mission is completed. Know it, and don't stay around so long that you are no longer welcome. Focus on style, verve, creativity, and sex appeal. Capricorn and Cancer play roles, along with Aries and Libra. Have luck with number 9.

*Sunday, November 21 (Moon in Pisces to Aries 11:12 a.m.)*     Be stylish. Wear bright colors when you make personal appearances. Highlight color coordination, publicity, and showmanship. A "different" kind of romance is on the horizon. Keep recent resolutions concerning health, diet, and exercise.

*Monday, November 22 (Moon in Aries)*     Attend to a routine that could include home repairs. You will be considering a new direction—where to go and what to do when you arrive. Make concessions to your family without abandoning your principles. A Capricorn plays a major role.

*Tuesday, November 23 (Moon in Aries to Taurus 7:16 p.m.)*     Good news relates to the work you do at home or outside. Accent versatility and diversity. Keep your plans flexible. Someone who shares your basic interests will pay you a meaningful compliment. Your morale will be on the upswing. A Sagittarius is involved.

*Wednesday, November 24 (Moon in Taurus)*     Go slow, be meticulous regarding details. Be aware of your legal rights and permissions. The focus is also on cooperative efforts, partnership, and marriage. Someone who once repelled you could now prove attractive. You may say to yourself, "Such is life!"

***Thursday, November 25 (Moon in Taurus)*** On this Thanksgiving, there will be many anecdotes that reinforce your spirit of giving and receiving. Gemini, Virgo, and Sagittarius will play major roles, and one of those persons could "carve the turkey." Your lucky number is 5.

***Friday, November 26 (Moon in Taurus to Gemini 5:25 a.m.)*** The full moon in Gemini represents your eighth house. This relates to mystery, intrigue, and the financial resources of your partner or mate. The emphasis is on your family, home, beauty, style, flowers. Tender loving care is required for someone you think much of—be generous yet subtle.

***Saturday, November 27 (Moon in Gemini)*** On this Saturday, keep an eye on number 7 in matters of speculation. At the track, choose number 7 post position in the seventh race. Spiritual values will surface. You will make amends to someone you slighted without intending to do so. A Pisces figures prominently.

***Sunday, November 28 (Moon in Gemini to Cancer 5:11 p.m.)*** Within 24 hours, you will perceive potential for the future. You will be speaking to someone from a foreign land; learn what you can about "strange customs." You exude universal appeal. People are drawn to you for help in solving their dilemmas.

***Monday, November 29 (Moon in Cancer)*** There is a distinct possibility of a journey abroad. At the very least, locate someone who can represent your talent or product in a foreign country. Expand your horizons. Don't be satisfied with the status quo. An Aries will play an outstanding role.

***Tuesday, November 30 (Moon in Cancer)*** On this last day of November, you will seriously consider going into business for yourself. Focus on independence, original thinking, and confidence in your own abilities. You will meet attractive, dynamic Leo and Aquarius people who help build your morale.

## DECEMBER 2004

**Wednesday, December 1 (Moon in Cancer to Leo 5:50 a.m.)** Be optimistic about the opportunity for "international recognition." Look beyond the immediate. Dare to dream. A romantic relationship is serious and could get too hot not to cool down. What a way to start the month! A Libra figures in this scenario.

**Thursday, December 2 (Moon in Leo)** The spotlight is on romance, creativity, and the ability to imprint your personal style. Take the initiative. Wear bright colors and make personal appearances. Your instinctive knowledge of showmanship surges to the forefront. Leo and Aquarius will help in career or business activities.

**Friday, December 3 (Moon in Leo to Virgo 6:01 p.m.)** By tonight, you will know more about where you stand in connection with a partnership or marriage. Accent comfort, security, and assurance. You could be enjoying an excellent seafood dinner tonight. A Cancer will be the chef.

**Saturday, December 4 (Moon in Virgo)** What a Saturday night! Your wishes can become realities. Warning: Don't ask for more than you can handle! In matters of speculation, stick with number 3. Sagittarius, Virgo, and Gemini will play memorable roles. Accent your Scorpio personality!

**Sunday, December 5 (Moon in Virgo)** On this Sunday, spiritual values surface. You will be convinced that you do have a "guardian angel." Review, rewrite, do research. What had failed could now succeed. Taurus, Leo, and another Scorpio will play sensational roles.

*Monday, December 6 (Moon in Virgo to Libra 3:47 a.m.)* Prepare for change and a variety of experiences. A secret meeting could relate to "the rest of your life." Obviously, be attentive, alert, and sensitive to trends. What had been kept hidden will be revealed; write about it. A Virgo figures prominently.

*Tuesday, December 7 (Moon in Libra)* The emphasis is on luxury items that can help beautify your home. Pay attention to a Libra who makes a dramatic assertion: "At times I can hardly keep my hands off you!" A domestic adjustment could include an actual change of residence or marital status.

*Wednesday, December 8 (Moon in Libra to Scorpio 9:45 a.m.)* Within 24 hours, a mystery will be solved. What had been regarded as "treacherous" could now be a "laughing matter." Protect yourself in emotional clinches. Don't lead with your chin or heart. This message will become crystal clear tonight. A Pisces figures prominently.

*Thursday, December 9 (Moon in Scorpio)* In your lunar cycle high, circumstances take a dramatic turn in your favor. Highlight your personality. Exude confidence and sex appeal. Someone who once took you for granted will now plead, "Let us give it another try together!" Don't repeat past mistakes!

*Friday, December 10 (Moon in Scorpio to Sagittarius 11:55 a.m.)* Complete a project. Don't give up the ship! Events will transpire to bring you closer to where you want to go. People will be drawn to you tonight, hoping you can resolve their dilemmas. Do what you can, but know when to say, "Enough!" A Libra is involved.

**Saturday, December 11 (Moon in Sagittarius)** A moneymaking idea pays off. Check invoices. Investigate further possibilities for increasing your income. It is possible that you are growing a "money tree" in your backyard. Leo and Aquarius will figure in this sensational scenario. Your lucky number is 1.

**Sunday, December 12 (Moon in Sagittarius to Capricorn 11:42 a.m.)** The moon is in Sagittarius, which represents your second house. This means you will retrieve a lost article and earn more money. Remember: To get a smile, give a smile! Capricorn and Cancer will play significant roles and have these letters in their names: B, K, T.

**Monday, December 13 (Moon in Capricorn)** Forces tend to be scattered. Your popularity is on the rise. Don't attempt to please everyone. Ask questions. Highlight your intellectual curiosity. Perceive a situation in its entirety. Leave details for another time. A Sagittarius plays a key role.

**Tuesday, December 14 (Moon in Capricorn to Aquarius 11:10 a.m.)** You will retrieve what was lost 48 hours ago. Your financial picture is brighter than you expected. Revise, review, and rebuild. This can be your makeover day. Change the way you look via your hairstyle and wardrobe. A Taurus will play an exciting role.

**Wednesday, December 15 (Moon in Aquarius)** Lucky lottery: 5, 15, 22, 18, 3, 12. There will be a change of itinerary. Be aware; adjust your schedule to meet different demands. Be analytical about a romance. It is mostly positive, but do not leave everything to chance. A Virgo figures in this scenario.

303

**Thursday, December 16 (Moon in Aquarius to Pisces 12:24 p.m.)** Attention revolves around your living quarters. Improve your "comfort status." A domestic adjustment is highlighted. A change of residence could be involved along with marital considerations. Taurus, Libra, and another Scorpio play roles and have these letters in their names: F, O, X.

**Friday, December 17 (Moon in Pisces)** Wait and see! Refuse to be chided into a snap decision. Time is on your side if you play the "waiting game." Work backstage; find out what is happening behind the scenes. Pisces and Virgo play dramatic roles, adding to the mystery of the day.

**Saturday, December 18 (Moon in Pisces to Aries 4:52 p.m.)** Nothing happens halfway. Know this, especially in connection with "emotional entanglements." The pressure is on, professionally and romantically. You can run, but you cannot hide! Powerful people are behind you and will back you to the hilt. Your lucky number is 9.

**Sunday, December 19 (Moon in Aries)** On this Sunday, there will be more recognition of spiritual values. The Aries moon is in your sixth house. This relates to special services that you extend to people who require them. You will be a dominant figure in your circle, perhaps even the "talk of the town."

**Monday, December 20 (Moon in Aries)** Give serious consideration to gaining independence, perhaps going into business for yourself. A "different" kind of romance is featured. Speak from the heart, and expect the same from the "other person." Leo and Aquarius top today's scenario.

**Tuesday, December 21 (Moon in Aries to Taurus 12:52 a.m.)** Lie low, be subtle. You do your best work tonight while "invisible." This means keep out of sight as much as possible. Be realistic about a relationship; avoid self-deception. Capricorn and Cancer play instrumental roles. Your lucky number is 2.

**Wednesday, December 22 (Moon in Taurus)**    At the track, choose number 3 post position in the third race. Luck rides with you. You could be the main attraction at a social gathering tonight. Keep recent resolutions about your general health, exercise, and diet. A Gemini offers sound advice.

**Thursday, December 23 (Moon in Taurus to Gemini 11:33 a.m.)**    Within 24 hours, you will realize that legal decisions go in your favor. Focus on cooperative efforts, civic activities, partnership, and marriage. Be willing to revise, review, rewrite, and rebuild. You get the proverbial "second chance"—make the most of it!

**Friday, December 24 (Moon in Gemini)**    On this Christmas Eve, you learn more about loved ones and about your own feelings. One of your gifts could be a mystery novel. You will enjoy a wide range of presents. Show appreciation without being obsequious. A Gemini will play an outstanding role.

**Saturday, December 25 (Moon in Gemini to Cancer 11:39 p.m.)**    Focus on your family. You will enjoy being with loved ones, and there will be an abundance of foods and beverages. There will be many Christmas anecdotes. One guest will relate the serious side of this holiday. To all, a merry Christmas!

**Sunday, December 26 (Moon in Cancer)**    The full moon in Cancer represents your ninth house. This relates to philosophy, religion, and faraway places. Terms will be clearly defined. You will know where you stand in connection with love and marriage. A Pisces plays a major role.

***onday, December 27 (Moon in Cancer)*** What seemed long ago and far away could practically be at your doorstep. Don't sell yourself short. You have much to offer, and people you care about will show their appreciation. Capricorn and Cancer could dominate today's scenario. Your lucky number is 8.

***Tuesday, December 28 (Moon in Cancer to Leo 12:15 p.m.)*** You will be finished with one phase of activity. Be thankful—it is the right thing to do. Someone you once loved will make a surprise appearance; maintain your emotional equilibrium. Aries and Libra will play outstanding roles and have these letters in their names: I and R.

***Wednesday, December 29 (Moon in Leo)*** Accent feeling rather than logic. Strive for balance. You will be sensual and seductive, but maintain high standards. Don't give up something of value for a temporary thrill. This message becomes crystal clear tonight. Lucky lottery: 1, 12, 28, 4, 7, 47.

***Thursday, December 30 (Moon in Leo)*** Proposals that include career, business, and marriage are received. Decide on direction and motivation. Final answers are received as a result of meditation. Someone who "thinks the world of you" will say so in no uncertain terms. A Cancer is involved.

***Friday, December 31 (Moon in Leo to Virgo 12:34 a.m.)*** Steer clear of people who drink to excess. Have fun, but control your own intake of adult beverages. You not only will enjoy yourself, but will provide others with laughter and inspiration. Many of your hopes and wishes could be fulfilled, if you so permit. A Gemini plays a pertinent role.

## HAPPY NEW YEAR!

## ABOUT THE AUTHOR

Born on August 5, 1926, in Philadelphia, Sydney Omarr was the only person ever given full-time duty in the U.S. Army as an astrologer. He also is regarded as the most erudite astrologer of our time and the best known, through his syndicated column (300 newspapers) and his radio and television programs (he was Merv Griffin's "resident astrologer"). Omarr has been called the most "knowledgeable astrologer since Evangeline Adams." His forecasts of Nixon's downfall, the end of World War II in mid-August of 1945, the assassination of John F. Kennedy, Roosevelt's election to the fourth term and his death in office . . . these and many others are on the record and quoted enough to be considered "legendary."

# ABOUT THE SERIES

This is one of a series of twelve
Day-by-Day Astrological Guides
for the signs of 2004
by Sydney Omarr.

# SYDNEY OMARR'S®
# ASTROLOGICAL GUIDE
# FOR YOU IN 2004

## *SYDNEY OMARR®*

Brimming with tantalizing projections, this amazing single-volume guide contains advice on romantic matters, career moves, travel, even finance, trends and world events. Find year overviews and detailed month-by-month predictions for every sign. Omarr reveals everything new under the stars, including:

- Attraction and romance
- New career opportunities for success in the future
- Lucky numbers and memorable days for every month of the year
- Global shifts and world forecasts

...and much more! Don't face the future blindly—let the Zodiac be your guide.

209214

## **Available July 2003**

Available wherever books are sold, or
to order call: 1-800-788-6262

The Ultimate Guide to Love, Sex,
and Romance

# SYDNEY OMARR'S®
# ASTROLOGY, LOVE, SEX,
# AND YOU

Whether your goal is a sexy seduction, finding your
soulmate, or spicing up a current relationship, this all-
in-one volume will guide you every step of the way—
with a little help from the stars.

Includes:

- An in-depth description of each sign for men and women
- Compatibilty forecasts
- A fantastic section on romantic dinners for two, featuring
a complete kitchen-tested menu for each sign
- Myths and symbols associated with each sign
- An introduction to each sign's shadow
- Ratings on which signs are the most passionate
- and much more

206932

Available wherever books are sold, or
to order call: 1-800-788-6262

S456/Omarr